THE
IAN FARRER
MYSTERIES

'WARNING'

Please be aware, that this book has Course Language, Sexual References, and descriptions of Autopsies and Murder Scenes.

The Ian Farrer Mysteries

Mayhem

Murder

&

Revenge

A Trilogy

By
D. R. McGregor

Original Published by:

Genesis Life 55 Books™

D. R. McGregor - 2024

Christchurch,

New Zealand

ISBN: 978-1-7386119-0-4

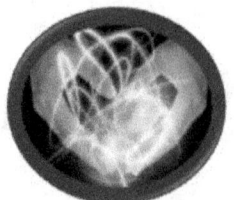

**Genesis
Life 55 Books™**

Part 1

'Our Demons Within'

"Mayhem"

****

Part 2

'The Demons Return'

"Murder"

****

Part 3

'A Deadly Revenge'

"Revenge"

****

About The Author

Born in Australia, graduated from High School and spent most of my teenage life and early twenties in the Royal Australian Air Force. I have a Degree in Psychology, Education, and a Post Graduate Degree in Human Sciences, Behaviour and Health as well as a Degree in Teaching. Investigates and specialises in Criminal and Forensic Psychology. I do not practice or work now but I have worked in many areas. I am married and settled in New Zealand.

I have three grown children and a grandchild. I am a family man, first and foremost. Hobbies are golf, fishing, reading and being an author. I started writing at 32; I never really wanted to publish anything but did Self-Publish three books in 2008. Of the three books; two were Non-Fiction and a Self Help Book. This book is the first adventure into full Psychological Crime Fiction, taking almost two years to complete. I write when something inspires me for the ideas to flow. Have read many works from varied authors and believe we can never read or learn too much.

My favourite quote is: "We are placed on this earth for a purpose, and the three most important things in life are the day you were born, why you were born, and the day you die".

My biggest inspirations: a r e f amily, friends, and the larger Universe of Life.

"Imagination is more important than Knowledge"

Albert Einstein

"Behold, I send you forth as sheep to live among the Wolves"

Mathew 10:16

Acknowledgements

*A big thank you to all who read the rough draft and made constructive comments and recommendations that made this story flow and give meaning to the Trilogy.

*To my family for their patience and understanding,

*The Detectives, Police, and CSI personnel who helped mould this story; your input has been invaluable.

*To those fellow Psychologists and authors who allowed me to use their talents and comments to bring forth the understanding of the Sociopath and what makes a Psychopath.

For My Family

"The Detective's Code"

The Detective has no right to conduct business on
behalf of or entrust t h e   w o r k
t o   any other intermediaries. The credibility of the
Detectives cannot be without confidence in secrecy.
There is always only one truth. Professional
confidentiality is universal and has no time limitation.
The Detective cannot be relieved of his/her
client, by neither the authorities nor anyone else.

-   **"Anonymous"** -

Preface

A good thriller, murder, or crime story usually begins with a beautiful woman, a tranquil scene, and somewhere within the first chapter a body. As an author, I tend to take liberties with my imagination and allow myself the freedom of creativity. As children, we would do this all the time in our lives whether in daydreams or our playtime pretending to be that hero, a cowboy or a soldier who could never get shot or die. Our futures are melded on the ability to believe in the unbelievable and to be able to distinguish right from wrong, good from evil, justice, and crime, and what causes the urge to kill or commit crime.

As a psychologist and having studied Forensic Criminology. The substance of this Trilogy has been taken from varying files, cases in many countries over an extended period, cases brought to me by colleagues and associates, it has been embellished so that the story flows, thus a story of fiction. Any names or references to persons living or deceased or to places or landmarks are completely coincidental. This Prologue will give you a basic understanding of the *"Serial Killer"* and what drives them. Along with many underlying stories of betrayal, death, jealousy, and the need for power and money, all go hand in hand within this fictional story.

I have tried to compare past *"Serial Killers"* and their unusual thinking and give an insight into their thinking. I have used famous well-known serial killers as well as those from many years past, I have also in areas noted the thoughts from experts far more experienced than myself. Within our Psyche, there is a fine balance between good, bad, sane, or insane.

We all walk that thin cotton line throughout life. Where do those urges come from? Why are they so powerful? If we all experienced this urge, would we be able to resist? Is it genetic, hormonal, biological, or cultural conditioning, nature, or nurture? Do serial killers have any control over their desires? We all experience rage and inappropriate sexual instincts, yet the greater proportion of us have an internal cage that keeps our inner monsters locked up.

Call it morality or social programming; those internal blockades have long since been trampled down in the psychopathic killer. Not only have they let loose the monster or demon within but, they, the criminals are virtual slaves to its beastly appetites. What sets them apart? Why do a significant percentage of psychopaths end up in prison, instead of in psychiatric hospitals? The psychopath is only capable of sadomasochistic relationships based on power, not attachment. Psychopaths identify with the aggressive role model, such as an abusive parent, and attack the weaker, more vulnerable self by projecting it onto others, such as playground bullies. In a substantial percentage of bullying cases, the bullies are acting out what happens in the family home, and in some instances go on to be criminals or psychopaths because of that early tendency to violence. There are murderers or criminals whose a c t s of murder and violence, questions both morality and what the psychopath thinks and how he/she acts and appears in general. So, we must ask the question, do they appear normal? Do ordinary citizens leading normal everyday lives become Psychopathic? If they were your neighbours and you did not know their backgrounds, would you believe they are capable of the crimes they committed?

There are individuals who are so psychopathically disturbed, that, in my opinion, no attempts should be made to treat them, and this is also, the opinions of others more professional than I. The reason being many psychopaths will read psychology and psychiatric books and become skilled at imitating other more 'sympathetic' mental illnesses, such as schizophrenia, bi-polar, but they are also paranoid about their looks, their image in public and being accepted. They will use any means possible to manipulate their evaluators. Do psychopaths ever legitimately hear voices in their heads? According to the research, most functionally psychotic individuals do not experience command hallucinations, and those who do generally successfully resist them. Is serial murder ultimately a quest for sex, power, or both? It depends on who you ask. Some believe that sexual domination is an expression of the need for power.

Dr Steven Egger, Associate Professor of Criminology at the University of Houston at Clear Lake in Texas, as well as Professor Emeritus of Criminal Justice at the

University of Illinois at Springfield writes, and I quote, *"Sex is only an instrument used by the killer to obtain power and domination over his victim,"* Unquote.

According to **Ted Bundy**, he is quoted as saying, *"Sex was not the principal source of gratification. I want to be the master of life and death; murder is not about lust, and it's not about violence. It's about possession. I'm as cold a motherfucker as you've ever put your eyes on. I don't care about those people. He wanted total control over his victims: Possessing them physically as one would possess a potted plant, a painting, or a Porsche, or owning the victim as an individual"* Unquote.

Others believe that a deviant sexual drive is the cause, and power is the tool to achieve sexual satisfaction. Some killers will identify with perceived sources of power, to siphon off some of the feeling of control and omnipotence for themselves. Some will indulge in illusions of religious grandeur, be it Christ or Satan.

Charles Manson for example and his cult followers believed he saw the end of humanity. His philosophy of the upcoming Apocalypse was the true motive behind the killings. He told his family that *"Helter Skelter"* was coming. According to Manson, *"Helter Skelter"* was the uprising of a racial war between "Blackies" and "Whiteys". In history we can look at **Hitler**, and his exploits as a serial killer. By the end of the second world war, **Hitler's** policies of territorial conquest and racial subjugation had brought

4

death and destruction to tens of thousands of people, including the genocide of some six million Jews, in what is now known as the *"Holocaust"*. Looking at *Hitler* many believe given his crimes and the inhumanity of his crimes, *Hitler* was early on linked with "psychopathy", a severe personality disorder whose main symptoms are a great or complete lack of empathy, social responsibility, and conscience. Probably, many would argue that *Hitler* suffered from the *"Dark Triad"*. This label is applied to someone who has the worst traits of narcissistic personality disorder along with antisocial traits, (which includes Psychopathy and Sociopathy) and a high tendency for Machiavellianism.

Stalin (700,000 executed, unknown number from beatings and torture, and then his genocide estimates the number of deaths range from 2.5 million to 10 million. *Pol Pot* and the reign of the *Khmer Rouge* in Cambodia saw 2,000,000 executed, and professionals the world over have asked were these men sane or psychotic, or did they do it for power, satisfaction, sexual pleasure, or only plain madness and why? Macabre mutilations excite the lust murderer.

For them, killing triggers a bizarre sexual fantasy, which had developed in the dark recesses of their warped minds. Since the perpetrator's sexual history is that of solo sex, and he/she finds interpersonal relationships difficult, if not impossible, he/she reverts to masturbatory acts even when a real partner (his/her victim) is available. Masturbation generally occurs after death when the fantasy is strongest. Because the fantasies do not involve an actual person but a symbolic, sacrificial victim, the violence can escalate after death. "Mutilations often occur when the victim is already dead, a time when the killer has ultimate control over the victim. I should reiterate here that not all criminals are male, some of the most sadistic and macabre murders to occur in history were by females. To name a few, *Aileen Wuornos, Kristen Gilbert, Myra Hindley, Belle Gunness, Nannie Doss*(aka *'The Black Widow'*).

Many serial killers admit to an abnormally strong sex drive. *Edward Kemper*, who would often behead his victims before raping them, said, *"that he had a very strong sensual drive, a weird sexual drive that started early, a lot earlier than normal"*, yet he fantasized about dead women, not living ones. *"If I killed them, you know, they couldn't reject me as a man. It was making a doll out of a human being ... and carrying out my fantasies with a doll, a living or dead human doll, the first pretty girl I see when I go out is going to die."*

The most disturbing thrill *Kemper* got from murder was the sexual excitement in decapitating his victims: *"I remember there was actually a sexual thrill ... you hear that little pop and pull their heads off and hold their heads up by the hair. Taking their heads off, while the body is still sitting there, that'd get me off,"* he said.

Kemper went on to say: *"With a girl, there's a lot left in the girl's body without a head. Of course, the personality is gone."*

Those annoying personalities, that serial killers find so troublesome in their victims explains, why they go to such extreme lengths to depersonalize the bodies of their victims with horrifying mutilations. What is it about a personality that these killers find so threatening, that they need to obliterate it? A question that no-one can answer. For some of those killers, sexuality is equated with sin and death by overzealous parents who were anxious to keep their sons from becoming promiscuous. Their libidinous drive was channelled into other deviant behaviour.

In his book *"Serial Killers" Joel Norris* wrote *"the killer is especially savage with respect to the bodies of his female victims; police should look for evidence of feminine physical traits on the suspect. Does he have especially fine hair, are his features disproportionately delicate?"*

Through his extensive research and interviews with five notorious serial killers, *Joel Norris* shows that *"serial killers have specific biological and genetic makeups that can be identified as early as five years of age".* It is a line of thought that the motivation of serial killers is often explained in terms of the need to expel: to expel the feminine, to expel the gay person. It is believed this was one of **Hitler's** motivations, while with **Stalin** and **Pol Pot**, it was the power and control. The question (and the problem) becomes not masculinity but femininity, or femininity's invasion of masculinity. Somehow feminine qualities are to blame for the killer's psychosis, when historically, almost all aggressive acts are masculine in nature. This targeting of the "female within" is nothing more than the serial killer's attempt to blame the victim. Before they begin killing, many serial killers display a fascination with death. This is not unusual. Perhaps if their antisocial personalities had not gotten in the way, serial killers may have become doctors, scientists, morticians, or even artists. **John Wayne Gacy** worked in a mortuary, sleeping in the embalming room, alone with corpses, but was fired after corpses were found partially undressed. The victim's, no-matter what the scenario or situation are the criminals' puppets, to use, and do with them whatever they want. Forgive me if this preface was long winded but I needed the reader to understand the thinking behind the perpetrators in the Trilogy.

PROLOGUE

Now for our story, this story is of a fictional village known as Oemen Lake, Lakes County, set in Montana, a place of tranquillity, pine trees, and crystal-clear blue water that fills the lake which are fed by the snow of the Omen Mountains, which run the full length of the lake on the western side and form the backdrop to this iconic utopia with a population of 22,459 people, which swells to 40-50,000 when the ski season open. Although it appears there are two lakes it is one eighty-two miles in circumference, but, in one part a pine covered hill sends it tentacles out into the lake which forms a large lake area, which can be seen to be shaped like a boot like Italy. The northern side of this area has a small settlement of homes known as Talon Point. Further around the edges some forty-one miles another isthmus of land juts out on which a small group of houses sit, this is Big Bear Village. The road to The Big Bear ski resort starts here in this village. Some eleven miles further down the eastern side is the Native Indian Tribe's reservation, which incorporates a large island in the centre of the lake which the Spokane Native Americans call *"Skaltamiax spukani saka'am se'ułku"*, translated roughly meaning "Man/woman of Sun, Moon & Water". The locals just call it "Moon sun". It is rumoured there are tribal witch doctors buried on the island. The main fictional township of Oemen Lake, which has a shopping mall, bars and motels is twenty-one and a half miles further on the southwest side of the lake.

This idyllic setting where the only problems law wise encountered are a few traffic violations, parking tickets, family troubles, accidents, and robberies as well as the occasional drunken disturbance; nothing really exciting that would call for even, a small section, in the local weekly paper. This was soon to change and become a nightmare for the town Sheriff and his deputies. The Sheriff an alcoholic detective who found life in the bottom of a bottle, and who had transferred from the big smoke due to a robbery and shooting that went badly, seemed his past had caught up with him in Oemen Lake. Bodies were soon to be a common morning awakening. Residents started to go missing, when they are found, some had messages cut into their backs for the police which keep them guessing, all poisoned in mysterious circumstances. Oemen Lake was about to become a hell full of demons.

'Oemen Lake' The view from the Causeway

"An eye for an eye only ends up making the whole world blind."

Mahatma Ghandi

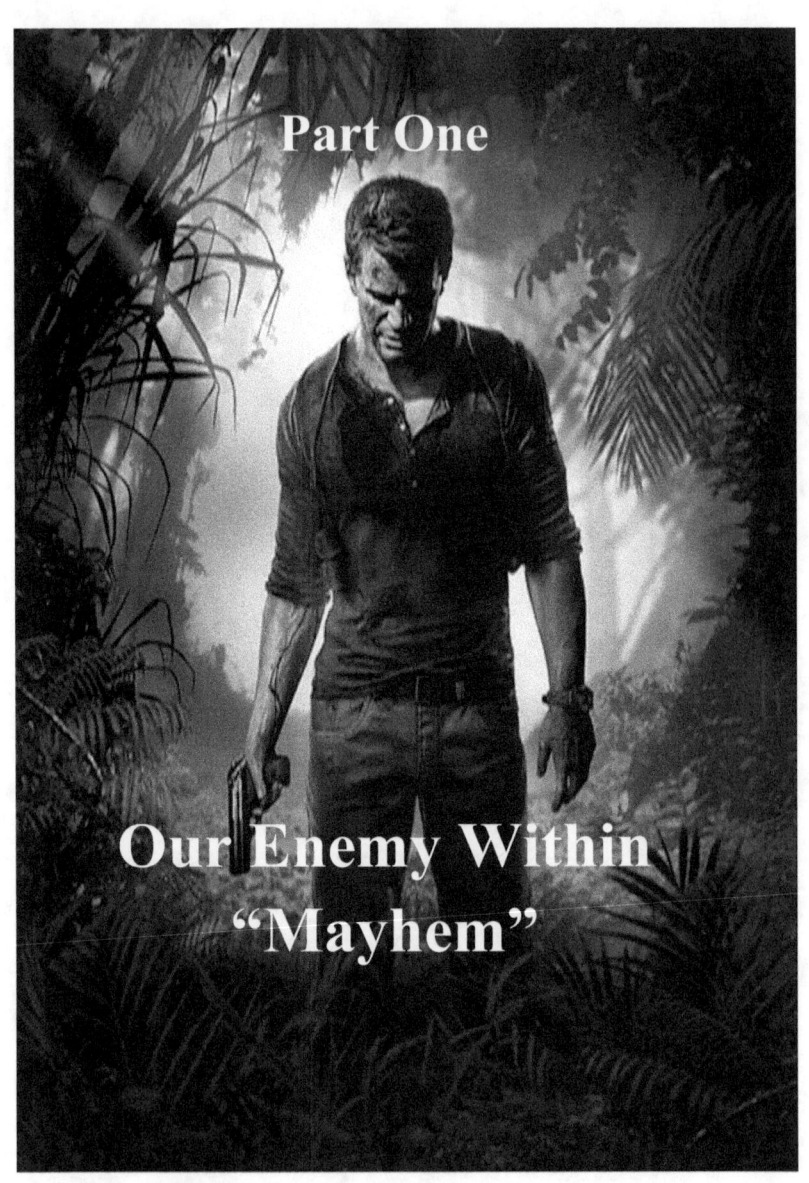

Part One

Our Enemy Within
"Mayhem"

1

On that cold stainless-steel table, the lights made it shimmer, like the moonlight on calm still water, but within the darkness of this room, eerie shadows cast onto those cold stark bare walls, lays a silky smooth and tanned skinned female body. Glistening from the table's reflections, she seemed ensconced there, the epitome of beauty, enticing any man to ogle and be spellbound and become lost in the moment as to what a futile attempt it would be to have met this beauty under better circumstances. I stood back in the surrounding darkness, with just the sheltered overhead light beaming down upon her body which the mid-section was covered with a white sheet that was soaked in blood, but the imagination was unyielding. My eyes carefully seeing each contour of this beautiful creature, God's creation no more than twenty years old, taken from this world by a person or persons unknown. They have a sick and regrettable disease that needs a cure, and what they have committed to this creature of beauty is ignominious. Why kill innocent people for the joy of watching them die. This was the first death of a young woman in this area in five years and I was starting to feel ill.

I am Sheriff Ian Farrer; I could not believe I was again standing watching an autopsy on another victim. I had come to the realisation a robbery and shooting that went bad at my earlier station was my fault, I was a drunk, a soak, and my own personal demons had control of me. The split from my wife and the divorce mainly due to my job, the hours I was forced to keep, and my drinking, was enough of a demon to raise its ugly head alone. My real sense of reality was not what it should have been. I felt disjointed from the real world and that I was always in a daze and could not put the fantasy or the reality into their respective areas within my mind. I should have probably taken time off and allowed myself the time to grieve or to celebrate, whichever way you look at a divorce.

I had cases building up, like speeding tickets, domestic disturbances, drunk and disorderly all the normal small-town misdemeanours and all needing attention, and it seemed everyday a new batch were arriving. There was a feeling of doom building up within me, I left my last position fed up with looking at people who had expressionless faces and had died unnecessarily due to another human being's demented reasoning for murder and mayhem. Why was there a part of humanity in such a bloody hurry to start culling the young and old alike? It was as if a huge majority of that part had suddenly forgotten the difference between right and wrong, good, and evil, crime and justice.

The problem with dealing with the criminal mind is that they never really know what is right or what is wrong they are just caught and suffer the consequences of their actions. I was on the wrong side of 45, a Degree in Law as well as Forensic Criminology and Psychology, no children, but I cannot blame my ex-wife for that, no advancement I was at the top of my game but stuck in a rut; like a train on tracks going nowhere. Six foot three, overweight, greying and developing a short temper. I was really feeling sorry for myself. Uh-oh! God, do I need a drink. This stark cold room was giving me the shivers; I have never, and I am sure I will never become used to being down here in the crypt of the hospital, where life and the living have no real meaning. It always reminded me of some medieval castle, so cold, dim, and uninviting, waiting for some humped back to walk in crying as he dragged a leg behind him,

"The bells, the bells, master".

My mind was running away with a vivid imagination, the alcohol was making me hallucinate about things that were not real. How can one's mind work that way? Maybe that is what happens to the criminal? I suddenly thought of the two offers I was given, one as an Attorney, sit in an office with a plush and affluent law firm; or do what I am doing a hic town Sheriff. What was I doing here watching this beautiful young thing being hewed to find out why she died? I cannot wait to be sitting in a courtroom watching the prosecution of the son of a bitch who did this.

I had no woman to keep me warm and comforted, had not had sex in two or three years, so long ago I have forgotten when. I may need to buy a book on what to do, if ever I was that lucky again. I was a true picture of self-pity, drunkenness, and a fear of impending doom a proper stuff up in life. 'The Lord', ran out of good parts when he made me, I was the cast-off parts from some elaborate set of indestructible, ornate set of men, who could never do no wrong, or evil, were so good and always followed orders. My imagination was so full of crap, a herd of cows do not shit that much. Suddenly, my thought pattern broken by the distant sound of a phone ringing, little did I realize through my drunken hangover, that the phone was mine, the Pathologist asked;

"You going to answer it?" I stared at him with an anger building up inside, I gruffly shouted;

"Just slice and dice arsehole and hurry up and tell me how she died!"

In my time as a police officer, I have seen some macabre and terrifying things, from headless corpses that criminals had had sex with, to half eaten bodies, by the sick and degenerate Psychopaths and Sociopaths who lurk in the shadows of our world, but the murders were starting to get to my sense of reality. The victim aged between twenty and twenty-five of small build blond or brown hair but blue eyes. She had been gutted from neck to stomach and some organs removed namely, kidney, lung, and heart, as to how she was murdered was yet to reveal itself. The messages carefully sculptured into her back, with a vertical and horizontal lines both hewed somewhere around the message whether left, right, top or bottom.

The lines were like ploughed furrows, no more than three to five millimetres wide and two to three millimetres deep, the skin and muscle tissue removed. This procedure we calculated to the best of our knowledge was, so as not to cause excessive bleeding; the cuts were of perfect proportions with the edges exceptionally clean and sharp. When we found the victim, the wounds on her back had been sterilised and very well dressed. As for her front that area was closed with fine sutures. The message which I was still to have interpreted was *"Angere"*.

I surmised it meant *"Anger"* it had a line carved underneath. The use of a surgeon's s c a l p e l was needed for this, no 'Jack the Ripper' here. The reasoning being that the murderer knew a few things about medicine, and surgery, and he was a sick, sick individual. It was frustrating trying to calculate what this person's thinking was or even his mindset.

The body had extraordinary a m o u n t s o f mutilation compared to some of the corpses I have had to endure, except for the weird markings carved on their backs it appeared there was no sexual assault although their vagina had been examined by a n object and traces of a sterile fluid such as cleansing alcohol was present. It was also that about one to two pints of blood had been taken from the body and the two bodies we had, had all recently undergone bone marrow tests, and a small skin graft off the right or left inner thigh had been recently performed, why?

The Pathologist was taking samples for toxicology, and hopefully this would help. The body when found near the head of the lake, North of Talon Point had no identification, or belongings within the vicinity. When the area was cordoned off and a very thorough and strategic search was conducted no evidence of identity could be found except for tyre tracks which the CSI's had taken plaster casts off.

The phone still ringing; I had thoughts of my wife and why she had left me, and I repeatedly sought solace in the bottom of a bottle preferably Jack Daniel's or Jim Beam, but whatever I could lay my hands on at the time, I would drink and drink, and did I need a drink now. That phone was driving me crazy. I hoped the answers would all fall into place quickly. I am dreaming as usual as I am full of bullshit, I surprise even myself, and whenever in my career as a Detective has there been a case where the evidence fits so easily and quickly.

I was getting to be as bad as the arseholes we pursue. What had I become? There was real concern within the office, a sense that this case may be beyond us, and that my work was not interesting to me anymore. Eventually I answered the phone it crackled, and static made my head ring with pain. I moved through the double swinging doors to the stark corridor of the morgue, with its polished hospital crème coloured linoleum, it was my partner calling; I did not need her castigation of me this early in the morning or at a time when I needed a drink.

My Deputy here in Utopia was a woman, and I really had trouble understanding. Joanne Mary Dwyer was 38, beautiful, about five foot eight, long brown hair, deep brown eyes, never married, only to the job. We had been partners for the two years I had been here in Oemen Lake, a difficult woman to really understand

19

and try to get close to. As colleagues, getting too close was not advisable. Frowned upon, you had that feeling of guilt if there was ever any truth in the matter. It was like a stigma, they would remark;

"You're screwing your partner, and how can you work together, sleep together and still could either of you have clear open uncluttered and independent thoughts on a case?"

Because you loved and admired someone with whom you worked, and they were female, you occasionally had the odd tumble between the sheets, even though it was not the permitted thing. If some of the higher brass heard about it, they would, not only be jealous but also angry that the tumble in the sheets, may lead to a case being compromised. Mind you given half a chance I would be into Jo like a cat up a tree at the sight of a dog, she would not have to ask me twice. I just treated her as a workmate, but deep down I had strange feelings about and for her that I could not explain. We had never really been close until recently when my divorce was final, she tried to help me, and I had shut her out completely and depended more on the bottom of a bottle.

She had specialized in serial murder and psychiatric crime at the academy. Her time, in the force was well spent, a degree in Criminal Psychology and was well versed around "Profiling". Jo had the great ability to sum situations up and look outside the square, no tunnel vision on anything, and she could see things from all sides, as this was not what all of us in life would do. Most of us tended to see things in a coloured world when they were black and white, no shading, and no fog around the edges, they were as is and would remain that way.

2

The shadows of the late afternoon were making their way slowly across the cold stark buildings. Like long slender fingers of dread, stretched into every nook and alleyway en-masse, giving the town an even colder and shadowy unnerving feeling. Amongst this ever-increasing darkness, stood a stranger, elegantly dressed in pinstriped suit, dark tie, and white shirt, did not have an austere look about him. Considering the cold and drizzle though, he had no overcoat, but a dark coloured woolly beanie which was stretched down over his ears, he looked completely out of place with the way he was dressed, as winter was just around the corner, and we already have had snow.

He shuffled around in the three-day old dirty snow, which congregated on the footpaths edge, looking intensely at what he was doing and the marks he was making with his shoes, which were now covered in slush. The snow had fallen three nights ago, and the temperature had been colder than predicted, so it still blanketed some areas, like crisp clean white sheets, intermittent with bare grassy areas where the snow had already melted, especially across the open park areas opposite our office heading down to the lake's edge. The stranger was waiting, patiently; any nervousness was hidden by his continued scraping the snow away from the area in which he stood. He reaches into the pocket of his suit jacket and withdrew a packet of Camel cigarettes, tapping the bottom of the packet, he retrieved a single cigarette, placed it between cold and numb lips. His first attempt to light up was unsuccessful, so cupping his hands around the lighter he made another effort, this time being more successful. Slowly dragging on the cigarette so the burning end was visible in the fading light, he slowly allowed the smoke to ventilate out his nostrils; combined with the air of his warm breath, the scene was like that of a magician doing some form of an illusion.

There was another unusual item which made this stranger stand out and give him that out of place reality, he was still wearing sunglasses, even though now, the darkness grew quickly, and the streetlights flickered into life. Those lights now were giving the area a strange false light that of a low incandescent sense of security; one of which could be easily extinguished, by the push of a button or the flick of a switch. Still drawing heavily on his cigarette, he spun on one heel in a half circle and started to walk down the road going south, crossing over Mall Avenue.

The drizzle was now starting to get a little heavier, and it glistened on the shoulders of his suit from the streetlights intermittently as he strode out. He quickly glanced at his watch, took a long drag on the cigarette, and then threw it to the snow filled gutter, where it extinguished quickly in the slush. On reaching Entrance Parade, he crossed the road, his pace quickened and again he glanced at his watch. He had just passed the bus stop outside the Youth Backpackers Centre. He knew that just passed the West Woods was his target. He arrived at five after six and stood opposite the main entrance to Lakes District Hospital, she would be strolling through those doors at any moment.

He had surveyed the area, parked his car inconspicuously and walked to where he was. He had planned everything to what he thought was perfection. He had not planned on the weather being so inhospitable, he cursed himself for not having an overcoat, and the darkness arriving so quickly had also caught him unawares. Suddenly the doors of the entrance slid open and four females in nurse's uniforms walked out, giggling, all trying to talk at once and gently pushing each other in a playful, jovial fashion as they progressed out across the entrance pathway, heading towards the car park. The stranger was now sweating slightly, his palms clammy, his stomach in knots, he suddenly felt ill.

"Why now?" he asked himself in a quiet whisper. Three months of planning and watching, same routine, same time, same friends, nothing was going to change. As with the others, they were all victims of their own character. Their schedule, life and daily routine set in concrete. Nothing changed for any of them from one day to the next, go home, shower, and have tea, sit in front of the television watching some soap on television, then maybe bed, unless they had a friend over, as some of them had. Then he had to sit in his car and watch or to get a clear view of the shenanigans going on from a window vantage point. He had seen it all, breasts, dicks, pussy, all on full display, unaware they were being gazed upon, caught up in their own serene world of excitement, be it all of seven minutes or not. Suddenly there she was blonde, hair long and sleek.

Her uniform, he thought, did not do that body justice. He had already viewed her in her glory, some weeks earlier on a night she had had her lover over. The stranger had sexually relieved himself outside her bedroom window at the site of her. She said goodbye to her colleagues and started down the road heading south to the car park where her car was usually parked, this was a familiar routine. He watched her closely, her hips swinging side to side, that lovely backside making erotic motions under that uniform, it brought back such memories. He could now even feel himself becoming aroused all over again.

She shook her head side to side and it made her hair fly around her neck and settle down her back. He was now fully aroused as he surreptitiously watched he; he could feel his manhood hardening in anticipation of what was to be, he slowed just slightly, he reached for his pocket and retrieved a small plastic bag, opening it he wet his finger and dipped it in the bag, collected the white powder, then gently putting it to his nose, sniffed heavily, shook his head, licked his finger and breathed out a huge sigh; he resealed and replaced the bag in his pocket and hastened at high pace again, as he had slipped behind some twenty or more yards. The car park appeared, her car was second in line in the second row, next to his, what good luck, he thought, he had planned this down to the most minute detail. She crossed the newly gravelled surface her shoes making the usual crunching sound; he quickened and was behind her in an instant, his left hand with swift and agile movement was over her mouth; his excitement was pushing against her rear, his right hand under her arm pit holding her still. He could feel his excitement, three feet from her car; he had made his move, an impetuous one, so quick, but so well executed. With his knee now in the small of her back, he pushed her against the rear door of her vehicle and with his free hand removed a syringe from the breast pocket of his jacket, the plastic cover quickly removed by his teeth revealed a fine needle.

He glanced at the side of her neck and at the bulging vein, plunged the needle in and syringed the contents in. Her eyes quickly glazed, and her legs became jelly like, she felt a sudden urge to throw up, but this quickly passed. With an awareness of what was happening but not being able to feel or control the situation, she was slowly laid on the back seat of a strange car, it had a smell about that she was unable to place. She was aware of her surroundings and through the dim light of the falling darkness she could see and hear all but had no feeling or control of her body. The figure lurked over her, but unable to focus entirely on the details of the facial features, or even what they were wearing and to that point whether they were male or female. She glanced down along her arm and could see a small needle had been inserted into her vein on the back of her hand, although she had felt nothing. He was amazed at how he had been able and so quickly, effectively and without little worry over power and extricate her from the area beside her vehicle to his. He had been able to administer the small amount of Propofol quite quickly and insert the intravenous needle without too much difficulty. Now he needed to continue quickly and leave the area before being seen. Suddenly things started to become dark her eyelids heavy and then nothing. He placed the bag of saline on the rear shelf behind the back seat and connected the tubing to the needle, adjusting the flow to what was needed, then sterilised the injection point of the tubing and inserted the needle, the whole time keeping an eye on her breathing and gently lifting her eyelids to check her eye movement.

He placed an oxygen mask over her nose and mouth and adjusted the oxygen flow while he slowly syringed the contents into the tubing. Within seconds she was anaesthetised and ready for transportation. He felt proud of his accomplishment as he had done with the earlier victims; he felt a feeling of elation, as well as satisfaction. He then moved to the driver's seat, started the car, and drove off into the engulfing darkness.

3

As I answered the phone; it was as though Jo was speaking at a hundred miles an hour, I told her,

"Slow down, my head hurt" she had no sympathy for me at three in the morning". She asked;

"Had the autopsy been completed yet," I said;

"He has not even begun, the useless prick."
There was a small pause on the end of the phone, and I knew that there was more to this conversation,

"We have another body" she blurted out;

"I'll pick you up in ten"
suddenly the phone went dead. I stood in disarray, not sure what to make of this. Another body, this bastard was really starting to work overtime on the body count. I slowly walked the lonely cold corridor to the lifts, pushing the down button for the ground floor there was a rattle and a clanging, about time they replaced these I thought. The lift arrived and the doors opened, on entering my mind a maze of differing thoughts and unconnected questions with no answers, a drink would be good now, and I fumbled for my smokes, forgot, I had given them up. I pushed the 'G' button the doors closed, the rattling and clanging began again and in no time at all I was on the ground floor. The doors opened and I headed for the main entrance, shit it was already sleet and hail, tonight was going to be a cold one. Lakes District Hospital was as usual, busy, and the ambulance bay was full. I stood under the veranda waiting for Jo. Little

did I know that at some time earlier a new prey was being stalked and ended just like hunting deer on the very spot upon which I stood; a fact I was soon to become aware of. Fifteen minutes later I was sitting in the car watching lights flash by in the opposite direction. Our red and blue light mounted in the centre of the dashboard reflected off the windscreen, more like a bloody disco ball than a police light, and gave me a false sense of security, it also felt like one of those hypnotic wheels that go around and around in never ending circles.

"You had better get yourself together", Jo said, and gave me some of what I think was perfume, to try to quell the alcohol smell. We were heading for Dunfern Road, near Shanks Point Village, another body found there about two hours prior. Why is it all these idiots, or psychopaths, who murder, kidnap, or do crimes of major proportion, find the places they choose, that are usually quiet and nothing exciting happens. I am not saying it happens all the time but over the last two to three years, I had noticed the trend. Those towns or cities and their outer suburbs, like some bloody soap opera, where everybody knows everybody, and who is up whom and who is doing who and why. It is the sort of situation you would think any sane minded criminal is going to avoid, but no, they still in some way, cause these sleepy little towns, cities, or suburbs to become the centre of attention overnight.

Most of the local police, were probably born there, went to school there, and grew up thinking this was their entire world. Probably went away to University or College, worked somewhere, and came back, then decided they want to be a cop, went to the Police Academy, and guess what, they returned right back here. I came to this quiet little piece of heaven two years ago after the problems with the intention to retire to one of these towns, it would suit me no rat race, hustle, and bustle to worry about, just sleepy little hideaways. My mind fucked up, but through the haze, I was starting to go over the case we had in my mind, which was ripely stewed or pickled, not sure how far it had gone, and I was never good at cooking anyway, but the drink was doing its job, which was fine by me for the time. Its haze was slowly wearing off, and my head hurt, my tongue felt like it was three times its normal size, and as dry as a desert. I would give my left testicle for a drink at this moment, no I would not I may need that testicle sometime in the future, was I dreaming? My phone rang; I answered it was our pathologist at the hospital, our first body turned up North of town, on a wet and cold December afternoon.

They had named her from dental records, Teresa Caldwell, Twenty-One, Single, Blonde hair, Blue Eyes, she had a cross, no distinctive marks except what looked like forceps had been used on her vagina, but this was inconclusive. Blood and toxicology test proved she had had Propofol, and other forms of anaesthetic administered plus Fentanyl. So far it seemed she may have been dead maybe two weeks before being found. The word *'Avoutrer'* means *'Adultery'*, what was that all about?

4

Her hair was dirty, face felt on fire. Her hands and feet bound, and she had difficulty feeling anything. Her eyes stung as if she had been swimming in a heavily chlorinated pool. Tears streamed down her cheeks as the realisation of what had happened to her finally hit her. Unfortunately, she remembers only leaving work having a joke with her workmates and getting to her car then a hand put over her nose and mouth, she felt a jab in the side of her neck, the rest is hazy to say the least and she awoke here in the present.

There was a shuffling in the distance as her senses not fully alert yet but started to become more instinctive. Blinking rapidly, cleared her eyes, but she could still smell and taste the odour of something that she could not discern as to what it was. The shuffling became louder and suddenly the door creaked, a medium built male walked in wearing what looked like hospital scrubs but the light was dim, and she could not clearly make it out. He stood at her feet looking at her, she could not see his face, and it was hidden by something, although his piercing green eyes were clear and bright.

"What do you want with me?" she shouted in a hoarse voice, which did not sound her own. She noticed he a white powdery substance under his nose, and she knew in an instance what that meant. In a muffled but deep raspy voice he said;

"You are now mine to do with what I wish. I have no plans for you at present as I am only just halfway through my game. Be patient wee one, our turn will be soon".

With this he turned and left the room, closing the door as he went, somehow, she recognised his voice, but her head was not fully clear, and she could not be sure. The small amount of light only dimly lit the room. She raised herself up as best she could onto one elbow and peered through the half-light at her surroundings. It appeared to be some sort of cellar, like a wine cellar.

There were large barrels in the corner, four that she could see. Further round there were one, two, no three tables with white sheets and something was covered by the sheets. Fear suddenly overtook her body and thoughts, her instincts now kicked in the fight or flight reaction. Shocked and hurting, she scrambled to sit up straight, her adrenalin pumping wildly and from this vantage point had a much better and fuller view of the area. Although the light was dim and shadows cast over much of the floor and walls by objects within certain areas, there was only one door, no windows.

The smell she could not name prior, was that hospital smell, it was strange they were so strong in this cellar, but then she had no idea of what was happening or what was going to happen. She did not scream or yell for help as it had seemed impossible and a waste of time and energy, from what she had seen when she awoke. The other fact was this arsehole had surely planned this so well

who was going to hear her fleeting screams. The
sound was like someone who had metal tips
on the toes of their shoes. Then a metallic sound
came from the other side of the door a key in a lock and a
bolt was slid back . She quickly lowered herself back
down into her original position. The door opened and the
male had changed into white, clean, and crisp coveralls
and wore a surgical hat and gloves. Suddenly, Catherine
Rhind had that feeling of impending doom, he was going
to kill her; she would not be going home, seeing her
friends and family again. She was going to die in this
forsaken hole in the ground, and the worst of it was she
knew who he was, as she went to sit up before she could
mouth the words, he hit her hard it stung, and all went black.

5

We were almost at the scene, I looked in the car mirror,
what looked back at me was something unrecognisable,
and that appeared to have just been collected from the
gutter. The snow was starting to get heavier, fuck it, all the
yuppies will start arriving to ski and we have two murders
I thought to myself. Then thinking more deeply maybe
I deserved to be one of those who are the victims
of economy fallout and must be homeless. Okay I have a
job, an income, but I do not deserve either, my life is shit.

The Police radio squawked into life, asking;

"You on your way boss?" I replied,

"Yea, what is the problem," the voice came back

"This one has a note for you, shoved into her mouth!"

We arrived on the scene. Southeast side of the lake by the boat ramp, the third body had been discovered. I slowly ascended from our car with my head pounding and my tongue urging me to find a drink. A polystyrene cup pushed under my nose with the smell of strong coffee filling my tortured nostrils. I turned to see who had given me this pitch-black shit; I caught a glimpse of Jo, pouring herself one from a flask. I knew she was trying to help but "Jack D" was what I needed now, not coffee. We now had a third.

"Any information about her yet?" I queried.

"Yes Guv, locals had done their homework on this one as she had been missing for some days, disappeared from the car park, at Lakes hospital about 2 days ago".

"Any CCTV footage we can use?" I asked.

"We have not checked yet Guv but will ASAP".

"Who was she?" I asked in a monotone voice. Catherine Rhind, Twenty-Five, Single, blonde hair, blue eyes, had a cross on her back, vertical line above the cross, the word *'Blasphēmāre'* engraved in her back just like the first victim.

"She was also operated on and some organs missing. It is a bit messy", he said in a rather soft tone.

I shouted;

"Why has this area not been cordoned off, it is a bloody crime scene after all".

33

The young constable quickly cordoned off the area with yellow police tape, and his sheepish look made me smile inside. I had once been in his position and did not do the trivial things. The CSI's quickly kneeled beside the body and opening their kits of magic delights, all the things that may or may not reveal the cause of death, how long it has been in this state and any other pertinent information. Suddenly one spoke;

"Dead at least a day, liver temperature tells between 18 to 24 hours, rigor was well on its way and the bruising around her wounds was beginning to darken with black and blue hues. Her injuries are the same as the other bodies in the Morgue".

As he finished his quick summation my mind galloped ahead. There was no pattern forming or so we thought, until this body was found, in a dark and rather forgotten area, this time of the year. The ground was damp and everywhere there was large pools of water, dark, still and no reflection and gave off an eerie feeling as the snow settled on them.

This was eight days after the first body. Now this new corpse threw theories into overdrive and any pattern we had produced, was right out the window, or so we thought, as it started to sleet, I cursed silently, as I knew heavy snow was not far away and our crime scene would soon be compromised.

I asked myself,

"Did we have two killers working as individuals or in tandem? Was there a copycat killer loose?"

My mind raced with notions of what our next step would be. My head hurt from the amount I had had to drink the night before and breakfast this morning. The press was already here, how did they know so quickly, bloody leeches? It is amazing how they can be at a crime scene in droves before we even know about the crime. Yes, I agree they do help us out from time to time, printing stories, helping with notices etc., and that all goes towards the apprehension of a criminal. I do not down on them but they in such a case as this, could give us breathing space. It is as if they expect us to have all the answers and solve crimes within minutes.

Then when the shit hits the fan because they have put their own slant on a story, we get the kick in the arse from upstairs, when it was those shiny arses that arranged the media releases in the first place. I feel I might be starting to get jack of this whole job either that or getting too old. I walked over to where the local boys had set up the perimeter now around the scene, the forensic team and coroner were on the job and the flashbulbs popped everywhere, or so it seemed to me. Nothing clear as to what was happening; I had also not really had a good look around either. I told my deputy dressed in shirt and tie under his raincoat and looking quite respectable compared to me;

"Move the reporters back as this was a crime scene."
He looked at me stupid and said;

"What reporters?" I said;

"The ones taking all the photos." He looked at me quizzically and said;

"Farrer, you are drunk again. Why the hell don't you get your shit together?"

"We have had a hard day and no sleep for thirty-six hours", I yelled at him in return, which was a complete crock of bullshit, but it sufficed for the time, even though I knew it was a futile argument, he to, had his own demons to deal with.

This man was Deputy Hal Myers, former Homicide Detective Inspector, demoted from state and transferred under somewhat suspicious circumstances for shooting an unarmed kid in a robbery. A mean son of a bitch who would do anything to get me busted, as I did not back him up some two years prior when the incident happened, and the shit hit the fan. He had had it in for me from that day. He stood about six foot six, some three inches taller than me, built solid with a deep Irish accent to be specific. He was born of a family who had a long history of Police; at most times I thought he was still on the clan vs. clan ideal from old Ireland.

He hated being here but was seconded some years ago, and it basically had become permanent. When I arrived as his boss, to say he was pissed would be an understatement. He has resented my presence and on occasions made life a little difficult. He knew though that I knew a few things about his past endeavours, and should he try the back hand with me he would be a lost cause, pension, and all.

Here in this sleepy little nook of Oemen Lake, he had earned a reputation to be known as the *'Directory Interviewer'*. He would use a phone book to get a confession. I will leave it to the   imagination how that happened. It was also rumoured; he was not immune to a little game of *'Russian Roulette'* with suspects. I still believe that was what happened to the young fellow he shot, nothing was proven though, only rumours. He had a bad habit of chewing gum and spitting it everywhere. He was a good cop though, knew his job, and got results even if they were a little unorthodox at times. The flashes were from the Forensic photographer from Mayville laboratory in the capital, who had reflective mirrors set up to give him light. I suddenly thought about the little mind rant I had had earlier about reporters when we arrived, I felt like an absolute idiot.

Just Forensic photographers, not reporters, who would be so dumb to get those two confused, I ask you? I moved slowly over to the scene, gingerly making my way down into the shallow drain where there was a hive of activity, there was more bodies moving around here than a swarm of bees around a Queen.

   "This is a crime scene not a Friday night stroll. If you are not directly involved in this case, then fuck off my crime scene". I roared, I took a deep breathe a sip of the coffee, which near choked me, it was so hot. I made my way over to the body.

A young police officer asked,
   "If I was Farrer?"
I nodded and he handed me a blood and mud-spattered transparent plastic envelope, it was a plastic evidence bag, in it was a letter written to me, the handwriting

was very neat and had some form of special lettering:

"Remember me Farrer, for I am your nemesis,
  You will never be allowed to forget the years.
  I am out and at it again.
  The nights will be long the booze will get sour,
  So, remember you are going to suffer."

The message meant nothing; years ago, I was based in Northampton County, Pennsylvania, New York, and before that in Randolph County, Arkansas, through my fuzziness I could remember no case like this one. I needed a drink. This son of a bitch was not only testing my resolve, but he was also murdering and mutilating the future mothers of this town, who in turn were someone's daughters. This was a case I had hoped would go away in two to three weeks, a month at the most; here I go again fooling myself that the cases we are given are simple and straight forward in a small hic town. I was just so full of shit. I looked around at the scene we were a part of; this death should not be here it is completely out of place. Why would a murderer pick a town such as this to take the lives of innocent young women who had yet to begin their lives? Everything just seemed so out of place.

There was no rhyme or reason, and I am sure everyone gets that little niggly feeling down deep in their stomach, that something is not kosher. I melded things around in my head and realised this man was not killing them for sport, or for fun, he had a purpose and a good reason.
The murder was not of this area. He was dumping them here and in other places for a reason and had made no real

attempt to cover up the bodies or even conceal them, he wanted them found. He was murdering them somewhere else because he had to make sure of his power, his absolute control over them; they were his puppets as were we now. To murder here would have left too much to chance and thus his control was gone. This murderer was about to make a drastic mistake and I was about to have his balls for my afternoon tea. My shoulder was giving me hell and I knew I was under the knife sooner or later and could not delay it any further. I was hoping above all hope this case would be over signed sealed and delivered, but I have no crystal ball, and the office will function without me, I hope, when the day comes, I must have the injury fixed.

I was drumming my fingers on the dashboard as we returned to the office. This bloke needed to get his thrills from the murders, he was not from here or around these parts, as he is smart and knows, he may be recognised and that would cause big problems in his plans. There was a definite feeling low down in my loins, that he was not finished, and that there were more to come. There was also a feeling that there was more brewing here, something behind the scenes and these murders were only part of a bigger picture. There were layers to this, I could feel it, like a Chinese whisper, things exaggerated out of control and secrets laid upon secrets and as I thumped the dashboard, I said aloud;

"This arsehole is mine!"
Jo jumped and the car slightly swerved.

6

The post-mortems on the victims had arrived on my desk. Our temporary office set up we had was not great, we had been moved from our barn on East Street, and it was like a rabbit warren, the ironic part of the move was we were almost next door to the local lawyers. It had its great benefits though, it was good and handy to everything we needed, and just a brisk walk across the street around the corner and the "Cone & Pine" bar was there, no more than a hop skip and jump away, I was in heaven. You could walk across the street through the small park and be at the lakes edge.

There was the ugliest wood panelling that ran the circumference of the office of about four feet in height. Above that and reaching to the ceiling was glass, a smoky coloured cheap type. I had never really noticed all this previously. My desk was a piece of board with four legs. No drawers, no racks, no shelves. Look more like it would be suited in an interrogation room. At present, it was covered in papers, files, notes, and coffee stains. The ashtray overflowed on the papers with extinguished butts and ash. Three chairs the metal fold up type placed strategically around the walls. At least I did have a good chair and I had broken this in, in many ways. Lights were two fluorescent lights covered in fly shit and only one bar of each worked, they flickered annoyingly. Air-conditioning was a group of windows if we ever managed to get them open. It was now ten am, fifteen days after the first two victims. I had called a meeting of those involved in this case. On the case board, we had photos of the three young women and a map of the area and markings where the bodies had been found. Through bleary hung-over eyes, I was pondering over this when Deputy Barrelli came into my office. Now here was a good cop, been a cop for seventeen years, and most of it in the state police, sharp mind, married with two kids. Over the last two years since I arrived in Oemen Lake, I had spent a lot of time with Eugene and Katrina. I had felt like I was part of the family. Little did I know at this stage how much truth there was in that statement? His kids Ayden and Gina respected me and even called me Uncle Ian, which I found to be rather enjoyable; it gave me a feeling of worth. Eugene hot headed at times, but that was his Italian heritage I suspect, tended to be a loner on some parts of an investigation, but his paperwork was thorough, and he always kept impeccable notes.

He was the sort of bloke you wanted at your side when the chips were down, and you had a real scrap on your hands. Jo, followed, and then Deputy Coney a twenty-five-year county police veteran, not tall in relation to the rest of us, had an easy-going attitude at most times. Was an absolute arsehole to get his paperwork up to date and needed help nine times out of ten to make sure it was all together. Married with three grown kids all married, and four grand kids, I thought he would have probably retired by now but once a cop always a cop they say.

He had the attitude shoot first then ask the questions, he also had a chip on his shoulder and an axe to grind as he had been in the area longer, when I was given the Sheriff position.

Like Myers he has never really forgiven me for that and like Mayor Majors hated my guts. He had a characteristic limp which no one seemed to know why.

"What the fuck smells in here?" he said, as he walked through the door, Barelli as quick as ever said.

"Your arse." We all smiled at the remark. Coney was referring to me due to the promotion, believing I had arse licked or brown nosed my way there. The last one in was a detective from the Special Investigations Division of the National Crime Office, Grant Macey, he was a twenty-year veteran but still a Detective, which I found strange, but did not question the fact with him. He was assigned to aid us in this case, as the entire bodies found suit his ability in criminal psychology. A hard face and deep green eyes, solid man, but gentleness about him, he did make me feel uneasy. This uneasiness was making me twitchy. I had had dealings with Macey before and some of his methods and certain tactics left a bit to be desired, but he got the job done and just within the letter of the law. He was born and raised on the streets of Lincoln County, in his early days was a street kid, streetwise and I suspect has a rap sheet somewhere. He has a good nose for working out the improbable but sometimes I believe, he has an inside running in things and this is why I have this twitch on certain items such as evidence and statements he produces. Jo briefed the squad on the results of the post-mortems. Barelli had a strange look on his face, one of, I have a question but not sure how to ask. It may have been my 'Jack Daniel's' haze, but I am sure he had picked something up in what Jo had said. I waited as Jo profiled what she believed to be the make-up of this killer.

"He is about thirty-five to forty, Caucasian, well-mannered and smartly dressed, strong and athletic,"

"How the fuck, do you know that?" Coney said, who did not trust this profiling shit. I gave him a stare of sheer contempt. I would like to get rid of him but could not, as I need them all. This team worked on a shoestring budget allowed by the county council. Jo continued,

"He must have medical training of some form as he takes the blood, and body parts and leaves hardly a cut or suture out of place. The bone samples taken are clinical. The cuts in the back are with surgeon precision and are also cleaned and dressed for ten to sixteen hours before we find the bodies".

She stops and breathes deeply, then continues;

"The incisions in the front from the breast plate to the just above the navel line are precision and with extreme care taken. He is in no hurry, it seems. It maybe that he carries out the mutilations somewhere else then stores the bodies in another place awaiting the right moment to dump them. He also plans where he is going to leave the body as it appears he wants them found as well as to taunt the Police." She takes another deep breath;

"The pathology tests showed gauze residue on two of

the victims. The victims are alive when he takes the blood and the bone marrow. Injection sites are visible on the right arm and left hip area of the victims. This person is playing a game with us, but more, so it seems with Farrer. We are going to need the background on what this maybe about."

This comment went right over my head as I had a headache that was splitting my head apart, so it seemed. I needed this to end and get out of the room for a drink and quick. Jo pauses to take another deep breath this was rather intense stuff;

"The reason his age is around the age I said is, the victims were carried to the sites where we found them, and they were murdered somewhere else as previously said. The actual murder took place in a very clinical and clean environment."

"Thank you," I said.

"A lot to take in and study on our Mr X." I looked at Barrelli,

"What is it, Eugene? You have had a quizzical look on your face for the whole of Jo's brief," no answer, I left the subject alone.

"Jo, could there be more than just the one perp?" I asked quizzically, hoping the answer was short and sweet.

"Yes, certain items and results from DNA show two maybe even three but we need to finalise the results", she said. Macey stood up and said;

"Have you all looked at the map and where the bodies were found?"

We looked at the crosses on the map and the words that were cut into their backs, they formed a pattern of sorts but nothing I could put my finger on at once. Macey went over to the board. Studied it for what seemed minutes but must have only been a few seconds; I was hoping he would say nothing, and we could leave, I had a fervour for a drink. Then with a positive and almost glee sound in his voice he said,

"Look, photo one," he said,

"The body was found here, had blue eyes, cross on her back, vertical line, and the word *"Avoutrer"*, which means *"Adultery"*. He drew a vertical line next to the cross already in place on the board.

"Victim two, found here horizontal line, and a cross, blue eyes," he formed a cross and drew the horizontal line below and the word *" Blasphēmāre"*, which means *" Blasphemy"*. Suddenly Coney jumped to his feet, shouting;

"Dante! It is all about Dante's nine circles of hell, well I think it is". He exclaimed as he sat down quietly, and then muttered;

"There must be more, we have two, Blaspheme and Adultery, there is Lust, Greed, Anger, Violence, Treachery, Fraud, Gluttony and Limbo, there are nine in all, and they are associated with the deadly sins also".

"We have "Anger", I stated;

"It was on the body in the morgue".

"Macey was livid his thunder had been stolen, his face filled with rage, and he went red, he glared at Coney and me then shouted;

45

"Shut up you son of a bitch, I found it not you!" We were startled by the outburst, it seemed Macey did not like being shown up.

I challenged him on his attitude but allowed him to go ahead and told Coney in a silent manner with a look of let him finish. He had put the two words and crosses etc on the map, he marked the area I mentioned, and although there are areas missing, we had three areas of nine. If this was right, then we had six victims to come. What was it about the colour of the eyes? I needed a drink more than ever now, the "Cone & Pine" was looking so good.

7

The Forensic boys as well as the Pathologists were working overtime on this one. I was in the Pathology department of the Lakes Hospital and getting what is and what's for about the key factor in the case which is the DNA; "Deoxyribonucleic Acid which happens to be a chemical, a nucleic acid, which is at the basis of every living thing", he exclaimed,
I am lost already but I dare not show this jumped-up little pox doctor's night watchmen, or I could be here for months, and the night is getting on, closing time is so close, last orders will be called soon. How pathetic is that thinking, I am worried about a drink and three young women have lost their

lives to this jerk off?

He continued in his monotone commentary,

"Our DNA or genetic makeup can influence certain psychological factors such as personality traits, or aptitude in certain areas. This person or persons when we get their DNA, we are on the road to solving this case. The problem is trying to separate all the different fluids etc. that have b e e n found on the bodies of the victims," yes, we can show DNA it is special, because it is at the basis of who we are, I thought.

"No other human being on the planet shares the exact same DNA formation except for familiar bodies, e.g.: Children inherit 50 percent of their DNA from each parent, but unless they are identical twins, they do not inherit the same DNA as each other. If your parents' genes combined were a deck of fifty-two cards for example, you would receive twenty-six of them. So, this son of a bitch once we individualise his DNA, I have his arse in a sling" I exclaimed;

   "Is that right?".

He just looked at me. At last, I said;

   "But we have fingerprints do we not?".

   "Not really, they are only partials and so far, they all belong to the victims or unidentified person or persons." his voice on saying that, was sombre and really gave me no real confidence in trapping this perpetrator soon.

We had had no luck on where the victims are murdered, how he moved the bodies and was it a scalpel or just a very sharp type of knife he used? Why did he want the blood, and skin and tissue? W h y t a k e t h e o r g a n s ? These questions and a thousand others went over and over in my head which was now hurting. I had the feeling a real boomer of a headache was just around the corner, but a cold beer would fix that, I thought, my mind again racing, and my thinking blurred.

"Was there any blood at the scenes?" I asked;

"No, we told you that, only small amounts from the weeping wounds, not enough for the body to have been killed there, which is why the job is so bloody difficult." He exclaimed with contempt. I was now running out of ideas. Tyre tracks I thought, but dare not ask, not the mood these guys were in, otherwise I may have worn a beaker or two and then there was the chance of anything else that had the ability to be thrown was handy.

My phone rang;

"Farrer," I stated with complete superiority.

"Farrer, Jo here, and do not have that tone with me it is wearing very thin, are there any further updates?"

"No", I stated, and I realised I was taking it out on the squad, which is not good.

We needed something, a break of some kind just to get us in the right direction. I knew the upper floors would be on my back in the morning, and I had nothing for them. The next day I steered well clear of all, I needed to think, so went and sat down by the lake's edge. I went over everything, my life, my marriage, my career, and this case. Was I losing it I thought? I had not had a drink and my mind was clear, my phone rang;

"Farrer, Jones here the Lab Tech, we have used ABO for the blood, and we may get a result."

"What is ABO?" I asked hoping not to get one of his

monologues, which was too much to ask;

"We determine who the blood belongs to, by their blood group, A, B or O etc."

"Why did you not just say blood matching, would have been simpler." I exasperatedly asked.

There was no answer, and the phone went dead.

I headed for the office. Four fifteen in the afternoon and was sober and thinking straight, Jo was amazed. I ran into her outside and apologised for my behaviour during our short conversations, she shrugged and showed with her eyes, it is okay. We were sitting on a bench overlooking the park down the street from our office building. Jo looked at me;

"You have to think, Ian, the note, means you have had this sort of thing before as the killer knows you."

"Dinner?" she asked, we had planned to meet for dinner, she left; I sat there staring into space. My mind started to wander again as I went back over earlier cases I could remember, but nothing came to mind in that moment, my mind danced between thoughts ex-wife, my career, this case as it did hours earlier and where I was at this very moment.

Why do I keep going over all this, is it a type of omen? I sat for a long time pondering everything; what I must do to get my life back on track. I drove home slowly, showered, dressed, and left for Jo's, but time seemed to stand still. Before I knew it, I was at Jo's apartment sitting at the dining table, drinking a glass of water. I must be in a dream. I looked at Jo, who was in the kitchen preparing dinner. I asked in a quiet mousy voice;

49

"Where did the last four hours go," it was now eight p.m. She explained;

"I suppose you had gone home had a shower cleaned up and arrived here twenty minutes ago for dinner?" Those four hours was a mystery, and somewhere in the foggy haziness of my head was the answer. It was not the first time I had lost time like that. It had to be the booze. We ate dinner in relative silence each with our own thoughts, our own feelings of what we wanted from life. After dessert, Jo and I sat in front of the fire on the large Persian rug, dinner was great the first decent meal I had had in weeks.

She had done well for herself and was a compact woman, married to her job, her apartment was neat everything orderly and tidy. It was like a new place, so clean, hygienic. Put my place to shame, clothes everywhere, empty takeaway boxes all over the place, papers here and there and sink full of dishes five to six weeks old, booze bottles everywhere, I shuddered at the thought. I must get my head straightened out and quick.

I gazed into the fire and tried to get my mind off my apartment, and she asked;

"What are you thinking about."

"The letter," I stated,

"Somewhere in my past files I must have clues to all this and why has three young girls had to die because of me."

She looked at me and, her eyes said it all before I knew it, we were in an embrace on the floor, the protection of our clothes had disappeared, naked to the world, as we had arrived at birth. Her body was soft and smooth, she smelt of roses in full bloom. Her breasts were large, and her legs I had not noticed before were long and strong, from all the exercise she did, she was a powerful woman. I stopped and looked at her;

"We should not be doing this, it is unprofessional."

"Shut up and make love to me now!" she said,

"Before I lose the plot, tonight forget the job, your troubles, your life, tonight it is just us."

I kissed her passionately all over, fondling every area of her superb body. I kissed the silky-smooth skin, which glistened with the flickering fire light. I ran my tongue up her back to the nape of her neck, taking my time slowly to watch her reactions to my intimate moves. I caressed her breasts with my mouth and tongue and searched the valley between them with my now moist lips. I allowed my eyes to travel over her entire body. It made me aroused at the site of her, she was enjoying what I was doing, I had not been with a woman in three years, and this was so pleasurable, and I felt at ease. I again kissed her and followed the natural contour of her body down to her hips and along her strong legs. I fondled the inside of her thigh and again kissed her buttocks; she raised her hips and her body writhed with pleasure as did mine.

Her breathing as mine became rapid we entwined like two vines in a forest and we became one, bereft of inhibitions. Her lovemaking was intense, we explored all there was of each other, and it was well into the next morning before we finally went to bed and cuddled up together, satisfied with each other's fulfilment and contentment. I was awoken by bright light piercing my eyelid, it was sunshine, it hurt my eyes as well as my head, and it had been a long time since I had woken up sober. I felt warmth next to me and looked across at Jo, who was smiling.

"How do you feel?" she asked, in a sultry, seductive kind of way.

"I am not sure," I said;

"As this is unprofessional, and we are partners. I have not made love for three years since my wife left."

"It showed" she remarked, and gently kissed my cheek.

"I have to get to the office, as I feel somewhere in my past lurks the answer to this case."
I had made a conscious decision also during our lovemaking to sober up and rearrange my life. Jo had showed me the way, and I aim to do it right. I went to move but she pulled me back into the bed and we again made love so passionately I was lost in a world of pleasure and ecstasy. I arrived at the office a bit after one pm, and Jo was already there, she glowed, Coney looked at me and said;

"You must have got a shot in the arse last night you look reasonable for a change."
I shot a glance of resentment at him and felt as though they all knew about Jo and me, just then Eugene came in, and asked;

"Could I speak to you alone…. please."
The others left and he closed the door. I showed for him

to sit and asked,

"Did he want coffee?"

"No" he said;

"I want out of this unit."

I looked at him and was going to say why, but thought he must have reasons, and my mind flashed back to yesterday, when he had the look on his face, which I could not explain.

"Boss, I know the two victims, and I do not want to go into details, but I need off this at present. I will name the two I know, addresses etc., but no more."

I looked at him with what must have been a look of shock as well as frustration.

"I cannot let you, we do not have enough manpower now, so I am sorry, you are going to must give me more than that." He went silent and seemed to stare at a point above my head. For a moment then looked me in the eye and said;

"One is Catherine Rhined age 23, I have or should I say was having an affair with her for the last 3 months."

There was a short silence, then with a gasp;

"Fuck me! Eugene, why did you not come to me earlier?" I blurted out without really thinking.

"I broke the affair off with Catherine, two weeks ago; I had not heard from her since and naturally assumed she had accepted the end of the relationship."

"I think you will find the other girl is Teresa Caldwell, she is Katrina's niece who we have not heard from in months, and she only contacted us when she was coming to stay."

"Katrina (Eugene's wife) was like her mother, as her parents murdered some six years ago in a carjacking in New York when on holiday."

"Your wife" I said looking at him in disbelief,

"I gather does not know about the affair."

"She does now," he said in a low tone.

"How" I shouted in a very pissed off tone?

"A messenger arrived this morning with a photo and a letter sent to Katrina, postmarked yesterday."
I slumped into my chair my head in my hands, why have I decided to go cold turkey. I looked at Eugene,

"I will keep this between us, I will have to tell Jo and no one else, but you cannot leave the case. You will have to be the office runner no field work, OK? You also realize you are a suspect in the eyes of the Department."

He acknowledged with a slow nod, and I could see tears welling up in his eyes as well as a feeling of disbelief and relief all at the same time. I told him to take the day off and sort out what he was going to do; he left and closed the door behind him. This was the last time I was to see him, but I was not to know this at the time. Later that day I spilled the whole thing to Jo, she said,

"You will have to suspend him, he cannot work on this case, he is tainted with suspicion, a conflict of interest".
I roared;

"Who the fuck am I going to get, we have a squad of four, I do not trust, Macey, Coney hates my guts. I think I am falling in love with you, and my best snoop man confesses he was having an affair with a victim, head office would love this, and Coney would nail my arse to the wall if he knew, and God knows what Mayor Majors would do. No! It is in here; it stays here, for the time being at least. I must see Katrina; I need to verify Eugene's whereabouts, for the last two weeks."

"I will see Katrina," said Jo.

"You sort out Eugene, it appears we need him". I was starting to feel regrets for my night with Jo and deciding to go cold turkey on the grog, I needed a smoke, and I had given them away eleven years ago.

Jo asked, as she left;

"Are we on for tonight?"

"I will let you know,"

I said with a low but unconvincing tone.

8

Somewhere just outside of the town in an old disused engineering factory, with so many rooms and areas, it was also unique as it was carved out of a sheer rock face, the factory was built into the rock about two to three metres and this rock formation formed the back wall of the factory for at least three quarters of its length. The stealth figure was unpacking surgical instruments onto stainless steel trays, and carefully covering them with sterilized white linen cloth. Another person moved with agility and was about to perform another macabre murder. The streets of town were quiet it was three fifteen in the morning, when a sleek new BMW, Dark Blue in colour drove slowly through the quiet suburban streets.

Her boyfriend had just dropped off Sally Donald, as her parents did not like her current boyfriend, her mother feared him, and her father did not trust him. Along the low-lit street, she was unaware that a panther like person was pursuing her, he was in a clean-cut suit, no overcoat and a woollen beanie pulled over his ears, again he wore sunglasses, sniffing something as he walked in a shuffling pace along the wet pavement. He quickly glanced back along the street and across to the opposite side. Sally was in a good mood as her and Damien had had an enjoyable time and it was great, she felt on top the world. She thought to herself, stuff mum and dad, I am Twenty years old, working, I am going to get my own place and Damien and I can do whatever we like. Just then, her instincts kicked in and told her to look around, she spun around and coming at her was this dark mysterious figure, brandishing a knife, the blade could be seen by the streetlights, shining, clean and had a slight sparkle about it.

It was long and wide, with a slight curve in the blade and a sort of cut away piece near the tip, giving the appearance of an up turned point. She instinctively turned and started to run shouting,
    "Help Me" at the same time.
The pursuer grabbed her from behind by the hair and she fell heavily to the left into a large bush. The pursuer was

on top of her before she could do anything his hand clasped over her mouth, she was dazed, and her head throbbed from hitting the trunk of the bush. She kicked out at the assailant, but he was too strong. Sally then smelt an odour and she was gone everything went dark for her. The figure picked her up with ease and carrying the limp body over his shoulder ran back from whence they came. Under the dimly lit street, if anyone had seen him and what he just completed, they would not be able to give a good description of either party.

The large dark figure carried a parcel over his shoulder, and it appeared to weigh little, because of the ease at which he moved. The car he was driving was in a side street; into the back seat the body of Sally was delivered. Two hours had passed and when Sally awoke, she was in what looked like a cellar, but a hospital also, everything was white and stainless steel, except for parts of the walls which were carved out of rock. There was a distinctive smell though, one of oil and grease. There was also another more distinctive odour, one you would associate with a hospital. The lights above her were like that of an operating theatre. Sally, just for a moment felt safe and her screams for help have been answered she thought.

Her attacker had run off and someone had brought her to the hospital as she had passed out. Then a shadow appeared over her, it was her attacker she recognized those deep penetrating eyes, she seemed to recognise the person who wore a surgical mask and gown. When they spoke, it was as if they had some kind of machine-like voice; she had heard before when people have operations on their throats.

The attacker moved to the foot of the table and Sally could only just raise herself enough to see the person. She then felt cold steel on her vagina and felt the instrument forcibly opening her. She then felt a needle prick deep inside her and she was starting to feel sleepy and a feeling of numbness. The instrument removed from her; the assailant moved to the other side of the table. Sally was numb she was unable to feel her legs, she felt completely vulnerable. In the central office of Philadelphia County central records, Ray Barry was filtering through some old case files. I rang on the off chance that even though it was four o'clock on Friday there in Philadelphia, he might be consciences enough to be in the office. He answered;

"Hello Detective Barry, can I help you?"
I said;
"I hope so, Farrer here."
"How did you go with the information I sent you?"
"It's on the wire to you, we identified the other girls for you Farrer", Ray said, he also explained a case that might interest me.

"Remember back in 1980, the kid that was a ball short of a full pool set, by the name of Elroy Arthur Smith?"
"Not off hand".
"Well, he died about nine weeks ago; he was the character that was trying to recreate the perfect girlfriend from body parts of the dead in the funeral home in

58

Monroe County. Bodies were disappearing from the funeral home and turning up in pieces, spread across County after County. They all had amounts of blood missing and small skin sections. You would have to remember him; he was a real fucking nutter, remember your regular Dr. Frankenstein".

I could not recall the case quickly although I had a vague memory about it; I was still not clear in my thinking, as I had not rid myself of all the brain pickles. Ray continued,

"He had an accomplice that we never caught, and Elroy would not give him up. We did know that he had some training of sorts in the medical area. I will courier the file it may be him as he threatened to avenge Elroy's capture". I sat in absolute silence, listening to all this and thanked him a lot. I asked;

"If he was coming back, as I now owe him a Coke or two". He said;

"I thought you were on stronger stuff."

"I told him I had given it away." We made a promise to catch up soon. I was trying to get a grip on what Ray had told me and to sort this out within my partially well sautéed brain when the receptionist ran in screaming,

"We have another". The look on her face was one of terror and fright . I sat her down and asked;

"What are you on about?" Taking a deep breathe she licked her lips and uttered;

"Barbara Waite has been found in the forest above Talon Point".

Barbara Waite, twenty-two, married, but separated, no children, had a cross and line identical to the other victims and the word *"Dalus"* meaning *"Fraud"* cut into her back. She also had been dissected, lung, left kidney, blood and one ovary removed. She apparently had been skimming from her employer, but this was yet to be verified. I photocopied the information we have gleaned, gave each of my team one of the names and told them to follow up their history, who they knew in town or where they were from. Just then the phone rang it was the Desk Sergeant at Lakes County Central, he said that in the last three weeks there had been reports of four women between twenty and twenty-five go missing under strange circumstances.

They were from various areas all in neighbouring countries. He would have just regarded them as missing persons except he had received the wire concerning the identity of the already found victims. I crossed to our board, looking at the map and filling in the names the board hoping they were just missing, not a victim. The hair on the back of my neck stood on end, it was now clear our perp was not going to stop at the three we had. Deep down in my lower bowel I had this feeling we are only just scratching the surface within this crime. What was his next move? I told the officer I would meet him in the Needles Café, arrangements were made, and he assured me he would bring all the information he has. I said;

"I promised to have the coffee hot". I quickly rang Jo, apologized that I would be late and told her of the developments. She wanted to know if I wanted her to come with me, I said;

"No, I would take Macey and Coney".

I rang Coney and filled him in, told him to be ready in twenty minutes to travel, asked him if he would contact Macey. I collected the file and my briefcase and walked to the elevator, there was still some others working. I pushed the button for the elevator to take me down to the garage level. While waiting I kept thinking of what Ray had said, Elroy's mate we had a brief description of him, but it was still fuzzy. The elevator bell rang, the doors opened, and I stepped in. Pressed "G" and the doors closed.

I watched the floor numbers tick down as I still had things going around in my head. Then the elevator came to a stop. I looked at the floor numbers; one was flashing, then a voice, a mechanical voice started, I quickly grabbed my revolver and dropped the file and my briefcase to the floor. Waiting for the door to open, I instinctively glanced around. I quickly run my eye over each wall and then backing up to the rear of the elevator and listened, gun still in hand ready for anything.

"Ha Ha Ha, Farrer, your nemesis is in, you have three
or four with a lot more to come within.
You need 6 maybe more for Dante to be happy, and 3
to console the sins.
Remember 11 years ago, the longer you take, the
more you fuck around, the more you will forsake."

The voice started again, and I grabbed my recorder from my pocket and turned it on, holding it up with my right hand still with my revolver drawn, safety off and ready. The message repeated 4 times. Then the voice stopped, the elevator started again. I placed the recorder back in my pocket but kept my gun ready. I reached the garage the doors opened, as I stepped out something came at me from above it hit me square in the chest, I fell to the ground, hitting my head on the concrete floor all went black.

I came to my senses realising that there was a crowd standing around me, I had weight on me, which seemed to be all wet, and a stench to it like death. I realized I was looking at what appeared to be the naked body of a woman covered in blood lying on me. She was laying with her back to me the right side of her head seem to be missing and what looked like parts of skull and brain hanging out the gaping hole. Macey was looking at me; Coney was to my right; I said;

"Get this off me and help me up for fucks sake."
I asked;

"What the fuck had happened and what was going on?"
They said;

"We were about to ask you the same question?"
I had been knocked unconscious and out for about five to ten minutes, as Coney could not raise me on my mobile when I did not pick him up. I told them about the voice and played the tape. The bastard had been in the building. The problem was my fingerprints were all over the woman's body and on the scalpel that had carved *"Haeresis"* meaning *"Heresy"* and *"HA HA HA"* in her back. It was strange; the words carved in their back corresponded to something in their past or present. How the fuck, was this arsehole getting this information. Considering we were struggling to get anything

ourselves; it just pissed me off this freak of nature was able to be always two steps in front of us. This body on top off me also had been gutted to use the expression, but not here as there was so little blood but enough to make a mess on me. I had to change, and my clothes were taken to the lab to be examined. The tape recording was also to be analysed. I could still smell the odour of the victim's blood on me. I went to the changing room removed the orange jump suit they had given me to change into and took a shower. No matter how much soap and scrubbing I did I could not get rid of that smell, and the thought of the poor girl who was so unceremoniously dumped on me. My head throbbed and I had a lump the size of a boiled egg on the back of my head. I sat in the shower dazed and confused and feeling sorry for myself, found myself crying like a baby and asking the question;

"Was this job getting to me after all these years?"

9

It was a strange type of day no real sunshine, a ghostly sky tinctured with grey, giving one the thought that it was going to rain, yet there was still an iridescent look about it. A gentle breeze swept in from the east, it had a ghostly chill about it. I had the feeling that there was a problem somewhere and we were about to find out about it. My head and body ached all over; I am still trying to come to terms with what had happened and the weather, the darkness, combined with my aches and pains made for a miserable day. My grandfather had a saying;

"When trouble brews or there is an ill wind or thought about, it will be black over Mother Cummins. "Mother Cummins", was his name for Mt Galtymore at his home in Tipperary, Ireland. Suddenly killing the silence my phone rang it was Jo. She said;

"There was another case developing the body is in the morgue and Bill is there".

My mind just went blank, and I have a feeling of dread. I had also fell off the wagon after the meeting of the body and elevator episode. I looked out from our new office that was spacious to say the least; better than the rabbit warren we were in, difficult to move in the middle of an investigation, but necessary as the team grew and the crime had become a well-known event. Each had his own spacious office, fully equipped with, large desk, computer, television, and video equipment.

There was a very expansive conference/briefing room, very well laid out even a bar, which I may frequent often, although slowly I am trying to dry out. I continued to gaze out my window, feet up on the windowsill, with a few moments to repose and think of what may be ahead. I felt sequestered in this office never to be allowed to roam or be free again. No new leads, the body count had stopped, we had a body yet to be named and the autopsy yet to be performed on the body that smacked me in the face. My head was still rather fuzzy from the knock, normally I would have had a real "Jack" attack but being dry at present, I do not remember much of the happenings of yesterday at all. I was told I had a concussion and should take some time off.

My attention drifted off into the past the thoughts of my wedding day, heaven on earth, love, pure and true, the nectar of life. I had alienated all around me to be plaintively maladroit about my existence. Things had become a nightmare. My wife found that living life on the edge as most law enforcement officers must do was just too much. Waiting for the telephone to ring or that knock at the door to say I was in hospital or to be interred on such and such a day was just what she did not want and retreated from my life forever.

I will always love her, and a special place will always remain in my heart and soul for her. The telephone ringing awakened me from my few moments of self-indulgence, to snap me back to the world of reality. I slowly picked up the receiver hoping above all else it was not a case. I was looking forward to at least another couple of trouble-free days.

"Hello" I said, in a less than enthusiastic voice.

"Hi Farrer, Bill here, I think you had better get to the morgue we have a weird one and they want us to investigate".

"Why?" I asked, again with that tone of I am not really interested.

"This woman they suspect has been poisoned like one of our bodies in our present case. No traces of a struggle, only rash type marks on the inside of the wrists. Like a chemical has been used to penetrate the skin to the blood stream and boom she is dead."
Bill said this with such enthusiasm that I felt compelled to go.

"Okay, this may be the one Jo rang me about. I will meet you there in fifteen minutes. You mean we have another crime, or it is related to the one we are investigating?"

William "Bill" Welding, a man of immeasurable talent in the legal profession. He could make a case out of nothing; he had joined us from the law firm next to our old offices. His memory was just full of case histories and could recall most of the evidence and precedents that would be needed for an indictment in a case. Twenty years of law had him tuned to the max. He knew how to use his skills and vent his ability in a courtroom. To watch this man at work was like watching a woman seduce a man. He could manipulate a jury and judge like putty in his hand, I am glad he was on my team and not opposing me.

It took me about thirty minutes to get to the morgue I had to stop at the store and get some 'Jack' that's "Jack Daniels" for the uneducated, I needed my morning constitutional before I could continue. I had four good swallows of what I had now found to be the sweet taste of the Lord's nectar, in my opinion, my dry spell was over, would I regret this later? That was the unknown. I believed that they should serve this at mass instead that cheap dollar a bottle shit they serve up. Yes, I have been to mass, not a lot lately, but it has been a while since confession, I did not want to turn Father Brennan's hair grey just yet, considering he was only forty-six. I walked the blue line along the highly polished floor of the Hospital heading to the Morgue. To my right was a yellow line that if you followed it took you to reception. The white line took you to the elevators to the upper two floors. The red line on my right led you around, I am not sure I have never had to follow the red line and I really have not taken much notice of what it leads to. The blue took me to an elevator, set apart from the rest a sign saying, "Staff Only".

It took you down to the bowels of the building where ghosts roam free, angels picking up souls to take them to heaven. The Grim Reaper after the bad ones to send them off to hell.

"Fuck, I was starting to sound like a Stephen King or Dean Koontz novel", I said aloud.

I should not read them and drink too. I will give up the reading it is not good for my health. I arrived at the elevator and pushed the lower ground floor button, threw two peppermints into my mouth, and the doors opened almost at once, Bill, was there.

"Hi, Bill, how are we on this bleak typical windy day."

"Farrer, you reek of alcohol, before you go in here, piss off to the bathroom and clean up, or else Buchanan is going to have your arse." Bill, said to me in a rather polite but effective manner. We reached the floor of the dead; I went left and headed for the men's room. Bill went ahead to the Autopsy area. In the bathroom I washed and cleaned myself up, straightened my tie and combed my hair. I had four or five gulps of water that almost made me dry reach; it had no flavour my mouth felt like the arid surface of a desert, not that I had tasted a desert mind you. I stood staring at the reflection of a person I could not really identify with. I decided to take a few moments to re-gather and compose myself, popped two more peppermints and re-washed my hands what for I do not know. You have got to change old man, otherwise you will not see sixty, and the reflection gave no discerning look of disagreement. I turned and left the bathroom, rather disillusioned with myself.

10

Sally Donald was turned over onto her side and the person started to cut at her hip, but she could feel nothing, and she was unable to move due to the restraints. She tried to scream but nothing came out. She felt nothing in her whole body. The person seemed to be cutting at the top of her leg from what she could just manage to catch a glimpse of. What seemed a brief time she saw the person carry what looked like a piece of skin to a tray and place it in the tray and place it into what looked like a large refrigerator on the side of the room to which she was facing. He then returned to the table and undid the restraints, Sally tried to force her body to move but nothing happened. He then rolled her onto her stomach and the restraints re-tightened. She imagined he was doing something to her back and maybe they were cutting at her spine. Sally tried to turn her head to look but could not roll her head in any direction. They then seemed to tear something it sounded like paper. The restraints re-released as she saw the buckle of the large belt around her shoulders fall by her face.

The person then rolled her onto her back and the restraints re-tightened around her. She then saw the person place two plastic bags with red fluid and another silver container into the fridge. They returned to the table where Sally was, still unable to feel or move, or shout out. Again, the person was at the foot of the table, and she felt nothing but could sense he was again at her vagina. She woke up in a room, which looked exactly like a hospital ward. Her body restrained with large belts across four areas of the body, her back was in terrible pain; her hip felt like it was on fire. She tried to move her leg and felt a darting pain from her groin; she looked around and saw a plastic bag of fluid above her and a tube running down towards her groin. She could only imagine what it was doing. She then realized she was not alone, on looking around she could see four maybe five other bodies all with the same apparatus attached on similar beds to hers. The smell was horrible, she suddenly felt her feet become loose and the belt around her thighs was undone. Because of her numbness, she had not realized this earlier. She wriggled a little then realized she was able to wriggle down the table she exhaled and freed herself of the bindings.

The tube into her groin pulled and the sharp pain made her cry out with agony, but there was no sound; tears welled in her eyes. There was also a bag attached to her gown she was wearing and a tube into her bowel area. The bag looked like it was full of urine. She gathered her thoughts and stood there quietly for a moment listening, there was not a sound heard, the floor, well smoothed concrete, cleaned and polished. The walls were some forms of white mat type material but all clean and crisp. The lighting was fully on; there were no cupboards, shelves, or storage of any kind. This was just a room with the beds, the bodies and equipment attached to each bed.

She went over to the other beds two of them the odour was rank, they were covered with clean white crisp sheets, she pulled the sheet part way back and it revealed half a decayed body lying there, it had been cut down the centre of the body, she could make it out only just through the decaying skin. She suffocated a scream when she saw the blackened emancipated body. She struggled to catch her breath; she felt nauseous and had to control herself from throwing up everywhere. The room started to spin; she grabbed the side of the bed to balance herself. What had they done to her and the others?

She then felt the tightness on her back and realized she must have a bandage on, she groped around her shoulders and felt large strips of adhesive tape, she then felt around the top of her hips, the bandage ran all the way down her back and covered most of it. She had sharp pains now and it felt like a cut across the back. She felt faint. Pulling her wits together and looking around and pushing back the feeling of vomiting everywhere, she went to the last bed on the right, the young woman about her age was in a bad way, she looked anaemic and there was no life in her blue eyes. She was alive. Sally knew she had to get out and quick to get help before whomever it had come back. The one other strange thing Sally noticed about this room was that it had no doors or windows just two ventilation shafts in the ceiling. There was a noise a metallic sound; she spun around to see her pursuer aiming a gun at her. There was a loud noise and a flash of bright light.

11

Back upstairs in the office, there was still a nagging feeling but I needed to pull myself together myself together and most of all get out of these uncomfortable jump suit things I had been given to wear when my clothes were taken for analysis. Macey walked in, said;

"Jo was on line three", I picked up the phone, took a deep breath and signalled Macey all was okay and could he close the door and bring me a coffee.

I punched button three and Jo's voice came through,

"Are you all, right? Coney rang and left a message on the machine as to what had happened. I was in the bath when the phone rang."

I filled in the gaps and was taking off the jumpsuit and finding clean shirt and trousers in the cupboard in the corner as I went through the details of the ordeal. She did not seem shocked. This struck me as strange but then she could not see what I looked like either before showering etc., covered in blood, head to toe. Coney returned with a pair of Police issue overalls, jacket, and a fresh towel for me, I said;

"I don't need the overalls I had spare clothes in the cupboard".

I went ahead to pass the image of the body and the stench that had been lying on me for what seemed like an hour. I could not for the life of me understand fully what had happened, not yet anyway. The voice on the tape kept going through my head and the reactions of Coney, Macey, and Jo. Monday arrived, I had not had the best of weekends, and the horror thoughts were still going through my mind of that body on top of me. Upstairs wanted me to see the head shrink, to see if it had affected me, and how I was handling the situation. It will have to wait I had said, I now have four unexplained deaths, all connected and four missing that I am not sure of, and in some way, they are connected to my past.

The brass higher up was talking of replacing me and calling in the FBI, this I was afraid of and leave a half-finished investigation. I stated;

"What happens you take me off this case and this psycho goes on an absolute murder spree, I do not think we can take that chance." Coney and Macey knocked on the door, I waved them in, and they seated themselves in front of me on the far side of the desk, like schoolboys being sent to the headmaster's office.

"You OK Farrer,"

"I am,"

"Well, we visited that copper on Saturday and he gave us the names and descriptions on the four missing girls." Coney reeled off the names;

"Sally Donald, age twenty, single, lives with her parents, still missing, no clues, and no evidence. Bridgett Carmichael, twenty-three, single, lives with two others in a shared apartment. Anna Piress, twenty-five, single, vagrant, released from custody to appear in court never showed up. A warrant issued, as she was to stay at the shelter, they said she never made it there from the courthouse. Apparently, her boyfriend picked her up from jail, but she did not arrive at the shelter".

This sparked a thought in the back of my aching head.

I said;

"Continue".

"The fourth girl was Deirdre Zastes, twenty, single, lives with parents."

"How many of the four are blondes and have blue or brown eyes?" I asked. Coney looked through the more detailed descriptions and said;

"Sally Donald still missing and Bridgett Carmichael, both blue eyed blonde hair. The other two are of Italian and Spanish parents".

"This is starting to add up a bit, the body on top of me, fit any of the descriptions we have".

"No", was the reply.

"But boss we have a body and the Forensic report on the body. It shows that she was at some time in the same clinical environment as the others had the same sort of operations on her, and she had been shot, through the eye, thus the mess at the back of the head. Forensic said she had been dead at least three weeks. The blood was not hers; it was a watered-down mixture of two other types".

 He went ahead to finish the brief,

"She was also shot while lying on top of you", continued Macey, as he was relaying this information it made me feel even worse.

He continued;

"Fragments of her skull, and brain tissue were found imbedded in your jacket, and on the floor beside you. One single shot, close range. The bullet luckily missed you and ricocheted off the floor and lodged in the rear wall of the elevator; it did not do a JFK thing and go through anything else before it lodged in the wall".

Macey continued;

"The bullet is from police issue; it was your gun, which fired the shot. The tests on your hand for gun residue was positive, the other thing is your gun is now missing. This whole thing seems a bit bizarre now boss"

"How are you connected with all this?"

"We will know when the file arrives; it apparently is an old case that has similarities to this one. How do they know it was my gun?"

"You know all our weapons are tested and the firing pin, barrelling and numbers are recorded as well as any other distinctive markings, department regulations". Macey was looking at me with a look of total amazement that I had forgotten that fact. What he did not know was I had a second gun same calibre, make and model. Carried it just in case, and I just nodded.

"If this girl was dead three weeks, which means he may still have others. Have we found any others yet?"

"We are still working on that, this girl was a bit of a mess, and they have to try to reconstruct her face etc., so we have something," said Coney.

"All the families of the other girls have been notified, from the notes I left on your desk?"

"Yes, Jo has not been seen this morning though," said Macey;

"Nor has Barelli" tuned in Coney.
I said;

" I had spoken to Jo, but Eugene I had not had contact with since Thursday when I gave him the day off".

"What is the matter with him?" asked Coney,

"He is as jumpy as a jack rabbit when that Natalie woman's name is mentioned."
I told him not to worry it was none of their business, the whole thing is a need-to-know basis. Just then a young, uniformed officer came bursting through the door;

"Sir, your wanted downstairs in the first-floor men's room ASAP." He looked as white as a ghost and was quite out of breath.

"What is the problem?" I asked, he said;

"Captain McLean wants you there now!" McLean was head of the Fraud division in County Central, why was he here and always trying to stick his nose into our business, if he thought that a homicide might cross his territory. Macey and Coney followed me to the elevator, I thought twice will I ride in this or go down the four flights of steps, I decided to hold my breath and use the elevator. We arrived on the first floor there were uniforms and plain clothes cops everywhere, you could have mistaken it for the entrance to the Policeman's Ball.

I forged my way to the door where McLean was standing with an ashen look on his face.

"What is your problem?" I asked;

"It is not mine mate, but you have a big problem in stall three." Coney, Macey, McLean, and I went inside, there two uniform boys at the entrance to the urinal area and two more further on at the doorway to the stalls. I could see Matt Lawrence from Forensic, facing the other way and he looked ill. I reached the stall door first, glanced around, and slowly pushed the door open. There was the horror of horrors; slumped in the corner was Eugene, half his head missing plastered all over the wall. His stomach ripped open and his insides neatly laid around the front of the toilet bowl. His eyes glazed and bloodshot, wide open and they seemed to have the look of horror in them, blood everywhere, his small intestine hanging out the front of his shirt with his heart wrapped in it and sitting on the toilet bowl lid, with a tag attached in bold print, *"HIS HEART WAS NOT IN HIS JOB"*.

I felt my breakfast in the back of my throat; I took a deep breath turned, pushed my way past the others, standing there with ashen coloured faces and looks of disbelief reflected their feelings. I ran to the opposite stall, I threw up; it felt like I had vomited all of what I had eaten in the past six weeks.

The look on Eugene's face, that of horror, the sight of it, I vomited again. I sat down in the stall with sweat and tears streaming down my face;

"Why?" I asked.

"What had he done, who could have done this?" I then out aloud asked;

"Was it connected to our investigation? Was it connected to the girl in the car park? Did we have another set of murders?"

My mind would not stop racing. This was my fault; I had to end this. Then I thought of Katrina and the kids.

Had Jo spoken to them? The Forensic boys had started when I came out of the stall. I washed my hands and face, rinsed my mouth, and looked at what and who I was and trying to get answers from the reflection in the mirror, I had no idea at that moment who the man in the mirror was or what truly was happening, I washed my hands and face again, rinsed my mouth and took four big gulps of water.

This case was so full of empty vessels, clues that took us nowhere, we kept chasing our tails and biting our own arse with no feeling. Sooner or later things had to fall into place the puzzle had to be finished. The face looking at me from the mirror seemed to be talking sense and was more clued up than this drunken shit. I admitted to my image that I was a washed-up soak, and I needed to get my shit together. I had lost a good man and a dear friend. I know deep down I was not to blame, but that made it no easier. I left the bathroom p a s s i n g t h o s e s t a n d i n g t h e r e a n d I d i d n o t e v e n r e c o g n i s e o r a c k n o w l e d g e t h e m , and walked slowly along the stark corridor, down the small flight of steps, the side door was unlocked, I went outside, it was snowing, I didn't care my shirt soon b e c a m e soaked and hair become straggly, I could not feel the cold, I was too angry to feel cold. I turned, stared at the lake, and face upturned to the sky, I swallowed a deep gasp of air and roared as loud as I could;

"Fuck you, you son of a bitch. I am going to get you and mark my words you will fucking suffer!"

12

Linda Forrester, sitting at her desk at the chemical company. She was due to leave for a private meeting in fifteen minutes. Linda was the Legal adviser on the patent and registering of the products the company produced, worked from home, and did most of her work by the internet. Linda, forty-two years old, married, two children, Tammy fourteen, strong willed fiery and very independent. Robert, the complete opposite to his sister quiet achiever type he was sixteen. Dean Forrester, forty-six, was the company's Manager, and had been for nearly fifteen years. He was a Biochemist by trade and started the company just outside Oemen Lake, knowing that it would be a boost for the town as well being a wonderful place to live. The decision was a good one, it had made he and Linda rather well off over the past six years since the products went on sale. Dean was hen-pecked by Linda who was a bit of a control freak. Everything had to go her way, or the event or conversation did not go ahead. Dean had found solace in his work up until two years ago when he met Cerise Blackwell, thirty-five, five foot eight, brown hair, blue eyes, and a body of lust.

Dean and Cerise had been having a torrid affair, primarily based on lust. In the last three months though things had started to get serious between them and Dean was looking at plans of leaving Linda. Tuesday afternoon October twenty first, Cerise and Dean are exploring the areas of the human body once again in the small motel in Pale Top Hills, the next village, not far from the factory. Their rhythmic movements each were enjoying the other. Cerise was groaning with ecstasy as Dean, and her climaxed. They lay there cuddled up together when Cerise asked;

"When are we going to make this permanent Dean, I am sick of the sneaking off in the afternoon for a quickie, and no real fulfilment. I am running out of excuses at work, and Ray is becoming very suspicious of what I am up to."

Ray Beale owned the trucking company that shipped all the products internationally for Dean in as well as around the county and interstate. That is how they met. There was a discrepancy over an account and Dean went to Ray to sort it out. Cerise was the Accounts Manager and thus it all fell into bed from there. Ray Beale was an initiative-taker. A driver who eventually brought his own truck and then another and another and so on until he now has a fleet of twenty-three trucks travelling throughout the country, twenty-four hours a day. He had known Dean since he was a youngster and Dean had grown up with Ray's own son Mark, who was killed in a fire about ten years ago.

If Ray knew about Cerise and Dean, there would be hell on earth, as Ray treated Linda like his own daughter. Ray's wife Gayle was like a mother to her. Linda's parents had been killed just after her twenty first birthday in a boating accident off Port Villa in Vanuatu. Dean looked at Cerise and smiled;

"You know I cannot rush this it will take time and we have to be careful as to how I go about it, Linda will be like a bull in a China shop and with Ray and Gayle getting involved it could become messy." Cerise realised he was right; time was of the essence in the situation and the timing needed to be perfect. They again rolled over on top off each other, and Dean was caressing the neck of Cerise with his lips and their foreplay and lovemaking continued to well after four. Little did they know that sitting in a car, not more than thirty metres away was Phil "The Prick" Mews, a rather shady character, who had spent time in the slammer for theft, larceny, robbery with intent, and a few other misdemeanours?

He was now an unregistered private detective who seemed to do odd jobs around the restaurant, 'The Wander Inn' owned by a gentleman named Stewart Madden. Linda had found him through her enquires with some unsavoury characters that had frequented a restaurant that a good friend of hers owned in Libby, Lincoln County. She knew that Stewart Madden had been in love with her since High School and that the feeling was never returned although she had led him on like a prick teaser a few times. Stewart was forty-three, single, six foot six, and built like the preverbal outhouse. Linda had not seen him in this light before and had she not loved Dean so much, she would have been in Stewart's bed in an instant. He would not have to ask twice; he was to be surprised and little did he know he would not have to ask at all. Linda knew that Stewart had some underground friends, she had told him about her suspicions of Dean, and he may be having an affair.

In walks The Prick, probably the worst person she could have got involved with. Phil Mews was as ugly as sin itself, two front teeth missing thanks to an accident in Prison, the rest of his teeth yellow and stained from smoking. Always seemed to have a three or four-day growth beard, hair that needed a good wash, and cut although balding slightly in the front. He was a real no hoper.

13

Sally Donald awoke to find her whole body ached, her back was on fire, she could not move. She was back on the original table, but she was alive. She seemed to be facing another way and noticed that the girl who was in the last bed had gone, and so too had the decaying body she had seen. There was still a rotten stench, but also an overpowering smell of disinfectant. She tried her arms and legs but could not move she felt the wide belts cut into her skin. Her mind raced with what had happen, her right arm just above the elbow felt as if it were burnt, but she could not see it from the position she was laying in. The metallic click sounds again, it came from her right, she turned her head as far as she could just in time to see a section of the wall close, and the masked, gowned figure come into the room. When the door closed, you could hardly see the opening, the figure had entered the room through. With menacing eyes and a slight frown on the forehead the person leant over, Sally;

"You know you got the others killed, don't you, with your little escapade. You made me angry, and I am pissed off."

Sally smelt a familiar aroma from this person; she could not put her mind into gear to place where or when she recognized it from. It had a sickly, sweet aroma. The figure slowly withdrew and then in a voice that made Sally tremor with fear.

"Your time is near, my dear, Farrer is now starting to

realize what we are about".

Even though the person spoke with a very educated sounding voice despite the machinery used to disguise it, Sally was still trying to place the smell; the eyes also had something about them. Unfortunately, the disinfectant smell had taken over again, and the aroma was lost to her.

The figure went over to a table at Sally's feet. She was unable to see what was happening, then, suddenly she was hit in the face with what felt like water, she opened her eyes to see a blonde body, naked being carried out the door over the shoulder of her captor. She realized in an instant that the fluid she felt was not water but blood from the body that they had taken from the room.

As it disappeared, she saw the cuts on the back of the body; it was a cross and a word *"Glotonie"* with a horizontal line under it, Sally had no idea what the word meant. She now had a fair idea why her back felt the way it did. She shook with fear, her mind was racing, she had to get out, and she had to get help. There was a small noise and a low hum started, Sally felt cooling air on her face from the vent above and the stench in the room started to dissipate. Suddenly, the figure was back at her feet, undoing the belts; a strong hand grabbed her by the shoulders, and she was raised up into the sitting position. She was then hoisted over this person's shoulder with what seemed relative ease. She glanced around the room there was only the empty tables and equipment left. The thing she would remember most was the smell. That odour she believed would stay with her for the rest of her life, which may not be long. They went out into a corridor and the door closed, behind them.

The corridor was long and narrow; there were small lights at intervals like Christmas lights just enough to be able to see where you were going. The walls were decaying concrete with what looked like wire stretched over it everywhere, the supports were or columns at intervals she thought where either there to brace the wire in place or so it seemed or were part of the structure.

What appeared to be windows were painted over and the other doorways that Sally could see in the very dim light were many but few and far between. Some had wide plastic strips hanging over them, there was a stench a musty wet smell, that aroma was coming back as well. There was some of the rooms with lights but mostly dark. In the dimming light she could not be sure really of what she was seeing. Eventually, after what seemed to be a long time. Sally estimated they had walked at least two to three minutes, they ascended wooden stairs and came into a room; well-lit although there were areas on the walls that had shadows, or the lights were shaded by something to cause this. It had two doors from what she could see at the far end of the room and a window, which was half covered from the bottom up. Her head was starting to hurt from the position she was in and the manner she was held. Her back was now on fire as the garment covering it was rubbing against what she believed to be cuts. She had to keep her wits about her, memorize this place if she could. Through the top half of this window, she could see it was dark outside or what appeared to be outside as she imagined the lights, she saw were from a building close to where she was. The person took her through the far side door again leading to another corridor this time not as long, but the stench was unbearable.

A lone light globe on the wall lit this area. Wires ran the full length of the walls and constructed the same as the earlier hallway, this time with less doorways but they were wider. The aroma was also constant, and she started to think where she had smelt it before even though her mind was fuzzy and was still recovering from what had happened down in that dungeon area, when she first came to. They turned a corner a short distance a door opened, this room was like a bedroom but dimly lit, a bed in one corner and chair, table and what appeared to be a television in the other, but the light was so dim Sally could not really make it all out clearly.

The aroma in here was strong; it felt like it burnt the insides of her nostrils. They went through an archway and into a small alcove area. She noticed video equipment, and what appeared to be a dark room, with a low voltage red light hanging on a cord from the ceiling, it had what appeared to be another cord hanging from just above the globe. Then a door opened, and they entered a room that Sally recognized. She heaved a long deep breathe, she did not want to be back in here, there was so much she could not see but knew there was bodies, dead bodies in this room. Was she to become the next one lying under one of those half sheets? She tried to fight but there was no feeling, she was numb, then suddenly he lifted her off his shoulder in one quick movement. She was put on the table in the centre of the room and her hands were then handcuffed to a bar, which was bolted through the table, her ankles had the same thing done to them, she looked around there were two other bodies lying on what seemed to be operating tables, she was sure they were dead as the others were, but these had been moved around, the tables were in different positions. There   was blood everywhere, both   where blond, although you would not have guessed with the amount of blood streaked through the long strands which hung over the table's edge.

One of the bodies had a small sheet covering the lower half but her breasts large and full seemed to hang lifeless to the side and covered in blood. The other completely naked no covering. Blood was everywhere on this body, her breasts where missing, part of her face had been cut off it appeared. Sally looked away in horror, bit her lip hard and stifled a scream. She continued to look around, her senses now alive and everything she could see was being recorded into her memory. The windows in this room were all covered and blacked out. It had that hospital smell. The figure walked over to a trolley and came back with a syringe, filled with a milky liquid.

"This will make you sleepy, you will be my message to Farrer, to show him I mean business, he still has to find the other bodies to make the hunt complete, and if he has understood what I was aiming at then he will see that I have all in front of me and he cannot win."

In the room over her captors left shoulder, on the wall to her right covered in newspaper clippings showing ghastly pictures of these dead girls with markings carved into their backs.

There was a headline in the centre;

"Police Call Case - Dante's Revenge".

There were at least thirty paper cuttings on the wall, all referring to the murders, differing newspaper header masts on each. It suddenly hit Sally even in her frenzied, foggy minded state before he gave her the drug and it started to take effect, she realized she was in the den of a murderer. She knew she had to get away now, at all costs.

Her instincts told her to go along with this person until she could seize an opportunity. Sally started to wriggle and tried to scream but then realized she had something over her mouth. She kicked out and lashed with her hands at the figure, but to no avail. The figure stepped back, and Sally suddenly caught site of a wristwatch or bangle that was familiar in some way, just as she felt a blow to the side of her face she fell across the table. She felt the needle as the fluid pushed into her vein in the back of her hand; the strength of this person was unreal. They had managed to give Sally the needle even with all the struggling and moving. Her face hurt and she could feel her eye and cheek swelling. Sally started to feel sleepy, but it came to her in a flash, she knew her captor, and all went black.

14

In central records in Helena, Ray Barry's interest in the information I had given him and what he had collected for me had sparked his imagination. He had read the old case files; and was perusing mountains of paperwork, case notes, evidence notes, court transcripts the works. Ray had even perused the cold case archives, looking for anything that may help. He called me twice to ask about certain areas of what was happening with things, and I brought him up to speed.

I asked;

"Any chance of you coming here, one of my young investigators has been killed in a most macabre fashion by this person and I need another set of eyes on this"

"I thought you would never ask," said Ray.

"I cleared it with my superiors yesterday, they said only if you required help".

"I will be on the first plane out in the morning, and I will bring all the other files with me. I will fax you with my arrival time. This will be like old times again man".

Ray Barry, a former Homicide cop had seen it all, married with 3 kids, he was the real family man. He warned me when I moved to Oemen Lake that Christina was not going to go along with it and my marriage would suffer. He also had empathy and the ability to talk to members of the public easier than I did, and that is why we were such a successful team, the good cop bad cop scenario, when stationed together in Philadelphia. I have to say though it was not always that way. A man, who stood about six feet four, quiet nature and spoke with an extremely well-educated tone, I had never asked Ray about his background and felt it was too late now anyway, suddenly I thought of Eugene and his wife and kids, as his boss I had better see her. I had been there on many occasions for dinner, and she had made me feel like part of the family.

Katrina even tried to get me hitched up with her sister on a blind date, not that I did not like Evelyn, but my divorce was just over, and I needed space. I decided now was as good a time as any to go. I drove along the suburban streets thinking about this whole stinking affair and how it was starting to affect so many people. I had picked up some flowers and candy as well as a bottle of wine. I am glad that I did not have to break the news to her the Doctor at the hospital had already seen to that and explained briefly what had happened to me. I pulled up the driveway of this nice two-storey home in a respected area of town, it was a picture-perfect scene with snow laying deep and the colours of the house and lights all reflecting off this white blanket. The white fence could not see the neatly mowed lawns and well-kept gardens for snow, the beautiful trees, and shrubs, were laden with snow, Ayden came out to greet me; he was Eugene's youngest, and still to start school. Katrina was at the door, red teary eyed from crying.

I gave the candy to Ayden and the bottle of wine and asked

him to take it inside. He looked at me and said with his big brown eyes wide and shiny,

"My daddy has gone to live with God, he will be happy there, won't he?" I almost started to cry, I felt the welling up in the back of my eyes, and I took a deep breath and replied;

"Yes". Katrina put her arms around me, and I cuddled her tight, I hated this part of the job.

"Ian, why has this happened?" I did not have an answer and could only look her in the eye and shake my head. I stayed and had dinner and we talked and reminisced about the fun times we had and how Eugene was always the joker etc. We both cried a little, we both fell silent at times with our own thoughts and eventually I had to leave but I made her promise if she wanted anything, call. She agreed, I told her I would pick her up for the funeral, but I will contact her and let her know a time.
I returned to Jo's and lay beside her thinking of who may be next and what was happening to me and why?

I then thought of Ray arriving in the morning, I hope he has produced something positive. The phone rang, I looked at the clock, it was two forty-six in the morning, Jo answered;

"OK, be there in fifteen minutes, I will ring him and pick him up". She hung up the phone, turned over and faced me and said;

"That was Macey we have another body, close to here, you heard me say I would pick you up so, have a shower and we will arrive at the scene."

I understood what she was trying to say this was getting hard now, with this relationship. At the scene, again, it was busy. Forensic had started and the local police were milling around as if they had all lost their dicks somewhere and did not know how to find them. This body was east of the city near Big Bear Road heading to the forest, as we had been informed by the desk Sergeant. Coney rushed over;

"They have found another body through a phone tip off, just off the main road near Big Bear Ski Field, Macey and I will go there now". I said to them;

"When you get there ring me, I want to know what is on the bodies, is this all of them, or are we missing something."

We now had seven bodies it would seem in the pattern as well as the unidentified car park corpse and Eugene made nine, how did they all fit together? The Big Bear Road body was again a blonde, brown eyed about twenty-three. She had a crosscut into her back and a horizontal line below it close to the small of her back and the word *"Limbus"*. I looked at Jo and said;

"When Ray gets here in the morning, we will have to have a complete run down on what we have and also on what evidence we have and if we have any suggestions or suspects."

Almost 3 hours rolled past as we surveyed the area. The Forensic boys were just about finished. The snow had started to fall and seemed to be getting heavier. I cursed as our crime scene would be obliterated by this. Colin Miles, one of the top boys in his field came over;

"Farrer, I have looked at all these bodies, they are killed somewhere else and dumped. There are no tyre marks, just footprints leading to the spot then he seems to retrace his steps thus causing the double effect on the footprint."

I looked at him, and asked;

"Would you like to join our team for this one? We are having a briefing in the morning."

"I will be there, 9am ok" he said. I acknowledged;

"That would be fine". My phone suddenly started ringing;

"Hello",

"Farrer, its Coney we have another one here, twenty to twenty-five, blonde, brown eyes, cross in her back and line below the cross and the word *"Violentia"*.

"Have the forensic got any idea of time of death."

"Three to four weeks ago at a guess" he came back with. I told him about the meeting, bring whatever he could get, tell Macey also.

15

The funeral for Eugene was on as well tomorrow, so with the meeting, I think we will need to have a bit of resolve about us. Jo looked at me, the sun was coming up, I had not realised the time and our meeting in effect was only an hour or so away. I told Jo to ring Coney or Macey back and tell them it was this morning; I would see her in the office as I would have to pick up Ray. I rang the office and asked if there was a fax for me from London. There was and it had Ray's details on it, they read it to me,

"Arriving six fifteen in morning", I looked at my watch, fuck; he has been at the airport over an hour already. I tried his phone but no answer, so I left a message to say I was on my way. I arrived to see Ray sitting on a baggage trolley, reading what looked like a file.

"Sorry man" I said with a smile on my face.

"No problem, I caught up on some more reading". We travelled back towards the office and Ray filled me in with what he suspected was happening, he had not heard about the other bodies, and he was interested in this "Dante" theory. The other query he had is why blondes and only brown or blue eyes. I told him we are having a meeting this morning and will go over all the evidence we have so far.

"This one is a blinder Ian; I cannot put any sense to the whole thing yet and how he is connected to you or your past." Ray was looking, out the window as we pulled into the underground garage; he seemed preoccupied, with his thoughts. Then without warning he said;

"Why would the killer risk the security and the trouble to come into this building unless he or she knew their way around."

"They would have to know the elevator you were on was the only one that came to this floor, the surveillance cameras, where not operating that day, and that there was no risk of being seen here; you told me it was bugging you as well, and I have been questioning that fact since."

I gave him a quizzical glance,

"What do you mean?"

"We will have you had your team checked out. Who is working with you? Who has helped you? Is there anyone with a grudge?"

My mind raced with all the faces of the people I had dealt with over this case in the past weeks, Ray had opened a can of worms now. I at once disqualified Jo; but then why? She was part of the team so, was I? We rode the elevator to the third floor in silence where we had now set up a headquarters for this investigation. Greeting us at the door was a plain clothes Detective from the Homicide division of the County Investigation Squad.

"Hi, what can I do for you" I asked.

"Is your name Ian John Farrer," he asked.

"It is" I replied.

"You are under arrest for the murder of Julie Anne Crow."

16

Detective Chris Mills arrived at our office from Helena. The District Attorney had appointed him to interview everyone, formulate a report, and investigate our systems and measures we have in place for the investigation and whether this was too big for a local sheriff's office. The reason being during our recent investigation it appeared information was being leaked to the media by person or persons who had no interest or connection to the cases. The first thing was, he enquired as to what the 'Dante's Seven Sins' connection was all about. First person to progress to the room that had been set up for him, to enable him to conduct this as I call it a 'witch hunt' was yours truly. I entered the room went ahead to the end of the table and promptly took my seat.

He looked at me, while he shuffled folders and papers. Opened his laptop, shuffled some more papers and I had had enough with a very forthright and evil sounding voice I stated;

"Fuck you man, I have an investigation to conduct and not sit here and watch you try and sort out what you are going to do. Ask your fucking questions and hurry up about it!" He slowly looked up eyeballed me for what seemed like hours, and suddenly asked;

"How long have you been sheriff here in Oemen Lake?" I took a deep breath and said slowly,

"About two years".

He shuffled some more papers and then asked me;

"Please explain the Dante theory and what Dante is and how you and your team connected this to the victims".

I looked at him with a disbelieving glance and uttered;

"You are shitting me, right?"

He just shook his head in the negative aspect and gave me an evil glance. I knew then I was going to have to go through the whole thing. So, I started on the explanation of what Dante was all about as explained to me by Macey, I also quoted off my notes. I tried to also incorporate the deadly sins. I started that the names in Dante's Inferno, were associated with a discovered body with a cross and line.

"Annabelle Tate had *"Limbo"* and from what we understand it means the person's soul or self-resides within the unbaptized and although not sinful, she did not accept Christ. Without baptism she lacked the hope for something greater than rational minds can conceive."

I looked up from my notes, taking a breather I stopped.

"Keep going" he said.

So, I continued, slowly and more deliberate as I explained the second circle.

"In the second circle of hell are those overcome by *"Lust";* Dante condemns these carnal male factors for letting their appetites sway their reason. Judy Hampton had this engraved in her back, again, with a cross and line. This means she will be one of the first ones to be truly punished in hell".

I slowly took a sip of water and again looked at my notes

and continued;

"The great worm Cerberus, guards the gluttons, who suffer gluttony and who are forced to lie in a vile slush produced by ceaseless foul, icy rain", I slowly took a breath and stated that upon some investigation I found this little gem, Dorothy L. Sayers writes that, and I read from my notes;

"The surrender to sin which began with mutual indulgence leads by an imperceptible degradation to solitary self-indulgence, which includes not only overindulgence in food and drink, but also other kinds of addiction. We have no body with this word yet".

I paused and slowly looked at him, he was feverishly writing, so I continued;

"The fourth circle is *"Greed"*, we are told to see the souls of people who are punished for greed. We have no body for this either, yet. So that is two of Dante's Inferno that are yet to appear".

I studied him closely, this detective Mills showed no emotion, and not uttering a word, just nodded and I started again.

"The fifth is *" Anger"*, this we know was the mutilated body of Rose McHenry, it was disgusting and showed the perpetrator's real anger and that he has truly a mental problem. Her body was not a pretty site, she also had the circle and line as well. I should say that the words were spelt out in Latin on their backs we had to translate them".

He asked;

"Could I have a copy of the Latin words at a later

time, as well as the photographs of the victim's backs".
I nodded agreement. I began;

"In the sixth circle, those who say the soul dies with the body are trapped in flaming tombs".
Pausing for a moment before continuing I took a deep breath and explained how this body was found and the circumstances. Telling him she was found on top of me and the steps leading up to this situation, he continued to make notes. I said;

"This body had *"Heresy"* on the back again with a circle and line, we are sure it was Julie Ann Crow. I am going to have a full run down on this at a briefing tomorrow, so do you want me to continue?"
He replied;

"Yes" in a most perturbed tone. I continued even though I was feeling rather shitty and getting sick of his attitude, or what little he showed.

"The seventh circle is *"Violent"*. This body was also badly mutilated, and her hair was shaved off, it was not pretty, and her face had been badly battered".
I snarled and went ahead to the next;

"The next was *"Fraud"* and yes, we know what went on with her when we did the background check. She had the same circle and lines as the others.
I will say here, he had done his homework and knew what to look for in his victims. This and the ninth circle really do punish sins that involve conscious fraud or treachery, the last being, *"Treachery"*, which we have no body for yet making three missing from the nine".

I did not stop him, I let him continue so I could get out of here as this was not getting anything done and I am sure that he was not going to use this information in his report as I could see no real connection with what he was supposed to be reporting on, and this information.

"With the seven deadly sins of *Pride, Envy, Gluttony, Lust, Anger, Greed,* and *Sloth,* they have as you have heard in some areas have been used on already discovered bodies, so we are hoping that we do not end up with sixteen bodies. I hope I have been briefed enough and that we can now continue?"

He continued making notes, then said;

"I will need to look deeper at this, can we continue this tomorrow?"

I stood and left the room without saying a word, or even looking back, just leaving him making notes and shuffling papers. I went into my office thinking of life, was I hiding from life or just from myself. I started to think about how Eugene had died, and life deals up shit. Life can be cruel as well as fun; one must pick the time to have fun and who with, when the cruel side of life happens, deal with it and get on with life otherwise you will wallow in it for too long.

As I was self-assessing myself the secretary from the front desk brought me a file. I opened the cover and here was what I had not expected so soon, another case of mysterious murder with seemingly vicious intent and guile. As sheriff, what had I done wrong that this was happening in this small quiet community? I wanted to solve this case and not have the state troopers or FBI just walk in kick my arse and send me packing.

I perused the file and thought a person who unlawfully kills another human being, with malice commits *"mens reus, acteus reus"* (Guilty mind, Guilty act), the two cases were now this. Were they connected, a question I was asking myself as I read the Pathologist's report. This I hoped would have some clues or even a definitive answer if possible. Was I asking too much, or was I just being naive?

17

While Cerise and Dean played in their love nest, Mews was listening with his boom microphone and filming the whole thing with a camera he had planted in the air conditioning vent of the room before they arrived. He had known of this for about three weeks and had planned it well, which was surprising for him. Dean and Cerise left the motel and went their separate ways, in their own vehicles; Mews retrieved his camera, and returned to his hovel he called home. He had bought a rather lot of sophisticated equipment thanks to his employer for editing videos and dubbing etc. as well as computers and software to enhance the entire process. Mew's time in jail had not been wasted he had completed three courses on computers and editing of movies, sound, and programming.

In the back-room Mews loaded the tape into one of the machines, he had his own blue movie, and the sicko decided he would masturbate while watching it, not once but twice. Later he finished dubbing and splicing the tape. He sat and watched it again, with a smile at his handy work, he had, a movie with sound and motion that was going to make him rich. Linda Forrester had already paid him thirty thousand dollars and he had bought almost seventy thousand dollars in equipment, which she agreed to pay for when she had the evidence. Mews had decided if she can afford that, she can pay anything. His next move was fantasy, he was going to try and extort her. Little did he know that Linda Forester was a step ahead of him? Through Stewart she had found out Mews had jumped parole and a warrant for his arrest was out. She also knew that if he tried to double cross her that there were people who could make him do a disappearing act quick. Linda had become so obsessed with her theory on Dean's affair she was starting to live a fantasy life. She was going to get even with anyone that tried to stop her, or that came between her and Dean.

The facade she put on in front of everyone hid the real Linda Forester underneath. The phone rang, Linda answered;

"Forester residence".

"Hello missus, Mews here, I have a sexy tape for you to watch and you and I could get hot with this."

"Mews you sick bastard, just meet me at the planned location with the tape."

Mews started to laugh and then with a serious voice,

"Fuck you lady, I want half a million dollars now or this tape goes to hubby. I have pictures of you I will work with them onto the tape and you and Stuey boy will be fucking in that hotel instead of your husband and his bit of crumpet. You get my fucking drift." Linda knew that he would try this;

"Do you know the name Charlie "Chico" Hemming?"

"Yea, he is my parole officer, why?"

"Well Mr Mews I have his number and I know that he wants you bad and there is a nice warm bed waiting for you back in Greenock Prison".

Mews' end of the phone went quiet, there was the longest pregnant pause Linda had heard of, but she knew who ever spoke first loses the game. Finally in a stunned sounding tone, Mews replied;

"Okay, bitch you win, but you fuck with me or allow Chico to know where I am, I will have your fucking tits for breakfast." Linda laughed, and hung up the phone, she started to shake, she knew now that things were serious, and that she was going to need help. Stewart was waiting for her at the restaurant in the back booth. He gave her a coffee, and she explained the situation.

"You idiot'" he said.

"This guy will kill you given half the chance. Why the hell didn't you just do as I said and ask Dean straight, was he screwing around?"

Linda sighed deeply, Stewart was right, but it had gone

too far now to turn back. Stewart pulled out his mobile and dialled a number, be here in ten minutes bring Alfredo too; we are going to need some backup.

He stared at Linda with an icy look;

"I can take care of Mews, you will have to deal with the broad that Dean is screwing. You work at a chemical factory look up and see what are not traceable but deadly."

"What are you saying Stewart? I must kill this woman."

"Yes, if you do not then, Dean, will do it again to you." This was a side of Stewart that Linda had not seen before.

"When did you become so violent?"

"When you walked in and asked for help with your husband's infidelity." Linda knew that this whole thing was now going down and that she would achieve her dream.

Dean would remain faithful; she had decided she would have Stewart on the side for a while as payment to Dean. Dean's lover would be out of the picture, and all would be sweet. She was now living her fantasy out in true life. Her obsession with the situation had taken over control of her thoughts and judgment, she had become her alter ego, obsession and fantasies all rolled into one. Stewart's friends arrived; he took them aside and explained what they had to do. He returned to the table;

"Where was the rendezvous with Mews?"

Linda told him;

"The old Judson sawmill out on the North Pine Road about ten-mile past Strathaven Lodge on the east side of the lake about 22 miles from town. There is a room at the rear that some homeless people sometimes use, we were to meet there at nine o'clock tonight."

"Okay go boys, we will see you there,"
He then looked at Linda;

"After this is over, I am going to have my payment!"
Linda would have gladly given it to him there and then if
he had asked.

Her obsession now was with Dean as her husband and
Stewart her lover, she could not of dreamt a better
scenario. She was so proud of herself. She returned to
work to pack up for the day. Dean arrived just after, not
even knowing that Linda had been away since he left.

"Ready to go home" he asked.

"No, I will see you later on, I have some things to finish
off and the girls and I are grabbing a bite in town."
Dean just nodded acknowledgment and went to his
office. Linda saw the light on her phone for a line light
up she knew he was ringing Cerise.

The small factory and offices at the south end of town
were quiet. Linda went out to where the chemicals in
the laboratory were kept. She searched through the
drawers and cupboards for a sampler bottle and found
them in the second cupboard. Filling the sampler to
about two thirds full of her perfume, she then found the
Chemical cabinet, from this she took the first two bottles
she saw, one of Potassium Chloride, and one of Boric
Acid. The latter is used in keeping the ants,
cockroaches away from the laboratory. The Potassium
Chloride is used in another area of the factory where
they are experimenting with fertilizers, which they hope

to be a side-line to the business. What a combination poisons and fertilisers. Linda put ten mils of the Potassium Chloride which of course in this form is odourless and colourless into the sampler bottle, it bubbled, and the liquid still had the perfumed aroma emanating from the small neck of the bottle. She then placed fifteen mils of the Boric acid in, this slightly changed the colour. Chemistry at school was never her strong point, so she was guessing as to what she was doing. Although she had a quick look through some of Dean's books in his study; she did not understand a lot of them and the chemical terms. Who cares she thought if the bitch dies? She then added fifteen mils of Sodium Hydroxide, acetic acid, and sodium acetate; this became a base buffer solution.

Linda then realised that there was too much, so she poured an amount of the liquid down the sink an odour lingered from the plug hole she turned on the water quickly, the smell was rather over whelming, so she turned on the exhaust fan above the sink. She then turned back to the workbench she carefully smelt the neck of the bottle and it had a sweet strawberry scent. This is okay she thought. She packed up all the bottles etc. she had used and cleaned up the area turned off the fan, the fumes had disappeared. At the other end of the factory was the sealer unit where the bottles were pressurised and sealed with a small pump action applicator.

They were then labelled and packed. Linda tried to do this and then decided it would be fitting to put the most expensive label of all on the bottle, she had previously steamed this off a bottle perfume she had bought the day before. She then boxed up her potion. She picked up her case and coat from her office and left the factory saying good night to the security guard, which she had forgotten about.

Driving through town she found the Seven Eleven store open; she bought gift paper and card with ribbon. While sitting in the car she wrapped up the gift and placed it in her briefcase. Whoever this woman was that Dean was fucking was going to receive a gift, a very deadly gift.

18

The young police officer looked at me with a look of contempt. He asked me to place my hands behind my back, as he read me my rights. I asked;

"Can we conduct this here in the building as I am in the middle of two investigations at the moment."

"That has already been arranged the Commissioner and Mayor Majors at county are here to question you."

"What! Fuck, he is not with us, why is he doing the interview?"

My blood boiled with rage I knew that this was not going to go smoothly. Ray quickly went to my office dumped the briefcases and grabbed the murder file off my desk. He returned just as we were heading down the corridor. The young officer looked at him and an exceptionally low authoritative tone;

"Sorry sir, no civilians allowed."

Ray flashed his Senior Inspector badge at the young buck and his face turned red.

"Majors orders were he was to come alone".

"That will be the day," said Ray, and continued his rant;

"Who the fuck does this Majors think he is? The King of Turd Island, this is a Police building not some out in the boondies hideaway suburb office where a night   stick and   phone   book   are   the   interviewing techniques." His   face   red   with   rage   as   he   made   the   statement. Just   then   the   huge   frame   of   Majors   appeared   in   the doorway of interview room four.

He   looked   at   Ray   and   bellowed,   which   I   reckon   they heard   on   the   third   floor.

"Fuck off, you bastard, this is my birthday, and this son of a bitch is going down." Ray moved toward Majors, and I stepped in front, I said;

"I   am   not   going   in   there   until   he   is   allowed   and   my attorney."

"Stiff your attorney Farrer, you arsehole, I have got you this time, murder, covering up evidence, misleading   Police, tampering with witnesses, do you want me to go on?"

I looked at him with contempt and just kept my mouth shut. Ray was on his mobile to our legal department; he nodded that Steve Barlow was on his way up. Steve, a former prosecuting Attorney, was now our man on the spot for preparing cases for the Court and prosecuting them. Just then there was a knock on the door, Steve entered, a smiley man of mild manner, about six feet and maybe a little overweight, but he was a whiz with the law books.

Never, married and thirty-seven years of age. Everyone wondered whether he was gay, I knew that he had been in a very long-term relationship with a lovely lady which he kept quiet and his personal life to himself. The reason for this was his job. The characters that he had to deal with some had long memories and carried grudges just like Majors. Steve looked at Majors and asked;

"Has he been read his rights, and why is he still cuffed considering he is now in police protection?"
Majors grunted and signalled that the cuffs could come off.

"What is your interest in this case anyway; it is out of your area is it not?"

"Fuck-up, smart arse, the girl this dick killed was my niece, so that makes it my jurisdiction."
Steve looked at him and started to laugh;

"You are the biggest fuckwit I have met, and the charges here will not stand up, as they have been brought by yourself in an area outside your jurisdiction. Not only that you idiot, but it is also a special investigation case, and the Forensic report shows she had been dead at least three weeks." Steve continued to bait Majors;

"The report also shows she was freshly shot on the scene but that never killed her she was strangled to death." Majors stepped over towards Steve, he raised his arm and before any of us could do anything he brought it down hardon the left side of Steve's head. Steve reeled across the room and hit the far wall hard.

The young officer Munroe, who had just told us his name, rushed over to restrain Majors; he was flung to the other side of the room. I leant back in my chair and put my feet up crossed on the table, drew my gun aimed it at Majors and said;

"Sit down you great lump of shit, you have just about put yourself in the cooler for a long time."
Majors glared at Munroe and roared;

"Why, has he still got his gun?"
Munroe just looked at him with a great deal of contempt. Ray pushed Majors into the seat opposite me.

"Get away from me you shit head, you do not touch me."
Ray gently leant over Majors left shoulder, dug his thumb into the neck of Majors thus causing the blood flow through the artery to be slowed the more pressure you put on the slower the flow, until eventually, you can cause a person to pass out.

"If you ever, call me a shit or bastard again as long as I know you, or you have the pleasure of my presence again or you ever trouble Farrer or anyone in your care as a Police Officer, I will personally see to it that you go up the river for life".
Steve in the meantime had slumped into the seat at the end of the table still soothing his bleeding forehead, nose,

and lips.

He glared at Majors; the look was that of a man about to blow steam out his ears.

"You ......You........fuckwit" he blasted out.

"I am going to have your badge, your head, and your arse for this"

"Leave it Steve" I said.

"I can understand how he feels he hates my guts his niece was found lying on me in a compromising position, with half her brains splattered all over me, and he needed a scapegoat. Because of his hatred and his grudge against me I was his patsy".

We all sat there in complete silence for what seemed like hours, then Ray said;

"What the hell made you think Farrer killed this girl?"

"Just the situation and the place and time his gun etc."

"How did you find out about the gun, we only found out about that in last couple of days and it has not to be released".

"We got a phone message from someone who said he was a Forensic boy from here and gave us all the details."

"Did you get a name?"

"No".

"Well, this Julie Crow was another of the victims of this sick bastard we have been trying to catch" Ray said;

"Where did you get the idea that I was tampering with evidence and hindering enquires, Oh Let me guess this mystery Forensic man?"

I rolled my eyes and looked towards the ceiling, I was

110

asking for a divine answer or for a sign that would tell me, and this man the mayor and a man of law was not stupid. When you receive information like this, you check it out before jumping to conclusions. I then looked at Majors and told him;

"I want to know all about this Julie Crow, who she was, where she lived, who she slept with, what she ate for breakfast Tuesday three weeks ago, do you understand?" He said;

"She was my brother's daughter she had been missing for about 5 weeks; the last to see her was her boyfriend, Damien Rourke. I will tell you; he cannot be part of it as he is my son from another relationship. We cleared him, he had an alibi as to where he was the night she disappeared. He was in Fairborn County over seventy miles away at a function there was twenty or more witnesses. We also knew that she was having a bit of a poke with some other guy down here but did not know who and of course when I got this other info, I put two and two together thought it made four, but it made three."
He looked at Steve.

"Well, if you are going to charge me here is as good as place as any".
He then removed the magazine from his gun, cleared the chamber and left it open. He handed his gun, bullet clips, and magazine to Ray. Steve looked at me then back at Majors and with his finger pointing at him;

"Listen you arsehole, I am going to do nothing due to the circumstances, but if you step out of line again at any time, I will mention this. Is that clear?"

Majors nodded, I told him;

"Make sure the rest of the info on Julie Crow was on my desk within the next two hours. I gathered up my thoughts, looked at Steve then across at Ray.
Majors left with Munroe following like a lap dog. Majors walked like a man, who had been castrated, defeated by his own maturity. I had a chuckle, then said;

"Steve, it is about time we brought you up to speed on this case care to join us for the meeting this morning."

We made our way to the new room that had been set up for this case, I walked to the front of the room, Ray took a seat to my right, Jo, was directly to his left. Coney sat on a desk at the rear with Macey on his right. Colin Miles from Forensic seated almost directly in front of me, and Steve seated himself next to him. I quickly explained what had happened in the other room and told them what the outcome had been. On the board behind me was the following set out in order, as we knew it. Jo had put them up in order of find, all the details we knew and photos of each, I am glad I did not have to do this considering the shit I had to go through with Mills.

Victims:

Annabelle Tate, 24, Single, Blonde hair,
Brown eyes, she had a cross on her back with one horizontal line. Had the similar injuries and some body parts missing, as the others except, had only been dead pproximately 48

hours before she was found. The word *"Limbus"* meaning *"Limbo"* was carved in her back. Was taken off the walking path along the lake in the early morning. No witnesses but her handbag and phone found in bushes along the path to the north of town.

Teresa Caldwell, 21, Single, Blonde hair, Blue Eyes, she had a cross, with a vertical line on the right of the cross. No distinctive marks except what looked like forceps had been used on her vagina, but this was inconclusive. Blood and toxicology test proved she had had some form of ether and other forms of anaesthetic administered and some form of poison on her wrist. Had been dead at least two weeks before found. *"Blasphemia"* was the word carved in her back, *"Blasphemous"*. Left her employment and went missing. Alert raised when did not turn up for work on the Monday morning.

Barbara Waite, 22, married but separated, blonde hair, brown eyes, had a cross with one vertical line, to the right and the word *"Dalus"* meaning *"Fraud"*. Been dead 72-96 hours, had organs missing also, it was later found

113

she had embezzled $35,679 from her employer. How did the murderer know? Her car was found near Talon Point, but no significant clues as to where she was taken from.

Natalie Benton, 21, Single, blue eyes, blonde hair, cross on her back had line, horizontal below the cross. Found in downtown Oemen Lakes had been dead no more than 12 hours. Word carved in her back *"Volentia"* meaning *" Violence"*, we knew she was Eugene's niece and had not been heard of for probably 4-5 weeks. No other information.

Catherine Rhind, 23, Single, Blonde hair, blue eyes, had cross on her back, and line to the right of the cross vertical *"Avoutrer"* meaning *"Adulteress"*. Dead at least a week, injuries are the same. We know some of her background and who her friends and latest lover was, she was an adulteress.

Judy Hampton, 22, Single, Blonde hair, Brown eyes, had a circle on her back, had one line horizontal above the cross. Had *"Lascīvus"* meaning *"Lust"* carved on her back, possibly dead at least 96 hours, we investigated and found that she was the town bike and would have sex with anyone, anywhere, anytime, again how the hell did they know her background unless they had first-hand knowledge.

Rose McHenry, 23, Single, Brown Eyes, Blonde hair, had a circle with two lines one vertical to the right and a horizontal one below the circle and again *"Angere"* meaning *"Anger"*. Had been dead approx.36 hours, this one was a tip off. Her injuries were the same the other victims, organs missing, sliced up. She had a police record for assault. Not known exactly how or where she was abducted. We also had two deaths that we are not sure whether they are associated but happened during this investigation.

Eugene Barrelli, 39, married, two kids, wife Katrina. Was having an affair with one of the victims. Former Navy Seal, with the Police Homicide for 7 years in the Special squad. Description of death was not needed the photo was enough and the memory of his heart sitting there w r a p p e d i n h i s i n t e s t i n e s with that note and the rest of him exposed was just too much. He had been dead about two hours.

Julie Ann Crow, 23, single, blonde hair, green eyes. No marks, just *"Ha Ha Ha"* inscribed on her back along with the word *"Heresy"*. She had been shot with Farrer's gun at close range on the night of the incident with Farrer but had been dead at least three weeks. Full report and other information on her, from Majors were arriving by lunchtime.

Missing: Sally Donald, blonde, blue eyes.

Even though we had a list of 10 victims we knew about, my gut feeling was that we have not seen the end of the list.

We all just sat looking at this list, and the things it meant, we really had nothing to go on they only had the blonde hair in common, four had brown eyes, three had blue and the one with green eyes. It did not have Eugene's eye colour there. I asked if it could be put up. I then asked;

"Why did you put up the information about the affair Jo?"

She looked at me with a gaze of contempt,

"He is dead, he was associated with one of the victims, he was also on this case, and he had contact with Julie Ann Crow's family over her disappearance before her body even appeared. The most important thing one of the victims was his niece. Somewhere along the line all this ties in."

She finished and had a look of real anger and betrayal on her face, I was looking for an excuse, and I looked at my watch. It is time we all got ready to say goodbye to Eugene. We had b e e n at this for over two hours,

116

and I had had enough. We had gone through everything over and over, but still could not really tie anything together. I then relayed the forensic information we had received on this poisoning case. I looked around the room, and then said;

"We are going to have our arses hanging out, two murder enquiries that are I believe not related. I will work out teams later and let you know who works on what". I asked Jo;

"If she could make sure that our investigator shit stirrer Mills has a copy of all that was in the presentation?" She had a look of disdain, and I knew I would have to smooth that over quickly. I sat and thought about the past few days, and what had happened over the past weeks, the murders, the mayhem and the accusations, the bodies we had and the ones we still had to find, how many more must die? I came to Oemen Lake for the peace and quiet; shit here I am up to my balls in murders.

19

I reached the room where on that cold steel table laid the body of a beautiful, brown-haired woman. She was drop dead gorgeous. I thought how could, anyone kill a creature of the lord like this, this job was really starting to get to my senses. Dr Albert Miller, Pathologist, was already performing the autopsy as I walked around the table, looking at this thing of beauty.

"Any ideas doc, on what killed her?"
Dr Miller looked up at me with those black eyes of his, like the entrances to a coal mine. His look scared the shit out of me at any time; he was the "Grim Reaper" himself in my humble opinion.

About fifty-five years of age, I knew nothing of his private life, jet-black hair, bushy eyebrows, that when he spoke or smiled, they seemed to ride up his forehead, and make it look like he had a toupee stuck there. His hands were well formed, and fingernails seemed manicured and clean like that of a female. He was a weird one in my opinion. He started to give his opinion;

"There is no distinguishing marks on the outer body, other than a small surgical incision under the right breast, which I believe at this time was for a Biopsy of some kind I will know more once I have her open. She has not been sexually assaulted, a small red rash on both wrists, which show an allergic reaction to some form of preparation. Skin, blood and toxicology and biopsy tests will tell me more."

He spoke in a deep authoritative voice, rather like a schoolteacher.

"So, you have at this point no fucking idea how she died?"
I said looking at him across the table with a rather agitated expression.

"We now have this girl we have yet to name. With

118

what would appear to a lame duck, like me, are suspicious circumstances and you cannot even give me an educated guess."

"Mr Farrer, I can only go as fast as I am able, this is a precise science, and we are short staffed and overworked." I looked at him then turned from the table and walked towards the far wall, leant against it with my head starting to throb, shit I need to get out of here and have a drink. I stood there for what seemed an immeasurably extended period, thinking, then turned, and started for the door;

"Doc, how about I send my man down here to go over these two bodies with you, would that help as I need some results?"

"Is he a registered Doctor?" he asked.

"To bloody right he is, Forensic Pathologist just like you. His name is Gary Mathews, I will get Ray to contact him and have him here today. Is that okay?"
He nodded to the affirmative, and smiled and there goes those eyebrows again. I bid him farewell, and Ray and Bill followed me out. Returning to the office I asked Ray to contact Gary and recommend to him of what I want him to do. Bill was to contact the other team members and ask them to come in at nine tomorrow. We need to start on this new case and get some answers as there was evidence, DNA, and blood cultures we were waiting on for the rest. They left my office and again I had solitude and time to think.

I opened the bottom drawer and pulled out my rescue bottle of 'Jack'. This was the one for times like this. I slowly unscrewed the cap and looked at the bottle long and hard, asking myself,

"What are you really doing here and with your life?"
I took a long swallow and leant against the window frame looking down on the visitors' two stories below. I knew I was drinking excessively and breaking my own vow to cease. I made my way back to the desk, but something stopped me to see the ominous calm on the lake, our new location was on Granton View Avenue, and looked out across the lake.

The grey cloud which had covered the place during the day, had given way to a smart breeze from the northeast, a black cloud had been ominous there all day, and though the lake was calm and sheltered, it was open to a storm should one start, it would come in from the Northeast down the valley and we would be right in the guts of a gale.

I turned and sat in my chair looking at all papers, photos, files, and unopened mail as well as the rubbish being old takeaway packets etc., lying on my desk. I lost all track of time and next I looked out the window, the veil of night had arrived. I was a bit surprised at the absence of the moonlight, which had lately bounced with delight off the lake's waters, as the weather had been unseasonably good. The moon's beams were like Tinkerbelle fairies dancing on the small waves as they rolled along the shore.

The sight was one of unabated and terrifying splendour. The huge black cloud that hung on the horizon most of the day had changed shape. Instead of a long wisp like a dark evil veil of a sorceress, it had now formed into a large daunting archway, likened to the gates of hell.

Beneath this vast and magnificent portal, flashes of sheet lightning passed noiselessly. Behind it was a dull and threatening roll of thunder that started with a low murmur and built to a deafening crescendo.

The rain had started, and was smashing against my window, like a thousand demons trying to enter. The roar of contending wind had suddenly whipped the water of the lake up into a frenzy of gushing waves that now barraged their way upon the rocks of the wall that ran along the promenade, giving no relief to the foreshore. This had all happened in the moments I stood gazing through the window into the night.

The lights that were on in the street suddenly disappeared; everything was now black, desolate, and extremely eerie. Bill came to my office door;
    "This is a real fucker of a storm, have not seen one come up this quick in ages"
He joined me at the window, I gave him a spare glass and half filled it with "Jack". Before too long Hal had joined us, glass in hand. Gazing upon this gloomy expanse, I again heard their voices, a worried tone resounded from them.
    "This is a demon storm," said Hal.
    "Someone is going to die tonight that be for sure".
The sound sent shivers down my spine, from the whistling wind as it sped its way between the buildings. As the

wind and rain lashed the windows, making an unnerving sound that left me with an uneasy nervousness. We all turned and gazed into the darkness of the office looking for some form of light. I glanced back out of the window; the wind was forcing the rain sideways across the lake. It was so strong; it bent the trees on the foreshore road sideways, like reeds along the side of a swift flowing stream. Winter was here with a vengeance. Lightning strikes lit up the sky at intervals, we had a death storm brewing, and the lightening was bouncing its light off the black menacing rolling balls of clouds, as they gathered their fury.

There was a howling from the wind as it weaved its way across the rooftops of the close-knit buildings around us. A loud clap of thunder hit, and windows shook with the ferocity of the blast. Anything not tied down was going to be whipped away with the power of the wind gusts. We walked blindly through the unforgiving darkness, looking for some form of light; each lightning strike lit the office up with a feeling of unforgiven dread. The heavens now opened fully; rain, hail, and lightning mixed with the wind. I glanced through the sheet-like rain outside and was glad I was inside at the time; I pity those commuters awaiting a bus or walking to their vehicle.

I looked towards the small jetty and boat ramp and with the force which the mountainous waves were now pounding upon them. White spray shot to the heavens and exploded by the wind blowing the foamy heads around like baubles on a swaying Christmas tree. The waves were even encroaching over the jetty, leaving large pools of dirty foam as the water receded back into the darkness. I had not seen a storm this ferocious in a long time, I glanced across at the pines and vehicles moving as if in slow motion, in that fleeting moment, I realized that being out there, at this time could end up in death. That uneasy feeling suddenly engulfed me, and I shuddered. Hal had said the storm was a demon storm, and death would linger after it. I dreaded going home if this were to keep up; my office couch looked inviting and safe for me that night.

20

I had rung Katrina and showed what time I would be picking her up for the funeral. She sounded very down and upset which was understandable considering she was attending her husband's funeral. The rest of the team had organised to carpool, and we would all meet back at Eugene's and Katrina's afterwards. I arrived to pick up Katrina, she gave me a hug, but it was not the hug of an emotionally distraught person, but, that there was more to it. I ignored my thoughts thinking that my imagination was just running wild. Ayden and Gina were upset and just climbed into the back of the car without saying a word. Katrina got in and as I did up my seat belt I glanced across and flashed me a smile.

You could see the hurt in her face, both from Eugene's death and the fact of his infidelity. I struggled with this last thought as Katrina was beautiful, former cheerleader at college, voted the darling of the region at twenty-one and nothing had really changed her. Two children and many good years of marriage and she was still something to behold. She would have passed for twenty-one she looked that good, I started up the car and we drove off slowly down the street heading for the one thing I hated about this job the funeral of a fellow police officer, and especially this one as he was a mate and partner.

He had been a confidant and a leaning post during my rough times as well as a guy who knew when and what to say. We arrived at the small Chapel for the service the Police escort and guard of honour were in place. We all wore dress blues and white gloves. Eugene would have made some smart remark; I could hear him in my head;

"Look at this lot, dressed up like a pox doctor's night-watchmen." I must have had a smile on my face as Katrina asked;

"Why are you smiling?" I just glanced and she realised I was thinking of Eugene.

During the service, I seem to have shut myself off, the coffin stood on its trolley at the front, and I could hear off in the distance the sound of tears I heard Eulogies as if they were coming in waves from outer somewhere; none of this seemed real. I then heard my name mentioned and felt a slight dig in my side. Katrina had brought me back to reality; it was my turn to pay tribute to a friend and colleague, I cleared my throat tears had already started to well up in my eyes.

I could feel the hurt and the loss as I began to speak:

"Eugene Roberto Barelli, how do you define a man's life? He was a father, a husband, a friend, and partner. He was a confidant to us, a friend to us all. Never did I hear a bad word about anybody from him. His quick wit and one liner always made dreary cases seem fun and made us all remember that we are only human. A man of few words, but in silence we held him in great esteem. He knew his job; he knew his place in this world."

At this point I realized I was crying, and the tears were rolling down my cheeks I had trouble holding back my emotions. I looked at the coffin, and realized I could not finish the rest of what I wanted to say. So, in a low muffled voice emotions welling up in me I said.

"I will miss you my friend, go to your place of peace, I will think of you often."

As I looked up there was stone silence, and I felt all my hatred for the person who had done this. Coney and Macey and I were on one side of the casket, Eugene's brothers, and Katrina's brother on the other, we lifted it slowly and walked up the aisle to the door. Four altar boys lead the way with the priest following, then us. The sun shone through on us. I was not a religious man but felt that somehow God was taking a special interest in this occasion.

A figure stood in the doorway; I caught a glimpse of it

shortly before it again disappeared to one side.

We came out into the bright sunshine, and placed the casket in the hearse, I glanced around looking for the person who had been at the doorway, nothing. As we drove slowly in the procession to the graveside I was thinking of the figure, who was, it seemed strange, the actions of this person, was it my imagination, was I starting to see things that were not there. I hoped that this would all hurry up, as I needed to get out of this sad event and get my mind onto other things. At the grave the usual passages the usual passages and protocol followed, the rifle salute rang out and the flag folded neatly in the correct manner and handed to Katrina. I had controlled my emotions with thoughts of the case, and then away on top of a small rise in the centre of the road stood a figure in front of what looked like a blue BMW.

I could not see clearly, as the sun streamed into my eyes, I shaded them just as the figure got into the car and reversed over the rise and out of sight. I was now sure that this figure was the one at the church, and what were his reasons for being evasive? Was this the killer gloating over his victims as they went to see their maker? My thoughts were not rational; was my mind playing tricks, or was it? As we were about to leave Ray came to me;

"Did you see the vehicle on the rise up there?"
I acknowledged his question with just a nod. I was not the only one with a wild imagination. At the house, we all gathered to farewell Eugene, this part of a funeral I have never understood since my parents died.

Why does everyone, gather and say what a great bloke

he was how good he was? When he was alive half of these people would not have gone out of their way to say good day to him unless they had a reason. It was late when the last person left, Katrina looked shattered, I carried Ayden up to his room and put him to bed. Gina had already gone to bed. I checked on her then went back downstairs. Katrina had made me a fresh coffee, sat on the large sofa looking into the flickering flames of the fire and my thoughts went to Eugene and Katrina as to how often had they been in this position in better times during their marriage.

Katrina sat beside me, there was silence for a prolonged period and then she leant across and kissed me, I looked at her and she again kissed me, this time more passionately, I returned the passion, and then realized who she was and what I was doing. I said;

"No, Katrina, we have just buried your husband and I know you are feeling low, but this is not right he was my friend."

She looked at me with sad but a feeling of surprise in her eyes,

"I have had feelings for you for a long time Ian, and I knew in my heart that Eugene was being unfaithful. I am not looking for sympathy I am looking for a man."

With this I decided it was time to go, she looked at me and said;

"I am sorry, please stay you can sleep down here in the guest room, I promise I will not disturb you, and besides I would feel safer."

I awoke early, showered, dressed and on entering the kitchen, Katrina had fixed me a breakfast I had not had for

127

a long time, eggs, bacon, toast, grilled tomatoes, and coffee. Ayden was watching cartoons on the television and Gina was getting ready for school. Katrina looked at me and apologised for last night. I looked at her and said;

"Any other time other than last night maybe, it was a bit much on the day of his funeral."

She nodded and returned to her lunch making for the kids. I arrived at the office feeling the best I had felt in years, Ray met me at my office door, and we went in. He started by showing me notes he had made yesterday after the funeral. He wanted to look at the notes the killer had left me with body five and with Eugene.

I pulled out the evidence envelope and showed Ray the note, he was particularly interested in the bit about;

"I am your nemesis, you will never be allowed to forget 11 years ago". He then said;

"The last three words also made interesting reading, *Ha, Ha, Ha,* as this was carved into the back of the body that had landed on me at the garage downstairs". We had heard how that was done with a cable attached to the doors of the elevator and the body as the doors opened, it released the cable and boom, the body hit me. We agreed though the killer had to have known I was coming down in that elevator at that exact time and I was alone. He had to have been in the building. The other note that was of interest was the wording on Eugene's heart;

"His heart was not in his job" Ray had remembered something from years ago about a case we had worked on. He was still trying to piece it together and as he left my office he said;

"I will see you later I want to check out a few things."
I asked if he would send in Coney, Macey, and Jo. They
came in and I invited them to sit. I had Coney in just as a
diversion, it was a bit unfair but at that stage, I needed to
clear up things. I slowly looked at them all but was particular
in not showing any of them a longer glance than the others. I
then asked;

"How did you know about the Dante and his sins
theory?"

21

I woke early again in the morning shaved, showered, and
dressed. I made myself a good breakfast, which I had
not done in so long. I had cleaned up my place, it was now
spic, and span respectable, I could not believe the change I
had made in myself over the last weeks. The drive to the
office was pleasant the aroma of freshly cut grass and the
smell of pine as I headed down the Avenue towards the
Office. If I had known what was awaiting me at the office,
I would never have even entertained the idea of getting out
of bed. I walked out of the elevator confronted by a mass of
flashing bulbs and microphones stuck under my nose. I
glanced around and could see my colleagues all looking
bewildered by it all. I yelled at them.

"Second floor now! NO Press past this point, I will have a
statement in fifteen minutes." I re-entered the elevator,
punched the second-floor button just as Jo and Macey

made it through the doors.

Coney was taking the stairs, as was Ray. We arrived at the second floor the doors opened and there in our discussion area was the Mayor, the Commissioner, Captain McLean, and Bourke the local honcho who is supposed to stand for us in County Council but spends more time in the brothels than doing his job.

"What is happening on this case Farly" said the jumped-up little arsehole of a puppet politician,

"That's Farrer, and you know as much as I do."

"Bullshit", he said.

"You have eight bodies and in this so called 'Dante' thing and two others and you have done fuck all about it".

I looked at him ten bodies as far as I knew when I awoke this morning it was six plus Julie Ann Crow and Eugene.

"Where the fuck, do you get ten bodies from?"

I was starting to get irritated with this son of a bitch and his arrogance. He was here for political gain and nothing else. I glanced at Jo just as a red faced and exhausted, Coney entered the room, he had forgot our offices were on the second floor, and he was not that fit or young anymore. Ray followed looking much better than Coney.

"Well, where did the ninth and tenth body come from?"

Jo stepped forward and handed me a file. It was a report that another body found just outside of Berwick House, the day of Eugene's funeral.

The on-call staff had handled it in our absence and filed a

report, which had arrived on my desk this morning. Her name was Alexia Hamilton, twenty-one, single, brown eyes, had one horizontal line below a cross and *"Fastosus"* meaning *"Pride"*. She had the same markings injuries etc. as all the other women. The estimated time of death was about four days ago. I was now really starting to be pissed off, with this bloke, eight innocent victims maybe ten and he was playing with us, especially me. Bourke came over to me,

"You had better fix this up quick Farrer, get this prick behind bars, and so all the women in this town and the County can feel safe again."

He glanced across at the Police Commissioner from Helena; we now had all the brass here at one time or another, more for the fucking media than to aid in the investigation.

"What are you going to do, is Farrer doing the job properly or just fucking us around?"
I moved across to him and looked him in the eye;

"Listen you jumped up little fuck, I would like to find one piece of dirt on you, and I would have a field day. You came from nowhere, no on e knows you, so shut the fuck up."
I moved a step back and looked at him;

"I will do my best; my team are working overtime on this case. I will get this bastard and hang his balls from your door knocker if you like."
McLean stepped between us and intimated I should take my team aside for a moment.
The hierarchy stood in a huddle, and a lot of nodding and

glancing across at us was going on.

"Look we have better things to do than stand around here listening to all this crap and playing with ourselves. We have nine murders in about fourteen weeks; this prick is frustrating us all. Why don't you high priests of the press go and fix the vultures downstairs up and let us do our job?" I said in a rather acerbic voice.

The mayor, who I thought as a reasonable sort of bloke although, could be a proper arsehole. I had a run in with him. He had presented me with a special commendation a couple years back. I had since had dinner with him in connection with other matters. He walked over to me;

"Do your best Farrer, we will handle the pressure and extra costs". As they entered the elevator Bourke (it was his wife who the mayor had fucked and had the child who was Damien), turned and glared at me;

"Good to see you have cleaned up your act; you now at least look a bit human, *Ha Ha Ha*".

I was fuming and would have knocked his fucking block off given half a chance. I turned to the team, well we have nine victims, and we need a suspect get on with it. Ray took me aside and said;

"Did you hear the last three things that arsehole Bourke said?"

"No", I replied.

" I was too bloody livid to even listen to the prick."

"Ha, Ha, Ha, does that seem strange to you, who is he? Do we know anything about him?"

"Get on it Ray, find out whatever you can."

132

I looked at Jo and knew I would have to talk to her about us.

22

Loneliness is hard to take when you have been with someone for a long time, and then, your life is suddenly, empty, and pathetic. The loneliness, it eats at you like a gnawing animal at a bone, it overcomes your rationale and every thought of reality. I took another long gulp and re-screwed the cap on to 'JD' bottle. Replaced it in my bottom drawer with a photograph of my wedding, I closed and locked it, I should do that with my life. Just then I heard a cheery voice coming along the corridor, Kerry "Alvin" Masters had arrived on the scene; 'Alvin' as he preferred to be called was a nickname. He was so full of life. He poked his head in my office;

"Hi, Ian, what is on the plate for today?"

"Tomorrow, nine o'clock for a briefing."

He nodded and left, whistling that bloody chipmunks' song as he went. Meanwhile in another area of town, approaching eight fifteen in the evening, the sun has long gone, and shadows stretch across the sky when Linda arrived to meet Stewart.

"Where the hell have you been, we will be late and that will fuck everything up."

Linda just ignored him and drove off as Stewart settled

himself into the passengers' seat. Twenty-five minutes later lights out they slowly drove along the road leading to the sawmill, luckily it was a moonlit night, so they had good vision. Linda pulled the car around the back of a rotting log pile and turned it off. She started to shake and feel extremely nervous.

"What happens if something goes wrong Stewart, what will become of us?"

"Bit late to have second thoughts now baby. The boys are in place, and all is set. What did you brew up for Dean's girlfriend?" Linda threw a glare of absolute contempt;

"Do not refer to her as his girlfriend, she is dead hear me, she is DEAD!!!!" This outburst even surprised her. Stewart was a bit taken aback by this sudden show of anger.

"She has her present from Dean; I left it in her mailbox which is why I was late." He smiled at her and touched her leg with an affectionate pat. Suddenly there were lights coming down the road. "Here we go," said Stewart, as he leaped out of the car and ran across towards the factory.

Linda stayed in the car crouched down in the seat but enough so that she could see the doorway to the vacant room, where the plan was to go down. Mews, got out of his car carrying a paper bag, he looked around with a suspicious glance and looked straight at the car. Linda froze thinking he had seen her, but he moved off in the direction of the doorway. He entered; there were two loud bangs and flashes of light. Seconds passed and Stewart appeared, with the paper bag. He walked swiftly to the car,

134

got in and said;

"Drive, now! I have your tape, let us get out of here and back home."

Cerise arrived home a bit late about nine forty-five, she cleared her mailbox, and found the small quaintly wrapped parcel with the card attached.

"To my bed partner, an angel forever" she knew it was from Dean but had no idea the angel forever part meant forever.

The gift which was an expensive bottle of de Francoise' perfume. Cerise showered and stood in front of the mirror admiring her body, when she decided to try the perfume that Dean had sent her, she sprayed a small puff of mist into the air and smelt the sweet smell of strawberries with another aroma in the background. This is nice she thought, Cerise sprayed some on her left wrist it tingled, and she then rubbed her two wrists together; there was a tingling sensation, which she thought was rather a turn on. Cerise then went ahead to do her makeup ready for when her lover, suddenly there was a noise; a dark blurry figure came in the room from the direction of the spare room. She suddenly felt queasy and very dizzy, suddenly she wanted to vomit, her wrists had turned red where she had placed the perfume, her head started swimming, she threw up all over the basin and mirror, and her whole body started to quiver, and blood was trickling from her nose. Her mouth was now full of blood, and she was vomiting blood, she felt blood running down her naked legs and onto the marble floor.

135

Her head was now feeling immense pain pressure and she was no longer able to focus, she grabbed for the phone but over balanced and crashed into the wall, knocking the handset off the cradle and left it dangling by its cord. Dean was waiting at the restaurant for Cerise, he thought it strange that she was running late it was not like her. He went to the pay phone booth in the foyer of the restaurant and rang her phone, it was engaged. Maybe something has come up; I will try again in five minutes he thought. Five minutes went past, and it seemed to Dean more like an hour. He again went to the payphone and tried Cerise's number, no answer. He started to worry.

He left the restaurant, and thought about going to her apartment, but remembered that Cerise had warned him about the snoop old Petra Wood the local know it see it all bitch, who lived in the ground floor apartment. Whoever arrived she would open the door and peer out gazing at anyone who did not live in the building. Cerise's last boyfriend she brought to the apartment could not even get past the front desk, and the apartment block's security man. Petra believed he was a cat burglar she had seen on "Most Wanted". Three times she had him arrested for the same thing, it got too much in the end.

The Police were also sick of her calls. He tried her again as he drove home, I hope all is okay he thought. He pulled up the drive of his home, pushed the button to the garage doors and drove in closing the door behind him. Linda's car was not there; she must still be out to dinner with the girls. Good he thought I could try Cerise again from the study phone. He quickly went into the house through the garage entrance and headed for his study. Turning on the light he thought that is strange maybe Robert has a Chemistry exam, as he found some of his books and journals left open on his desk. He quickly packed them up making sure to mark the pages just in case he had not finished his work. He rang Cerise's number again, still no answer.

"Fuck it" he said out loud to himself.

He thought to himself I will go to bed and try and get in touch tomorrow, she better not be two timing me and have the phone off the hook. Linda in the meantime had arrived home, just as Dean was climbing into bed. He quickly turned out the light and lay there in the dark. Linda snuck in and undressed, went into the bathroom, and showered, a few minutes later she climbed in next to Dean and little did she know he had fallen asleep while she was in the shower. Next morning sitting in his office going through the mail Dean could not think of a reason why Cerise had not called or answered the phone it was still busy when he tried this morning.

He rang Beale's trucking finally, and asked to speak with her;

"I am afraid she is not in yet sir." replied the receptionist.

"Thank you, I will try later," said Dean in a rather worried voice.

He sat back in his large leather chair contemplating whether to go to the apartment and risk the old snoop and her busy body ways or just wait for her to contact him. He decided on the later. Two weeks passed, Dean had not heard a word from Cerise no messages, her phone was still engaged, her work had a leave application which had been approved and assumed she had taken the days off two days ahead of her plans. Mr Beale had no problem with it as she had not had holidays in three years. He was a bit worried she had not contacted them but then again Cerise had done this before. When she needed some time alone to think she just went off somewhere did what she had to do and came back refreshed. Dean then remembered they had planned to go to London for ten days on a trip together, under the guise of a business trip to promote a new product, then on to Paris and Rome.

He thought maybe she has gone alone to think about the content of what their conversation was about the last afternoon they were together. No, there was something wrong, something did not fit right here. He decided to ring the Police under a guise and say that she had missed several meetings and her telephone was engaged all the time. The call went through to the local Police Station. Coney took the call. He took down the details and passed it on to me. Two deputies were assigned to visit the apartment. They interviewed the Guard at the desk, he noted he had not seen her in days, but then he is not always on. They ask him to go with them to the apartment. The old snoop Petra stuck her head out;

"I knew she was trouble, the little slut, she was nothing but a whore".

She mumbled loud enough for them to hear.

The two officers ignored her but told her they would be back to see her if anything was wrong. On arriving at the apartment there was no answer at the door. They asked the guard to open it with his master key; they also rang for back up. As the door opened the smell was unbearable, the first officer went in slowly, covering his mouth with a handkerchief. He searched through and found the body in the bathroom, he quickly returned to the doorway. He coughed, then said;

"You better get the boss and Forensic here this is not good. There is a body in there and it is just covered in blood."

Five minutes later two Detectives were on the scene as well as Forensic. They entered the apartment and started to look around nothing seemed out of place.

The Forensic boys started the gruesome job of photographing and checking the body.

"Any ideas?" asked one of the suits.

"You had better get the boss and his boys in on this one as there is something strange about this, no tell-tale sign of a struggle or cause of death, other than she has bled from every open orifice in her body, as though she has had a massive haemorrhage."

She had the words *'Dies Irae'* meaning *"Days of Wrath"* and a cross on her back. The body was removed back to Lakes Hospital. This was the body we now had in the morgue. We now had positive identification as Cerise Elizabeth Blackwell, thirty-five, single, worked for Beale Transport and lived in Big Bear Village. On arriving in the office, the next morning, I set up a board with what details we had and went over everything that may have had a bearing in the past few days since the body was discovered.

They had interviewed Ms Petra Woods who seemed to know the entire coming and goings of all the residents and what times they even went to the toilet. She had informed them that Cerise was a slut, a whore, would bring men home at all hours and then these men would leave at all hours. When checking the log of the security guard none of this information fitted, as there was only one visitor on four occasions that had signed in as 'John Doe'. The security guard explained that the residents pay for their privacy and who comes and goes if they sign the register, it is not important what their names are so long as it is signed and a time registered.

There had been only one visitor two weeks prior about seven thirty in the evening signed in but not out, "John Smith". This left us with little to go on other than the old biddy was a sticky nose trouble making old bitch out to waste our time. Fred and Ray had gone to Beale's transport to interview her workmates as well as Ray Beale. I decided I would go and look around the apartment with Bill, Gary was helping Dr Honan with the autopsy so hopefully we will have a report soon. Beale Transport, one of the largest in the county, transported everything from sheep and cattle to chickens as well as fertiliser and fuel; they were licensed under law to carry it all. Ray was sceptical about some of the information the staff gave him.

They had informed him that Cerise was a bit of a loner, although the girls had the feeling that she had been having an affair with a married man. The reason for this, women's intuition, she had been secretive in the lunchroom about her private life and was a close friend of the owner of the company, although he was not the married man. They believed she was going off on some afternoons to meet with him and have these sordid afternoon delights. Not one of the women there though could give us a name or a description.

The receptionist told Ray;

"He called there often for her, and they would recognise his voice as it was so smooth and deep, rather sexy sounding. If his voice were like him, he would be a stunner."

Bill asked her;

"How could she judge a person by their voice?"

"Experience man, I have been a receptionist for fifteen years you get to know things."

Ray Beale told them;

"That it was not unusual for Cerise to take off; she had done this from her early teens. More so though since her parents died. It was like a relief. She would go away and think out problems then come back full of life and ready to start again."

This left a lot of unanswered questions and loose ends. How was it this woman could disappear and no one asked any questions? Who was the mystery man that kept ringing her? Was she having an affair with a married man? The unanswered always gave me a rumbly gut, and it made me think of too many scenarios. There was some secrecy behind this also. What was Ray Beale's, angle was this little trip of his Accounts Manager a ploy to cover up illegal dealings of some kind? With a firm as big as this, maybe we needed to be checking with other departments, whether they had anything on the firm.

My mind was racing, as the information we have been given was leading us nowhere, and I needed some air and a drink. I found a nice quiet area in the bar far enough but close enough from the office, sat myself down and ordered a double 'Jack' and beer chaser, also known as a widow maker. My phone rang it was Bill;

"Where are you boss, we are heading for her place now?"

I suddenly remembered I was going to check out this woman's apartment.

"Yes", I replied and hung up. I threw down the drinks and left the cosy little bar. Cerise Blackwell was an organised person; everything in the apartment had its place. The furniture was well set out, photographs were all aligned. I sat on the large leather sofa and eyed the whole place over and got the feel for it. There was something here, I could feel it. I decided to ring and get Gary down here. This did not feel right.

I went into the bedroom; the clothes she was going to wear on the night she may have been murdered were laid out neatly on the bed. Her robe was impeccable, dresses, in coordinated colours, blouses the same. Underneath on the shoe rack, shoes to match the outfits were set below in order. I checked the dresser drawers, as I went, I was reading the report of the autopsy, I had copied and stuck in my pocket, this must be murder, I cannot see how a person could bleed like this from a disease.

There was a knock at the door; Gary was standing there looking at me with a folder in hand.

"You got here quick" I said;

"I thought you were still out of town".

"No, I came back last evening as I had this for you, but you had retired when I arrived as it is not quite complete, I thought it could wait."

I opened the red file and started to read;

"No distinguishing marks on body other than a one-inch scar under left breast. Result of a biopsy for tumour growth, benign. Both wrists one quarter of an inch above joint had large red skin contusion and rash.

This was caused by some form of chemical reaction with the skin's own cells. Dies Irae' meaning "Days of Wrath" and a crosscut on her back. She had haemorrhaged in the stomach, lungs had been burnt by some form of chemical. Stomach lining did not exist. Bloods build up showed high traces of Chlorine, Boric Acid and compounds found in the production of fertiliser, or sprays.

White cell count was excessively high, Platelet count non-existent. Toxicology and skin samples showed excessive breakdown in the body's immune system. If she had not died, would have ended up with permanent brain damage

143

as cell damage in this area was excessive. Result of death, in preliminary autopsy awaiting confirmation of test results, but preliminary result Internal poisoning, by Acid and chemical compound formula of unknown origin.

Also, in the advance stages of Staphylococcus Aureus (Toxic Shock Syndrome) maybe 6-9 months to live, victim was also pregnant. Approximately 12 weeks entering second trimester, Foetus showed signs of severe distress, she would have lost the baby within 2 – 3 weeks under a normal miscarriage."

End of report.

Dr. A. J. Clements – Chief Pathologist

....

I now knew that there was something in this place that killed her, and we have missed the obvious. We needed to search the insides out of this place I thought.

Gary searched the bathroom, while I continued in the bedroom. In a rubbish bin in the corner by the telephone stand and bedside lamp was a box, wrapping paper with ribbon. I pulled out my surgical gloves and retrieved the box, the screwed up wrapping and ribbon from the bin. It smelt odd and there was, what seemed like lipstick smeared on the side of the ribbon as if someone had tried to tear the ribbon with their teeth. The paper wrapping, I was hoping would carry some form of print or trace of what the odour was.

The box was a perfume box that was a bit out of place in the organised and very neat and tidy room. I glanced at the wardrobe as I place the items in each in their own evidence bag, tagged them and continued. The wardrobe was like that of a department store, as I had already noted everything matched the shoes below, all colour co-ordinated and skilfully placed and hanging correctly. Not at all like my effort, all scrunched up and even if shirts or trousers had been cleaned or ironed, they would need doing again after they were forced into the cupboard in a miss match manner. My shoes thrown in covered in dirt and all in the bottom area of the cupboard or some other part of the room with a do not care attitude. Seeing her neatness, I felt a little ashamed of my untidiness. My search continued without any other eye-catching evidence or anything that would relate to the case.

23

The box had been a sampler bottle of perfume expensive, but the spray unit did not match the name of the perfume and looked like the sort of sprayer from the local Company.

"Ian, come here quick". He came from the bathroom carrying a small bottle atomiser;

"I think I have found the killer perfume," he said.

"This was out of place in the bathroom she had make - up and other toiletries, but this should have been there on the dresser with the others." I agreed.

I showed him the box and wrapping now all we need to know is who sent it. In here somewhere there must be a card, as this was hand delivered.

It took another hour of searching, but we found the card, inside her pillow slip on the bed. We now had a name Dean. We also had found the potion that had killed her we hoped, Gary was taking it down to the local hospital's pathology department to analyse it. We also knew that it came from the Company right here in town, but was it brought over the counter. Was it deliberate or just a coincidence? I left the apartment knowing that in my gut there was still something there and until I was sure of the missing piece, I was unable to put my finger on what was going on in that apartment. The next morning, I was surprised to see Gary so early; he had been up all night doing the tests.

Gary had found that the chemicals found in Cerise Blackwell's body matched those in the bottle of perfume. He had also found out from one of the nurses in the Laboratory that the label on the bottle of perfume was wrong. "Strawberry Passion" which this one smelt like came in a red strawberry shaped bottle with a strawberry label. This was not the right bottle or label. She also told

Gary that it did not come as an atomiser only as a screw top drip bottle. My visit to the factory this morning will be more than intriguing. The telephone rang just as I was about to leave. "Ian it is Hal, the locals have found a body in the old, abandoned sawmill. It has that Cerise's name on a piece of paper in his pocket. He has been shot twice. He looks like a pimp, but an ugly son of a bitch." I told him I would be there as quick as I can, I would have to organise transport.

The secretary at the desk told me that the young officer at the front desk was at my disposal, I asked her if she would ring and cancel my appointment with the factory manager and I would be in touch later. We arrived at this old sawmill, I went into this back office, there lay a body, shot twice, once through the chest and one between the eyes. He was ugly before that had happened though; Hal was right. Dean Forrester sat in his office pondering what was going to happen now. He had found out about Cerise's death from the gossip in the lunchroom. He also had this Sheriff Farrer coming to see him, why? Cerise and he were so careful about their affair, and how they made sure that they were never followed, change motels all the time, although it had become a bit of a routine lately. He had no clothes at her place, not even a toothbrush, nothing. His secretary then buzzed him;

"Mr Forrester the appointment you had with a Mr Farrer has been cancelled he will contact you later."
Dean became even more agitated now, how long it was going to be before he found out what this was all about. He tried Linda's line, there was no answer, where

147

was she at this hour of the morning. He asked his secretary if she knew.

"Mrs Forrester has not come in this morning Sir." Dean rang home, no answer just the machine. Where the fuck was, she, was she behind the death of Cerise with her fucking jealousy? He suddenly froze, could she have found out and went to see Cerise.

She had said on many occasions if she ever found out he was having an affair, she would kill the woman he was with. He knew though that she would not do it herself she would need help. Her office, somewhere in there may be a name that could help him. He grabbed a coffee at the machine and went around the corridor towards Linda's office. The blinds were closed, and he knocked no answer. He knocked again louder, still no answer. He asked her secretary, could she open the door, as he needed a file that his wife had. She explained that Mrs Forrester was the only one with a key.

"Fuck!" he said to himself, what game is she playing? If she is involved at all, I may be jumping to conclusions he thought. This Farrer character might be coming here just to check something with the factory or one of the employees why am I paranoid?

He thought long and hard, no-one knows of my affair no-one. He looked at his diary;

"Shit, fuck, shit", he expressed aloud he also had a board meeting to attend at ten o'clock. That is all he needed, with all that is going on. He knew he Would be unable to back out of this, so he prepared his folders and notes for it. Linda Forrester had left home early this morning to meet with Stewart she had decided that she was so on a high after the last couple of days she could wait no longer. She drove slowly into the back lot of Stewart's restaurant and parked. She entered through the kitchen and went up the stairs to his apartment above the restaurant.

Linda was on the brink of excitement as she knocked. Stewart answered the door, and she undid her fur coat and was wearing nothing underneath. Her clothes were in the bag she was carrying. This is how she wanted to surprise him. Stewart stood there looking at this forty something women who had had two children but had looked after herself and was a real beauty. He invited her in and closed the door behind her. Linda slipped the coat off and let it drop to the floor. Stewart removed his shirt and Linda saw his washing board stomach muscles and glorious chest, his broad shoulders, she moved to him, and they embraced. Stewart lifted her with ease and carried her through to the bedroom the whole time kissing each other. He laid her on the bed gently and removed his trousers, no underwear thought Linda. Stewart slowly moved over her body kissing her tenderly, making every inch of her body writhe with pleasure. She had never been so excited and turned on in her life she wanted him.

He looked at her;

"Patience", was his reply. Linda felt him touching her legs as his mouth slowly wet her now erect and hard nipples which were about to burst with pleasure. She could wait no longer for the pleasure of this man. She was wet and ready for him. He slowly lifted her buttocks, and the rhythm of life began with lust but gentle and loving movements. Their lovemaking lasted for almost an hour. Linda was so fulfilled she had multiple orgasms, she thought why she had not screwed this man at school and the other times she had led him on. They lay together thinking of the events of the past few days and congratulated each other on achieving their respective dreams. They were lost in their own world and that was all that mattered now.

Finally, Linda said;

"I must get to the office, or they will think something is up as I am rarely late."

"Will I see you again" asked Stewart.

"My darling you can have me whenever and wherever you want" she replied.

They kissed and Linda ran off to the bathroom to shower and dress. Stewart came in, as Linda was about to finish in the shower, he climbed in behind her and started to caress her passionately,

"Anytime anywhere" he said.

She looked at him and smiled. She turned to the wall and Stewart again showed his strength and power lifting her off the shower floor holding her up while they made love again in the shower.

Linda arrived at work; everyone looked at her in surprise to see her arriving so late. She went to her office, unlocked it, and asked if there were any messages. Her secretary recommended her, that her husband was looking for her and wanted a file that she had. She opened the door closed it and leant against it thinking of the escapade this morning and how fulfilling it was. Then asked herself why Dean would want one of her files. What was he up to? She threw her briefcase on the desk and hung up her coat. Picked up the phone and called Dean's office, his secretary answered and told her that he was in a board meeting. Shit she thought, I should be there. No, fuck it, not the way I feel, I do not want those old farts bringing down my euphoria. Linda sat in her office contemplating how she was going to get away from home this evening to meet with Stewart. Oblivious to what had happened this morning with the discovery of Mews' body. All she could think about was her time with her lover. Dean sat at the boardroom table with the other executive members who just seem to ramble on about absolute shit.

24

We left the site, returned to our office, and awaited the reports and the tape. Bill came in with an armful of lunch packs for us all. Gary, Fred, and Alvin joined us. We had a quiet lunch, discussing a few theories on this case and what the tape may hold. We all concluded that it had to be something to do with an extortion case as this Mews guy was not the most likeable looking guy and, on his history, as relayed to us by the young policeman, it seemed the most probable answer. We had the final Forensic and

Pathology report for Cerise Blackwell. It read the same as the preliminary report except that the Pathology report also showed advanced signs of 'Staphylococcus Aureus' and Toxic Shock Syndrome, and that she was 12 weeks pregnant. This started me to think we now had a motive. The lover did not want the baby, somehow knew that she was dying so just sped up the situation. Was I guessing? Or was I on the right track? Was this a jilted lover or a jealous one? Whatever, I had a gut feeling that Mr Mews was related to this whole affair and the tape was vital.

The next morning the tape arrived on my desk. I thought well, I hope this shows what I think it will, I placed it in the recorder and pressed play. I could never have hired a better pornographic tape if I had tried. This bloke had made a movie of Cerise Blackwell and some male we had yet to find, having the fucking time of their life. Just then the rest of the team walked in. I stopped the tape rewound it and started it again.

"Well, well, well," said Alvin.

"This is nice, can I have a copy? This is excellent quality sex material. You cannot hire or buy anything as good as this, as this was real no acting."

We all laughed although this was serious, we could not help but have a smile with this lovely piece of arse poking in the camera and humping the life out of some prick. Fred had called the local detective and his deputy up and they found Dean Forrester as the guy getting it on with the deceased.

They acknowledge that if Ray Beale knew, Forrester's arse would be hanging from the local chestnut tree. We watched the tape through three or four times to see if there were any other clues on it. The only thing we got from it was a few new positions to try out. We had a motive and a reason for the death of Cerise and Mews. My interview with Mr Forrester was now going to be remarkably interesting. I rang the company to make an appointment and told his secretary that I was they're following up a lead on some company insider trading on stocks and needed some time to talk to Mr Forrester.

It was a ruse, but I did not want him becoming suspicious and fleeing. We now had a lot of evidence but no real suspects other than Forrester. I still could not see him knocking off his delightful sex partner. As far as Mews went, yes, as he had the evidence that could cause Forrester a lot of embarrassment. Mews may have been the culprit for Cerise's death.

The poisons in her body though led back to Forrester as the company had those chemicals readily available. Was there someone in the factory jealous of Forrester and his little afternoon sojourns? This also led to his wife did she know? I had dismissed this though as how would she know Mews. The other thing how would Linda Forrester know about chemical compounds to mix up the poison? I would have to find all this out. I called the team together, that afternoon and laid out my theories to them and asked for their ideas. They produced some remarkably interesting scenarios. Some that I would not have even thought of Fred's was the best and worth following up.

He proposed;

"What if Linda Forrester was screwing around, she found out her husband was doing the same thing. So as not to get found out herself, she planned the whole thing with Mews. Forrester must be worth a mint. She divorces him gets half his fortune, humiliates the shit out of him with the video and the after math of a divorce trial. She has access to the poisons; she works at the factory."
He continued at a slow pace with his thoughts;

"The only floor in this plan is I do not think she killed Mews; this was a professional hit".
Alvin also had a theory along the lines of Fred's, but he turned it around.

"What if Dean Forrester knew about his wife and planned the video with Mews. He killed Cerise to set his wife up for a jealousy motive and for reasons only known to him, killed Mews. Maybe so he could blame both murders on her."
I was impressed with the two scenarios as both when put together, showed that somehow the Forrester's were involved, and the factory was the focal point for all of this. We went over all our evidence.

I arranged for Hal and Fred to interview Linda Forrester, Alvin and I would see Mr Forrester and I wanted Gary to look over the factory for evidence of the poisons. Bill in the meantime was to find out what ever he could on the Foresters, their backgrounds, who would get what if one died, what the situation of the company was and most

154

of all which one stood to gain the most. Next morning, we arrived at the factory. The five us I must admit looked like a raiding team as we descended on the place. Dean Forrester met us in reception, he asked the receptionist to show Ray and Fred to Linda's office and Gary around the factory. We went ahead with him to his office.

He offered us coffee but we both refused.

"Mr Forrester, we are not here about your company or anything to do with it at this point. My colleague and I are here to question you on the death of Cerise Blackwell!"

"I am afraid I have no idea who you are talking about" was his answer. I could not help noticing how cool calm and collected he was over the whole thing he never blinked an eyelid when he gave that answer. I looked around he had a video machine, without asking I went ahead to play the tape and then asked him;

"Is that not your arse fucking the life out of Cerise Blackwell?"

His whole demeanour changed. He knew he had been caught out and not only that he had lied to the police.

"Yes, Cerise and I were having an affair. No one knew and then she turns up dead. I have no idea how or why. She was supposed to meet me for dinner the night she apparently died and when she never showed I suspected that she may have been followed so just went out and then home again as we had arranged. She never called though to confirm what had happened and every time I called; I received a busy tone."

"How long had this been going on?" I asked as I

155

stopped the tape.

"A while I could not tell you exactly, where did you get the tape anyway as Cerise and I never ever made any tapes?"

"We found it on a sleazy little shit called "The Prick" better known as Phillip Mews."

"I do not know him have never heard the name."
I tended to believe him on the latter answer as we had hit him with some hard evidence, and he had coughed up more than we had expected. I did not think he would hide anything now we had found him out. The other thing was that he was nervous now about the whole thing.

"Are your men interviewing my wife on the same matter?"

"Yes, but we need to know who she has been playing around with, to eliminate you both from enquires otherwise there will be more questions to be asked." He looked at me strange,

"Do you mean to tell me that my wife has been playing around too and there is a tape of her too?"

"We have no evidence on your wife as we do on you Mr Forester; by the way did you know that Cerise was pregnant as well and very ill with a fatal disease?" This shocked the hell out of him, I had played all my cards, as I now needed the full picture.
He slumped in his chair, gave me a look of absolute shock and horror. He broke down;

"I had no idea she was pregnant she had said nothing to me. What was the illness she had?"

"Staphylococcus Aureus – Toxic Shock Syndrome, she

had had it a while from using the tampons over a prolonged period. It is estimated by the pathology and other tests she was in the last stages they believe. She would have had to have known." I stated.

He was now quite emotional, and we decided that we had enough from him. We left him to wallow in his own grief, despair, and embarrassment. Alvin and I left and decided to see what Mrs Forrester had produced in the way of evidence. We met Gary at the front door and as we went out into the car park, he looked at me with a sign of glee in his eye;

"They have it all, the compound, the bottles, the applicators everything. The poison scent was made here in this factory. I interviewed the head chemist; he checked the log for the chemicals. There was about one mil of Nitric acid missing and about the same for the Boric and other acids. There was also an atomiser and bottle missing. The sealing machine also logs times and dates on the computer, as this is how they keep a record of production. On the night of Cerise's death someone used the machine."
I said to Gary;

"We need to see Mr Forester again, for that night where he was, also Mrs Forrester. I will bet you a pound of horseshit to a bottle of "Jack" they were not together, and they have no real alibis. I also want the other staff members all interviewed but do not drop the hint of what we know about Mr Forester".

Ray and Fred joined us, and they had some interesting

157

information they had gleaned from Linda Forrester. She knew about the affair; she also had an alibi for the night Cerise was killed. We needed to check it out, but as Ray relayed the information, he was convinced that she was not anywhere near the apartment of the victim that night. I was still uneasy about the perfume bottle and the wrapping, gift box etc. We still had nothing from the local Forensic crew on any prints, I asked Gary to follow up as quickly as he could as I needed to match them up with either of the Foresters or this Mews. If they had nothing to do with it, then the results of that test would clear them to a certain extent.

Why do cases get so complicated and end up with so many scenarios and so much evidence that points to one plan, but at the outcome the answer was staring us flat in the face the whole time?
My phone rang;
  "Hello".
  "Ian it is Bill, I have a heap of information on the Foresters, are you coming back to the office?"
  "We will all be back there in about an hour or so, okay?"
  "I can tell you there is some interesting reading amongst some of this." with that he hung up.
I told the rest of the crew to be back at the office within an hour as Bill had some information for us to go on with.
  "I will be a bit longer Ian," said Gary.
  "I will check on the Forensic report on the items we collected from the apartment and then be back at the office." I nodded that I agreed.

This was going to be a long day. Back in the office, Bill had all the information for us, I told him;

"We will wait a little while until Gary gets here so hopefully, he will have other information for us as well." We all grabbed something to eat and a coffee. Gary was not long; Bill grabbed another coffee while Gary also prepared himself one. Bill started;

"Mr & Mrs Forester have insurance policies on each other totalling five million dollars. Mr Forester's net worth is close to forty million dollars although he does not really know that. The reason being is that he owns twenty percent of the company in his own name, with shares and profit that is close to twenty-eight million."
He took a deep breath and continued;

"The twenty nine percent the family trust owns is fifteen percent his, and ten percent for his wife. The balance of the trust is in four names, their children get one percent each, and that is about three million. If Mr Forester were to die his wife inherits all his estate and the two kids get an extra five percent of the trust. If Mrs Forrester dies, he gets four percent of her amount the balance is split between the four names".
He continued;

"The other two are family members, Dean Forester's brother and his wife's sister. Now here is the fun part. If either is found out for infidelity or for any reason divorce proceedings are brought by one against the other the trust amounts are frozen and neither gets anything. The trust is then split up between the four, the two children and the in laws."

He took another breath and had a slurp of coffee; this had thrown a new light on things the in laws could be in this up to their neck as they stand to inherit millions. The stupid thing is though nowhere in the paperwork, we have, is there any mention of a brother of Dean Forester. I asked Bill;

"Where does this brother come into the equation?"

"What do you mean?" he replied.

"I have no record of Dean Forester's brother, on record. I have Linda's sister here and all about her but there is no mention of a brother."

"This is where I am about to get to the nitty gritty. Forrester is not Dean's real name, it is Marsden, and he was adopted when he was three years old by, Betty and Donald Forester. His real parents were killed in a sightseeing helicopter crash in Regina, Saskatchewan, Canada. The two brothers were split up. Dean was the eldest at three the other was a baby and he lived with an aunt. Now we are unable to find any record of him at all. He seems to have disappeared off the face of the earth. You want the good guts now".

He took a deep breathe, paused and with a slight smirk said;

"The old biddy that was the one who knew it all at Cerise Blackwell's apartment block, she is Linda Forester's sister."

"Linda's former name was Woods. It is a tangled web we weave, so much ambiguity. It appears that somehow Linda found out about Dean and Cerise. I believe the sister was the one that told her. As far as Dean knows Linda's sister lives in Sydney, and he has only met her once at the wedding some fifteen or sixteen years ago. I would say a bit of a dysfunctional family."

25

The agenda the board had was not being followed, there was side conversations going on everywhere and the Chairman himself seemed as disinterested in the whole proceeding as Dean, the only thing Dean thought was a bit strange was that the Chairman Mike Grant kept giving him the beady eye as if Dean were to utter something to start the whole thing off. Suddenly there was a hush as the Chairman asked;

"Is there any other business we need to discuss urgently at this present time, as I know a few of us have pressing engagements elsewhere."

Dean sat there absolutely fucked, the meeting had not covered any of the items and either he had slept through the whole fucking thing, or there was to be no meeting. He glanced at his watch and noted they had only been in the room forty-five minutes. These meetings usually take four to six hours. Who gives a shit he thought, if they want to do this, then I have no problem; I am only the lackey here. The only time he would start to worry is if the company started losing money. It was strange though that they all seemed to want to finish off the meeting so quickly maybe they had a hidden agenda. He returned to his office and slumped in his chair. There was a knock at the door.

"Come in" he bellowed, Mike Grant the Board Chairman walked in and helped himself to the large leather seat to Dean's right.

"Well Forrester, I will come straight to the point as I only have a few moments, as I have another meeting to attend. I hear you have been screwing around and that you have been seen with another woman other than your wife. You realise, as General Manager and major shareholder that should this be true the Board will take a dim view of it and so would the other shareholders. The board prides itself on family values and discretion".

This straightforward approach took Dean by surprise. He was short of an answer for a brief time.

He then looked at Grant and with an authoritative voice;

"Listen I am the Owner and General Manager here, and my name has a handle to it that is Dean, Dean Forrester, not Forrester, what I do outside this office and company is none of yours or the fucking board's business. Furthermore, if you had that farce of a meeting just for my benefit then you have fucked up badly. Do you get my fucking drift or do you want it in triplicate. Remember prick, I own sixty percent of this Company and my wife a twenty percent shareholder, the other being my family Company who owns ten per cent. Your arse is mine so do not push me. You could be replaced by the

town drunk if I see fit so fuckup and get out."
Mike Grant, looked at Dean with a disdain frown;

"You little upstart, I would like to get rid of you, but I know I cannot worse luck." With that he turned and left. As he approached the door Dean had a last shot;

"Next meeting I am going to ask for your resignation and the board, you are just a bunch of freeloading shits, and if you ever want to see me again, make an appointment, now piss off."

Dean was now fired up and not really prepared for any work; he had a florid look about him. Those arseholes treated this company like a toy, they get paid around two hundred thousand a year to have ten meetings and they play around. Dean had not seen a performance like he had this morning. Was there something on in the background, which he knew nothing about? He was starting to become paranoid; he had this incident with Grant, Cerise was dead, and he could be implicated, and where the hell was Linda?

He left his office and went ahead to Linda's office. He knocked; she was there he could here papers being shuffled.

"Come in" he entered; she looked at him with a pleasant smile and rushed over and gave him a kiss on the cheek.

"Sorry, I left early this morning, but I had to check out a couple of things as well as call at the post office and County Offices to make sure the plans for the extensions had been processed through to the department okay." Dean looked at her. Her excuse was plausible although it had a touch of bullshit about it as he knew that the plans were already at the planning department, but he did not question her any further. He kissed her back and said,

"I will see you later I have a few errands to run, and the board meeting has broken up for today, do you want to meet me for lunch?"

"That would be nice," Linda replied.

"Okay I will see you at 'Pierre's' at one." With that Dean left.

While all this was happening, I was having trouble putting this mess together, I had a body here, that was shot twice, he had no identification on him except a tattoo on his left forearm of a square and compass design, rather like that of the 'Freemasons'. I thought this ugly looking shit could never be a member of that organisation, so that form of inquiry I think is out.

"We found this tucked away in the back of his trousers." said Ray; it was a small eight-millimetre video camera cassette.

"This was also there a thirty-eight special no registration number; it had been filed off."

The young local police officer came over with two shell casings that were found near the doorway by the stairs. He looked at the body.

"Holy shit, someone finally nailed 'The Prick'." he said with a startled and squeaky voice. "Do you know him?" I said as I threw him a glance of amazement.

"Yea, everybody knows Phil 'The Prick' Mews. He has been up in court and up the river more times than I have had sex" looking at this young bloke I thought with an inward smile that is probably only two or three times anyway.

"Well, he is a dead prick now, and is not going up the river anymore the morgue will be his next internment." I stated with a rather melodic tone and a smile.

"I want everything you know about him on my desk by last thing today, we may have a connection. I want this tape transferred to a CD as soon as possible and brought to my office." Ray came over;

"He was shot at close range with a forty-four, he never stood a chance the Forensic boys dug the two slugs out of the wall over there. He has no skull at the back, it has been blown off and fucking great hole there and his spine is splattered over the machine o v e r there. This was a calculated hit, no sign of a struggle. My opinion, he was spying on someone, they found out and the hit arranged."

"The tape will tell us," I remarked in a solemn tone.

26

I returned to my office, the press had all gone, the area was empty, and I had time to think. I must tell Jo that I have decided to break it off between us, as it was not right working together and having a relationship. I also was in two minds at even staying with the force. The team came back down, I yelled out for Macey and Jo to come to my office I needed to know how they figured out the 'Dante' thing to clear up the doubts. I asked them again, they said;

"Go up and look at the board for yourself, the pattern of the bodies, the places, and the lines on their backs, crosses, circles, and the words. Wake up Farrer and smell the roses, get back to reality, it was there you only had to look, and I still read books, maybe you should try it." Macey said in a very disgruntled tone.

I went up to our room and looked hard at the board I took down the last three victims, and looked at what Macey and Jo could see, and they were right it was there, you only had to look. I replaced the other three victims, as they should have been, and the pattern was complete I returned to my office and wrote out apology e-mail to all my staff for my actions and especially to Macey and Jo for the doubt. Jo came in after reading the e-mail;

"Are you coming over tonight," I asked her to close the door and sit down.

"Jo, I care for you a lot, but I cannot work in the capacity I am in while having an affair with a colleague. I know you love your job, and as soon as this is over, I am transferring or leaving Oemen Lakes, I have not decided which yet." She looked in pain;

"I love you Ian, why are you doing this?"

"I have told you the reason Jo; I do not want you to leave either as this, I would say, will be your job, when I go. It is what you wanted".

166

"You bastard, our nights together meant nothing, my feelings for you mean nothing", she got up and went to the door turned and looked at me;

"Fuck You Farrer" and left. Luckily, the phone rang it was Katrina, this was all I needed now was another love-struck woman.

"Ian, I was clearing out Eugene's things and I found a notebook of his. I think you need to read it."

"I will be over in an hour." I hung up the phone. I caught a glimpse of Jo entering the elevator, I ran out to try to talk to her, but was too late.

I arrived at Katrina's, and she opened the door almost at the same instant I was about to knock. We entered the kitchen and I sat at the dining table, she gave me a small hard cover book, blue in colour. She put a coffee in front of me and left. I opened the book and started to read, skimming over most areas in the first ten or so pages but really taking in the following notations;

"Tuesday, 8am, received phone call from ... he told me that the woman I was getting info. From was also a prostitute, working for a big wig in a private escort service. I followed this up and found that two of the other victims had also worked or was still working for him. I asked who the person was; he said he did not know, just that they were well connected and high up, lots of cash."

"Thursday, 2pm I met with Catherine, fucked our hearts out as usual, she then told me what she really was, she too was connected to the service, and she were

frightened as three of the other girls had died in the last couple of weeks. I was starting to piece together things I will have to talk to Farrer, I must tell Katrina about Catherine and that it was part of the job as I needed to get close and inside to get the information and verify what my snitch, Benny had told me. "The team had a meeting Jo and Macey started to put things together as I had, but I kept my mouth shut. I told Ian about affair. I had challenging time in relation to Natalie, she was working from the escort service also, and she was a victim." I needed to get some more information on this big wig that runs the show".

This Bourke is connected and some other high officials. Benny said Mayor and County councillor maybe involved. Will see Benny again tomorrow."

The notes went on for four or five pages.

I contacted Benny, he met me at three, I was shocked to find out who the bastard was, can I connect him to the murders, as I do not believe he is doing them. Someone is setting him up as revenge and Ian knows both arseholes. Will know more tomorrow.

There were a lot of other notations and dates times etc, Eugene had the names of the victims, in his book before we had even found them. They all worked for the same escort agency or had ties with other prominent figures within town. I rang Coney;

"Told him I wanted to know all about this place, who runs it, who owns it, names of the girls working for him etc.

Told him also to get Ray to ring me at Eugene's, if I am not back in the office when he returns."

Katrina came back in when she heard me on the phone.

"Can it help you?"

"You bet it can", I said, and gave her a long kiss and hug, I said;

"I will come around tonight I needed to talk to her. She asked;

"Would you like dinner?" I said that would be nice". I raced back to the office and up to the second floor with Eugene's book burning a hole in my jacket pocket because of the information it held. I am going to nail this bastard, for the things he has done.

I put all the information onto the board, by each victim, dates times etc, and what Eugene had written in his notes. I even went as far as to put his name now as a victim of this prick, and the information about his affair times etc. Julie Anne Crow, she was supposed to be a victim in this and was part of the puzzle, but something had gone wrong, or his plans had not been to his liking, it threw him off the pace. She was a victim but used to side-track us. I needed to talk to those concerned. I read a bit more of Eugene's book.

I found Benny's phone number and address, scribbled in the back. I made my way to his address. The place was a run-down boarding house on the outskirts of Pale Tops Village a small ski lodge for singles, but also with winos and street derelicts littering the corridors, one of those back street buildings you never see from a Main Street and usually visitors and tourists never see, it was a dodgy looking place, I really could not see the skiing set staying here but each to their own. Maybe I should have brought backup. I could not believe the sight on the second story landing, a man about thirty giving himself a hit, there right in front of me. He looked at me with his drug filled eyes;

"You want a hit man, fucking good stuff."
I knocked the needle from his hand and smashed the kerosene bottle lamp set-up he was using to heat up the spoon of heroin. He jumped at me with anger, I flashed my badge and pulled my gun from its holster;

"I didn't come here for you, and I could not give a rat's arse about you or your problem."

"Well fuck you", he said.

"You have just destroyed five hundred bucks' worth of my fix."

"Tell me where Benny lives, or I'll fix you where you stand" he seated himself back down on the step and said;

"Room two three one, but he isn't there hasn't been for days." I asked;

"How do you know?"

"Because I'm kipping down in there, he disappeared after that cop got it".
I cannot believe I did not know about this place and the going on here, especially in my town. I went to the room and looked around; it smelt of stale urine and that familiar smell of kerosene. It was a mess, old newspapers spread over floor to look like carpet, and there was a small

table to the right with handwritten notes laying on it as well as small bags with a white powder in them. I gathered them up and put them in an evidence bag, they may come in handy later. I quickly looked over them they seemed like dates and times for drugs drop off, this was a heroin or crack house, Benny was the tie in distribution.

The bloke on the stairs must have been a customer. The small room off to the left was a kitchen a dining table was placed against one wall and all over the table were more bags of white powder all numbered and dated. The numbers corresponded; with the notes I had found in the other room. On the bench was a black satchel, took out my pen and lifted the open flap, inside was bundles of money, different denominations, twenties, fifties, hundreds. I withdrew the bags from my pocket and threw fifties them along with the ones on the table into the satchel.

A quick calculation I estimated around twenty thousand dollars. I rang the boys at the drug squad from the next county, informed them of the address and what I had found. I searched the other rooms and the main bedroom there was a double bed with soiled sheets and blankets. The blind on the window was down I released it and it flapped up quickly around the roller. The sunlight showed dust floating around in the rays as it beamed in.

The room had a smell worse than the other areas of the house. I found a suitcase; it was Benny's it had personal notes and details of different people, time's, places etc. There were some old clothes in it and still hanging in the cupboard seemed like most of Benny's possessions judging on the state of the building and the room. Benny had disappeared; I had to find him. Just then, the drug boys came busting in guns ready, they got here quicker than I expected. I held up my badge identified myself and told them why I was here and that I had called it in. Gave them the satchel and started to leave thinking to myself, where was Benny?

27

I walked slowly through the streets, the sun was out and shining bright, but the wind was cold and chilling it was like a mother in law's breath, blowing through you instead of around you. I was pondering over all that we had on this case, how we could tie it all in together. There had to be a connection between the bodies, the drugs and money, the whole thing stunk of corruption, money laundering, people smuggling and black-market organ selling, how was I going to connect the dots. We knew that some of the victims worked for an escort service that was run by a high, powerful person, well-heeled, and with huge amount of cash. We knew that Eugene had found out about this person through his contact this Benny, who had now disappeared, and through his mistress Catherine Rhind. All the clues to do with the 'Dante' theory, was this a clue or just a ploy. We had all this written on the board in our case room and we all knew that there was only one maybe two pieces to put all this together. We also knew that there had to be more bodies to complete the puzzle. As I walked, I also thought about Jo, and how I felt for her, but I had made the right decision. I thought about Katrina, she had lost her mate, husband, partner in life, even though he had his faults and was unfaithful deep down she loved him deeply. I felt for Ayden and Gina and how they had lost a father in such a gruesome and despicable manner. The sight of Eugene's body came back to haunt me his guts hanging out everywhere from where his heart had literally been ripped out of his chest. His brains splattered all over the toilet wall and the note attached to his heart and his intestines. Was this the work of our killer, of Benny or someone else? How close was Eugene to it all, why did he not confide in me over all that he knew?

My mind swept across the victims and the cruelty they had been put through; their bodies mutilated in someone's sadistic game. I was starting to feel the propinquity of the situation and the reason I am targeted. This whole thing was one large enigma. At that moment my mobile rang, I was rather hesitant to answer, as it could be Jo to lambaste me again, the press to hound me, or one of the cronies from the other day to ask what it is I am doing about this case. I answered, it was Coney, his voice had a quotidian sound, he remarked;

"Where are you Farrer, we have found another body, but this one is alive." I felt my heart drop with the news of another body, then as my mood started to accelerate, to one of excitement.

"Was she able to talk?" I asked.

"She is in the hospital, Ray and Jo are on their way over now, and do you want me to pick you up?"

"Yes" I replied;

"I am on Inverleith Ave, on the corner with Dalkeith Place." I hung up the phone and rammed into my pocket as I started to run across the grass, towards the corner, a break in this case, was the woman able to talk, could she name this bastard?

The hospital was about two minutes away as the crow flies driving, but a good twenty-minute walking. We had to hurry. My mind was racing. Coney was very quick in picking me up. We put on the siren and light and rushed through the midday melee of traffic; we headed down the street, turned left against a red light. Ahead of us was traffic, everywhere, Coney knew this town like the back of his hand; he cut right and around the roundabout, squealing tyres as he hooked the car to the right it lurched over then hard left with the feeling we were going to roll.

He swung on the wheel, oversteering on the opposite lock, the car righted itself, and he accelerated down the street. We came to another intersection he again yanked on the wheel turning hard left, again the car fished tailed out he applied opposite lock we again righted, and the hospital was about half a mile straight ahead. We weaved in and out of the traffic, cars pulling over to allow us through.

We crossed lanes against the lights veered up the

narrow driveway, how we avoided hitting traffic must have been the will of God.

The car again lurched as we avoided going right up the arse of the car in front. I could not believe that people on hearing a siren or seeing a Sheriff's car lights and sirens going would not pull over or get out of the way. I was amazed at how Coney could even see where he was going. I looked at Coney;

"We are not on a mercy mission for fucks sake, what is all this about?" He just smiled and continued to drive, we screeched to the right and onto the long horseshoe driveway of the hospital; Coney hit the brakes the car pulled slightly to the right as it skidded to a stop. Smoke was all around us from the tyres locking up, but unbelievably we stopped right at the front door. Five minutes flat, which was good, I thought to myself as I put my brain and stomach back in place. Leaving the car, it started to rain; I cursed hoping this was not a bad omen. I do not remember; but in the hospital corridor heading through to the emergency department; before I really came to my senses. I saw Ray talking with a doctor.

"Where is she?" I asked with anticipation.

Ray led me to a private room, where a blonde-haired girl lay. Deep blue eyes were looking off into space, as she looked at me with a frightened and quite petrified look on her face.

"Hi, I'm Ian Farrer, Sheriff of Oemen Lake, how are you?" She replied in a quiet monotone;

"OK", and I nodded and softly asked,

"Can you tell me anything?" She rolled over slightly onto

her right side, and I could see bandages covering at least two thirds of her back, the doctor was beside me at this time and said, *"Invidere"*, meaning *"Envy."* She was not the last of the puzzle though, *"Sloth"* was still out there. Ray came in as I touched her hand gently and said;

"Your OK now, we will get him"

My spirits lifted, I asked as gently as I knew how;

"Could she describe her experiences and to her whereabouts or where she was kept. The last few days of where she had been, as well as her best description of her captor, as we had a break in this case?"

28

I sat there in stunned silence, this whole thing now was a fucking spider's web, we were going around in circles and the web was getting bigger with each day.

"We need to look at all we have and follow up on Linda Forrester's alibi for the night of the murder. We also need to know Mews movements as well. Has anybody searched his place yet?"

"That was on the agenda for today boss." acknowledged Alvin.

"Get over there quick go through that place with a fine-tooth comb there must be something there that can link this together. I believe our friend Mr Mews is the link to either Mr or Mrs Forrester."

I followed on by saying,

"We also need the report on his autopsy, Gary can you tell me what you have got from the perfume bottle and box etc."

Gary looked across at me and said;

"Nothing Ian, the prints are those of the victim.

"Whoever made up the stuff used gloves or wiped it clean. We have got zip."

I knew then that the Foresters, whichever one was in the loop was responsible for these two murders a n d were not working alone. There was too much that added up, and a lot more that didn't, this was too well planned and executed to be a one-person crime. The other thing that kept gnawing at me was why Dean Forrester had made the calls to Cerise's place and when there was no answer for such a long time and he kept getting the busy tone, why he did not call the phone company or the police. I had to work that one out.

Were he and his wife in this together to go for a divorce to claim the trust inheritance and split it? There was a lot that I was contemplating. I decided I would front Petra Woods with what we knew and shake her tree a little maybe she could enlighten me on the matter, and maybe spill her guts as to what she knows. I arrived at her apartment with Ray, we knocked there was no answer, Ray went and collected the passkey from the security guy. He followed, as he needed to know what was happening so he could report to his superiors. We opened the door, the smell was horrendous, and I looked at the security guy

"Do you smoke?"

" Yes why?"

"Then light one up or get a cigar and smoke it." Ray and I entered the apartment covering our mouth and nose with handkerchiefs, and there in the small room off to the right was the dead body of Petra Woods. My theory and hopes just flew out the fucking window.

Linda was sitting at her desk trying to sort out in her mind now that she had covered her tracks thoroughly the night, she had made her potion and delivered it to Cerise's. Should she ring Stewart and let him know that the police had been to see her and that she had told them she was with him. What had Dean told them? She was in a real quandary and starting to panic slightly. Then the little voice in her head told her to calm down that everything was okay, and she had no worries. Linda rang Stewart; she relayed to him what she had told the Police.

"That is okay, do not panic just remain calm there is no way they can link you or I to the deaths and they cannot link us to any of the evidence they may have. You were careful when you put the potion together you followed my instructions?"

"Yes, I made sure everything was as you stated."

"Okay then, we have nothing to worry about." Linda told him that she was having lunch with Dean, that the Police had also interviewed him at the same time.

"Dean has more to lose than you Linda and now he has been found out about his affair he is going to be a bit jumpy so as we discussed keep your cool."

Quarter to one, Linda left the office to meet Dean for

lunch. As she drove along the radio was playing a Phil Collins' song, "In the Air Tonight", she started humming and thought how apt it was that song was on. Linda related it to her and Stewart. As she pulled into the car park of Pierre's she glanced around but could not see Dean's car. Running late as usual she thought. He will be late for his own bloody funeral, he was late for our wedding, he was late for both births of the kids, and he is a late one when making love. Lateness should have been his middle name. She smiled to herself at the way she had produced such a thought.

In the restaurant, she was seated at a window table; Dean had booked and rang that he would be late. Linda ordered a dry martini and a bagel until Dean arrived. One thirty and he walked through the door. He looked all tense and very worried.

"What is the matter?" she asked knowing full well he was in the shit up to his neck over this affair, and what made it better he did not know that she knew all about it. He ordered a double scotch no ice no water just straight.

"I have something to tell you and I need to do it now!"

"You know the lady that was found dead the other week in her apartment, well I was having an affair with her. Her name was Cerise Blackwell, she worked for Ray Beale." His scotch arrived he skulled it and ordered another. Linda acted the part well, of the shocked wife.

"How long" she asked in a surprised voice.

"I do not really know probably eighteen months a little more" he replied.

179

"This is why you are buying me lunch?"

"No, I needed to tell you after the Police were at the office this morning as they suspect me of killing her."

"Well, that would be a surprise if you had the balls to do that. I do not feel hungry anymore; you can eat on your own and do not bother coming home tonight. You can ring me tomorrow; I need time to think."

With that she finished her drink, picked up her coat and walked out of the restaurant. She got in her car and drove off and when she was out of sight, she could not but laugh out aloud and at once rang Stewart to let him know what had happened. They planned to meet that evening at his place.

Dean was left lamenting in the restaurant and what his future held. He really was in it. He had lost his lover; his wife was probably going to sue for divorce, which meant his job and his lifestyle. His kids and life as he knew it was now one large pile of horse shit. How could so much happen, in such a short space of time, and he not really have a handle on it all. He also had the feeling that the board knew this too. He suddenly had the feeling that Linda had taken this too easily for her, and he became suspicious. What if she was doing the same thing and this was a plot to discredit him. He was now paranoid about the whole situation. His wife was not that good, she was obsessed with him, and she would do anything to hang on to him but "Murder", No! No way.

The report on Petra Woods' body was that she died of an embolism. She had been injected with an air bubble that killed her. No prints, no sign of a scuffle, no sign of forced entry. She knew her killer. It again came back to the Foresters. Dean Forester though, I am reluctant to say he was the murderer, as he had not seen her since his wedding and the information we had was to this effect, he did not even know she was in town. That left her sister, but why? Then looking at what Bill had collated she stood to inherit a small fortune if the sister and Dean were out of the picture. This left Mr Mews how did he fit into all of this. We had another team meeting. We all sat around, and I asked;

"Who had any ideas or theories on the deaths?"
I looked around the room expecting one of them to at least produce something. The whole team had blank looks.
I decided it was my turn to at least put up a theory.

"Mrs Forester and another person are the instigators of these crimes. There seems to be a pattern. For instance, Mrs Forester stands to inherit a small fortune if her husband and the sister are out of the picture. She has achieved one of her goals. That of her sister, I do not believe she did the sister in, she has an accomplice that is doing the dirty work and she is paying the bills."
I again searched the blank faces looking for some sign of recognition that at least one of them agreed even in part with my theory. I continued.

"The other thing that sticks out here is also, that Cerise Blackwell was murdered because she was having an affair with Dean Forester. I again come back to Mrs Forester. She had the means, the motive, and the opportunity. What we need is the accomplice, and how they planned to get away with it."

I decided we would set up a sting operation as we needed to have one of the Foresters make a mistake. I believed that Mrs Forester would panic; I had no idea what made me think she was the instigator of the whole affair, call it a gut feeling. We needed to check out her movements, who she meets with when and where, but she was not the architect behind the Dante murders or was I not giving her enough credit. We also needed some evidence that she had the opportunity to be involved in the murder of the 'Prick'. I decided it was time that the rest of the team woke and smelt the coffee.

"Alvin, what do think of my scenario?"

"Well boss you are way off base, but then again you are rarely wrong, so I must go with it. What do you want me to do?"

Finally, I had some thoughts on the matter even if they were not what I wanted.

"Alvin, I want you to follow Mrs Forester, I want her every move if she eats you eat, if she shits you shit, do you understand?" He nodded and got up and left the room. As he was going out the door, he asked;

"Do I start now?"

"You bet your arse you do; I want you to be with her from like yesterday, okay?"

"Fred, I want you on Dean Forester's arse, the same thing wherever he goes you go, okay?"

Fred acknowledged me with a positive nod of his head. I knew he understood that he was to start right away as well.

"Gary, I want you to go over the apartment of Cerise Blackwell again, I want every square inch of that place searched and tested. I want the bottle dusted again, the wrapping everything. The reason, the perpetrator must have slipped up somewhere, and I want them in my custody as soon as possible. This case is starting to get like a can of spaghetti as there are too many leads and not enough ends joining up."

Ray finally looked at me.

"I must agree partner; I believe you're right about Mrs Forester. When you look at the evidence and the way things stack up, she could carry all this out. The other thing is she is obsessed with her husband, which was clear enough in the interview with her."
He looked at the others; he was looking for some kind of acknowledgment. I finally said,

"We need a sting operation as already stated, we need somehow to set up the Foresters and see who cracks first."

I had already planned the sting and all I needed was to have the information that Alvin and Fred were going to bring me. Mrs Forester was having an affair I was sure of it. She did not like hubby having one, due to her fantasy and obsession about him. She had some contact with knowledge of underworld people like Mews.

The sooner we had the information the better. I will call another team meeting in two days we should have a pattern by then also the names of the people that the Foresters see. I am going to need the co-operation of someone at the factory as well. The poison was manufactured there. Whoever made the lethal potion also delivered it. This whole case really did have the odour of death about it. Greed, obsession and the jolly green giant, jealousy was all part of these murders. Who had the most to gain, over the next two days I needed to be a sort of mystic with my crystal ball. My little under worked brain cells will be working overtime. Alvin was following Linda. He was like the local peeping tom. He watched her every move, wrote down all that she did and who she met.

He found it strange the first thing that Linda did was to go to a motel on the outskirts of town. She would have spent almost an hour in there, who was there she is meeting. Alvin was at a loss did he go in and check what was going on or just sit tight? He had no idea that Linda was getting rid of the evidence she had that could connect her to any of the crimes that had been committed. A little womanly charm also worked on the desk clerk, as he scrubbed her name out of the register and pocketed ten grand for his trouble. Linda was starting to think was this all worth the trouble the worry and the money just to fulfil her obsession. Finally, she left the motel, Alvin knew he was going to have to contact me somehow and let me know of the situation. We would have to get some men over there and go over that place with a fine-tooth comb. Again, that gut feeling came back that we are just that little bit too late and the real damaging evidence was in that motel room. Alvin called in and we arranged for some of the local boys to follow up and give the place the real once over.

Linda in the meantime had now gone to the mall this was going to cause Alvin some problems as this place was packed and it was like a herd of cattle all were going opposite ways to each other and no one really knowing where they were going or what they wanted. He fought his way through the throngs and tried to keep Linda in sight. What was it about a woman shopping she seem to be moving with ease through this sea of bodies and yet Alvin was going three forward and then seemed to be carried five steps back with the movement of the crowd. It reminded him of a beach as the surf came in wave after wave and one trying breach each wave was hit again and again by the incoming then outgoing current.

Finally, some breathing space, but he had lost Linda.

"Shit," he exclaimed with anger and pulled his mobile out of his pocket, he was at a main window to the outside and could see, just as the snow started to fall.

"Farrer, Alvin here. I lost her in the crowd at the mall. It is like a mad house down here and I get the feeling she knew that she was being watched."

I thought for a moment then replied;

"Watch her car, which may be the only means of transport she has."

Alvin retreated out to the car park, her car was still parked about seven spaces down in the opposite row. As he sat in the driver's seat of his vehicle trying to gather his thoughts and senses, there she was, getting into a taxi.

"You bitch," he said out loud.

The taxi drove past Alvin, and he slipped low down in the seat at the same time starting his engine. He pulled out and followed at a discreet distance behind the taxi, the snow falling he cleared his windscreen with the wipers. Ten minutes later they arrived at a restaurant. Lunch thought Alvin, and then he noticed a sign in the window closed. Linda walked right through the front door as it was opened for her. A rather tall, distinguished gentleman came out took a quick glance around and went back into the restaurant, closing the door behind him. He dialled his phone;

"Fuck, Farrer this is Alvin do you hear me?"

"Yes, what is it?"

"She has gone into some restaurant down Learmonth Terrace, just up from the corner with Dean Terrace, and the place is closed. It is as if she had prior knowledge that the place was closed, as if it were just for her. I do not like this, Ian." I calmly agreed with him.

"Stay there and watch I will be there as soon as I can. Ring Ray or try and reach him on your radio and see if he can come and sit with you till, I get there."

I will have to make sure all is okay as we want this to go down smooth no fuck ups. I need a couple more pieces of information before I will feel comfortable with what I knew. I needed to check out what Mr Dean Forester was up to. This lady going to a closed restaurant gave rise to a real positive outlook to our theories. I would bet my balls to a pound of beef; the owner of the restaurant is the one that helped her organise all this and he is Linda Forester's lover. I realise this was assuming a lot and as I say assumptions if wrong can get you killed. But in my business, you must go with gut instincts, brainwaves

186

whatever takes your fancy, that you believe to be correct. You are only going to get it wrong every now and again. I called Fred to ask what the other Forester was up to.

"He has not left his office. I can see right through the window into his office, and he has sat there staring at the wall for over an hour now, without moving." Was his reply; I now felt sure that our main culprits were in that restaurant. I informed Fred he was to stay there and keep a real close eye on our friend. If he leaves, follow him but do not intercept. I was hoping above all that he went to the restaurant as well that would tie this whole thing up in a nice little package for me if I were correct. I called the office and told Bill;

"Get a search warrant for the Forester residence, the restaurant, and the complete factory of Francoise National. I need them in less than an hour, I will also need arrest warrants for Linda Forester, Dean Forester, and Stewart Madden alias Marsden."

"I will do my best Ian," was his reply. Alvin reported back that Mrs Forester was leaving and she appeared to be upset.

"Follow her do not worry about the person or the restaurant." I informed him in a rather jocund sounding voice. I must admit, if I was right, then I had every right to feel most nonchalant about the case even have a little vanity about oneself. Fred rang to let me know the warrants would be ready within fifteen minutes. I summoned the whole team back to the office for a brief on how this whole thing was going to go down. The surveillance over the past few days had paid off.

We had the movements of both the Foresters; as well I had all I needed on Mr Madden/Marsden. This man was a piece of works. It was right he was the brother of Dean Forester, but the other skeletons that came out of the closet under closer scrutiny made my neck hairs stand on end. He had worked for Carlos Manzelli, better known as the "Father". Carlos was in the laundry trade, and I do not mean clothes.

This man could launder anything from a simple dollar to body parts. He was the family's main man in the southern areas of France. He answered to only one-man Frank Neopolie, in Sicily. Now Frank was the "Godfather" or so he thought, he answered to no-one. We had no factual evidence on any of them until Mr Madden showed up here in Oemen Lake about a year and half ago. This was going to be the bust of a lifetime. I wanted Stewart Madden; he could turn over Carlos, who in turn would give us Neopolie. The only problem I did not like about this whole thing was that they would all have to be given a deal to get us Neopolie. I honestly do not think Mrs Forester knew about Madden's past or who he was really connected with.

The other thing in this spider web of deceit was how did this all fit into the bodies we had and who handled them, was Madden the mainstay in that to throw us off his other business. Carlos for example had twenty-one charges against him for fraud, forgery, money laundering, pandering and murder, which as far as we know counted nine and human trafficking. The problem we had there been no tangible evidence of the facts and his smart arse highly paid lawyers always seemed to get him off due to some glitches or inconsistency. It had taken us three to four days to have everything in place to move on this case. I still had the Foresters under close surveillance. I was uneasy at the nonchalant way that Linda Forester went about her daily routine knowing she was under suspicion of murder.

There were some within the department that had the opinion of disapproval with my motives as to how I was working this case. Fuck them, I oversaw the investigation, and I knew that if I rushed it, I would lose the ladder to the big boy himself. Alvin reported in;

"Boss this lady has not left the house now for two days, I have seen no movement inside and the curtains are all closed."

"Keep on it man, she is there and playing it cool now, neither she or her husband can make a move and are both shit scared of what we are going to do next. Okay?" He replied;

"Yea Okay" but his voice was unconvincing.

29

I had one provocative question in my mind why Sally was still alive? The next three weeks she recovered well from her ordeal, and we kept a guard on her in a private room. Ray spoke to her about her ordeal, and she gave us the full story of how her boyfriend Damien Rourke had dropped her off and she was grabbed. She explained the appearance of the rooms and the corridors etc.

She was found just south of town in Tothernwell Pines Forest, by some hitch hikers, naked and wandering around in a daze. They took her to the hospital; the deputies had interviewed the hikers and taken statements. We did not push too hard although we needed as much as possible, we knew we had to take our time with her. We did not need another victim, so we had a catch twenty-two situation; we are damned if we do, and damned if we do not. The whole thing started to piece together. Ray came to me;

"I am going to check out this Damien Rourke, Majors mentioned his name as well",

"Ok" I said. We are so close, I hope.

I read the reports again, the statements; I needed to really sit down, and map this whole thing out, as the killer seemed to have now made mistakes, or was a deliberate ploy. I again perused Eugene's book for any clue or piece of information that fitted the puzzle. We knew that Dean Forester had set himself up at the office and had been sleeping there for at least two weeks since he told his wife of the affair. We had the warrants for the arrests, but I was not ready to move, not just yet anyway. Ray reported in;

"Madden is on the move"

"Follow his arse mate wherever he goes as the drill goes." Ray acknowledged.

"He is heading for the airport, and he has no luggage"

"I will arrange a ticket for you just let me know where he is going, flight etc. as soon as you can."

I sat at my desk pondering this situation over, my head now starting to throb; alcohol deprived cells, where was this prick going?

I started to draw the case in tree like form on my desk pad. At the top of this pile of shit we had Dean and Linda Forester. We knew that Dean was screwing around with Cerise, who was connected to Ray Beale; he was connected to Madden, owning part of his restaurant; now this is where my gut started to really churn over. Somehow, and I am not sure yet, Beale was connected to Majors and Rourke Snr, and Cerise and Dean were in on all this. That was my theory now but there were a lot of holes, big enough to drive a big rig right through the middle.

Ray called;

"He is on a flight out of the country, it leaves in two hours. We need to follow him on that flight".

"Go and I will fax an authority now for a return ticket, as well as an accommodation and meal allowance voucher. Stick with him Ray, this bastard has the answers to a lot of questions." I quickly filled out the proper forms, flipped open our bible that has all bus, airline, taxi, train and any other type of transport's names and numbers and special authority codes in. I faxed off the authority for Ray and put a note at the bottom.

"Please report to me every five to six hours, I will not move until I hear from you as to what is happening. I will also contact the local authorities once I hear from you, to meet with you for help. Good luck." I rang Coney to tell him of the development and what I wanted him to do. He was to get a warrant with Bill and search Stewart Madden's restaurant and residence while he was overseas. Gary in the meantime had produced some prints on the atomiser under the cap near where the tube connects to the actual spray button that sprayed the poison.

They matched those of Linda Forester. He said there was only one and it was not good but the main of the print was enough for seven points in fact for the computer to give a ninety percent match. He was going to need another fresh set of her prints at some time to get a full and perfect match. I decided this was the time to bring Mrs Forester in. I rang Alvin and told him to sit tight we were on our way.

Gary and I drove out to the Forester house and met with Alvin. Coney called to say he and Bill had all that we needed, and they were heading for the restaurant. If my hunch were right Mrs Forester would not be here but wherever Madden was heading, somehow, she had given Alvin the slip. How wrong can a person be? We knocked at the door almost bashing it down I was thumping that hard. I sent Alvin around the back. He yelled out over his radio in such a loud voice that his speech was slightly garbled, but I picked up the main of what he was saying;

"Boss, get your arse around here quick." We all sprinted around the pathway, to where Alvin was standing looking through a pair of open French doors.

The sight was not nice. Linda Forester, if it was her, she had large areas of flesh showing, it was as if something had eaten her. Her face was, well the right side was non-existent, the skull was showing through and that even showed signs of parts missing. Her arms and chest had huge like blisters, which had burst, and the skin had left large weeping, bleeding red raw craters. It was like the special affects you see in some horror movie this corpse walking along as large pieces of flesh fall off.

Then the skeleton keeps going until it crumbles. The sight of this woman, and how the flesh, was just eaten away. The smell was so offensive. I have smelt burning skin before, even the smell of an exhumed body, but this odour was extremely putrid, it felt like it was searing the insides of my nostrils and my eyes started to water. I looked around Alvin was the same, just then Gary yelled;

"Get out all of you it is an acid, and the fumes will make you ill."

We all rushed to the fresh air, out through the doors whence we came. For a few moments I sucked in some deep breaths and Gary advised;

"Do not wipe and I repeat do not wipe your eyes. This is sulphuric acid, and it is reacting with everything around it as well as there is another acid or chemical involved."

"Ian I am going to need the special team from Helena Central here. This is more than I can handle on my own."

"Get what you need. Is it Linda Forester?"
One of my young local Officers walked over toward me with what looked like a letter in his hand and pushed it toward me. It was a suicide note.

"Dean, my darling, I am unable to have you. I have loved you Dean with all my heart for as long as I have known you. From the first day I met you I knew you were the man for me. Please forgive me for what I have done; my obsession to hang on to you and my fantasy about Stewart has gotten me into this mess. I killed Cerise with a poison I brewed up at the factory. The Police knew and I was unable to control the panic that had built up inside me.

Please explain to the children that I love them, and I will always be with them. I have written a letter to Mr Farrer, which he will receive in the mail telling him about Petra and Stewart. I am sure they already know. I go to my maker with a heavy heart knowing I had not been the wife you wanted as you needed to have an affair with someone else to get fulfilment. My jealousy was overwhelming when I found out.

I planned and schemed for weeks, and the result was too many people getting hurt. I had an affair with Stewart to get back at you and to try and make you feel jealous of me, and to understand how I was feeling.

I have destroyed myself in this manner so that there

will be nothing of me left for you to worry about ever again.

All my love, now and forever,
Linda.

I stood there in an absolute dolefully frame of mind. I felt like I was glued to the spot where I stood. My mind had this incessant little voice going around in my head,

"You were too late Farrer, you fucked up Farrer, she is now dead Farrer." I needed a drink, as this case was now just so inscrutable, I did not know which way to turn. I had no idea of where to look and what to do.

Stewart Madden had to relate to all this so did Mews and it tied in somehow with our friends on their way out of the country with Ray in hot pursuit. How the fuck was I going to break this to Dean Forester? Just then I felt ill, nauseated, I turned and threw up all over a rose bush, my gut was heaving and so was my whole body. This was getting too much to handle. Too many bodies!

30

I was sitting at the table drinking freshly brewed coffee when the phone rang. It was Katrina asking if I would come over. I was hesitant at first but decided what the hell, why not. I told her I would be an hour or so as I had some things to follow up on. I had read the files that Ray brought from central, but the files held nothing that I could conclusively say was a tie in between this set of events and the case that Ray thought it had a similarity to. Eugene's book raised more interest for me, in the person or persons who were well connected. I suddenly remembered what Ray had said at the meeting with the Commissioner and the Mayor etc. Bourke had made that remark of *"Ha Ha Ha"*.

This started me thinking about the passage in Eugene's book concerning the escort service. I wondered if Bourke was the big wig, he had connections in high places being in Government. Was a noted visitor on frequent occasions at brothels, the vice boys from central had had some of them under surveillance a short while ago due to another case concerning a drug and murder case? Caught on film on many occasions he was entering and leaving the establishments. He also had money and lots of it. He will need checking, but discreetly. I had a clear head and the clues and evidence in this case were starting to come together.

I was glad we followed up this Rourke as was mentioned he had a connection to two of the victims, Sally Donald, and Julie Crow. I thought maybe I had better approach Myers; his local knowledge would be an immense help and not only that he had the connections to follow up this Rourke character in a discreet manner. The other thing that kept popping up was this, could a cop be involved, even one of my team? This thought I had to keep to myself, as it was a touchy area. I would expand more with Ray on this one as he was from out of town and I could trust him, I will talk to him when he rings me. Was it that Eugene found out the connections and put it together approached someone on the matter, thus getting them cornered? After all he was killed right here in the building.

I left home and headed for Katrina's, just as the sun was going down, although it had been an overcast day and sleet was falling and it was fucking cold. I stopped on the way and picked up Chinese as well as a bottle of wine, I hope they had not eaten, I knew the kids liked Chinese. I pulled up the driveway and walked to the front door just as the garage door went up. "Mum said to put your car in the garage if you like" I looked at her and, decided why not. I drove in and Gina closed the door behind me.

I collected the food and wine and went ahead through the internal access into the house. Katrina was at the sink.

"I collected dinner on the way hope you have not eaten" I remarked.

"No, I was just making a salad and we were going to have hot dogs" said Katrina, with a smile. Gina set the table and we all sat. We laughed and joked over dinner and Ayden asked;

"If I would put him to bed when it was time." I smiled and said;

"Yes". Katrina flashed me a smile that said thank you. I rang Myers and asked if he would like to join the investigation considering that he had such closeness to the case. He accepted my offer and we agreed to meet in my office at ten the next day. In the meantime, he was going to find out all he could about this Damien Rourke from his end and bring it with him. I rang Ray to let him know where I was and that I had asked Myers to join us. I also ran my theories past him; asked if he could think over what I had tried to piece together, whether it all seemed plausible. I put Ayden to bed and returned to the kitchen to finish the dishes; Katrina was in Gina's room helping her with her homework.

I poured myself a coffee returned to the living room and turned on the television, hoping that there was some kind of sport on. I was lucky; Soccer was on, so I settled down to watch. I must have drifted off to sleep brought out of my slumber by the feel of a warm breath on my neck and a pair of arms around me from behind.

I looked up and Katrina's eyes said it all. She came around to the front of me she was wearing a red see through negligee, my heart started to race; the sight of her body had started to excite me. I thought of Eugene who we had buried what seemed only yesterday but in fact was nearing on ten months. Time has just flown by; this case has really taken up my time. Katrina had beautiful firm medium sized breasts, and the body any man would want.

Her hips were slender, and she had a small scar about three inches long just above her mound of mousy pubic hair. I gathered that she had had her children by Caesarean, considering where this was. Her legs were the ones that men talk about they seem to go on forever. I just sat there in absolute awe of her beauty. I asked,

"Are you sure about this?"

"I have never been as sure of anything in my life as I am of this" I looked at her;

"What about the kids?"

"You have been single too long Ian; the kids are long asleep, and I have showered and all while you drifted off down here."

It was like a dream come true, I remembered my night with Jo, I knew that was over even though I had some feelings for her. Katrina knelt between my legs and looked at me, with a look of what I interpreted as lust, why did I use that word. She slowly undid the belt of my trousers and gently removed them, my socks, and shoes.

Running her hand up my legs to my crotch that was now about in full fever pitch, she came up to my chest opening the buttons on my shirt and kissing my nipples. Slowly tantalizing me, she removed my shirt, and I lowered her straps to reveal her well-formed breasts. Overcome with passion my inhibitions were gone. I fell under her spell and the night was now heaven. I awoke with a smile on my face, Katrina had showed me things that at fifty-three I had no idea you could do with your body. It was a night of passion that I wanted to last forever. I looked across at her sleeping, and admired her body as she laid there, her back to me, I was fifty-three she was forty-one, could this work? She had been married to a cop so knew the circumstances, the consequences etc. I ran my hand down her spine to the base, fingers gently caressing her buttocks, she moaned and turned over, looked at me and I was away in pleasure heaven again. I asked her;

"Where do we go from here, what would the kids think and have we a future?" She smiled and said;

"Yes, the kids have already asked about you staying here forever, and I told them you would have to ask Ian yourselves."

I went and showered, dressed and the whole time was thinking about what had I done, could this last, was I dreaming, or was it real? I entered the kitchen the kids were there smiling at me at they said;

"Stay forever". I went over and kissed Katrina and turned to them, I said;

"I cannot replace your dad, but I will try my best to be a dad, remember though your dad will always be with you."

I had breakfast with them and then headed for the office. I told Katrina I would drop some things off later in the day, but I would not get rid of my place just yet until, we were sure. She agreed. Myers was waiting in my office when I arrived; Coney was only minutes behind me.

"Thanks" he said.

"Think nothing of it; you are a good cop, maybe a bit overboard at times, but still a good cop." I looked at him as I closed the door and glanced at Coney.

"Are you two going to be able to work together on this as I need both of you co-operating?"

"I do not have a problem," said Coney, Myers looked at him and nodded,

"I can work with this man as he is honest and calls a

spade a spade, and digs well", we all laughed. I laid out my thoughts to them again and we collated the information that Ray had gathered; I saw Jo enter the office, giving us unusual glances as she took her seat at her desk.

I ignored the looks; we are so close now I could taste this bastard. Rourke, was the adopted son of Sarah and Jesse Rourke, had no priors, was a centre and played soccer, if he had not blown a knee. He lived in Big Bear but was born and raised in Hawaii. He was six feet four inches tall weighed about two hundred and thirty pounds. He had a job as a bouncer at some illegal nightclub in the outer suburbs on weekends in Helena. His main job was a medical attendant at the hospital. He had had three years medical school training when could no longer afford the fees working two jobs he left. Was well known had respect in the place where he lived, also at his places of employment. This person was starting to sound like the man we wanted, but what we had was circumstantial, we needed to follow up. I looked at Coney;

"Tap his phone, twenty-four-hour surveillance on him".

"Right", Ray, before he left had followed through on Bourke; he was relatively unknown until he entered politics. There were some rumours around that his money had come from unsavoury sources and that he had run his election campaign from this. He was fifty-two, married but widowed about five years ago. Had two daughters that had nothing to do with him since their mother had died, one had dropped right out of sight.

Information on him was sketchy we needed more.
I said;

"Tap and surveillance as well" Coney looked at me,

"You are going to tap a member of parliament's phone and keep him under twenty-four-hour watch?"

"Fuck yes" I exclaimed.

"The information we have got and from a previous case he is a constant visitor to brothels, money probably from the drugs or the brothels, could be connected to the escort service, I just have a gut feeling." Bill and Hal looked at me with a look of disbelief,

"I hope your gut is right, because if you're wrong, he is going to have your guts for supper".
Hal exclaimed. I then said;

"A cop is also involved but I will follow that one up. Let me know if you get any further information. What we have discussed stays here nowhere else ok." I opened the office door and walked out into the room the team were all looking at me with quizzical looks.

"Hal Myers has joined us for the rest of this investigation". Coney looked at me and shouted as he turned to face his desk;

"Well fuck me!"

31

Sally Donald was still in the hospital when I went to visit her. We still had her in a secure room with twenty four-hour guards. I had this feeling that if we did not keep this up, she would be dead. I also knew that somehow this Damien Rourke was involved. I asked her about him, she told me she had met him about six to eight months ago, through a friend of hers. I asked who the friend was and what she told me made the hairs stand up on the back of my neck. She explained how she had come to know her friend, that it was at a party about two years ago that was thrown by some grey-haired big wig, who was in politics or something and was throwing money around as if he was making the stuff. There were a lot of important people there, some I recognised from newspaper photos.

The name she gave me was Annabelle Tate. I asked if she realized she was dead and one of the victims of this person who had grabbed her. She seemed unaware of Annabelle's disappearance, as she had not seen her for a couple of months. Rourke had rung her one night and asked her to go out, he explained he was a friend of Annabelle's and that she had told him I had just been dumped by my old boyfriend and needed some cheering up. I thought nothing of it and decided why not. I suppose I should have rung Annabelle, and checked, but he seemed to know all about me, and I was convinced he could have only got what he knew from her. We had gone out and he was nice, kind, a real gentleman. I asked if they had had sex and she said no. On a couple of occasions, she had tried to seduce him, but he was not interested at that time it was too soon into our relationship he had remarked, they just kissed cuddled and basically got each other off without actual sex.

I thought that a bit strange for a young male full of testosterone that he did not want to get his load off with a pretty girl like the one that was laying here in front of me, especially when she was throwing herself at him. She continued to tell me how he had dropped her at the end of the street, and that the reason for this was her mum and dad did not like him because he would not meet with them. I persuaded them to give him time that he was shy.

It started to dawn on me was this the man. Sally told me about his car, I knew then it was he, a blue BMW, she said his dad and this big wig all had the same make and model. Was he the one at the funeral chapel and the grave or his dad or this big wig? This was now a can of worms. I was shaking with anger but had to keep calm as she continued.

I asked her what-coloured eyes the person had who grabbed her she said;

"Cold expressionless piercing blue ones". What colour hair, she could not tell me as he wore like a surgeon's full head cap and facemask. I asked;

"What colour were Damien's eyes and hair?" She said;

"Light green and hair was brown. Damien could not have done this I know he wouldn't hurt me." I consoled her and said;

"I have to ask these things." The eyes had me a bit sceptical but then I wore glasses as well as contacts when needed and they can be coloured.

She described the place she was kept in it sounded like a disused wine cellar or basement of a disused building or warehouse. To set it up as she described would not have been cheap. The person or persons involved in this needed cash and lots of it. There would be no cheques involved; credit cards etc. all had paid been for by cash. The instruments she described, the drugs would all have to be stolen from hospitals, Doctors surgeries or brought in the underground economy, the latter is where I feel these maniacs got all this.

You would not be able to order this as records are kept. I will follow up on it anyway. I thanked her for her time explained that we were going to keep her here for another week or two under doctors' orders and she thanked me. I asked;

"Had her parents been to see her?" She said;

"Yes, could you contact Damien and ask him to see me". I said;

"I would try" knowing all the time that he was not getting within a fucking bulls roar of her. I left the hospital and rang Myers,

"I want you to go to Judge Herring, now, and get a search warrant for a Damien Rourke's apartment, ask Jo or Coney they have the details, and the reason is the suspicion of multiple Homicides." I then rang Ray and told him what she had said, he said,

"Colin has found something from Sally's feet, to do with where she was held."

"Ok", I said and hung up.
I rang Colin at Forensic and asked what he had. He told me

"She was kept in a place that was once a place that had been used for the storage of chemicals for treating timber. The soles of Sally's feet from the samples taken had traces of Chlorine Dioxide, Hydrochloric Acid, Arsenic, and Formaldehyde. There was also residue of copper and some zinc. Also, a minute but still enough to cause the small burns and redness on her feet of Sulphuric Acid, he suspected an old car battery factory or a place that held and destroyed them could also fit the scenario.
I said;

"Thanks anything else you get let me know" He quickly butted in;

"I haven't finished yet, I tested the feet and bodies of all the other girls including tissue and blood samples. They all matched Sally's for the same composition of chemicals, so guess what buddy, find this place and you may find your killer." I quickly rang Hal, and asked,

"If he knew of such a place," he said,

"Yes, the old, abandoned sawmill just south of the rail line on the old road, before the forest road to Lookout Point. There is a gravel formed road at the end is an old sawmill, it was also used dumping old batteries; been closed for years. The reason being they were pumping the waste into the Oemen Creek that feeds the western end of the lake near Pullmans Point; the Environment boys stung their arse over it. The fine broke the company."

"Thanks," I said;

"Guess where we are going in the morning, can you arrange for a warrant, see Ray and hit Judge Herring for it he is doing another for me at the moment, tell him both warrants are connected." We are finally getting a break, I went home to Katrina's that sounded funny saying that, and had dinner, I made telephone calls to the team informed on sketchy details of what we had, I did not want them to know everything, so I told them each a different piece. I made a note of whom I told what to and the details of each message. Jo said,

"She would be late tomorrow as she had a doctor's appointment woman's thing"

I thought nothing of it at the time.

32

I stood up and wiped my mouth and looked around for a tap I needed to wash up. Just then Gary came over and patted me on the back.

"You are not the only one Farrer; we have all had a bit of a heave. It is the fumes from the body. I have opened all the windows and the other doors in the room to get some air going through. I have also put ice around the body to try and stop the decaying process from progressing to quickly until the boys get here." I looked at him,

"I fucked up Gary, I should have moved quicker. My gut kept telling me there was something wrong with all of this, my head kept telling me through the alcohol haze that she was in this up to her neck, and she should not have died."

Gary patted me on the back and pointed across the lawn to a faucet beside the path. I went over turned it on and splashed five or six handfuls of the refreshing icy water on my face. Her letter said that she had sent me a letter; I hope there were some reasons in that to make me understand all of this. Just then the Forensic boys arrived I could tell by the look on some of their faces they had not seen a sight like this before. I decided now was the time to tell Dean Forester, I had no idea how I was going to do this as I drove slowly towards the factory.

I had the image of Linda Forester's body going around and around in my head. Suddenly my mobile rang;

"Hello",

"Ian, it is Ray; you would never guess who our friend has just had lunch with." I thought for a moment then with a change of mood and a nonchalant sound to my voice;

"Mr Frank Neopoli.",

"Arsehole, you are one third right, there were three others at the lunch which makes it all so interesting, and the party consisted of Mike Grant, Ray Beale and Carlos Manzelli."

I pulled the car to a screeching halt on the side of the road.

"Tell me that again," Ray repeated the names and I sat there wary at the prospect of what this meeting was all about. I filled Ray in on Mrs Forester and told him to keep up with Madden. I felt more reposed now at the new evidence we had gleaned from our investigative efforts. I had decided that Mr Forester had nothing to do with all of this but was a victim and the object of an obsession by a jealous woman as well as being used like a pawn in a game of chess. The latter I concluded from the information I had received from Ray. I knocked on his door. His secretary was not anywhere to be seen. I entered his office; he was not there but I could see this was not only his office but also his home.

He had a bed set up in the corner and had been having a takeaway meals as there where motley coloured food discoloured food cartons and boxes all over the place. The office looked rather squalid considering who Dean Forrester was and his position. It also looked like someone had been rummaging through the desk and filing cabinets.

The whole place was in disarray. Alvin rang to say that the coroner had removed Mrs Forrester to the morgue and the Forensic boys will be a while yet. I informed him I had not found Mr Forester. I asked;

"Is Fred or Bill there?"

"Yes, both of them why?"

" Could all three of you be in the office not tomorrow but Thursday at nine am? I think I have figured this whole shit pile out. In the meantime, tell Bill I want information on Mews and Madden any connections aliases etc. I want you to follow up on a Raymond Beale of Beale Transport. Tell Fred he is to find out about Carlos Manzelli. We need all this Thursday. I have something to follow up, I will be in touch."

This was a time I needed some space to think. Before I had time to really get myself into a relaxed mode my phone rang.

"Ian it is Gary, preliminary tests on Linda Forester, she used the same set up as Cerise Blackwell, except they were seven to ten times stronger. There was also an enormous amount of Sulphuric Acid in the mixture. From the test so far, she must have used between three to four hundred mils."

"Okay keep at it see you Thursday"

With that I hung up. The next day at the Forester home, somewhere in this house was the clue I was looking for to connect all this together. I sat in the large dining room, surveying the area and trying to get a sense of what went on in this house. I moved around the house slowly room by room, using all my knowledge and senses to pick up anything that might be out of place. Downstairs seemed rather normal and except for the blood stain on the living room carpet and the odour of the decaying body still lingering, the carpet was also drench with something the Forensic boys had sprayed to alleviate any more acid problems, but there was nothing I could see or feel that would make me think that there was anything wrong. I continued upstairs looking at the artwork on the walls as I ascended. I reached the first landing and surveyed down onto the foyer area.

There again I could see nothing that was out of place. I went up the small number of stairs to the top floor and looked both left and right deciding which way to try first. I went with my instincts and went right. I walked along the rather wide hallway to the end. I peered out the window that looked out over the expansive gardens. I turned around and walked slowly back. The room on my right was a child's room, well-kept everything in its place, as it should be.

I went to the opposite room that again was a child's room. This one was a bit messy but that was nothing different. It told me that one child was neat and tidy and the other was not. I walked along to the third door that was to a bathroom. I entered and surveyed the area. The door off to the left was to a separate toilet. Another door further left led to another room, which I entered and again nothing in here looked out of place. I exited back into the hallway opposite another window that looked over the courtyard area. Along a little further was a set of double doors, I opened them, and two steps up was the master bedroom. I went up the steps and entered. On the right was a walk-in robe that had a door at the other end, which went into a separate bathroom. The bathroom was well appointed and well laid out. It consisted of a shower, spa bath, and toilet.

I left here and went back into the bedroom. I looked
around and still nothing jumped out and bit me on
the arse to say here I am the clue you are looking for.
 I sat on the end of the bed and closed my eyes,
picturing everything I had seen so far in the house.
I was at a point where there was an obstacle in
my theories and the clues, we had was blinding the
team from the truth. In this house was the bloody truth
and I was going to find it before that meeting
tomorrow.
Then it hit me; there must be a study, library office
of some kind. A house this size and the occupants,
their line of work, there had to be a room for their
work to be done at home. I was just a lousy cop,
but I had an area in my hovel for such things. I went
back out into the hallway, again looked around, there
was nothing. It had to be downstairs. I proceeded
down the stairs to the landing, it was then I noticed
the latch, I had not seen it on my ascent. I pushed
 the latch down and low and behold a doorway to
 stairs. I went in and up and found exactly what I
was looking for. A well-appointed office and library.
A lot of chemical books and manuals on chemistry,
files and papers neatly stacked. The computer on the
desk was still on, I hit the enter key and the
screen brought up the desktop. I clicked on the
folder;
  "My Files". It was Dean Forester's; it had
some remarkably interesting material. He knew
about Stewart Madden, his association with Ray Beale.

He knew that they had connections to the mob. It was all here. Ray Beale would transport their drugs around the country undetected in coffee cartons, vegetable boxes and the like, inside the fertiliser boxes. Reading this was like a dream come true. I would copy all this to hard copy, for the team in the morning. I searched for a USB, found it and went ahead to download. As this was happening, I had the sense someone was watching me. I spun around quickly to see Dean Forester standing behind the door slightly obscured by a bookshelf.

"Well Mr Forester, the information you have here could very well put a lot of people away for a long time." He came out from his hiding place; his mood was sombre, and his face was drawn.

"I know Mr Farrer. I have known all this for almost two years. I have lived with it for all that time. I could talk to no one as there was a mole in our company as well."

"I know, Mike Grant." I said with a rather brusquely voice.

"I suspected him, but had no proof, how did you find out?"

"He was seen in a meeting with an underworld boss in Sicily a couple of days ago with Ray Beale also." He slumped into the leather chair off to one side.

"I have some unwelcome news for you, your wife is dead. She committed suicide." He dolefully looked at me,

"I know I was here when you arrived. I had come home and came straight up here. I needed to copy this stuff like you have and I was turning it over to you. When I heard the commotion downstairs, I came out to see and could not believe what I was looking at. Believe me Mr Farrer I had nothing to do with her death and I am now so lonely and so fucked up."

"Join the club" I said to him. I looked at him trying to work out the next step.

"Does anyone know you have this shit?"

"No",

"Good then I can take you, the info and whatever else you have here into my office. That way you will be safe, and I know where you are and that no one is going to get at you." We finished copying the material. I checked it and then we removed it off the hard drive. Tomorrow morning was going to be quite interesting. I took Dean to my place and told him to make himself at home.

"Do not answer the door or the phone, do you understand."

He nodded that he did. I returned to the office loaded the USB onto my computer and copied the whole lot to the printer and made five copies. I collated them and then locked them as well as the USB in the safe. I rang Judge Murdoch, went over the evidence with him and asked for new arrest warrants for Carlos Manzelli, Frank Neopoli, Stewart Madden also Ray Beale. I then rang my opposite number in Sicily, Inspector Eduardo Panzarella, told him the story and said an arrest warrant would be on his desk by morning. He was not to arrest Neopoli until I rang him that we had the others. He agreed.

33

The team was assembled as needed I walked in slowly and went ahead to the front of the room. The folders for each of them in my hand as well as the warrants and the USB safely tucked away in my pocket. This was to be the ultimate moment. This whole case overnight seems to have just fallen into place. I looked at the team one by one each had that look of expectancy on it, waiting for me to lay out the whole sordid scenario from start to the present. I handed each of them a folder.

"Well let's have a look at what we have. Firstly, we know that Cerise Blackwell and Dean Forester where sheet tossing buddies. Secondly, we know that Cerise Blackwell was like a daughter to Ray Beale of Beale transport. Thirdly, we know that Mrs Forester was jealous and had a bad obsession with her husband. She was not in the mood to allow anyone to even look sideways at her husband. Fourth, she found out about her husband's affair, combine this with her obsession and jealousy, Cerise Blackwell was a walking target."
I took a deep breath and asked;

"Any questions so far?"
Without waiting I continued;

"Fifth, we know that Cerise Blackwell, was ill and dying, she was also pregnant. Sixth, we know that the poison cocktail that killed her was manufactured at the Forrester Company. We also know that Mrs Forester made up the potion that killed Cerise. Seventh, we have

215

evidence that Mrs Forester was also having an affair with a Mr Stewart Madden, who just so happens to be the long-lost brother of Mr Dean Forester. This whole thing starting to sound bizarre, you should have been with me last night when I put it all together."

I took a short break and skulled a glass of water.

"Boss, all this that you are putting to us now, how does all this fit together with Madden, and his trips to Sicily as well as the other evidence we have on him."

Alvin was squirming in his seat as he asked this.

"Patience all will be revealed very shortly." I continued;

"Next, we know that somehow this gentleman called Mews fitted into this situation due to the tape he had of Mr Forester and Cerise. Who killed him? Well now, here comes my assumptions and hopefully the information you have in those folders will back me up and we need a small amount of luck. Ray Beale is the transport for the drugs for the UK and Europe to all parts. Carlos Manzelli is the go between for Beale and the Sicily crime syndicate. He organises the pickups, the drops, payments etc. Stewart Madden is the money launderer; he recycles the drug money through his restaurant, why do I guess this because his restaurant is hardly ever open so how he makes a profit?" I paused, looked around the room at the faces staring back at me with puzzled looks. I continued;

"We also know that Manzelli is connected directly to Neopoli the kingpin of the group in Sicily. Now the cruncher, Mike Grant the chairman of the board at Forrester's' company, is connected in this also. Why?

216

He organised the shipments of products which in amongst those shipments were the drugs."

I needed a breather. I went to have a piss and to recollect my thoughts and make sure I was leaving nothing out, as this was now important. I stood looking in the mirror of the men's room, I stated out loud to myself;

"You certainly are no prime catch man, but you can work a case well."

A voice came from behind one of the stall doors,

"You're a vain arsehole too."

It was Ray who had come in for quick piss as well.

"I hope you know what you are doing man as the assumptions you are making in this case are a little far-fetched don't you think?" I looked at him and just walked off returning to the briefing room. I positioned myself up front again.

"Are there any questions before I finish and then tell you our next steps?"

"The one thing you must keep an open mind about this whole affair, I have put this together from information gathered by us, and what we found in relevant files, as well as the interviews we conducted."

They all shook their heads, and no one really could agree or disagree.

"Finally, we know that the trucks from Beale transport carried not only the stock but chemicals, vegetables, coffee, the works. They could travel from anywhere to anywhere no questions. Why? Because they were one of the largest transports in the country and had never had any real trouble with the law, or the transport

217

boys. Mews was a gopher for the whole operation he would source out the orders prepares the shipping sequences and organise the money to and from Madden. Cerise was murdered due to jealousy and obsession. I stopped, looked around and took a deep long breath, and asked;

"Are there any questions?" I then continued,

"Petra Woods was murdered because she knew too much not only that she was due to inherit a fucking fortune if Dean was found out about his affair. Mews was killed as he got greedy and wanted more money for his little porno flick. I believe that Stewart Madden and Linda Forester organised this. Stewart Madden killed Petra Woods, he knew about the will and its clauses."

"Are you all following any of this?"

"Carlos Manzelli, set Stewart Madden up in business and through the contacts he found out about his long-lost brother and sister-in-law. He also knew about the will as I said and knew of Petra Woods. He gained the confidence of Linda and seduced her into believing he was genuine. They knew each other at school, Linda has caused him some embarrassment on occasions, and he sought revenge. This took him twenty years, but he finally got it." I continued;

"This now leads us to Manzelli and Neopoli; they are turning over an estimated thirty million dollars a year off their illegal trade. Beale is on ten percent, Grant is on five percent, and Mews was on the same. All of them were making a lot of money. Then the penny drops,

Madden was syphoning the money through the brothels and his restaurant, and the missing women who turned up with the mutilations on their backs where at one time or another staff at Madden's restaurant or the brothels in the next county."

I looked around there seemed to be a sea of blank and quizzical looks, but no one was asking any questions. So, I just went on;

"We also know who frequents them regularly, Mr Rourke and his mate the mayor. Who I am sure are all connected in some form to each other? In the folder you will see bank statements and deposit slips for all this. Dean Forrester knew something was going on at his factory and it has taken him almost two years to collate the information. I had a little talk with him last night and he revealed all, including the information you have in that folder."

For a short period, there was silence except for the rustle of papers as they perused the files I had given them.

"I have arranged for arrest warrants on all those named on the top page of your file. My counterpart in Sicily will grab Neopoli on my telephone call. The others are ours. The one thing I forgot as well, Cerise was reporting back to Beale everything she found out about the company from Forester and Forester was using her to glean information. They were using each other and neither knew it."

"When do we arrest these arseholes boss and close down this operation?" Fred was keen to get on with it. I looked around and asked;

"Anyone got anything further to say on the matter." There was silence.

"Tomorrow morning at six am Fred you and Ray are to arrest Beale, charges, drug dealing, illegal transportation of illegal substances, fraud, and conspiracy to murder. We have a truck of his impounded in Helena. It has a load of perfume on alright, but also nearly six million dollars' worth of uncut heroin."

" Gary, you, and Bill will get Manzelli; the file tells you where he is. I have the privilege of fronting Mr Madden. The local boys are picking up Mike Grant. We will meet here at four thirty in the morning and go for it."

It was an early rise, but I wanted these bastards before they had time to scratch their balls. I handed out the warrants and wished them all luck. Ray looked at me;

"You are taking a chance going after Madden alone are you not?"

"No mate I have someone with me as well as back up from the locals." Little did Ray know that Dean Forester was coming along to confront his own brother.

We left the building heading for the restaurant. I had rung Sicily and they would have Neopoli in chains by now. We had enough evidence to put him away for a long, long time. I drove in silence as Dean Forester sat next to me in silence with his own thoughts, he seemed to be miles away from here and he had a look of anger on his face, which I needed to sort out, and keep him calm as he is our prize pawn in this whole thing. The one thing I had not told the crew that we had other arrests to make at the old sawmill tomorrow.

34

I slept well and felt contented, cuddled up with an angel. The next morning, we converged on the sawmill, two deputies had guarded the deserted factory all night. Six in the morning, the sun was about to create a new day, the night shadows slowly dissipated, and I felt good. We had arranged for about thirty local police to help. Colin and his Forensic crew of five had arrived about ten minutes before us. We were lucky in that the Ray had gained some old plans of the building from the county records, so after perusing them we split up and started our search.

This place was a bloody labyrinth of buildings, passages and even tunnels so we found. It was not only a sawmill and recycled batteries but also mining for something I had no idea what, that was not shown on the documents. The building, built into and on a high rock face overlooking the river. Ray, Hal, Coney, Macey, and I took the east end of the building as to what showed on the plans like storage rooms under the building and a basement that appeared to face the river. We entered a dark corridor that turned sharply left, luckily the torches gave us full light and we were able to clearly see all around us. We came to a solid door with a large sign painted on it saying *"POISON BEWARE"* in yellow with the old skull and cross bone below it. Off to the right was a tunnel and shining the torch down its gaping darkness, the torch hardly penetrating the thick blackness, we could see a junction.

"Shit!" I exclaimed.
Hal said;

"There is more bloody tunnels over here, and they are as dark as midnight, our torches are not strong enough, we need some spots in here. I had to agree. We decided to go through the door and radioed for some spotlights to be set up in the tunnels. There was a distinct odour of rotting flesh coming from the tunnels to the left of the door that Hal had discovered. It was vile, and I felt my stomach churning ready to throw up. The years had worn the door, but it was still in good nick. I looked at the lock and straight away, something struck me as strange. Hal,

"How long did you say this place had been closed?"

"Twelve maybe fifteen years"

"If it has been closed that long why is there a new lock on the door that looks like it was put there yesterday" Coney stepped up to the door and out of his jacket produce a short length of bar with a type of fork on one end.

"That's not issue" I said, he did not answer, he placed it through the "U" of the lock and levered it against the door, with one clean jerk there was a metal sounding crack and the lock fell to the ground.

As we opened the door, automatically the lights came on,

I stood there aghast, it led to a corridor that had clean and smooth concrete floors and the walls had like a form of "Michelangelo" soundproof tile. At the end was another door with the same sort of lock, Coney walked up and performed the same task. I opened the door the lights came on, and I was in a hospital operating theatre. There were the most sophisticated pieces of equipment you would ever want to see. Some hospitals did not have this much.

There was a large three door fridge on one side and two doors leading off on the left. What looked like windows blacked out? I went to the fridge and held my breath as I opened it, the smell was horrific even though there was the faint smell of disinfectant in the air, and it smelt like rotting food.

"Macey go and get Colin, and his boys." I said quickly. In the fridge, there were stainless steel tubes with labels of the dead girls' names and dates on them, stainless trays, with pieces of what looked like skin that was forming new skin, it was growing or so it seemed.

In the top section of the fridge were plastic bags filled with what looked like blood, Petri dishes with some form of substances growing in them, Steve was going to have a field day here. We went through the doors, Ray, and I the closest, Coney and Hal the other, we ended up in what looked like a sleeping quarter, there were papers and medical books everywhere, files on the dead girls, three names I did not recognise. There were hundreds of photographs stuck to the walls and notes written on each. I removed one from the centre and looked at the reverse side. We do not have this much information on criminals, there was the person's date of birth, their addresses, where they worked, blood type, illnesses they may have had, it just went on like a medical history on each. In the corner stood three four drawer filing cabinets, I opened them and low and behold they were full of files, medical files. This had me completely bewildered; files en-masse of people and I looked under 'F' and to my amazement there was a file on me.

"How the fuck was he able to obtain this?"
I stated in a startled voice. Ray went and looked in the second cabinet and sure enough a full history on him. We looked at each with a look of disbelief,
and I knew then, I wanted to catch this fucker, no matter what it took and my fervour to do this was greater than ever.
These files will have to be perused with such care due to privacy issues, as we had no idea where they came from and not only that, was this how they chose their victims and why? There was a note pad and address book sitting on the table closest to the second door, I had a quick look, one page was missing, I quickly grabbed a pencil rubbed over the under page and two numbers came up I knew who one was at once. I tore the page out and put the pad back on the table, the other page which was for me I filed in my shirt pocket. The whole place was just as Sally had described it. I went left and out into another corridor with the Christmas lights, I heard a shout from in front, I ran to a doorway into a room, crisp clean, white, very sterile.

Two vents in the roof, the smell in here was terrible, on two of the tables Hal had found the corpses of two rotting bodies, both looked female, and had been dead a long time. The skin decaying, dropping off the bodies onto the floor or table. The bodies were naked, lying on their stomachs; backs had the markings in place. In the corner were large translucent plastic drums, with some kind of ochre coloured fluid in them. I found a stick poked around in the first barrel and stepped back in horror a head and hand floated to the surface. The second barrel I did the same and a leg came bobbing up to greet me. I threw up in the corner, heaving my guts out. Why had he not used these bodies?

The odour was starting to become overwhelming. Coney a seasoned veteran, also threw up in the opposite corner, he pointed to the room he had just come out of. As I entered the lights came on, it was cold, I stopped in my tracks, there hanging on hooks around the walls were bodies, ten maybe twelve, all in varying stages of decay while others looked fresh. I backed out of the room Coney was still heaving; I would have joined him only I rushed back to the other room. Steve was standing in the centre of the room with a look of astonishment on his face.

"There would be close to three and half million dollars or more of equipment here. Surgical, research, you name it, it was here."
I nodded at the fridge;
"I want a preliminary report of this Steve on my desk as soon as you can"
Just then Ray, Coney, and Hal appeared, Coney was

225

green, I surveyed the wall of paper clippings as Sally had described, we had found the bastard's lair. We left the Forensic boys to it, we still had another place to visit, I knew Mr. Rourke would not be there, as one of my team would have made the tip off, it was obvious now. I knew who a traitor in the ranks was, but I could not play my cards yet. I left the boys to search Mr. Rourke's apartment and went back to the office; it was empty and quiet. I sat at my desk, how was I going to go about this with a person who had betrayed us.

Why had they associated with such people that would do this to young women? I was not going to like what I had to do. My mind flashed back to those rooms, and we had not even surveyed the tunnels yet. My god what was going here? There had to be over twenty bodies connected to this crime so far, but why, what was the purpose. Next morning on my desk as requested when I arrived was the preliminary Forensic report from Colin. It made interesting reading, how the equipment was used for the investigation into tissue matching, DNA, and the room was so set up as to start Biopsies and conduct experiments into culture growing and the re-growth of dead tissue and blood cells. Colin was amazed at the advancement someone had made into the area of finding a cure for Leukaemia; he detailed that someone may have been looking for a cure to Myelogenous Leukaemia.

He had found blood and other samples taken from two other people with the condition. The dead women and Sally Donald did not match these samples. From his studies and tests so far, he calculates they are from two males one late twenties with a mild case, and the other in late fifties with an advanced case. The test also showed that neither had had the traditional treatments.

He was also fascinated at how the person conducting the experiment had cross-matched DNA from the victims and the blood in the bags treated with extra red cells and Platelets to be ready for a transfusion. The barrel bodies where rejected parts or organs and were being broken down for disposal.

It appears they had run out of room, so the dumping of the bodies we found had taken priority away from their efforts in that gruesome place. The bodies in the cool room which was at a constant minus three degrees were from six to eight months old, or as fresh as two days. Whoever wrote these notes also said that it may have been a lucrative body farm, selling organs in the underground economy, made for a huge gain. In another area we found body parts packed in polystyrene boxes with ice surrounding them.

They were addressed to many areas of the country. Upon closer inspection of a liver, it had had recent surgery and packed inside was a sealed plastic bag having a white powder. The white powder I believed was either cocaine or heroin and this was all part of the one operation, and it was very well set up they were using the lab and the sawmill for experiments but also the lab was used for manufacture and cutting the drugs. The skin grafts used with a concoction of chemicals as well as cross-matched bone marrow, which was in the small silver anti-contaminant containers and cells to start a biopsy type culture.

He found expansive notes in the small room that followed in the areas of traditional studies into a cure for the condition but had changed some of the methods used to the ones described or recommended. Whoever this was is a fully trained, Pathologist/Biochemist and a very skilled surgeon, as the cultures and grafts taken, were with great ability. All this medical talk had bamboozled me, and I was looking for a link. Just then, Frank Coney walked in with a tape in his hand,

"I think you are going to love this Farrer". He put the tape into a machine and played it.

Voice 1: "The cops are onto me; I cannot get near that Sally chick to finish her off.

Voice 2: "You were supposed to give her enough to kill her, you got soft on her and now we are in the shit" I knew the second voice I was trying to place it. The tape went on.

Voice 1: "I will go down tomorrow with a truck and clean out the lab; I will need to know where to set it up again. What about the Cocaine shipments ready to go, we cannot discard the stuff, it is Madden's that women, and their partners".

Voice 2: "Set it up again it has cost close to two million to set this up, we have twenty odd dead, and we are no closer to a cure you idiot, and we have not been paid for the last shipment. Remember our friends overseas will not be happy if we cannot continue, they have huge investments in this. How are we going to set up again? I am dying; I have about two months on the outside to live. So, setting up again is not an option. Hang on the phone in the other room is ringing".

We heard a lot of yes and no over the tape then what I wanted to hear;

"How do you know Farrer was there, He what? Fuck there goes everything. You had better cover your arse and quick".
The second voice returned to the phone.

Voice 2: "That was Mac, he has informed me that idiot, Farrer has already found out or surmises he knows about our little set up and the drugs, if he knows about them, we are dead". Before he could go on, I stopped the tape I recognized the voice.

I looked at Frank;

"Get the team into the briefing room upstairs in an hour we have two arrests to make." Two o'clock, the whole team was in the room when I arrived, they all had puzzled looks as I surveyed their faces and could see that they were questioning why I had brought them in at this time. While I was waiting for them, I had our electronics division do a sweep of the room, they had found bugs, and I had suspicions because it appeared that our investigation was being stalled at contrasting times. Before I could do anything, my phone rang, it was the hospital, Sally Donald had checked herself out. I needed this like a hole in the head, as she could name Beale, Grant, Rourke, and Bourke. I had to hope they give themselves away during the interrogation.

35

Back at the horror site the Forensic boys had set up lights in all the corridors or tunnels depending on how you look at them. It was a maze and some of the details of substances found, as well as items which will need to be tested. This case was far from finished, and how many I thought to myself are involved in this macabre caper. I had had my suspicions but had no real foundation or concrete evidence to link anyone from that little escapade of a meeting on the second floor some weeks ago. Things did not seem correct or the dominoes in the right place for them to fall into line. The second Forensic report was a horror story. Fourteen more decaying bodies had been found down the tunnels, a full drug manufacturing lab had been uncovered in a hidden area, as well as articles of discarded clothing, wallets, purses, rings, and some rings still had the fingers attached. There was a twenty-four hour round the clock laboratory set up at the scene. The body count was rising; we even had identified bodies from all surrounding counties as well as two unidentified foreigners, with this I called in the big boys. This was a bloody nightmare.

No one in the team was sleeping well, or feeling the best, after what we had met. I know my mind was working overtime; State Officers had finally got into the fray, investigating the identified bodies from their neck of the woods. I prayed there were no more bodies or parts to be found. Colin walked in with a grey ashen look; he never spoke or uttered anything, just sat down staring out the window into the gloom that was now looming over the city. The shadows of darkness were starting to engross the buildings as the night slowly drew its blinds and to make it even worse it had started to rain again. I allowed Colin time to collect his thoughts but then again how was he going to do that with what he had seen in the past days. He slowly got up and rested both palms on the windowsill, slowly with a soft whisper;

"I cannot do this anymore Ian. The bodies just keep coming and coming and they get more grotesque each time. How could a man do this, even a surgeon would not carve up people like this".

He turned his head to look at me, his palms still firmly planted on the sill, the clouds growing darker and more fearsome outside, as the rain began to fall heavier.

"Take a seat" I stated as calmly as I could.

"We will get over this, we need to finalise all the reports and the numbers involved. I swear by almighty God, and I am not a religious man, that this fucker or fuckers are going to fry for this mate. Mark my words, this has caused me upheaval and I have seen some sick things in my years as a cop, but this is beyond reality".

He sat slowly and sullenly in the chair; his face expressionless.

"This is mass murder on a grand scale Ian, the results we

have, show it has been years that they or he has been doing this. There must be at least three, due to the differing DNA and fingerprints we have found that do not correspond to victims".

I looked at him with a silent uneasiness, and I had no preconceived ideas or any optimism about what he was telling me. I knew we had to act and catch this killer or killers, but how? We were all in a precarious predicament and knew that Colin was about to breakdown over the volume of work we had lumbered on him. It was a time, I needed to be forthright, but also subtle at the same time, trouble is when it comes too subtlety with me, I am like a sledgehammer, and as far as this situation was concerned my headfirst don't think attitude was not going to cut it. Fuck if ever I needed to a drink, it was now, but abstinence is what is needed, I need a clear head not only for Colin but my whole team.

36

The electronic boys also swept my office and all the team's homes, desks, cars etc. they found we had all been bugged. The bastards had even overheard my escapade with Jo and Katrina. I broke this news to the team in the form of a copied note, told them to say nothing aloud, their body language was enough it showed they were suspicious of each other, and there was turmoil in the ranks. I called for a bit of attention as we went over this case. I wanted them to listen to the tape. I indicated we were going to the park with another sign, they were not to say anything other than follow my lead. I started;

"Well, I called you here to say, that the investigation has stalled, the forensic report from our raids yesterday gives us no more than we already know. Have any of you got more to add."

They all shook their heads and said, near in unison no. I showed that they could now leave and meet me across the road. They were each to say something of where they were going. They left and shown to me that each was going to follow something up. I went via my office to grab my briefcase and the files I had. I arrived to see McLean going through my desk;

"What the fuck do you think you are doing?"
He looked at me with contempt "I was looking for a pen to leave you a note, my little voice told me,

"That was Bullshit", I want you in my office ten am tomorrow, I will see you there with everything on this case and I mean everything" as he turned to leave, I muttered under my breath;

"If I don't see you earlier arsehole!" He turned and asked, "What did you say?" I looked at him with a look of complete innocence;

"I will be there; you can count on it!"
I raced across to the park to see that the team had moved over to the other side of the park out of sight of the

building. As I arrived, they were arguing as to who had bugged the place, Hal Myers was at Ray;

"Can never trust an outsider", before anyone could say anything else, I told them to sit, stand whatever, this was going to take a while.

"This tape is from our surveillance work; Frank and I have heard it."
I looked at Frank;

"Any ideas?" he shook his head. I played them the tape they all listened intently to it. I then dropped the bombshell;

"When you go home there will be a guy from our debugging crew there, he will debug your places.
You are to say nothing in your cars, on the phones
or anything until he has cleared those devices.
Tomorrow at eight, we will be arresting the following,
District Attorney Aaron James Bourke, suspicion of
murder, consorting to commit murder, causing grievous
bodily harm, practicing medicine without a license,
kidnapping, being involved with the manufacture and
distribution of a banned substance and anything else
I will be able to come with later today. I continued;

"The messages that he was relating to a case eleven years ago. It was to do with a rape case, which turned into more but that is another story and Elroy Arthur Smith was involved. One Aaron Bourke was the Attorney at the time but under a different name. He forged evidence about the case and what we had on the prick that did it would not stand up in court because, Bourke made it to be a misdemeanour. I knew and so did everyone else what he had done. Now he is our bloody state representative. He disappeared after that case. We found out later the arsehole we had charged was some prick relation of the mob boss and related to his family in some way".

I slowly took a breath and went on to say;

"The connection never made. I perused the facts and the case; two innocent cops were out of a job because of me. He had already disappeared though and there was no trace of him. We realized he had been pressured by higher ups to get rid of the case quick. The reason I could not place the case when it was raised, or anyone connected with it was the different name."
I looked at Ray;

"You remember the case now Ray?"
He nodded in acknowledgment. The team looked in complete disarray at me, then Ray said;

"You are crackers Farrer, you want us to arrest a fucking District Attorney, on a hunch he was some arsehole Attorney under another name eleven years ago. He fucked up a case by evidence tampering and on the grounds of a voice on a tape".

We all returned to our separate offices or the conference room once the tape had finished.
Sitting in his office, sifting through mountains of files and papers, some we had given him the rest from Ray's search of the Archive records at central Steve was lost, he knew we had a case and that he had been to court on less, but this looked like it was going to involve some high-ranking

officials. How can we fight a member of state, and prove he is a brothel owner, people smuggler, drug lord plus so many other things, Steve's head was spinning. Then you had McLean the high-ranking cop, where did he fit into all this, because he did fit in a powerful way. Finally, the Mayor, God almighty could not have picked it better than these three for a case, and then the crooked lawyer and the cop who made the evidence disappear.

I had given Steve a heads up earlier as to whom our main suspects were, and that we needed to make sure that the cases were hermetically sealed as tight as a fishes' arse. Steve started to make a list of the crimes each may face in court, but we were going to need one of these men to turn and rollover on the other two. There was also the problem of who was kidnapping the girls and who was cutting them up. Not one of these three had the ability or the knowledge to perform surgery, let alone set up and undertake kidnappings. Steve turned and looked at the board in his office which resembled what was in our conference room; he needed to be able to connect the dots, with no hurdles in between. He decided he was going to offer one of these men a deal, who that would be, was the question, and besides that would I agree.

37

The details of this case were such, that when we ever get the case to court, they will plead it out, as they know we have little to go on except a tape, my gut instincts, dead bodies everywhere with no real identifying marks as to who the perpetrator was and no DNA, blood or prints to tie these three into the crimes and all their accomplices which were now piling up as well. Steve knew as a lawyer the evidence at best was circumstantial, but I, as a hot head, was very rarely wrong with my gut instincts.

Steve was going to need some form of precedent to firstly go requesting warrants be issued against three of County's elite, and secondly as soon as these three lawyer up we are up the proverbial. Steve started to prepare a synopsis of a deal to present in the hope they will agree to an offer and the one who accepts gets the deal. The deal was agreed, that being twenty years, minimum security. This all depends on the system, as it is renowned for its independence, and not really being subjected to deals that involve mass murder, drugs, kidnapping etc., but we need a squealer, to turn on the rest, so getting a Prosecutor to go to a Judge and agree to a deal could be pushing shit uphill.

Steve drafted the document and had it copied, one to me and one to the Court to be couriered and for the file. He sat back and looked tensely at the ever-darkening skyline, it made him feel uneasy, as if the darkness that now was starting to envelope the city, was a foreboding of things to come. The drizzle pattered on the window and ran down the pane like small rivers all flowing to a central sea. He stared at the streetlights that now had a fuzzy look about them due to the rain. His mind ticking over as he thought about what he had just done and did one of these heinous murderers really deserve some form of reprieve. Steve contemplated his future as a lawyer, should he join my team as a legal advisor or get out of law altogether.

This case had made him sick to the stomach, thinking of those poor women and what was done to them, give them the death penalty, he thought. There was a clap of thunder and Steve was jolted back to reality, he mused that it was going to be a bit of wait for the documents to be approved or rejected, so he hoped I had something more concrete to hang my hat on. We were back in my office, which thankfully, was cleared of bugs;

"Fuck me man, you are off your head. Are you on the slops again?"

I felt Ray had said it all for them, he continued his rant;

"You are going to arrest the top brass, Ian; do you cherish your arse and job because I do?"

I continued without answering him.

"The next person we will be arresting at the same time will be former Chief Brian McLean, on the same charges, except he has an added one tampering with evidence and hampering an investigation as well as illegal use of listening devices."

I quickly glanced at Ray; he was shaking his head in an unbelieving fashion.

This time they all started to walk away, shaking their

heads with disbelief, Frank looked at them and said;

"Wait there is more, I believe in Ian, this is ok, let's hear him out." I threw a glancing smile at Frank and thanked him. It was the first time since I had known him that he had called me Ian.

"We have Mr Damien Rourke in custody, unbeknown to you, the reason Steve is not here, is that he is organising at cutting a deal with him to give evidence on the other two, and the rest of this murderous bunch, he sent the details of the deal to the District Attorney to see if it will fly, as Steve is wary of taking this to court. He is going down, but he is never going to get out of jail, he just won't get the needle any time soon."

"We arrested him last night at the airport trying to board a flight to Zurich, he had a one-way ticket.
His real name is Damien James Bourke, son of the Aaron James Bourke. He is a fully qualified Pathologist, Surgeon and has just finished a degree in Biochemistry."
Colin laughed;

"I told you whoever this prick was he was good."
I interjected;

"The information you got Hal was nearly correct, but McLean had planted some of it. He had done his training in Switzerland where he was a respected Surgeon in the field of Biopsies, and Pathology. He suffers from a rare form of Leukaemia, like his father, he has a high IQ, and finished Medical College two years ahead of time, University one year and his medical residency eighteen months ahead of anybody else, Consultant two years later."

I took a deep breath and collected my thoughts, then continued making sure the team knew everything;

"Professor of Microbiology in Geneva and was doing research for the study of rare diseases. This bloke could have been anything!"

I paused surveyed the room and continued;

"Right tomorrow at eight, we will arrest his two accomplices, the Judge is listening to his statement now at county and will decide whether to issue other Warrants as well as have him indicted. I also just caught McLean going through my desk looking for this tape, and the file. I also found evidence in the bedroom area of the factory, with two phone numbers on it, I recognized McLean's straight away, I tried the other one and the number was the state capital representative's offices."

I pulled the evidence and the file out of my briefcase.

"I want you all to read the evidence I have a copy for each. When you have finished return to the office and shred it. You will then go home and say nothing. Frank, you, and Grant have the boss."

Ray, Jo you go to the State Capital, Hal and I have the mayor. You are to bring them here to the briefing room, where the entire evidence etc. against them will be set up. Make sure you allow them their rights and a lawyer; we do not want anything to go wrong." I left them reading, returned to the garage got in the car and drove home.

Katrina met me at the door, I told her we had solved the case and that tomorrow we would be making many arrests. In saying this was I jumping the gun, or did I need to bite the bullet for a little longer. I was sure that we would get Bourke to roll on his mates as he was shit scared when we interviewed him. The reasons are I just cannot come to grips with, greed and power.

The debugging guys had been and done their job, we made love passionately that night and I slept content. Next morning while going over the paperwork and file, I slowly sipped my coffee and felt that I had predicted the suspects' responses and how they will try and offset the blame and circumstances. Not one of them will take responsible for their actions, I assured myself of this.

The demons were going around and around in my head as I was concentrating on what the day would bring. This I feel was to be the epitome of my career, I hoped. I said to myself I was upset I had lost Sally Donald as she could have tied up the loose ends for us and we would not have to make any deals. It was sloppy work letting her walk out of the hospital, to who knows where.

38

On my desk I had eleven medical reports from the autopsies of the victims concerning the two cases we were investigating, although they appeared separate, they did intermingle in several areas, and the participants were involved in both scenarios. I finally decided to start reading the mind-blowing evidence contained within each report. The reports I have are all forensic autopsies and have legal implications as they are performed to figure out if death was an accident, homicide, or a natural event. Steve filled me in on how they came about weeks ago and the word autopsy is derived from the Greek word *"Autopsia"*- *"to see with one's own eyes."*

Our medical area at the hospital still had bodies piled up and even though I had eleven reports in front of me, some of them were only preliminary and not final as we are awaiting toxicology reports. The other problem we had was this all the bodies or was there more yet to be discovered. I opened the front file and luckily Simon, the pathologist working on the autopsies, had given me an overall brief of all the current autopsies even though they each had individual characteristics. The extent of an autopsy can vary from the examination of a single organ such as the heart or brain, to a very extensive examination. He continued with the examination of the chest, abdomen, and brain. The autopsy begins with a complete external examination. The weight and height of the body are recorded and showing marks such as scars and tattoos also are recorded. The women in this case all had Tattoos of differing types; they were all about the same age and height as well as weight.

Of course, they all had different Latin words carved into their back as well as a cross like the crucifixion cross. They had a line also; I am at a loss as to what this and the cross signified within the scope of the case. Also was the 'Dante' thing to throw us off guard or did it have significance within the bounds of what they were trying to achieve. I will have to question the defendants about this area as it plays a part in not only the crime but also the reasons why they would mutilate the bodies in such a manner.

At that moment Coney and Hal came in, so I stated what I was doing and if they wanted the files after me, they were welcome to them. I explained how Simon described the steps and processes thoroughly within the report. The internal examination begins with the creation of a 'Y' shaped incision from both shoulders joining over the sternum and continuing down to the pubic bone. The skin and underlying tissues are then separated to expose the rib cage and abdominal cavity. The front of the rib cage is removed to expose the neck and chest organs.

This opening allows the trachea, thyroid gland, parathyroid glands, oesophagus, heart, thoracic aorta, and lungs to be removed. I was wondering whether I needed to read these as it reminded me so much of Eugene's death and how he had been left in that toilet cubicle in that state. I took a deep breath and cleared my head as I needed to continue to be able to understand the sickness the bastards in my cells suffered from. I continued to read, following removal of the neck and chest organs, the abdominal organs are dissected free. These include the intestines, liver, gallbladder and bile duct system, pancreas, spleen, adrenal glands, kidneys, ureters, urinary bladder, abdominal aorta, and reproductive organs. I remember the days being drunk and very hung-over attending plenty of autopsies. The sights and odours never worried me, but now just reading about them without the alcohol or a hangover made me feel queasy. I turned the page and continued to peruse the brief. The removal of the brain, an incision is made in the back of the skull from one ear to the other. The scalp is cut and separated from the underlying skull and pulled forward. The top of the skull is removed with a vibrating saw. The entire brain is then gently lifted out of the cranial vault. The spinal cord may also be taken by removing the anterior or posterior part of the spinal column. In all autopsies the preceding procedure was carried out. The organs were all examined by Simon to note any changes visible with the naked eye.

I was feeling ill, and the report was so in depth I am glad I can read this and not all eleven. This report tells me enough to go on with, I turned to page three and resumed reading. The organs are removed from the body; they usually are separated from each other and further dissected to reveal any abnormalities, the women examined had no distinguishing problems that could be seen on examination. All bodies had samples taken for slide preparations for examination under a microscope, also samples taken for laboratory toxicology reports. At the end of an autopsy, the incision made in the bodies is sewn closed, all organs were returned to the body. As I was glancing at the autopsy photos and trying to simulate them with the report, there was a pounding within my head like what happens when a migraine is about to strike you. The difference was I had no pain; vision was good then I realised what I had seen was the reason.

The line on all the victim's backs was that thin line we all walk everyday of our living life. From the day we are born to the day we die; we are asking questions why? This thin line was the divider between good and evil, sanity and insanity, truth and lies, we all walk it, and it takes little to tip oneself over that line. Could it be nature or nurture that dictates our end which is for each to discover. It is the cross and line and the way they are drawn, whether vertical or horizontal they mean the same. The cross being a symbol of good or Christianity, next to the line and under or alongside, the words of Dante or the Deadly Sins under that line. This maniac was trying to tell us, he was searching for his own destiny, his truth, he was a lost soul. Yes, he was experimenting and trying to find a cure, but the significance of the markings was too exact and too pronounced to be just a ploy to throw us off the scent, whether that be the human trafficking for prostitution, the illegal sale of body organs or parts and drugs. I am sure drugs are involved, as the amounts of money that was going through Mr Madden's restaurant could not be just from his twenty-dollar meals. This person or persons had problems with death, their own, they are too shit scared of dying, whether it is from the disease or being caught and shut away from reality, the fear of the needle, chair, chamber or locked away for life is something they are unable to fathom. Then there was the Forresters, who I wondered, whether they were involved in all this melee or was that a complete separate set of circumstances. The irony being if they were involved in this macabre set of murders why was there so many loose ends to their stories that the dots could not relate to the other victims. Yet there were some similarities, revenge, planning, jealousy, and infidelity.

The murderous spree they have been on has been to delay their meeting with the Grim Reaper; he is their enemy, their nemesis and the longer they went on the deeper and more gruesome this situation was going to get. They needed an outlet to release their fear. Why had I not seen this entire scenario prior, was my mind finally starting to recover from the pickled faze of alcohol, was I finally thinking as I should be? I could now use my brainwave as a tool against those we have in custody, make them realise we know what they are about and that death awaits them, no matter what!

I stared at the reports, photographs and the overview brief and knew I was right when taking all into account. The autopsies and all individual reports held more in-depth information as well as some toxicology reports and organ examination results. I resolved myself to finish reading and wondered whether to read or quickly glance at the reports to gain more information, I decided at this point I was not ready for the heavy going of a full report, after all I believe my epiphany on this matter was correct and the reports were only going to confirm it. My time had arrived I was going to give these fucking arseholes an extremely tough time, make them realise the trauma they had put the families through. It was time that I realised I had released my demons and the perpetrators of this despicable mass serial murder were about to feel my wrath.

39

We had Stewart Madden, Brian McLean, Damien (Rourke) Bourke, Aaron Bourke and Majors all locked up. Our cells have never had so many guests all at once. Our friends in Sicily Inspector Eduardo Panzarella had let me know that their end had all under control and 4 of the 6 arrested had been charged with conspiracy, murder, drugs, and human trafficking. They were also looking at other charges but that was up to their prosecutor, and they were also sure that each would have a lawyer trying hard to orchestrate a deal. The other two culprits were still being interviewed. The problem was Ray Beale and Mike Grant had slipped the net. This made an uneasy feeling with the team as they had the most power and contacts so it would be easy for them to fall off the face of the earth.

The big problem that he could foresee was the influence and inherent pressure that the Cosa Nostra could bring to bear on the justice system. They had special signals to recognize each other, offered protection services, scorned the law, and had a code of loyalty and non-interaction with the police known as 'Umirtà' *("code of silence"),* it was known they had judges and police in their pockets, who pissed themselves whenever approached by one of the organisation. I was glad we here in our small town and county had nothing that was close to that cloak and dagger stuff. I headed home and decided to let our captives sweat a little, and although not a bible man there is a quote, I admire by a man named Sartre, *"Existence precedes essence".* Most religions teach us that human beings were created by a higher power; others believe in the Darwin theory. Both have credence which would mean that they have some purpose or essence innate in them.

Now Sartre, on the other hand wanted to prove that humans create their essence from their own existence. If we think human essence includes consciousness or morality while you exist, then what do we call our captives who murdered, mutilated, and created a complete lawless society only answerable to them? F. Scott Fitzgerald said;

"I am still a little afraid of missing something, and I repeat that a piece of fundamental decency when parcelled out at birth is unequal".

It may be not that exact but in relation to the scum in my jail house, this statement pertains to them so well and makes me so angry, that innocent people must lose their lives because they need to feel the power over their death and to escape from their own end. I sat at the table staring at my dinner that Katrina had prepared. I studied the vegetables, nicely arrayed on the plate and the steak cooked to perfection but my appetite was not that important. There were other things gnawing at my gut which I was unable to really put a handle on. I knew I was not going to sleep well tonight, not only due to what and how we were going to make sure that those fuckups were going to jail for a long, long time, but give some closure to the families. I drifted in and out of sleep throughout the night, tossed and turned and eventually finished up in the spare room.

I finally showered, dressed, and made coffee. Headed to the office not realising it was only six in the morning. Fuck, oh well, the shit heads are going to get an early wakeup call. The office was dark, cold, and stark, Coney was seated at his desk, and he acknowledged me as I walked past his doorway;

"Good morning" I stated as I walked past.

"Your early he remarked". I replied;

"We need to get things started, those fucks in there are making my office and cells stink!"
Eight o'clock, the full crew were assembled; I set them up in teams and gave each a culprit to interview and take their statements. I briefed them on the interview techniques as I was not sure how much my team had been privy to murder cases.

I apologised if it sounded like I was asking them to suck eggs. I told them about using some empathy and try to prove some type of rapport with each before rushing

249

right into the interrogation. It is not natural for a suspect to want to tell us anything, especially when he knows that the game is up. Give them a cup a coffee, cold drink etc., and explain to them you have completed a thorough investigation that has led to them being arrested and you really do want to hear their side of the story. I emphasised to let them interrogate themselves, ramble on at first and give you their false statement about their involvement in the crime.

Lock them into a lie, and then start to pick it apart piece by piece. If you have done a thorough investigation, this should not be that difficult. Sometimes catching a suspect in a lie is just as good as a confession. Pay close attention to everything. You can pick up a lot of non-verbal and verbal clues you may miss if you have your head down in a pad taking notes, which is why you are going in pairs. Additionally, paying close attention to everything the suspect says and does creates added stress on them, which may lead to them breaking down sooner rather than later. Don't be afraid to offer an alternative "face saving" scenario. Make sure your scenario still holds a confession of the elements of the crime being investigated and does not create an affirmative defence issue.

I will be doing some research on your suspects. I will find out what is important to them their children, wife, job, fears of jail, etc, and I will let you know what I find and then use those hooks to your advantage. I was not going to get involved at this stage of the investigation; I wanted to read every file, every piece of paper no matter how insignificant it appeared to be. I wanted the charges to stick, the I's had to be dotted and T's had to be crossed. The County was going to be on my arse over this, as I think we may have stepped on their toes in arresting the shits as they may have wanted the glory.

"Fuck em", I stated out loud.

I completed my task but still had those doubts. Once this case is finalised, I may need to have a few days off, allow the brain to recharge and maybe then the nagging doubts will become clearer. Cases back in the big smoke never seemed this difficult or had so many twists and turns, but then again, I was in a blurred pissed state the whole time so how was I to know what was happening other than I was able to constantly get a drink.

I was, as is the team still baffled as to why the nine circles of hell were introduced into this case. Upon interviewing all the offenders, it seems 'Inferno', the first part of Dante's Divine Comedy. We also found that he was connected to my nemesis Elroy Arthur Smith, with whom he had a special affiliation. As far as the seven deadly sins went, Bourke gave the following on why he co-ordinated them with Dante.

"People have always been immoral, shiftless, and self-gratifying".

He rambled on that mankind both men and women struggled to find a conceptual system to put their spiritual shortcomings into action. He said *Pride* is excessive belief in one's own abilities. It has been called the sin from which all others arise.

251

He declared *Envy* is the desire for others' traits, status, abilities, or situation, Damien said that this really was aimed at him as he had a desire to be better than anyone else. *Gluttony* is an inordinate desire to consume more than that which one needs; he believed that two of his victims had this sin. *Lust* an inordinate craving for the pleasures of the body, this he could not abide as he was a sufferer of erectile dysfunction. He could never love as his father abandoned him and did not love him but used him. It was anger that manifested in him because he spurned love and opts instead for fury. He would rather call it *Wrath*. His greed for material wealth or gain, ignoring anything and everyone and he hated anybody who came under the sloth area as avoidance of physical work made him angry and the vicious circle started all over again.

In a funny sort of way, I had a feeling for him of sorrow; it seemed in his delusional mind that the world was against him even though he had such a brilliant mind and education. I believe really, as they say he has 'Daddy Issues'. Maybe he will get some help hopefully within the prison system. He was really worried about Ray Beale and Mike Grant; he explained that their tentacles were able to reach far and wide even into the prison system as he had already seen this in the past weeks. They had money and power.

Why the fuck was I worried about a murderer. I must be going soft in my old age. Any of those arseholes I would gladly, flick the switch, insert the needle, or pull the lever and I would do it without blinking an eyelid. They have murdered, mutilated, and seem to have no care or remorse, I was going to make sure their demons would haunt them for the rest of their days?

40

This case had baffled me for a long time, as we got further into the investigation it became clear that our every move was known to outside sources. We successfully, arrested Bourke and McLean; they stood trial but not for the crimes we had predicted. Yes, they were involved but would not reveal as to who was the mastermind behind the whole gruesome escapade. Damien Bourke received and accepted the deal and was convicted on eleven charges he was given life with minimum parole of 45 years, for his part in the murders and kidnapping's, he died in prison under suspicious circumstances. Bourke Snr sentenced to two life terms, for his part, he also gave state evidence on some underground characters who were involved in money laundering, drugs, illegal brothels, importing unlawful non-citizens for the brothels and other corrupt practices, when they had fulfilled their purpose in the brothels, they were used for the body parts.

Bourke did not though divulge the main source of the money behind everything before he died in prison, five months later of Bowel Cancer and complications with Leukaemia. Former and highly decorated Police Officer

Brian McLean given two life terms, he had killed Eugene, as Eugene confronted him on the day of his death and McLean killed him before he could tell me. McLean also killed Benny. McLean was also supposed to get rid of the money man, he was hired apparently to do the deed by the money man's wife. He did not divulge who she was, and we are still in the dark over this. Benny knew who McLean was, and McLean had set Benny up in the drug house and was skimming the profits; McLean was shanked and killed in a scuffle in the prison showers six months after his incarceration. He also took his knowledge of the money man and the wife's plans to the grave with him. McLean was the one who used his influence to gain access and copies of all the medical records and Police information we found in the filing cabinets within the tunnels of the sawmill.

The drugs involved were items of police evidence. All three were involved in running the escort service, out of Maddens' Restaurant where the girls worked from, Madden also tricked foreign ladies on the promise of jobs etc, to come to the country illegally; he knew their blood group etc., because his doctor had performed their monthly test for HIV, so he was able to get close matches with blood groups DNA etc. Mike Grant was the power broker in all this and was the one who ordered Sally's death. He also had a direct link to the Shaws and Forrester's. With this it made it a complicated spider's web, which really no one of us could connect to and was Shaw or Forrester the money men behind all this.

McLean had to have Sally killed, as she had seen Damien's face and a letter in his car addressed to a Damien Bourke at his address from a Swiss Medical Group, but Rourke (Bourke) genuinely loved her and could not go through with it, but he needed to make sure she did not know or say anything. The whole thing financed by the money launderers from the drugs produced, and the whole scheme financed by an unknown banker who was yet to show their hand, and to us was the real missing link.

We knew that whomever it was lived here in town. Trouble being, this was a tourist town, and a lot of the residents were permanent, but there were also those who were seasonal. This person was someone who creamed a percentage off the top for their initial outlay and cash backing. The person who had this amount of money was kept well in the background and we had no real hard evidence They needed Damien to perform surgery on some of their people for new identities etc., so they could lose themselves back into society and to continue to work.

The body parts we found were ready to be sold to foreign countries illegally and the ones filled with drugs were delivered by undercover policemen disguised as postal employees. The whole operation would have made in the vicinity of two hundred million Euros for the group. It is now three years since this case began and as for Katrina and I, we are now married and happy, my Sheriff's office has been decorated for the work on this case and our budget has been expanded to have two new deputies and two detectives. Our area has been extended and now covers not only our district but four others as well as the total county.

We travel all over to investigate crimes. We nick named ourselves "The E Office" in memory of our departed colleague "Eugene". Joanne and Grant transferred to the FBI, special branch; Hal Myers resigned as a regular police officer and joined the District Attorney's office as an investigator, Ray Barry, left his comfortable job, with his family moved to Oemen Lake, and is now our "Profiler". Frank Coney retired; Steve Barlow is our legal co-ordinator and Colin Miles our Forensic expert, he had a challenging time on this case, and although he almost threw in the towel at one point, I think we all felt like doing that, but he came through. I oversee this unruly lot; best of all I have not touched a drink in over two years. Oh yes Simon is our resident pathologist at the hospital.

This case though, to me is still open as the ring leaders and masterminds whoever they were behind this sordid situation was yet to be known; but not only that, two of the culprits were still at large, they, I believe were the true brains of this case. The money, corruption, and the number of deaths which we still have not been able to figure out, leave me feeling very cold and unnerved by this. Maybe one day someone will be able to rattle some cages and find out the truth behind all this and hopefully the demons which have caused us so much upheaval will never return to Oemen Lake. My mind was unsettled as I believed the main antagonist was still in town, and very close.

The next morning was the start of a new day, but it was cold and stark, light rain more drizzle than rain fell upon the ground, giving the concrete patio and steps in front of the office a look of mirrors. I entered the office and, was taken aback by the large envelope on my desk marked URGENT in red ink. I slowly opened it.

"Shit", I exclaimed another part of this case, my gut feeling was starting to surface, this is too much. This information had been sent through from the FBI. I read on; Isabella Shaw was a wealthy woman in many ways. She was married to one of the richest Merchant Bankers in Seattle, Washington, had a beautiful home, had a horse ranch in Nevada, an apartment in London, a holiday home on the coast of Spain,

"What else would a thirty-six-year-old woman, mother of three require. We should all be so lucky to ask this question of ourselves?", I muttered to myself.

Then suddenly Steven Shaw's name appeared linked to Bourke and McClean. Was this the mastermind? After a brief time, we finally figured the reason for the vertical and horizontal lines placed on the backs of the victims along with a cross or zero as well as the Latin words from Dante. It was the children's game "Tic Tac Toe" or "Noughts and Crosses".

What significance did this have with all the bodies, the drugs, etc. We still have that burning question;

"Was there more to this than meets the eye, and had we really solved the case fully?".

I pondered whether these were clues to the identities of the moneymen who backed this whole charade?

41

Isabella Shaw's mind was full of ideas of what she wanted out of life that money could not buy. Her husband it seemed paid no real attention to her; he was pre-occupied with his work and his Personal Assistant Ms Victoria Merrin. Isabella had been married to Steven, for what seemed like a lifetime but in fact was only fourteen years. They were childhood sweethearts and had gone through school and college together before Steven went off for three years to study a degree in economics and banking. When he returned, he did not seem to be the same man who had gone away. He was still her thirty-eight-year-old, six foot four, brown haired, blue-eyed hunk, who had a body which was so good she could not let anyone else have him. Her children were also her pride and joy. Josh thirteen, although unplanned he looked like his father, and already had the girls in his class admiring him. Brittany, twelve, was blond had deep mahogany brown eyes, and was growing into a beautiful young woman. The youngest and the shyest and most withdrawn of the children was Adam ten. He had his dad's looks as well and was already taller than Josh; he felt this was going to be the bane of his life. All this and Isabella was still unhappy, she needed a spark, something to get her juices flowing again, and have her interest in life rejuvenated. Her suspicions of her husband and Victoria were playing heavily on her.

Her imagination ran wild, like some form of pornographic movie in her head. She could see her young twenty-eight-year-old body firm in all areas, writhing like a sex kitten all over her man, he responding to her every move and enjoying it much the same as they used to at school then at college. She had had two lovers in her life Steven, and Mitchell. Mitchell was a casual fling while Steven was away at university. She had never told Steven about him, but she knew he had been unfaithful to her, as she had found out through her bridesmaid about three years after the wedding. She felt in her heart that Steven, unfaithful, not now they were married; other couples did that, but not us! Her thought pattern was broken by a knock at her bedroom door; it was Lily the house cleaner, asking;

"Would you like tea in here ma'am or on the balcony?"

"On the balcony" replied Isabella.

"Would you like to join me, Lily?"

"That would be very nice ma'am."

Lily left the room to prepare the tea; she found it strange that ma'am had asked her to join her for tea. In ten years of working for the Shaw's this was the first time. She had meals with the family but never tea like this. She wondered if Mrs Shaw was Ok. As Lily and Isabella sat on the balcony overlooking the expanse of the property and out across the lake and land. Lily was afraid to talk, as this was an uncomfortable position for her, she had never been in this position before. Isabella looked at her and told her to relax,

"Have you ever been unfaithful to your husband Lily?

"No ma'am." Lily replied, in a quiet tone, not sure what was to come next.

"Has he been unfaithful to you?" Isabella asked,

"No ma'am.," now Lil, wa s startin g to feel uneasy.

"My husband has; I know that for sure." Isabella spoke with conviction and a sort of sour tone to her voice.

"But ma'am, you must not think like that, your husband loves you and your beautiful children."
Lily was now really starting to wonder where this conversation was heading.

42

Steven Shaw, born Little Rock, Arkansas, ranked one hundred and fifteenth on the list of the richest two hundred. Self-made millionaire. He started out selling stocks and shares for a brokerage company. He worked hard in this first period, and it paid off. In December of 1987, he received a telephone call from a Japanese company Osyka Corporation. They wanted a broker to buy shares in some of the large Computer Companies especially in the manufacturing area. Steven did the deal and before he had realized what it amounted to, Osyka Corp., became the largest client he had as well as his employer. In the two years that followed he had made over 2.3 million dollars and wanted for nothing; his family wanted for nothing.

He had investments, three homes, four cars, and then there was Isabella's property, as far as he was concerned, he could have retired. He was not going to be his father, so he ventured out. He decided it was time to branch out, so with his knowledge and ability as well as the backing of Osyka he opened his own Merchant Bank, especially to serve the small investors and businesses. It was at this time that he became acquainted with our friends McLean, Bourke, and Dean Forrester. These two were to become as we know the main antagonists in this whole charade. Was Forrester and Shaw involved? In one year of business his company had achieved the largest growth rate in the banking sector, jealousy was rife, and yes, he now had enemies, in the other banking fields. His clientele read like a Who's Who of the crème d' la creme of the financial and business world.

His main aim though was his little clients who had trusted him with their money, and he had done well by them. Just over two years in business and he was turning over almost three billion dollars. He should have slowed up and let his directors take over some of the workload, but he enjoyed it too much. His personal assistant practically knew the business inside out. Little did Isabella know that he and Victoria had been an item for just over a year. He felt guilty, but Isabella had let herself go and she had terrible mood swings, which disturbed him.

The kids had even remarked to him "mum seems strange." Mention going to a doctor to her, and she would go into a fit of rage and withdraw. She would continue about him and his affair, so he played along not sure whether she knew or was assuming. He was not interested anyway, as he, had all he wanted, a wife, three great kids, a business which allowed an extremely comfortable & plush lifestyle, and a lover that was just as impressive. He believed he had everyman's dream, or so he thought. He sat at his large Oak handmade desk, going over the latest acquisition by one of his companies. Ian Bryant, forty-four, Accountant, Company Director, and Steven's assistant. Married but separated no kids. Went to school with Steven and played football together at college. Was a bit of a chump but knew his job inside out, he had saved the company almost seven million in tax last year, through his knowledge of the tax laws. He told Ian that he was to look after things while he was away for the week, especially keep an eye on Isabella for me, as I am worried. Ian Bryant knew of with Victoria, so it was only natural that the wife was suspicious, when he was going away for a week to a conference with his personal assistant.

Over the weekend Steve stayed at home, did some gardening, and kept busy around the house, he took no phone calls or faxes, and took Isabella and the kids out to dinner on the Saturday evening. Isabella believed this was the last dinner they would have together she felt it deep down in her heart that something was wrong. They returned home at about eleven and the kids went to bed. Isabella poured herself a nightcap; Steve just had a soda water and ice.
They went to bed and for the first time in months they made enthusiastic love, Isabella forgot all her inhibitions and

responded to Steve's every touch and move. They cuddled up and slept in each other's arms for the rest of the evening. Sunday, Steve rose early, showered, went, and collected the Sunday paper and was seated at the dining table to have breakfast when the rest of the family came down. The children all went up gave him a cuddle and said thank you for the dinner last night. Isabella remained quiet.

Monday Isabella took Steve to the Airport at seven am, saw him off on his flight to Paris, and returned to the car. It was now or never, she decided I have one week to set this all up and make sure that it all works correctly. She went to the city to Your PC World, bought a small laptop, and paid cash. Hurried on to another store-bought supplies of disks, paper, and envelopes. Went to a Pharmacy on the other side of town and brought a box of surgical gloves. She knew that Victoria was away, Steve was with her. She arrived at Victoria's apartment, how would she get in, she thought long and hard, then the idea hit her, how did Steve get in? Isabella put disposable gloves on; she had seen this on a police show on television so as not to leave fingerprints. She felt along the top of the doorway no key, looked under the mat no key, and then a plant took her eye. On the tag "Sobralia Orchid" Steve's favourite Orchid, she looked under the pot, she looked at the tag it was a small plastic envelope inside was a key. Isabella opened the door and returned the key to its location, then went inside. The apartment was luxurious, expensive furniture and fittings.

She wandered around looking in every nook and cranny making sure that she replaced everything back exactly as she had found it. The bedroom was enormous, and there beside the bed was a photograph of Victoria, Steve, and Ian. Taken in Hawaii at last year's conference the bed was a giant four-poster something that she had always wanted, and Steve had on many occasions admitted he did not like. On opening the walk-in robe down one side were all Victoria's clothes, the other a man's suits etc., all in Steve's size. There are many pairs of shoes, ties, and shirts.

The bathroom was expansive, giant spa bath in one corner; four headed large shower area, dual basins, and those theatre type lights across a full wall mirror. To one side of the left basin was a woman's facial makeup items etc. To the right a man's toiletries this baffled Isabella a bit as none of items were what Steven used, so this sent a small doubt into her plans. She photographed everything she could and left as quietly as she had entered. Next stop was to get the film developed. Then she went to the Colonial Inn and booked a room for three weeks under the name of Sorensen, this was Mitchell's surname. This was where she could plan and type up the letters and send them from this room and no one would know. Little did she know all his planning and everything would lead her to an undreamed-of end. Then noticing the time returned home so that she would be there for the children. She would continue tomorrow.

Isabella was working on sheer instinct, and she had to make sure that all was in place and that what she was doing was for the right reasons as she had doubts both, about her and that of Steven now. Why was he doing this what was his motive she loved him with all her heart and soul. The next thing she must do is copy everything as she needed to cover herself should anything-go wrong at all. Isabella had now suddenly worked out that Steven was in over his head not only with his affair but also those with which he was associating. The reason, where money was involved, these people cannot be trusted, and they must be kept under control. She realized that she should not have paid McLean until the job was finished. Why was he taking so long to get the job done. Little did she know he was in jail and that she would need to execute her plans herself. It was too late now as she drove along the street and turned into the driveway of home.

The equipment that she had bought she must hide it until tomorrow and a time Isabella will have to prepare to do what needs to be done.

Part One Epilogue

In this part one, we saw what Farrer had to face, in his new position as the Sheriff of Oemen Lake, his past unfortunately followed him there and caused no end of macabre events that turned this quiet little settlement into a place of death, destruction, lies and so many happenings that it made the whole town into a crime scene. For Ian Farrer there was no case like this one in his whole twenty plus years as a Robbery/Homicide Detective in New York. Drugs,

265

human trafficking, organ smuggling, prostitution, and murder all wrapped up into a small group of perpetrators that not only terrorised the town but the Sheriff's department as well. The whole scenario was a cobweb of deceit, secrets within secrets, and the main person or persons behind the whole scenario who were making the money were not even firsthand with what was happening. So many innocent lives were affected, and it made every citizen on edge as no one knew who was next to suffer the consequences of this group. Farrer had brought all this mayhem into the town, but he did not realise this at the time until the perpetrators, started linking him with the macabre demise of so many young women and the death of not only a trusted friend and work colleague, but a trusted member of a very close-knit community and family.

This was too much for Ian Farrer, but he was not going to let Eugene Barelli's death, hinder his quest in making sure he brought some form of peace and justice to the victims and their families and make those who caused suffering for those people to face a true judge. There were many undertones and other person's jealousy with vengeance against those who had caused harm or embarrassment to them; such is the aim of Isabella Shaw and others yet not named, as we will see in part two.

The thing about this is, that the demons, that Farrer thought were gone, return with even more of a vendetta out to prove who really is the "Demon of Oemen Lake?"

"Darkness cannot drive out darkness: only light can do that. Hate cannot drive out hate: only love can do that."

Martin Luther King Jr.

PART TWO

-Our Demons Return-
"MYSTERY"

Prologue Part Two

In Part One, you the reader learned that Farrer had retired or so he thought to a quiet tranquil little village miles away from the haunting big city. There were two things wrong with that scenario firstly, he became Sheriff of that tranquil setting and secondly, his past followed him there and caused him hell on earth with vicious macabre murders on young women and using their bodies to play a children's game and foretell of Dante's Purgatory.

Farrer's inner soul was threatened, his sanity absolutely unwound those perpetrators teased and guided him into a web of deceit and self-blame. The reader would have seen that Ian Farrer was a normal man, an everyday police officer just doing his job, but a shooting that went wrong in his past and haunted his every thought of his being caused him to seek the refuge of Oemen Lake. The problem was his past as you know eventually caught up with him and like serial killers of the past, all have one common thread, the murders must be separate events, which are most often driven by a psychological or sociopathic thrill or pleasure. It is good to keep in mind here, do we have a serial killer in Omen Lake; or have we just a psychopath at work? Ian Farrer thought he had solved the case to a certain extent in Part One and he was confident he knew who the main characters were, but this was to be an assumption he would come to regret, as he knew what happens when one makes assumptions, they can get you killed and the demons return to Oemen Lake for a purpose.

1

We are known as "E Office" a group of very resolute detectives, lawyers, pathologists, and forensic scientists. About eight years ago our quiet small town was the scene of the most horrific and macabre series of murders, all culminating in a blanket of secrecy to cover up drugs, prostitution, slavery, human trafficking, and the weirdest thing trying to find a cure for a sickness that one of the perpetrators suffered from. Overall, fourteen people lost their lives to this group of Psychopaths, who had no remorse as to the crimes they committed or what they were doing was causing heartache to so many.

Many of the victims suffered horrific injuries such as vertical or horizontal lines, with either a zero or cross carved into their back. They also had Latin inscriptions referring to Dante's *"Circle of Hell and Punishment."* It is strange that they used the name Dante or his circle as the name itself means in its Latin roots, symbolizing strength, perseverance, and longevity. The name that will inspire anybody to be steadfast in their pursuits, looking at the crimes those criminals undertook, Dante was an excellent choice. The ring leaders were not apprehended and the ones we did eventually have prosecuted were pawns in a larger game.

The Chief of Police, a highly decorated officer with over twenty-five years of experience, a restaurant owner, a very shady character who ran the drugs and was the pimp for the prostitutes, a contact in Europe who was the brains behind the importing of the drugs and the slavery side of the operation. There were others also involved that were of a lesser standing. But we still had not caught the money man or men behind this operation as that was the bug up my arse. I wanted those who supplied the backing more than anything else, even if it is the last thing I do as Sherriff.

I am Ian Farrer, Sherriff of the town of Oemen Lake, and even though the world goes on I have not closed the case on the deaths of the fourteen innocent persons who were the victims of these sadists. I have always suspected that the two most prominent families in Oemen Lake being the Forrester's and the Shaws were involved. I had to back off this thought slightly when Linda Forrester found murdered which we still must follow up on. Linda poisoned by a cocktail of chemicals that she used to poison her husband's lover.

We proved this and unfortunately it left lot of questions as to whether the husband was involved. This town and its inhabitants are more intertwined than the big city where I served as a detective for over twenty years. The problem was the bodies, the murders, the macabre and when it started to involve children, I drew the line. I sank my head in the bottom of a bottle and this led not only to divorce but a shift to Oemen Lake. I suddenly decided to go down to the archives and retrieve the boxes of files we had from those earlier cases as there had to be a clue in there of who may be the financiers of the whole project. Any small detail we may have overlooked, would be a start, just then Bill Dunham, a detective of twenty years and new to our team met me at the elevator. Bill six foot three, on the larger size, typical of donuts and beer and fast foods. Bill was divorced and now married to the job.

He fitted in well with the team and came to us after spending a winter here with his partner skiing. Bill had arrived right in the middle of the earlier case but did not have any input but followed the story in the media closely, as it reminded him of a case back in Austin, Texas in which he was involved. That case did not have the Psychopath side of things but had intricate twists within the case. He sent me a letter asking if I needed another detective as he was sick of the rat race and the involved crimes which there never seemed to end. He asked;

"Where are you off to in such a hurry," I replied;

"To the archives I want to retrieve the files from the case, as there is something gnawing at my arse, and I need to scratch that itch." He nodded and asked;

"Do you want a hand?" I agreed.

The elevator doors opened, and we entered I was still apprehensive of lifts after my earlier encounter with the flying body. The lift stopped on the first floor and Colin Miles our CSI and Steve Barlow our legal man entered.

"What is happening today?"

They asked in unison like parrots.

"Going to the dungeon to retrieve old files." I said.

"Meet us in the conference room in half an hour, I want to go over some things." I pulled my phone out and dialled Ray Barry our team's profiler and asked him to meet us in

272

the conference room also if he could bring Dr James Simmons our Pathologist and Dr Andrew Brian the other CSI along with him.

We found the boxes I was looking for and went ahead to lump them towards the elevator, when from around the corner Hal Myers appeared. He was now the District Attorney's investigator, he was part of the original team, so I asked if he wanted to be involved in what I was doing. He mulled over the thought for moments then exclaimed in an excited voice "bet your fuckin balls I would as I want to know who the money men were." I was glad he agreed, this meant we almost had all the team together except for Joanne and Grant who were now with the FBI Special Case Unit in Washington. It may be that at some stage I may require their input into what I was undertaking.

We arrived back in the conference room and went ahead to unload the files when my phone rang, I answered;

"Hello, Farrer here," the voice on the other end was one of panic and surprise it was Dr McMichael;

"There is a lady in the hospital asking for you."
My immediate reaction in silence was what the fuck would this woman want with me? I told the person on the other end of the phone;

"I would be there immediately," I hung up and must have had a look of mystery or one of loss on my face as I turned to the others in the room and said what had just happened. Hal and Ray said they will be tagging along as this may be the break, we have been waiting on to find out the money men.

2

Outside of the Lake Tavern and Motel, a dark blue SUV pulled into a parking space, with tinted windows which looked strange on a vehicle that old. Out of the passenger side a man alighted wearing a light grey suit, tall and had a full beard and wearing sunglasses, considering the age and state of the vehicle he looked out of place. The other was of medium height wearing clothes that was more suited to the type of vehicle he was driving, being jeans and a leather jacket and had a goatee beard also wearing sunglasses. As they met at the front of the vehicle they spoke then turned and headed towards the office of the motel. Upon entering the office Ruby, the receptionist greeted them with a smile and handed them a registration card each. Ruby watched intently as they completed the cards and noted one was from Greensborough, North Carolina and the other gent was from Tampa Bay, Florida. Ruby noted his complexion did not match someone from Florida as he did not have a tan which would be normal for someone from Florida.

The suited gentleman then took the key to unit twelve and went ahead across the motel car park towards the unit on the ground floor. The other gent went back towards the vehicle and then drove it past the office to the car park in front of unit twelve. Both men took briefcases and small carry bags from the rear seat of the vehicle, entered the unit, and closed the door behind them.

In the office Ruby placed the cards in the pigeonhole for unit twelve but as she did so take notice of the registration written on the card was for a vehicle registered in Colorado, her inquisitive nature alerted to this, so she checked the names Mr Ian Sommers, from North Carolina and Mr Michael Adams from Florida. She decided it may be a hire vehicle so took a walk around the path from the office past unit twelve and glanced at the vehicle. Ruby realised it was not a rental as there was no licence tag signifying such and the dilapidated state of the vehicle ruled it out also. Ruby quickly returned to the office and went into the back room which was the unit for which she and husband Thomas lived. No sooner had Ruby returned to the office unit than the front door of the office opened again and as Ruby came into the office the gentleman closed the door and asked if there were any vacancies. Ruby said;

"There was one unit available on the top floor if that would suit you?"

The man nodded in the affirmative and Ruby handed him a registration card which he completed, his name was Ashley Collins, from San Diego. She told Mr Collins his car park was to the right of the present parked vehicle; the unit number painted on the ground. Ruby pointed out that the unit was straight ahead up the stairs to the right and was number One One Two. At the same time, the vehicle the earlier two gentleman had arrived in, reversed out of their car park, and went ahead out the driveway, turning left and headed south on the main road. At the local diner a short distance down the road, Greg Manns was serving two gents seated in the corner booth facing south out towards the main street.

 A vehicle caught his eye as it past the diner. It seemed strange that it was just on dusk, and the sun had gone yet the man seated on the passenger's side of the strange vehicle was wearing sunglasses. This was the second strange thing that had happened in his diner this Friday. The two men he had just served were two of the richest people in Oemen Lake Township and had never frequented his diner before. He knew them as Dean Forrester and Steven Shaw.

Both had ordered hamburgers, beers, and fries which Greg felt did not fit with their status. Back at the motel the new gentleman was settling into his upstairs unit. He unpacked his bag and then a smaller briefcase that held a small calibre rifle in three separate parts. He carefully and meticulously put the weapon together, then slid the bolt back checking that the chamber was empty. He retrieved a small pistol from the briefcase and placed this on the bed next to the rifle. Two boxes of bullets he retrieved from the bag and placed them next to the rifle and pistol. He picked up his cell phone and placed a call;

 "I have arrived and setup in the motel. I am in room one one two and will await your phone call as to what and where this going down."

He then hung up and slowly crossed the room to the mini bar, retrieved a small bottle of bourbon and a can of coke from the fridge. He found glasses in the bathroom and taking one he poured the contents of the small bottle of bourbon unto the glass followed by the coke. He crossed to the window and looked out through the venetian blinds at the car park of the motel across the roof of the tavern and cast a glancing eye up and down the main street just as the streetlights flickered into life.

The light on the Tavern Motel sign flickered into life as well as the light in the office shone through the windows out into the carpark, casting an illuminated shadow of shielded light across the entrance to the motel. Ruby noticed the shadow of the gent in one one two standing at the window as he had opened the venetian blinds up, she turned and went about getting things ready for the night. The sign showed *"No Vacancy"* and Ruby returned to the family unit to prepare for dinner. The guest slowly closed the venetians and shut out the outside world for the time being. Back at the diner Steven Shaw and Dean Forrester tucked into their burgers and beer as they discussed the event that had happened over the past three years, Dean said;

"Things got out of hand and went farther than I ever expected. I never believed Isabella would or even could kill someone, let alone plan, and conduct the task." Steven agreed and nodding said;

"Yes, things had become a little hard to control or even get a handle on things."
Just as the conversation seemed at an end Dean's phone rang, he answered and only said;

"That's good, I will be in touch." The vehicle with the two men in headed along the main street heading towards Pale Hills Top Village.

277

They passed through the village and around South Arm heading towards Pullman's Point. Inside the vehicle they discussed what they needed to do when they arrived at the Old Sawmill;

"What if Farrer has found everything we had there" asked Ian Sommers. Michael Adams replied;

"I doubt whether he would have the brains to fully look thoroughly in all the rooms, there are the few that we closed off and there is no way they could ever find them. I believe we may have trouble as we do not know whether they closed off certain areas."

They arrived at the gates to the old sawmill, which on closer inspection were heavily chained. Retrieving the cutters from under the rear seat, they had come prepared for any situation, they also retrieved torches and two handguns. Striding up to the gates Ian chopped the lock off and went ahead to open the gates as Michael drove through, Ian closing the gates after him. The vehicle lights shone brightly on the front of the old building and in areas reflected of the rockface it caressed into. The vehicle pulled up at the side of the building so as it was out of site from the road and hidden enough not to draw attention. The two men then mounted the three or four steps to the main door, it to chained and locked. The lock quickly cut, and they entered the building, heading straight to the rear of the main room towards the corridors that branched off both left and right.

3

Arriving at the hospital with Hal and Ray close behind we headed for the lifts. I pushed the up button knowing we were going to the second floor. The doors opened we entered and pushed the button for the second floor. The doors at once closed, and we felt the slight jerk as the old lift rattled its way to the second floor. The doors opened and there was a sign showing floor number two, under it was an arrow pointing right showing "This way to reception," the other arrow pointed left showing "to wards one to four and rooms three to seven." I exited the lift and went right heading for the reception area. A nurse with mahogany brown hair and lovely smile greeted us.
I said;

"Dr McMichael called and said there was a patient wishes to speak with me, I am Sherriff Ian Farrer. She asked if we could wait in the side room, and she would page the doctor".

No sooner had we settled down in the side room off reception than in strolled a gentleman in a doctor's white coat and his name embroidered on the left pocket, Dr Geoffrey McMichael, a stethoscope slung around his neck as well as one of those hammer things for testing reflexes poking out of his left pocket. Tall man about mid-forties going slightly bald with a moustache and slightly greying hair. I bet the nurses swooned over him as he had that look about him. He introduced himself and I introduced Hal, Ray, and myself.

"Well Sherriff the lady pleaded that she needed to speak with you urgently she did not say what it was to do with or why it was so urgent."

I looked at him and must have had a look of bewilderment as he continued to tell us how this woman arrived at the hospital.

"She was in a car accident and her name is Sally Donald. She suffered cuts and abrasions as well as concussion we are keeping her here for the next two or three days under observation."

He stepped towards the doorway and indicated to follow him. We walked along the corridor past the lifts and past two rooms and came upon a third room off to the left.

There was a woman lying on the bed with cuts and abrasions on her face as well as her right arm in a sling. She tried to sit up, but the pain was a bit too much.

"I am Sally Donald; I escaped from the dungeon at the old sawmill, and you were investigating the murders that occurred here in Oemen Lake."

I agreed and she continued;

"About two weeks ago I received a letter from a friend who stills lives here her name is Lilly and she works for the Shaws. She wrote to me two three months ago. I am unsure exactly when, but it was from Lilly, but I had moved around a bit with my job and the letter followed me around until it caught up with me in New York, where I work now." She continued.

"Lilly wrote to me telling me that she was working for the Shaws, and she knew that Mr Shaw and another man took part in various deeds of harmful stuff. Yes, I escaped from the clutches of those men who murdered all those girls, and I ran and ran until I was so far away from here that no-one was going to find me. I changed my name and my whole life. The only reason I am back now is that you did not catch all the people involved in that murderous time."

She continued;

"I am here in the hospital as I was forced off the road about ten miles North of the lake on the Northern side of the causeway. I stopped at a truck stop diner about two hours from town to get fuel and a coffee, and there were two men ordering coffee also, one in a suit the other in jeans and leather jacket. They were driving a dark blue beat up SUV. There was a pause, and I indicated to her to continue, if she was able;

She started;

"I recognised the one with the goatee beard and I am sure he recognised me as they left very quickly. I left the diner and headed here, about half an hour from the diner the SUV, was on the side of the road. I went past but they pulled out from where they had been parked and quickly caught up to me ramming me in the rear, then passing me and near Two Ton Bridge they forced my car off the road into the gully."

She paused, winced with some pain, and shifted her position slightly in the bed. She then took a deep breath and with a look of uncertainty on her face and the look one gets in your eyes when frightened, she continued;

"They did not stop, and as luck would have it my car came to rest by a large tree which stopped me falling into the ravine."

She stopped and looked at me with a look of foreboding and took another deep breath;

"The man I am sure I recognised was Ray Beale."

My heart seemed to stop as I took a deep breath, and with a loud voice said,

"Fuck, what are they back here for?" I asked.

"Would you recognise the vehicle if you saw it again?"

"You bet she replied, as will have a white mark down the driver's side where they tried to run me off the road to kill me, I think."

We need to find that vehicle and if they are in town then trouble is brewing. I asked;

"Hal put out a call for the vehicle, we need to find it and quick."

I went ahead to ask how she arrived at the hospital?

"I finally was able to climb back up to the road and waved down a truck who stopped and gave me a lift into town and dropped me at the hospital. My car is still in the ravine" she exclaimed.

I looked at her in disbelief, questioning;

"Why did she run in the first place, why the hell did she not come to me and tell me all this at the time?"

"I knew that the police were involved and that I could not trust anybody!" she exclaimed, with a frightful look on her face. I nodded that she was correct that there were police and high-ranking officials involved. I asked if she still had the letter from Lilly? She nodded and pointed to a bag on the side table. I retrieved a letter from the front of the bag and saw the address was to an address in Utah, and then sent on to Sally in New York from her earlier employer. I looked at Hal;

"Put a guard around the clock on this lady, and no-one and I mean no-one except the three of us in this room are to be admitted seeing her."
He at once got out his phone and rang the station for a deputy to come to the hospital at once.

I sat in Sally's hospital room and read the letter she had received from Lilly. It read;

Dear Sally,

I do not know whether you will receive this, but I do hope it finds you. I know you contacted me and told me not to try and find you. You had a fear the men who had taken you and caused you so much grief would again try to get rid of you, thus you ran. As you told me about your fear and the consequences that may happen. I followed your instructions to make sure that I never broke the promise you asked of me. I now need to write to you as I feel I may be in danger because of what I know and for whom I work.

I do not in any way hold it against you for running as when reading the news report after the police arrested the culprits and they went to jail, I felt you may be able to return as we have known each other since childhood. I need you now to return to tell the Sherriff what you know as I am able now to shed further light on this matter as it

283

has not ended, I feel. I will understand if you do not return or even answer my letter. Please remember I will always be your friend.

Lots of love Lilly.

The letter shook me to my core. Here was a lady that may be able to finally give me the names of the money men behind the murders, drugs, prostitution, and illegal transport of body parts.

The young police officer arrived, Hal left the room to brief him on what he needed to do and that he and two others would be on shifts around the clock guarding this lady. He was told no-one other than Ray, Hal or I was allowed into the room except the Dr and nurse caring for this lady. The young officer shook his head in agreement and then gathered a chair and placed himself directly outside the door. Ray and I left Sally's room as I did, I said I would be back later to ask more questions and get more details from her. I cautioned her not to say anything to anyone and I would take her letter but return it to her once I had copied and verified it. I stated I would also be talking to Lilly and taking her into protective custody, because if the Shaws were involved I had an innovative idea who else may have been the other money man in this.

Could Sally Donald be the smoking gun that I was looking for to finally get the top men behind the macabre events that went on and the murders that occurred? Hal, Ray, and I returned to the office and went straight into my office closing the door behind us. I knew this would need explaining to the rest of the team at some time as I needed to verify things first and more than anything getting this right the first time so that the top dogs did not slip through my fingers again. I was like a dog with a juicy bone now, I had the evidence and just had to make sure that all the skittles placed in a line, and everything made watertight and that we were going to make arrests of prominent persons. That was my plan within my head, but was it going to work out that way? Sally returning made think of the Old Mill and was there any more secrets or evidence within those grey dark catacombs, and would we be able to make any charges stick against the ring leaders unless we could find more damming evidence against them. I knew in my gut who the others were but proving it was going to a problem.

The other thing that was causing me a little anxiety was that Ray Beal was back in town and that could also mean Mike Grant was here too. If those two were back then trouble was brewing as they had a lot to answer for as well as giving up the brains behind this whole fiasco, as I was sure they even if they put their heads together were not able to orchestrate and carry out what happened without a lot of money behind them as well the dirty cops we knew about and the others that were either dead or rotting in gaol. We had to find Beale, as I was sure he would lead us to who we wanted.

4

At the old sawmill, the two men made their way along one of the corridors, making sure that they did not disturb anything and to make sure they left no trace as they went. Knowing they will have to return within the next few days as if what they were searching for was still there, then it would take at least two days to do the task they needed to conduct.

They also knew they had to get rid of the top men who were involved as well as the Sherriff as he knew too much and was not going to let the matter lie. Ian Summers and Michael Adams might be why very slowly watching things that were around them for tell-tale signs that could give them an idea at what they were looking for. It had been two years since they were there and therefore things had changed, the walls and floor we are still the same, but the ceiling had moisture on it. They looked around for what could have been causing it and suddenly realised that the joint between the rock wall and where the building abutted up to it had moved and there was a slow drip coming from the joint as well as moisture running backwards along the ceiling.

They shone their torches along the joint and hoped that there would be no rain between now and when they came back for what they are looking for. Puddles had formed in areas of the floor, and this gave them a disconcerting feeling that things had changed in that period. At the end of the corridor or tunnel depending on how you viewed this rabbit warren, was the door they were looking for. Upon opening it and flashing their torches quickly around the room there it was in the corner the box that had the goods.

They crossed the floor and suddenly realised it was dry in here and that dust had settled on all and sundry and they were leaving footprints everywhere as well as disturbing dust as they walked.

"We are going to have to move quicker than we thought" Ian remarked.

"With all this dust and the trace, we are leaving if anybody were to find this place then it would not take long to figure out who was here and what we were after."
Both lifted the heavy lid on the wooden crate and there was their goal, six transparent plastic bags. They could not believe their luck that no-one had found it, although this room was deep into the rock and was used by the old miners as a tearoom, therefore no one would have come this far when they found the outer rooms and what had gone in those.

They lifted the bags out of the box carefully placing them on the floor, closed the lid which sent a spray of dust through the air making Michael sneeze. They opened the first bag and there inside were twelve plastic bags all about the size of a loaf of bread. The other bags were opened one by one to make sure all was still in place, guns, and packs of one-hundred-dollar bills totalling almost seven hundred and fifty thousand dollars. Jackpot Ian thought, as he looked at Michael,

"Why don't we take it now, instead of coming back for it?" Ian shook his head;

"Too risky at the moment as we have to get in touch with Steven and Dean first to let them know it is still here." Michael could not understand why either Steven or Dean had come looking for this little parcel themselves, as they had had plenty of time to do so.

The two placed the bags back into the box and again closed the lid, turned, and carefully followed their own footsteps out of the room and back towards the opening into the old mill main building. Suddenly they stopped about twenty metres from the entrance when someone shouted;

"Anyone in here?"

Then a radio burst into life what have you found officer? The young Officer leant slowly towards the radio mounted on his lapel and pressed the radio into life;

"A dark blue SUV parked beside the old mill main building, and the chain and lock on the gate has been cut. The gates were wide open."

A voice came back.

"Do not go any further we are sending backup now." The young officer turned to leave and suddenly a shot rang out and he felt a sharp pain in the lower right-hand side of his back, he fell but as he did there was another shot and it hit him, and all was black.

"What the fuck!" exclaimed Ian, looking at Michael;

"Why did you do that he did not know we are in here and all he has seen is the truck,"

"That is enough. He only must tell Farrer and that prick would put two and two together and this place would be swarming with cops within hours."

Both men entered the area where the young officer lay bleeding out from his wounds. Ian gathered an old canvas blind from the other side of the room and laid it on the floor, they rolled the officer up in the canvas and struggled with limp body back into one of the tunnels and dropped it there.

They quickly ran back along the tunnel to the room where they had found the box, retrieved the items inside. Carrying three bags each and the torches flashing everywhere as they ran back out into what was now full darkness. Dumping the bags into the back seat of the SUV, and quickly starting it up reversed out of the where they had parked it. Heading for the gate and turning right heading North.

"We have to dump this vehicle and hide the stuff, going this way we may have a little time as the backup for that cop will be coming from the other way from town", remarked Ian breathless.

"You didn't have to shoot him; he was only a fucking kid for god's sake."

They drove off into the darkness headlights off only park lights illuminating the way for some miles.

A ways past the hook below Talon Point they dumped the SUV in the lake over the steep embankment. The plastic bags they hauled off into the wooded area on the opposite side of the road, here they found a place below an outcrop of rock and placed the bags in that area covering with loose rocks and branches, they were about four miles from the Old Mill.

"What now?" asked Ian;

"We walk to Talon Point steal a vehicle and around the lake to the ski field and hold up there until I can get hold of either Steven or Dean, then they can hide us until things settle down."

5

In the radio room, Sarah was trying to raise Officer Turner on the radio. He had called in that he was at the Old Mill and that there was a dark blue SUV parked there as well as the chain and lock on the gates was cut and the gates were wide open. Sarah kept calling but no reply. Trevor Cithers walked into the radio room and asked;

"What is the matter?" Sarah explained that Turner was not replying, and she explained what he reported was up at the Old Mill.

"Tell Farrer now and get another car to the Old Mill asap." Trevor ran out of the radio room and headed for the rear door to the carpark telling one of the officers standing at the coffee machine;

"Forget that you are with me, now."

The young officer dropped his coffee cup in the sink and followed Cithers out the back door to the carpark. They at once got into a squad car and headed for the gate which opened automatically. Meanwhile Sarah came into my office;

"Sherriff, we have had a report from a young Officer Turner who was investigating why the chain and lock on the gates at the Old Mill were cut and the gates were wide open. He has not returned our request as to what he had or had not found, and it has been at least twenty minutes."
I told her;

"Tell Ray and Hal to meet me in the carpark."
I quickly grabbed my jacket ran out of the office and down the corridor heading for the carpark, I raced to the car, Hal and Ray were following me. We sped out of the gate following Cithers with lights and sirens blaring it was a good twenty-to-twenty-five-minute drive to the Old Mill and I was not going to spare the horsepower.

"Hal from the back seat asked;

"What the hell was the officer doing at the mill in the first place?" I told him;

"It has been routine now twice a day a squad car on their patrols is to run by the Old Mill and keep an eye on the place. I have always had a feeling deep down in my gut that we had not finished with that place."

I viewed him in the rear-view mirror, and he shook his head in acknowledgement. The rest of the journey was in silence except for the sirens. We arrived at the Old Mill, just behind Officer Cithers, we pulled up close to the doorway of the mill's main building. Hal went to check on the patrol car belonging to the young officer. Everything seemed in order. I went through the main doors and into the area I had frequented prior, nothing had changed except the floors were covered in dust and in areas mud with puddles of still oily water spread across the whole floor area, they had like a rainbow effect due to water and oil mixing. Off to the left was the corridor that led to the rooms where the whole macabre scenario of a couple of years ago took place. I went to the far left and down a corridor that had a slight inclination. I flicked on my torch which I had retrieved from my jacket pocket and shone it into the unforgiving darkness.

 The torch hardly penetrating the eerie surrounds, when suddenly up from behind came a stronger more powerful light. Ian had brought the big torch from the car and told me;
   "Put that little candle away, he had a real light."

Even then the darkness the torch still caused a reflection back from the curtain of black. We reached the room where the girls were worked on, going on through there we entered the death room and where we found the barrels. I turned and went through the archway into another hallway, heading towards the rear of the complex. Ian passed me and went ahead of me, we went a little further when I told him to stop.

Looking at the ground I noticed not only scuff marks but footprints in the fresh dust and mud heading slightly off to the right. Rounding the corner, we noticed that we had not been in this area before. Both Ian and I stopped looked at each other and even though we never said a word we realised things were different.

Following on we came upon a doorway which was open to a smaller room, with a large open box in the corner. Walking over to the box and shining the torch into it we saw that it was dry and clean inside, but there were marks where something had been sitting. Flashing the torch around and glancing at other areas in the room, there was nothing else within this room. Ian remarked;

"This room is somewhere we have not been, and we need to get the Forensic boys in here."

I tried the radio but due to where we were the radio did not work. Ian and I retraced our steps back to the main room, luckily, he had a piece of chalk in his pocket, which I always wondered why he carried that and never bothered to ask. He marked arrows on the wall to show the direction of the room and we were going to need lights and everything possible in here.

Part of the way back to the main area I tripped over something, and had it not been for the wall I would have fell flat on my face. I looked down and it was a piece of what looked like rolled up canvas, shining the torch on it the canvas went back into a partial cove within the tunnel. Ian and I pulled the canvas out into the hallway and unrolled it, both of us stepped back in horror as there was a body of a young police officer covered in blood and the canvas was red with his blood. I leant down and gently closed his eyes. Ian said he would go back and get help. I stayed with the body and continued looking around the walls and ceiling. There was no blood spatter anywhere which made me think he was shot somewhere else and placed here.

Some minutes later Ian returned with Hal and more torches. He said he had called for the forensic guys and more help.

He also exclaimed;

"I found blood and spatter on the walls further down in another area of the next tunnel, showing he was shot there and moved here." Just as he finished saying this, Hal arrived and advised that there was something going on here as there were skid marks in the gravel on the left of the main building. We were going to need the forensic boys to take tyre tread casts of the marks in the gravel. Also, the chain, gate and lock may carry fingerprints also.

Later that night, which was now early morning, the Old Mill was lit up like a Christmas tree, and the lights were now placed in the tunnels and all rooms. The forensic guys in their white coveralls were everywhere all working feverishly. I walked out of the gates and along the road to the South but could see nothing significant with the torch light. I decided to try and walk North of the gates and found tyre marks in the mud on the side of the road. Admittedly this could have been any other vehicle, but I was hoping above all hope that it was the vehicle we were looking for. I signalled the forensic boys to try where I was as the tyre marks may be the same as those near the building.

Little did I realise at that moment it was getting lighter as the dawn was upon us and the sun was rising from behind the mountain range to the East. It sent a reddish hue over everything even the lake water calm as a mill pond had a red tinge to it. Finally, we might be in for a fine day I thought. Hal, Ian, and I walked about a mile up the road to the North of the Old Mill, hoping to find something anything that would lead us to who this may have been in the mill and to who shot the young police officer. I know it was a stretch, but I had to think positive, and my gut was telling me this was Beale and Grant. I would need to find out what they did before coming here and did they attend any place in town or come straight to the mill.

Upon returning to town, I told Hal and Ian to check the Motels in town as well as the lodge, make sure to enquire within the tavern also. Speak to Ruby at the Motel ask if they were there to describe them and any paperwork they may have completed. It was a longshot but something I hope yielded a clue of sorts. I went to the other end of town, down past the diner and gas station, also making enquiries. This whole time thinking about the poor young police officer who was only doing his job and these bastards had taken his life for no obvious reason. Our demons had surely as my arse pointed to the ground returned.

6

Ray Beale and Mike Grant walked North towards Talon Point hoping to find a vehicle parked close to the outskirts, as they did not want to have to go into the village as things were getting a little heated and not going as planned. Shooting the police officer was not part of the plan and that made things so dicey now their plans had become one huge fuckup. If they could not get hold of Shaw or Forrester, that would also be a spanner in the works, as they needed to get hold of them before they heard about what went down at the Old Mill. Daylight was now looming, and its bright sunshine was a blessing as the night had been cold and both men were a little worse for wear.

Ray Beale knew Bernie Talbertson, he was an old friend and lived in a log cabin back in the pines somewhere around Talon Point. Ray thought to himself and wondered whether Bernie would be able to help them hide out for a bit. Besides knowing Bernie, Ray had a little dirt on him from their old days before Ray built his transport business. Ray mentioned this to Mike and explained;

"Admittedly Bernie had gone straight for many years but back in the day he was the man for running numbers and knowing who and how money could become clean other than putting it through a washing machine, if you get my drift."

Mike laughed and nodded his approval.

"First things first we need transport" exclaimed Mike. Then as luck would have it, they came upon a Jeep Cherokee parked in a layby. Mike walked around and looked inside the vehicle as Ray scanned the area for any sign of life. The driver's door was open but no keys, which was not a problem. While Ray kept an eye out for anyone in the vicinity Mike climbed in the driver's seat and went ahead to pull the wiring cables down from underneath the steering column. He found the two that he wanted and touched them to make a spark and the Jeep fired into life. Ray jumped in the passenger's side, and they quickly left the layby heading for where they had stashed the bags.

They collected the bags as quickly as possible, turned the Jeep around and headed for Talon Point. As they drove through Talon Point, there was not a lot of movement around the small town, except for the local store and gas station, which was only just opening. Ray realised that it was six in the morning, so it fitted well with what they needed to do, as the early morning helped in making sure they were not recognised. They sighted a phone booth on the northern side of the garage and pulled in close to find out Bernie's number and or address. Ray quickly flicked through the pages until he found the number and address and quickly tore the page out of the already dilapidated phone book. He returned to the Jeep and told Mike to find a quiet sheltered spot so he could make the call to Bernie to ask for his help. A little more than an hour later sitting in a side road that led to the boat ramp North of Talon Point Ray dialled the number and awaited an answer from the other end of the phone. The phone rang four or five times then went to an answer machine;

"Fuck" exclaimed Ray aloud;

"No answer went straight to his answering machine." Mike said;

"Well, it is still early maybe we drive up to near his place and try again later," Ray nodded in agreement, so Mike sparked the Jeep into life and went ahead to head back to the main road. Mike suddenly stopped the vehicle;

"We need to get rid of this vehicle and maybe cut across country to this Bernie's place as the authorities will be looking for this now, I am sure." he exclaimed.

Ray agreed so they returned to the side road, wiped down the dashboard and steering wheel, other surfaces that a fingerprint or DNA could be drawn off, especially the wires used to jump start the vehicle.

Ray looked at a map on his phone and found the road that leads up to the place he is looking for and found they were one to two miles away. There was a bushwalking path that ran along behind Bernie's a distance from his house so they decided that would be the way to go, they headed South as Ray had forgotten Bernie's house was South of Talon Point. About an hour later crouching low in the bush behind Bernie's, Ray tried his phone again. This time a male voice answered "Talbertson," Ray sighed with relief, and then spoke to the voice on the other end.

"Bernie, it is me Ray Beale and I need a favour from you."

"Ray, what the hell are you doing back here after what went down years ago, I do not want to get mixed up in your shit."

"You owe me big time arsehole," shouted Ray down the phone.

"Where are you?" was the reply.

"Behind your house in the bush near the walking track." was Ray's reply.

There was a moments silence then the voice said;

"Go to the shed on the far side of the property, the door has a red panel, wait inside I will be there in a few moments."

Ray and Mike quickly surveyed the surrounding area and then as quietly and swiftly as they could went ahead past the rear of the house and towards the shed as described. The shed was a good two to three hundred yards from the house and well out of earshot of anyone near the house or coming up the driveway. What seemed like hours but was only a few minutes Bernie arrived at the shed. He entered and there standing in front of him was Mike Grant and Ray Beale, although it took him a few moments to recognise then because of their hair length and beards.

"You have got some guts coming back here after what happened, where have you been?"

Bernie's voice was quiet but a noticeable anxiety was detected in it by Ray.

"We are back to retrieve what we left behind all those years ago, we needed to leave in hurry, as the heat in the kitchen was getting too hot."

"What do you want from me?'

Bernie blurted out in a louder more authoritative voice.

"We need you to hide us for a few days and provide us with some wheels, we can pay you handsomely for your trouble, Ray showing him the money bags and drugs they had carried with them, after ditching the vehicle. Then we can call it square if you like." answered Ray.

"Call it square, bloody hell you participated in all those murders, and I suppose you had something to do with the young copper who was shot at the Old Mill yesterday as well."

Mike looked at Bernie with a stern face and said;

"Either help us now or we will implicate you in the murders, as you know it would not be hard as the cops are still looking for all the perpetrators of those." Bernie took a step back and looked at Ray;

"You would do that if I do not help, you are both out of your mind."

Just then Mike pulled his pistol out and pointed it at Bernie;

"I will have no hesitation in sending you to your maker old man, so do as we say or take the consequences."

Bernie was in disbelief of the scene that was going down in this shed on his property his home. He had had no trouble with the law and yes, he had done things over the years that were not always quite legal but never murder or drugs of any kind. This was a new experience for him and one that was scaring the bejesus out him.

"I have no family as my wife died a couple of years back and my son now lives in Denver and the daughter in San Diego. I will help you Ray, but you must promise me that I am kept right out of your problems."

Ray looked at him and made the promise. Mike still holding the gun on him was not so sure as to his trustworthiness or whether he even would be helping of the goodness of his heart. Mike decided in his own mind once he helps us this man has got to go as he now knows too much.

7

I entered the office; it was early and no one else around. I made a coffee and stood at the window looking out across the lake at the Oemen mountain range in the distance just as the sun was creeping over the top. The sunlight danced on the lake surface like a thousand dancing stars glistening in the half light. Suddenly the sunlight passed over the boardwalk by the lake and cast shadows from the pines across the road and onto the surrounding buildings making shadows like an eagles' talons. At that moment I realised that our quiet small town was again in the grip of evil and where was it going to end. Hal poked his head in the doorway saying hi and continued to his office. Bill followed with coffee in hand and entered the office, took a gulp of coffee, and said;

"I interviewed the Tavern boys, and they knew nothing about the strangers as they had made no appearance in the Tavern, but they did say that Shaw and Forrester were in deep conversation for a long while, which was strange as they rarely frequented the place. I will be interviewing Ruby from the motel later today as well as have a look at their room as to whether they had left anything."

"You can't do that without a warrant, and we are not going to get that unless we have factual evidence to go on." I exclaimed.

"It is not going to hurt boss I am not going to touch anything, just get an idea of who they may be." he remarked with a look of rejection on his face. I dismissed this with a nod.

"Let me know how the Ruby interview goes?"

"Do you know if Ray contacted the family of the young officer, and explained what has happened?"

He shook his head that that had happened. I nodded with thanks. Just then Steve Barlow entered with a box full of files. He placed them on a chair and looked sullen as he spoke;

"I went through all the relevant files from eight years ago and this pair if it is them Ray Beale and Mike Grant, are a real piece of work and to nail them would be a full closure to that mayhem back then."

I looked at him and said;

"It would be the best thing that I could do for this town was to close this off. I have always known with a gut feeling that there was more involved than the ones we managed to put away."

"Bill, could you ask Ruby when you talk to her are they using any other names than their real ones. I suspect they are, and we need to know them." I continued;

"We need to go over Ray Beale and Mike Grant's associates from that time and if they still live in the area and addresses for them all. We also need to know what vehicle if they are still using the same one, they checked into the motel with?"

I was back looking out the window as Steve picked up the box of files and headed for the conference room, Hal, and Bill in tow. How many more are going to die because of these two and the others still connected to this case. I know that Ray Beale and Mike Grant are not the kingpins of this as they do not have the influence or the brains for an operation like this. My gut feeling was that they would eventually have to contact or meet with whomever that was. I was going to head over to Talon Point village, not sure why but had a feeling about that place. Just then the phone rang, it was a young officer from the front desk;

"Sir, we have a report of a stolen Jeep over in Talon Point this morning. It was taken from a layby while the owner was fishing South of Talon Point near the boat ramp."
I thanked him for the information and asked if he could write the details down and leave them at the front desk, I will collect on my way out. I realised I was still holding my coffee cup which had gone to just warm at this point. I considered getting a fresh one but something about Talon Point was eating at me that there was something over there that could be a clue as to where these two arseholes had gone. I asked Colin;

"Did you get any trace at all from the Old Mill?"
He answered;

"He was still processing the evidence, but he had the Patrol car's video and the officer's body cam if I wanted to view that as it had some interesting views on them."

I sat down in his office as he started the video; he turned up the volume, the officer's voice came across clear, that he had found the gates to the Old Mill open and the chain and lock cut. He went on to remark there was a vehicle parked beside the main building a dark blue SUV. He faced his cruiser towards the vehicle just as two men appeared from the building's side door. He said that there was two men, and they were carrying plastic bags, he got out of his vehicle switched on his body camera and suddenly there was a split screen, the camera from his vehicle and his body cam. He yelled;

"Stop where you are drop the bags and hands in the air." There was silence then the person on the left dropped his bags and quickly pulled a revolver from his belt two shots rang out and the young officer was down, his camera pointing to the sky. His cruiser camera still working.

The two threw the bags into the rear of the vehicle, as one jumped into the driver's seat the other walked towards the now prone officer, pulled out his gun and both from his body cam and cruiser cam the man shot him again. I stopped the video at that point and looked at the face of a demon. It was my worst nightmare, Ray Beal and Mike Grant were back in town and already causing murderous mayhem. I said to Colin;

"Can you make me stills of the two men's faces and especially the one that fired that final shot. I also want the SUV's make and model as well as the plate number?"

"I will have them for you this afternoon." he remarked, I nodded and left the room heading for the front desk to pick up the information the desk officer had phoned me about.

I was in my car when Andrew Bryan pulled up beside me.

"Want me to come with you boss, sorry I am a bit late, kids causing problems." I nodded to get in.

We reversed out of the car park and headed South towards Pale Top Village, from there around the South Arm up past

Pullman's Point, the Old Mill and Lookout Cove to Talon Point a forty-five-to-fifty-minute drive in all.

We arrive at the boat ramp where the vehicle was stolen from, and I walked down to the water's edge beside the boat ramp. This whole time my gut was churning I knew they were here and that if they were not watching me, they knew I was onto them. There was not much to go on where we were, so we headed to Talon Point, there I entered the store and asked about who reported the vehicle being stolen. A man late fifties walked over to me and introduced himself;

"Hank, Hank Miles, it was my jeep they stole."

"Did you get a look at them at all?" I asked as I introduced myself.

"No, I was down on the edge of the boat ramp fishing and of course you cannot see the parking from there. I heard a vehicle start and thought that it was strange as there were no other vehicles in the area when I pulled up. I came back up to find my Jeep gone."

"Can you give my colleague Andrew here your details and the details of your vehicle."

I exited the store and went to the corner of the building, not sure what I was looking for, when I noticed the phone book hanging with a page half torn from it. Picking up the phone book, I noticed that almost three quarters of the page was missing. I got my phone out and rang Colin, told him to drop what he was doing grab his kit and bring Ray with him to Talon Point, we may have caught a break. I kept walking around the area and noticed tyre marks in the soft gravel close to the edge of the concrete pad for the store come gas stations fuel pad. I was sure they were the tyres of a four-wheel vehicle.

"Got you now you bastards!" I exclaimed to myself in a muffled voice. Little did I know at that point just how close but how far I was from the truth.

8

In Bernie's shed that smelt of cow shit, two men sat and waited for their host to arrive. They did not have to wait long; the door flew open and there was a double barrel shotgun pointed at them.

"Bernie, you fuckwit, put that down!" exclaimed Ray.

"Not on your life Beale, I am not getting involved in your shit, and I want nothing to do with you or your friend. They just said on the news that a young police officer was shot dead last night at the Old Mill and two suspects are wanted in connection with the incident. It does not take a Harvard fucking graduate to work out it was you two."

"Look, yes we made a mistake, but we need your help and besides you owe me," shouted Ray.

"Owe you, you bastard I owe you nothing. You almost got me killed by McLean when he thought I was double crossing your little contingent of hell raisers. Murdering those girls and that copper was not smart. Now you have gone a killed another copper, I am not going to rot in jail

306

or spend what life I have left rotting in a cell because of you!"

Just then out the corner of his eye, Ray Beale saw a flash and heard a gunshot come from behind him. Bernie's face took on a distorted look and then the sound and flash of the shotgun and luckily it was pointed to the roof as Bernie fell towards the hale bails behind him. Ray spun around;

"Mike, you fucking idiot, what have you done? He was our only source of help, and you shoot the bastard. You are nuttier than a squirrel's shit and that is saying something."

Ray was sweating, they now had Bernie laying there bleeding and in pain. Mike walked up to Bernie and fired again, this time between the eyes. His brain matter splattered all over the bails with the impact of the bullet. His anguished look disappeared in a collage of red as blood went everywhere. Ray stood still like a statue petrified the gun was about to be turned on him.

Mike took a step towards Ray and said;

"He is not going to cause us anymore trouble now, is he?"

Ray Beale stood looking at the scene in horror, he had sidled himself up with a madman, he always knew that Grant had a short fuse but not to this extent.

"We are going to have to bury him, he has a glasshouse out the back from memory, we could put him in there until we decide what to do."

The two men lifted the limp body and walked it around the house, to the glasshouse at the bottom of the garden. Placing him under a row of shelves full of Orchids and Chrysanthemums they rolled him out of sight so he could not be seen from the door of the glasshouse. Then returning to the shed collected the shotgun and the bale of straw that was covered in blood and brain matter went ahead to the house. On entering the house, it was very neat and tidy considering a man lived there alone and had no female company for some time. Mike ordered Ray to take the bale around the back where they had sighted an incinerator and burn the hay, while he tried to find food and gun cleaning material to clean up the shotgun.

"Before you go," Mike said to Ray;

"Go in the kitchen or laundry and find some bleach wash your hands and arms up to the elbows, I will have GSR (Gun Shot Residue) on me. Leave the gun here it will need to be cleaned. That is two we have shot with it, and now it needs to be cleaned and reloaded."

Ray reluctantly laid the shotgun placed it on the sideboard in the hall, retreated out the front door and picked up the bale of hale, continued around the back of the house. He reached the incinerator and loaded the first of the hay into it and lit it, and just kept feeding it until all was gone. Returning to the house through the back door making sure he wiped down the handles as he went, leaving no prints. In the laundry he found a blue bottle of bleach and quickly poured it over his hands and arms, then with a cake of soap washed them thoroughly, while glancing around for something to wipe them on. Finding a towel in the linen cabinet behind him, wiped down his arms and hands till they were dry then wiped the taps, handles, and bottle thoroughly. He kept the towel, re-entered the main house and found Mike cleaning feverishly the shotgun and his pistol. Mike was wearing plastic gloves of which he had found a box full under the sink in the kitchen.

"Put a pair on and burn that towel, after you wipe everything down." Mike did not look up just kept cleaning and Ray muttered in a low tone;

"You are a fucking idiot this was supposed to be clean and quick and a place to lay low for a while. Now we have a body in the bloody glasshouse, God only knows who heard those shots I am not sure where his neighbours are. I know there are none in the front between the house and road, but out back and on each side, I am not sure. This is only a small property."

Mike Grant was head strong and did not think about consequences of his actions he had been like that the whole time Ray Beale had known him. He was also the one that told McLean to kill Barrelli, the police officer on the case if he did not do it then, Mike would and make sure McLean was set up for it. As it was McLean got found out anyway, and is rotting in jail as far as Ray and Mike know. Ray slunk away out of the room and out the back and headed for the glasshouse.

He entered and closed the door behind him whilst looking for a shovel. In the corner at the rear of the glasshouse he found an assortment of shovels, spades, picks, and other small implements. He picked up a shovel and went ahead to the far side of the shelves. He began to dig as the floor was earth and looked like it had been turned over before at some. time. He dug down about two feet when he struck something, carefully clearing away the soil he discovered a sheet, once white he surmised, now tarnished with brown clay soil. He cleared the rest of the soil off and pulled back the sheet, he gasped, and fell back against the shelves in horror. There was a body of a woman, although partially dressed in a nightgown and still in decomposition, so she was not in the ground that long. Ray muffled a yell and slowly left the glasshouse at a quick pace towards the house. He entered through the back door and went ahead at once to the room, presuming it to be the dining room due to the table and chairs, and saw Mike with a glass of scotch in his hand and a bottle of Glenfiddich sitting beside him. Mike looked up and said;

"I poured you one old man thought you may need one," Ray picked up the glass and gulped down the good part of the scotch, and in a stammering, breath said;

"You had better come and look what I have found." Mike looked at him and saw that there was soil on his gloves, quickly rose from his chair and followed Ray out the back door towards the glasshouse. They entered and Ray led Mike to the far side where he had discovered the body. Mike pushed past Ray;

"Shit, what the fucking hell have you done?"

"Nothing", cried Ray, I was digging a hole to put him in pointing at Bernie's body and found this."

Mike bent down and pulled back the sheet more and quickly recognised the necklace around the neck of the corpse;

"Fuck, this must be Bernie's wife!" he exclaimed. Looking at the corpse Mike uncovered more of the body removing the sheet slowly, and discovered a bullet wound to the chest.

"The bastard shot his wife and buried her here." Ray fell back on his haunches and stared at the glass panels on the side as they stretched from ground to ceiling and over the top. It was then he realised there was a pungent smell, he recognised it at once from the corpses in the tunnels at the Old Mill all those years ago. Rotting flesh, he quickly looked at Mike and with fear in his voice said;

"You realise they are going to find these two bodies and we are going to get stitched up for both?"

"Mike, we must get rid of them both otherwise we are going down and any plans we had have now gone out the door. You shoot that young police officer and Bernie, now finding his wife with a bullet wound in the chest, hell man this whole thing the plan to get the bags and piss off has blown up in our face."

The two men looked at each other and neither was able to say a word. Mike left and headed back towards the house as he past Ray he said;

"I need a drink and I must think, how we fix this and leave this damn place and never have to come back here." Ray followed in his footsteps slowly, turning back just before leaving the glasshouse at the half-uncovered body that he had no idea was there, and if he had kept his wits about him in the shed and at the Old Mill, they may be free and gone by now.

"What a complete fuck-up this is," he said to himself as he closed the glasshouse door.

9

Colin arrived at the garage come store about fifty minutes later with his kit and tried to swab down the phone booth. I told him about the tyre tread, and he was going to make a cast and take it back the office. In the meantime, Andrew and I entered the Store and asked the lovely young lady behind the counter whether she had seen two men driving a Jeep in the area in the past twenty-four hours?

"There was two men early this morning they looked a bit dishevelled and not what I would call locals. They asked if they could use a phone and I told them there was a phone booth at the side of the building."

I saw that she was not keen on having to deal them in the way she answered my question, which is the Psychologist in me coming out.

"Did they buy anything?" I asked. She shook her head in the negative and went about her business of reading the girly magazine on the counter.

I wish I had the photographs from the video we had from the officer's cruiser and his body cam, then I could be certain it was Beale and Grant. I told Andrew I was going to drive back down the road towards the place where the Jeep was stolen from and walk the shoreline as I had a hunch as to what our two friends may have done with the SUV they were driving. He nodded and asked;

"Do you want me to come with you?"

"No, I can do this I will not be long, you stay and give Colin a hand if he needs one." I drove slowly back along the road South towards Lookout Cove and back towards the Old Mill, although I did not intend going that far at least. My thinking was had they pushed the SUV into the lake and if so, where would have been the best place.

I came up on the steep embankment, not far North of Talon Point and close within walking distance of the layby where the Jeep was stolen from. Parking the car, I walked to the edge of the steep runoff and there to my delight below the surface of the lake was what I was looking for. I rang Andrew and told him to borrow Colin's vehicle and to meet me about three miles North of where he was, and radio the office we need a tow truck and a crane I had found the SUV. Andrew and Colin arrived together, I asked Colin;

"Did you get everything from that site?"

"Yep, there is nothing more I can do there."

They both walked slowly to the edge and looked over into the crystal-clear waters of the lake as the sun shone brightly giving a mirrored effect further out in the lake.

"I rang for the two truck and told him he may need a crane to get this vehicle out."

"Good, all we need now is some evidence of where these two have gone?"

"Boss, when you were back at the store inside, I heard what I thought may have been shots fired somewhere towards the hills, I could not be sure, but it did sound like gunfire."

"There is a lot of hunters around here this time of year and most of the folk who live in this area are either short term stayers who live in the big smoke and only come up here on holidays or some weekends. From memory there is only two or three permanents."

I answered him by saying;

"We can investigate that once we have this vehicle back in the garage and go over it. I will get a couple of uniform boys to go check on the properties around here, to see if there is anything we should be worried about."

As soon as I stated this, I had a gut feeling was this just maybe Beale and Grant at work. I thought to myself they would not know anyone around this area as far as I knew, and they would not be that stupid to fire off a gun so close to where they stopped for information. I at once phoned the office and asked if we could get two uniform boys out to the area to checkout if there were any problems or if it was just hunters in the area.

The office lady replied;

"That there were two officers at the South Arm of the lake."

I told her;

"Tell them to work their way back up to Talon Point getting them to check out the properties as they travelled towards the Causeway and then back to the office coming on town side of the lake back past Big Bear village as if it was their normal route keeping an eye out for the Jeep."

I said;

"To tell the officers to keep their wits about them even though I was not sure there was anything even wrong."

I looked again down at the vehicle in the water, then turned to Colin and said;

"It has been in the water a while will there be anything worth retrieving from the vehicle?"

I turned back to my vehicle and returned to the office, hoping that we had some information from the interview with Ruby. There was file on my desk with a note attached. Ruby coming in at three to see us as soon as the relief for the evening turns up. I browsed the file it was from the earlier case, one of the files they had found in the boxes we had brought up from Archives. Hal walked past and said;

"Ruby had arrived did I want to sit in on the interview?" I said; "I will be right along." I quickly went to the conference room and looked feverishly through the boxes until I found the files I was looking for, one marked Ray Beale the other Mike Grant. With a bit of a spring in my step I entered the interview room and introduced myself to Ruby.

"Ruby, I have a couple of photographs here I was wondering if you could tell me if you have seen them before, or more than that recently?"

I passed the two photographs over the table to where she was sitting.

Ruby looked at them carefully then said;

"This one is Ray Beale although he has a beard now and that one is Mike Grant, and he has a goatee. They both came to the motel and booked in under assumed names, but something twigged with me and although I was not one hundred percent, seeing these photos now, I can say with surety that was them." She continued staring at the two photographs, took a breath and said;

"The thing that was strange the vehicle they had driven in with had Colorado plates but neither of them was from that state according to their booking cards."

I breathed a deep breath and sighed deeply, looked at Hal with a look of disdained and said;

"Hell has returned, and we are in for another string of dead bodies I am sure of it."

Hal looked at me with furrowed brow and I could see in his eyes that I was correct, and this town is going to suffer all over again. I thanked Ruby for her helped and asked if it would be okay if we came to the motel and searched their room. Ruby had no objections as long it was not going to get her in trouble. I decided there and then I would toddle off over to the courthouse and apply for a warrant on what we know and then the search if it came to court would be legal. I was glad I was doing this it made it more realistic and this time I wanted these two bastards.

The other thing on my mind was if we managed to engulf these two, they may give up the other ring leaders to save their own skin. I know Mike Grant would was an absolute Psychopath and he would not care if things came to a shootout at least in his mind, he would think that he had beaten us. Ray Beale on the other hand was an absolute squib and would have no hesitation in giving up whomever to save his skin although, I was going to make sure he suffered for what he had caused this town all those years ago. I reached the courthouse, and went ahead to the Registrars desk, asking who the duty judge was today, he replied;

"Judge Morton." Fuck I thought to myself he was like a bloody rock and hardnosed arsehole who needed all the paperwork to be in absolute watertight order before he would even give a warrant a second thought. I looked at the Registrar and asked;

"Is he free?"

"Yes, he is in chambers, do you want to see him?"

I nodded and he turned and headed for a rear door. After what seemed a lifetime, he returned and said;

"The Judge will see you now as it is convenient with him if that is alright with you?" Convenient I thought, what a bloody joke, this upstart Judge must think his shit doesn't stink like the rest of us. I walked down the white linoleum polished hallway to the large oak door with the name plate slid into holder, Judge Morton, Presiding Judge.

I knocked and entered, the Judge was seated behind a large desk covered with papers and coffee cups.

"Do you not wait for permission to enter my chambers!" he exclaimed.

I quickly turned and went out again slamming the door behind me, thinking you fucking upstart. I knocked again and waited for the permission to enter which was delayed so I knocked again and this time the word,

"Enter" echoed from inside.

"Next time you want to see me Farrer, I suggest an appointment would be appropriate, and less of your theatrics as you showed by going back out when you were already in my chambers."

I looked at him and took a deep breath so as not to antagonise him as I was fuming under the collar, this is the

317

judge who let murderers off with life and half pied sentences when they should have the death penalty. Although Capital punishment is still legal penalty in Montana. The death penalty has not been handed down for some time. The last time the state sentenced a defendant to death was in 1996 and he is still on death row.

"What do you want Farrer?" he asked in a non-polite manner.

"I need a warrant to execute a search of a room at the motel as there are two suspects in town who were part of the murderous group that caused havoc years ago, and the demons are back in town already causing problems. They have killed one of my junior officers and I am not in a good mood."

He asked;

"Did I have the paperwork in order?" I stated;

"Hal would drop it in within the hour would he sign off on it."

He looked at me those narrow black eyes and sighed;

"I will grant the warrant if all is order, and knowing Hal that would be a given. But you that would be another thing again as you seem to forget the full detail in your applications."

I thought you arrogant prick, said thankyou and left as I was glad to get out of that office before, I blew a gasket. I returned across the street and took a little time to breath in the clean crisp air and to clear my head after that little fracas. He may well be respected but he can be a proper pain in the arse. I walked slowly back to our building and

318

climbed the stairs to the offices and sought out Hal. I explained what had just happened and he laughed;

"He can be cantankerous old arse at times, but he knows his stuff."

Hal agreed he would get the warrant typed up and across to the courthouse so Morton could sign it as I wanted to be in that room today. If there was anything, anything at all that would convince me more and give unquestionable evidence on Grant and Beale I was up for it. Although I had files galore and evidence up the jacksy for a conviction the more, I had the more the District Attorney can push for the death penalty. I was not going to let these two murderous fucks get away again. I phoned Andrew to see if they had the vehicle out of the lake yest and was it on the way back to our garage, also had he or Colin found anything at all at the Store and gas station. Just then I remembered I still had the torn page of the phonebook in my pocket, I unfolded it and perused the names to see if I could find a clue as to who the two may have been looking for.

10

Back at Bernie's Ray had found a bottle another bottle of Glenfiddich and was quietly trying to drown his nerves and think what their next move was. Mike in the meantime was searching through the house for any gun and ammunition or money. He found two sets of car keys, one to a Ford Explorer and the other to a Camaro. He wondered where they were parked unless they were in the barn way at the other end of the property down past the glasshouse. He threw down his last drop of whisky and said,

"He was going for a walk to the barn at the end of the property."

"What is there?" asked Ray.

"Two vehicles and I will find the best one for us to use, while I am gone you had better think about what we are going to do about those two in the glasshouse, and quick."

Mike left the room with Ray rolling the glass of whiskey between his palms, thinking what a bloody mess this whole thing had become, and why those years ago did he ever get involved. He had a good business, making good money was free and easy, lovely home a bit on the side and all was good. Then Steven Shaw approached him and told him how he could make a mint from being the carrier of the goods they brought into the town and help to distribute them. Why the fuck did he not just say no. He heard the back door close and with that he stood up and decided he was going to do nothing about the two bodies in the glasshouse, not just yet anyway.

He walked quickly to the back door and went out onto the porch and could see Mike off in the distance past the glasshouse and following a pathway come road down to what looked like a barn some distance away. He went down the steps and followed Mike, bottle of whisky in hand, taking mouthfuls every so often, thinking maybe if he got drunk, he would wake up and this nightmare might be over. Why did he even come back here, why did he let Mike talk him into this as things had not gone as planned and in the back of his mind, he had this gnawing feeling that all was not going to be good.

He caught up to Mike just as they reached the barn. It was locked but Mike had found a bunch of keys, and he gathered that one of them must be for the barn and the others for the house, car and that shed they were in at the start. Mike tried the keys he found the one that fitted the lock, he turned the key, the lock opened they pulled back the door they're staring at them was a Ford and Camaro. Looking around Mike found a screwdriver, he began to undo the plates on the Ford. He then undid the plates on the Camaro and placed the Ford plates on the Camaro. Ray watched this whole time not really taking in what Mike was doing, but then he had almost half a bottle of Glenfiddich on board at this stage.

Mike got into the Camaro and started it up, fired straight away and he pointed to Ray to open the door right up so he could drive it out. Ray pushed the door open, and Mike slowly drove the car out into the late afternoon sunlight. The sun reflected the dust on the bonnet of the Camaro and as he got out of the car he said to Ray;
    "Close and lock the door again."
Ray quickly closed the door up and pushed the bolt across and clicked the lock closed. He went to the passenger's side of the car and got in, Mike got back in and drove up

to the house parking the car at the rear as close to the rear porch as was possible so that it could not be seen from the front of the house.

They both entered the house and went into the kitchen retrieved the bags from the table and went and placed them in the trunk of the car, returning inside again.

"We need to find something to eat and then rest before we decide what to do. We are going to have to bury those two in the glasshouse before we leave otherwise, they will be found, and we do not want that," remarked Mike.

Ray searched the kitchen for some food and the refrigerator, there was little in the way of food and Ray wondered whether Bernie ate out a lot or was planning to go to town to do some shopping at some stage. Meanwhile Mike got out a map from the bookshelf in the living room and was looking at the best and quickest way from here to the border and onto Canada. They did not have much time, and they also had to fix up Shaw and Forrester as well, they would become a problem if they knew Ray and Mike were back in town.

Ray finally found a couple of cans of tomatoes and baked beans; he opened them and placed them in a saucepan on the stove. He had one last mouthful of the whiskey and gone ahead to heat up the food. He found plates and forks and set them on the table. He called to Mike who came in just as Ray served up an amount of the food onto each plate, Mike sat at the end of the table and filled his glass with a good half of whiskey.

"You know we must get rid of Shaw and Forrester before we leave, as they know or should I say did know where the bags where hidden. If they go looking and realise, we have beaten them to it they could very well spill the whole plan and what was going on at the Old Mill?"

Ray looked at him with bleary eyes, he had had too much to drink and the food although good was not helping his thinking.

"Why don't we just piss off North and cross the border and fuck them!" he exclaimed in a slurry tone.

"We cannot go without fixing them up or making good on the deal either way we must make sure of what was agreed upon, is carried out."

Mike was looking at Ray when he said this as well as trying to eat and keep his thoughts clear. Ray bleated;

"We cannot just kill them for fucks sake, there has been enough killing already, and we have two in the glasshouse one we know what happened the other well the mind boggles at what went on there."

Ray had found and cooked some potatoes and carrots and had dished them up along with the tomatoes and baked beans. They ate in silence and continued to drink the whiskey. Mike pushed his plate away from him he had cleaned it up, Ray was still slowly finishing his, when Mike said;

"We bury Bernie in a deep grave with the woman in the glasshouse and leave them there. No-one will find them for a couple of days, and we will be clear and free by then. I will contact Shaw and tell him to get Forrester and meets us at the disused boat ramp near the causeway and we go

323

from there what the next step will be. You had better grow a backbone Ray, as this whole thing could get very fucking messy quick."

Ray cleared up the dishes from the table and washed them over the sink including the pots. He made sure he was still using the rubber gloves, put the dishes away and the empty cans in the rubbish under the sink. Meanwhile Mike was wiping down all the surfaces in the rooms where they had been even though he and Ray had worn gloves all the time he was leaving nothing to chance. He knew the CSI's would look for anything that could show as to whom was at the house. He had made the mistake with the SUV in not wiping everything before pushing it into the lake but thought by the time they find it, the water will have cleaned any tell-tale signs. As for the Jeep he had planned to put that around the back for now and then park it in the barn with the Ford. It may come to pass that Ray may have to take the Ford and go one way while he in the Camaro the other both with different plates, although from the same owner's registration. He should swap the Jeep plates to the Ford to really throw everyone off the scent, although he knew Farrer was like a starving cougar with a catch in its mouth, once he got a taste of something he was not going to let it go no matter what.

Ray entered the living room just as Mike was finishing. He folded the maps and made sure the books were placed back as he had found them. He then told Ray to take the Jeep down to the barn and put those plates on the Ford but leave both cars in the barn for the time being. He was going to start to bury what was in the glasshouse, and as soon as he had changed the plates wiped down everything again and relocked the barn, meet him in the glasshouse. Ray obliged and went to the Jeep out front and went ahead towards the barn. In the meantime, Mike picked up his phone and dialled Shaw's number.

11

The two officers, Deputy Sherriff's Brent Cotterill and David Coventry, who were tasked with checking properties on the Eastern side of the lake had started with the Jones property, which was about ten-mile North of Talon point and a mile South of the Causeway crossing. The property was well back off the main road about two three-mile in. Luckily, there was no properties of the Western side of the road as it followed the lake closely up until about a mile from Talon Point when there were just a couple of houses on the lake itself. As they drove up to the house there was someone on an ATV coming towards them, they stopped and asked if he had seen anybody suspicious or a Jeep around anywhere. Jed Jones replied;

"No nothing but I am going over to the Patterson place to check on their house for them as they are coming up this weekend from the big smoke. If I see anything I will be sure to let you know, I will call the station."

The two Deputies swung the cruiser around and followed Jones out the gate onto the main road. He went along on the grass as they left him to check on the Patterson place. They passed the roadside letterbox of the Patterson's and Brent looked in the rear-view mirror as Jones turned into the driveway. The next place was that of old Jack Nutton, he was a cantankerous old bloke who kept to himself, but they had cause to have a visit with him due to illegal traps he had set a while back, he was as mad as a hatter.

What the reception they would get could be anybody's guess. They discussed their tactics with each other how to manage him as they had been there at least twice before. His house was much closer to the main road only five-hundred yards in and could be seen easily from the road. As they approached old Jack appeared on the porch at the front door shotgun in hand, this was not going to go down well.

"Don't bother getting out of the car or you may wear a load buckshot up your arse," was shouted from the porch. Brent turned on the loudspeaker and said they only wanted to ask if he had seen any strangers hanging around in the past two or three days. The old man retorted;

"No, now fuck off." The two deputies were not going to push their luck so backed the cruiser into the small park behind them and swung the vehicle towards the gate. They had to take Jack at his word as he would have shot anyone he did not know or did not want anything to do with. He was the sort of fellow that shot first then asked questions if you were still able to speak that is. They made a note of the calls made in their log on the computer in their vehicle and went ahead to the next property. Here they were hoping they received a better reception than the last one.

This property belonged to Greg Manns the diner owner. His wife would be home as she did not work at present as she was six months pregnant with their first child. This house was also set back on a long drive two mile in, but it had a small cabin halfway along which the couple rented out to skiers during the winter and holiday makers in the Spring and Summer breaks. Nice couple down to earth and very pleasant, the two deputies wondered how they got on with their cantankerous old neighbour, although knowing Greg he would not hesitate to protect his family if the old bugger did cause trouble.

They slowly drove up to the house, alighted from the vehicle, and approached the front door, opening the screen door first and knocking on the hand carved wooden door proper. Soon a pretty, very pregnant Vicky Manns answered the door;

"Can I help you?" she asked.

"We are wanting to know if you have seen any strangers or out of place vehicles in the vicinity in the past two to three days?" David asked.

"No sorry I haven't but I am sure I would have heard something if they had come up the driveway as Greg has just had the new gravel laid and it makes a noise when it is walked or driven on." she replied.

The two Deputies looked at each other then turned and saw that yes there was new gravel, but they had not noticed any crunching as they drove up, but then again, they were discussing old Jack and the confrontation with him.

They thanked her and made sure to tell her and to pass it onto Greg that if they did see or hear anything to let the station know. She nodded in agreement and thanked them for coming around. Both turned and headed back to the car as Vicky closed the door behind them, there was a bit of smack as the screen door closed hard. In the vehicle they made a not they had questioned her and what was said. They then went ahead around the curved horseshoe and headed out the driveway and that is when they did notice the crackling sound of the driveway gravel.

It was getting late, and their shift was coming to an end, they still had Bernie Talbertson's place and the holiday home of a couple who were from Washington state to visit, but they decided to call it and begin again in the morning. They noticed the cones and the road markings where the vehicle was in the lake on the right near to the Old Mill and wondered if that would come of anything. There had been a lot of chatter on the radio all day about it. The sun was getting low in the Western sky and made a shimmering effect on the lakes surface, as they drove down past Talbertson's driveway and then on past the Reiner's place. They passed the four houses to the North of Talon point and through the village heading towards the Old Mill. Brent said;

"Should we give the Old Mill a once over before we head to town just to make sure all is still lock and secure?" David nodded in agreement, and they drove up to the Old Mill, got out and checked the gate was still chained and locked and there was no sign of life beyond the gate, other than the Security Guard off to the left who had been placed on watch of the place.

He waved to them from his vehicle as they drove the cruiser back onto the main road.

"Should he not be inside the gates? Asked Brent,

"I know I would feel a bloody lot safer if I was behind a chained and locked gate considering someone got shot their recently." David replied;

"We might raise it with boss when we get back, I agree it would be a safer bet to behind a barricade than in the open like he is. Even if they set up in the main building and did hourly walk arounds would be safer."

They drove on down around the South Arm and headed back into town, where they parked the car at the back of the building and went ahead into the office. David asked;

"Did you get our logs we sent about those we had visited?"

The desk clerk nodded and laughed aloud about their run in with old Jack. Brent said they would continue tomorrow that they have two properties to check out and the houses by the lake on your way into Talon Point. He nodded in agreement and the two went back to the locker room to change and finish for the night. In the locker room was a group of the detectives all talking about the vehicle and how it was found and the two men that were wanted because of it. The two deputies looked at each other with an unknowing glance;

"Fucking Beale and Grant are back in town," shouted David.

"Do you mean to tell me that who we are looking for in the door to door we are doing on the other side of the lake." Just then I walked in and looked them up and down, before uttering a word they knew I was not happy with their outburst.

"Yes, that is who we are looking for and we want them badly so please do not go shooting the fuckers until we have had a chance to question them. Remember, they shot one of your fellow Deputies and were involved with the murders of those young women and the fellow police officer a few years back. So do your job and make sure you check everywhere, barns, out buildings, shithouses, anywhere they might be."

They got the message and replied sheepishly;

"We had no luck today but will take it up first thing in the morning. Boss would it not be better if that security guard at the Old Mill was inside the locked gates instead of outside on the side of the road?"

I had to agree that would be a better proposition and said;

"I will give them a set of keys to give to the guy in the morning." I turned and left for the day.

12

Mike stood up from the chair he was sitting on and said down the phone in no uncertain terms to whomever was on the other end,

"You be at the causeway turnoff to 41 tomorrow at two and bring that lousy fucker Forrester with you, do you understand?"
He slammed the phone down and went ahead out to the glass house and stretched his back as he walked towards the door. Inside the glasshouse he moved one set of shelves off to the right and another to the left leaving the two bodies exposed in the centre. He started to dig the ground was quite soft and was a kind of sandy loam it made for easy work, he started to wonder where hell had Beale got to, he had a simple job to do, change some plates, park the Jeep in the barn, and lock it up.

"Shit", he is useless he thought to himself. Along with Shaw and Forrester he may go also tomorrow into the dark depths of the lake. Beale had finally completed what he was asked to do and was on his way back to the glasshouse, thoughts pounding in his head, why did he get mixed up with this Psychopath, and he goes and murders the one real person who could have helped them out of this mess. Shaw and Forrester for sure were not going to have any part of Bernie's murder and were more than likely to shun both he and Mike for what Mike had done. He finally reached the glasshouse and went in through the door, Mike stood up quick gun in hand,

"Fuck, knock next time, I could have blown a hole in you." Ray stepped back quickly at the sight of the gun being pointed at him and was not sure if Mike would pull the trigger and dig a hole big enough for all three bodies. Mike threw the shovel at him and said;

"Keep digging, I will find another shovel, and some lime or fertiliser in here, there should be some considering it is a glasshouse for growing shit."
Ray caught the shovel with both hands, moved over and started to dig, the hole was going to need to be at least four feet wide and six or seven foot long.
Mike returned with another shovel and a bag of something over his shoulder. Both began digging and the hole was finally finished and even if they say so themselves it was a good depth and both bodies would fit comfortably in it. Mike got Bernie's limp body and rolled him into the hole and then pulling on the sheet rolled the woman's body in beside Bernie.

"He must have killed his wife. I am at a loss as to why they always seemed so happy." remarked Ray;
Mike did not answer, he grabbed the bag of whatever he had found out the back of the glasshouse and spread it evenly over the two bodies, then with the sheet the woman was wrapped in he covered them and said to Ray;

"Fill it in and make sure as you go that you stamp the soil down hard with the back of your shovel so as the dirt consolidates".

Ray obliged and started to spread the dirt over the bodies, it did not take long for him to finish the job. The extra soil he spread around the floor of the glasshouse as Mike started to move the shelves back into place to the approximate position they were in when he first moved them. After repositioning the shelves, he grabbed the broom and swept the floor gently to cover up their footsteps and the furrows made by the shelves being moved. It was getting dark now and they needed to get back inside. They had to fumble around in the dark inside the house as they looked for light switches which they had not even thought about placing before they started their little escapade outside.

Finally, Mike found a lamp and switched it on thinking that may be all they need at present as it would be normal for Bernie to only have minimal lights on not the whole house lit up like Times Square. They decided may be two or three would be more realistic. Ray went upstairs to look around and hoped to find a reason Bernie would kill his wife. In the master bedroom he found bottles of tablets on the bedside table, he could see to turn the lamp on by the now setting sun and moonlight slowly shimmering its way through the window at the head of the bed.

Downstairs Mike had gone into Bernie's study looking for a safe, guns, whatever he could find. He found files and papers on the desk, which he shuffled through slowly and came upon one file that piqued his interest. It was marked, "Shaw Developments," he slowly perused the contents, and realised he had stumbled onto something that was of great interest and now he had ammunition on Shaw. He realised Shaw and Forrester had been double crossing all the others connected with what had happened years ago. The bastards were creaming excess off the top of the money they were making from the drugs, and they had made millions which Beale and himself had not seen one penny more of than what Shaw told them. He was fuming and could not wait to tell Ray as this was going to make him go Psycho.

When Mike told Ray about his find, even though they had something like two million in the plastic bags there was according to the paperwork another five to seven million due to the other guys in equal shares. Though he was not happy about Mike and his hot-headed attitude as far as killing anyone, this was different, and he would not hesitate if Shaw gave him one excuse blow him away. He remarked Shaw and Forrester had better turn up at the meeting at the causeway and if they do not give a good reason for what they had been up to then they would be floating down the tributary and into the lake with a bullet in the head. After Beale was told what the other two had been up to, Mike and Ray went into the basement where there was a cache of weapons and ammunition in speciality type cupboards along the three walls facing them from the doorway. It just looked like something out a James Bond movie and what "Q" would be showing 007 before an assignment. Mike quickly threw the plans on the table in the centre of the room over the top of weapons Ray had already spread on the table.

Ray perused the plans with a very engaging gaze and looked up at Mike and was going red in the face with anger when he realised what he was really looking at.

"What the fuck is all this really?" he asked Mike.

"Well mate our so-called friends have been swindling us out of a fortune, if you look in the file, you will see that they skimmed about seven million off us, and we knew nothing. Ray saw the plans for the hotel development at the ski field that Shaw and Forrester had plans for with their money."

"That is why those two arseholes oversaw all the money and never explained to us what was happening or where the money was going only what they told us was out share. All the work we did and the people they got us to get rid of to throw the coppers off our trail as to what was really happening."

Ray, paused and seethed with anger before anything else was said. There was a pregnant pause and silence in that basement before Ray in a very violent tone;

"Those pair of fucks are going to get their due when we meet, I hope that they both turn up and we can get straight answers as I will have no worries in taking them out, but not before we get our money."

Mike nodded in agreement and looked at Ray with a knowing look that it was going to be a pleasure to make those two squirm to get the information they needed. As the time slipped on Ray went to the kitchen to prepare food and find that bottle of whiskey they had started to drink. Mike in the meantime rolled up the plans and started to sort out what weapons they would take and looked for a bag to collect them in. He had a spring in his step at the thought of what tomorrow may bring.

Meanwhile Ray had found steak in the Freezer and was taking mouthfuls of whiskey as the steak was thawing out in the microwave. He had also found tomatoes and other things to go with a good steak meal. He could hear Mike whistling down in the basement with the occasional smack of metal on metal as he must be collecting weapons of his choice. Ray smiled to himself knowing that things were about to take a turn for the better, although they were not out of the woods yet, but tomorrow was a new day and the sun would be shining he hoped.

13

Next day there was a light drizzle falling with the grey sky looking ominous as if we were in for a real storm or two later. Then there was a sweet smell of bacon cooking close and that took away the feeling of doom and gloom as I entered the diner to grab a coffee before heading to the office. Coffee in hand, walked slowly along the grey coloured pavement which ironically was the colour of the sky and that made for a real feeling of dismay. Upon reaching the station front door I glanced across the lake and thunderous clouds were building up over the top of the ranges and an uneasy feeling came over me quickly.

I turned and pushed the door open, entered slowly and passed the reception desk where the duty sergeant nodded his head in a type of greeting. I headed for the elevator to take me to the floor where the offices and conference rooms were, as I did so I was wondering what Grant and Beale really did come back for and what was so important that they had to return to the mine, as well as why in hell kill an innocent police officer whilst he was only performing his duty. I sat my coffee on the desk in the conference room and looked at the evidence board we also knew as our conspiracy board or crazy wall, or our murder map, of what we had recovered from the old files and what had been gathered from this new evidence. Laying on the table was the Forensic results of the vehicle pulled from the lake as well as the autopsy results from the young officer. The vehicle had no noteworthy evidence as it had been in the water for too long and the documents found in the glove compartment were the registration and insurance papers for the vehicle belonging to a Donald C. Barret of Denver, Colorado. We had contacted him and found that the vehicle had been stolen and was reported as such to the Denver Police. Luckily, they had sent a copy of the Police report to us.

The autopsy for the officer was that he was shot with a nine-millimetre handgun and the shell found at the scene and the bullet retrieved was from the murder of Eugene Barrelli eight years ago in this very office building in the downstairs toilets. McLean the officer in charge at the time was found guilty of that murder, he also cut Eugene's heart out to prove a point to me. I also remember the words in Latin somewhere from those days *"mens reus, acteus reus"* (Guilty mind, Guilty act), which really did say exactly what was happening at the time. I wondered how the gun managed to be in the hands of Ray Beale and Mike Grant, but then remembered they were in deep with McLean at the time so that solved that small question within my thoughts. I looked back at the board and tried to make sense of reality as to what Beale and Grant were up to and who else was involved. I slowly sipped the warm sweet coffee and suddenly my thoughts drifted back to those gruesome times and how my drinking and complete disregard for authority not only got me fired but put more of my team at the time in danger as well as nearly destroying what self-worth I had left. Just then Hal walked in saying,

"Morning boss, here are the full notes typed up from the interview I had with Ruby from the motel. You know a bit and the search I conducted there was nothing in their room but two bags of clothes and a folder of maps and information booklets on Canada."

A hole develops in the pit of my stomach, these two were going to get away with what they had done here in town again and piss off to Canada and be out of reach again. Then, I realised they had not finished here, because if they were why ditch the vehicle. My mind racing into overdrive, I looked back at our murder map and realised they would

338

need to be in contact with the brains behind the whole operation in the past, as these two did not have the capabilities or the money to conduct an operation of that size. It still puzzled me what the 'Dante' thing and the 'Tic Tac Toe' markings had to do with it all or was it just a smoke screen to cover up the drugs and illegal transportation, exploitation and organ harvesting from those women that went on.

I told Hal to put up all the photos of the earlier victim's autopsy photographs as this all had to tie in somehow with the case now. In doing this I was hoping to get read a read on who may be still involved here in town with what Beale and Grant were up to. Hal handed over the file on the interview with Ruby and as I read the information, I noticed she described another who had arrived at the motel on the same day but a bit later and was checked into the room above Beale and Grant. The gentleman's name was Ashley Collins from San Diego. I asked Hal had he any information the guy, he replied

"No, but I have contacted San Diego Law enforcement, FBI, DEA, etc to see what they come back with."
He looked at pains to tell me he had found out nothing, but I told him to keep on it as it may be something. I returned to my office with the files to peruse the information more thoroughly and try to connect the dots. It was like a large jigsaw that we had three parts of the border complete, but the internals were still unrelated pieces that just did not seem to fit. I also read the coroner's report from James Simmons and in it he described how the bullet had

penetrated the left chest and heart. Death was almost instantaneous.

I thought to myself thank God for that that he did not suffer any prolonged pain, his report was extremely thorough, and it was refreshing to see that, as he was new to our team. Colin's report was also incredibly detailed in its entirety on the motor vehicle and although there was no forensics available, we now know that it was stolen, but more than that it was a stolen vehicle, and we knew who had stolen it. As to why was still to be answered, although I had my suspicions it was to throw off any investigation from anyone connected with Beale and Grant, but that did not work out well for them. Ray Barry entered my office and sat opposite me.

"I have been looking at the board and trying to fit together the evidence we had, I may be going out on a limb here, but I believe also, looking back through the earlier files there was interest in Dean Forrester and Steven Shaw. Could they be the money men behind that whole operation?" He paused, then continued, "At the time we ruled them out as there was not enough to really go on, but it still bugs me how well-oiled and prepared the whole thing was, as well as it would have taken a huge amount of collateral to get the whole thing up and running". He paused, looked at me with a quizzical look then continued:

"Ray Beale and Mike Grant certainly would not have had the nous or money to get the whole operation off the ground, or the contacts or even the balls to envisage such an operation. But that is my thoughts and professional opinion only, take it how you see it."

I sat quietly for a moment, thinking deeply about what Ray had just said and it made sense, I could not for the life of me though figure out why we did not pursue those two further when we were conducting the earlier investigations. It had always gnawed at me that there were still outstanding strings attached to that whole scenario. I said to him,

"Ray go with your gut feeling on this, do not make it known you are looking into the two of them but on the discreet side of things look at phone records, bank statements etc." He nodded and left the office.

I rung downstairs to find out whether the two officers who were checking the properties on the other side of the lake had returned with any news. The desk officer told me that they still had properties to check and that they were following up on that this morning. I wanted them to report to me anything and I mean anything that was out of the ordinary. I had this feeling that Beale and Grant were still in the area, and they had unfinished business, which was going to cause me grief as whatever they were up to would come back and bite me on the arse as sure as my arse pointed to the ground. I rang Katrina to just say hi, as I was feeling a little on the gloomy side given the weather and we were no closer to solving this case or even knowing where we were at with the whole thing. All we had was a drowned stolen SUV and a murdered Deputy Turner, a break in at a disused mill and two men who had attachments to earlier murders and abductions, as well as trying to kill another woman more recently when they tried to run Sally Donald off the road when she recognised them both. My mind was racing, and I needed fresh air as well as a coffee, I left the building and strolled slowly towards the diner, with drizzle still falling but the dark clouds were accumulating heavier now, and I was sure there was a storm about to breach the quiet of sleepy lake. I reached the diner just as a clap of thunder belted out and the large windows of the diner rattled then there was a flash of lightening and another roll of thunder. The drizzle now turned to rain and became heavier, bugger I uttered to myself as I had left my umbrella and jacket in the office. I walked across the diner floor and ordered a coffee black no sugar to the barista who smiled and said;

"Not nice weather today," I nodded in agreement. I received my coffee and decided I would sit at the front window overlooking the lake and glance through the newspaper lying on the table. It did not have news I thought but then again, my mind was not really looking for anything as there was more going on in my mind than what the news was reporting. The storm was getting worse, and I cursed at it and decided to make a run for the office hoping not to get to drenched.

As I reached the office front door, underneath the veranda, I noticed a black Camaro parked on the opposite side of the road with the passenger's window slightly down and the engine was running as there was condensation coming from the exhaust, thinking to myself what a stupid thing to do with the rain coming from the direction it was would be going right into the vehicle and why sit there with the engine running, but then again they may have been waiting on someone to come out of the shops on that side of the road. There was a sudden flash from the top of the window and a sudden crunch above my head into the brick wall and another hit then with small pieces of brick falling around me, there was a sudden squeal of tyres and the black Camaro raced off into the distance through the rain, I was unable to get a plate but the vehicle was distinctive and surely there could not be many of them around this town. I was shaken and for some moments did not have my wits about me. I was sure that what had happened was shots fired and I was the fucking target.

14

Morning had arrived and Ray Beale sat in the kitchen of Bernie's place as Mike entered with coffee mug in hand;

"Shitty weather, but today we will meet with those two arseholes and get this over with so we can get the hell out of this town. But first I have a little surprise task to perform first."

Ray looked at him with a look of bewilderment and one of questioning what was he thinking. Mike went over to the bags on the sideboard and pulled out a rifle and silencer, he loaded a magazine into it and then with a snarl;

"Today I make amends with Farrer, he has to pay for fucking up the plans and making our lives hell." Ray sat in complete silence then said;

"Your mad, you bastard how are you going to get to him, he is a bloody police officer. What are you going to do just walk into the cop station and shoot it up until you find him then shoot him, hoping you get out alive?"

"No, you dickhead I am going to sit in the car while you drive and await my chance when he comes out." Mike said with a supreme air of authority about him.
Ray gasped;

"Why do I have to drive or even be involved in such a bullshit idea", Mike looked at him with a sneer on his face;

"I have been planning this all night and you are in this with me up to your neck, so yes, you are going to drive me and wait with me for our chance to kill this fucker".

"We changed the plates on the Camaro to use as a getaway car and now you are going to use it as a murder vehicle. What are we going to use to get away once we have dealt with Shaw and Forrester?"
Ray asked in a high-pitched voice.

"You changed the plates from the Jeep to the Ford did you not, that will be our vehicle."
Ray nodded but was feeling very unsafe about this whole thing. He was not looking forward to killing another person as there had been enough killing and Ray could really see no sense of killing Farrer, as that to him was suicide with a capital "S". Mike went outside and placed the rifle in the back seat of the Camaro, returned inside to the kitchen and finished his mug of coffee.

"We do Farrer at about eleven this morning then hide up at the causeway until three for Shaw and Forrester."

"How do you know they will turn up if they hear about Farrer in the meantime," Ray asked. Mike just looked at him with a look that made Ray shudder;

"They had better turn up because I do not want to have to go looking for them."

This was the worst Ray had seen Mike and he had never really seen him this angry or so determined to do anything. The rain was now very heavy, and Ray wondered whether this was a bad omen for what they

had planned to do today, although he knew that once they had completed everything they would be on their way to the border, Canada, and freedom.

At ten o'clock Mike told Ray to collect himself and meet him at the car, it was time. Ray went and collected his coat and headed out through the backdoor towards the porch and down the back steps to the car. He went around to the driver's side door and got into the car. Mike was already in the passenger's seat with the rifle between his legs. He had a smirk on his face and looked incredibly pleased with himself at what his intentions were. Ray started the car and they drove around to the front of the house and down the driveway towards the main road. At the end of the driveway, they turned left and headed South towards Talon Point and the Old Mill. Just as they passed the driveway next door, they noticed a patrol car heading up towards the house. Ray wondered why they would be visiting there as there was no one living there permanently, and the owners only came there some weekends and during the holiday periods. They kept on a steady pace as they passed through Talon Point and then the Old Mill, on towards the South Arm and around the bend heading North to town. On arriving in town, they found a car park right opposite the front door of the Police Station and noticed Farrer was walking heading towards the diner further down the street. Mike rubbed his hands together and Ray thought to himself, that Mike was not going to do this in the diner. The rain was much heavier now and there was thunder and flashes of lighting, which Ray felt uncomfortable about. Luckily there was tinting on the side and rear windows of the Camaro so they were hidden from both sides and the rear, but where they were parked there was no real reason to think anybody would look in from the front as there was nothing parked in front, and the next car park was the other side of the driveway to the rear of the florist shop and the ski shop.

It seemed like hours as they set there awaiting Farrer to return, and Mike was becoming more and more agitated. Ray put the wipers on to clear the windscreen, but the rain was heavy, and they battled to clear it fully with one sweep of the blades. There was no-one on the street on either side but then why would there be as it was raining so bloody heavy why would anyone be so stupid to be out in this. The door to the ski shop opened and a man quickly ran out and crossed behind the car to the other side of the road and climbed into a vehicle parked there. Ray held his breath that it was no-one who would recognise the vehicle they were in. Time was going so slow, and Ray wondered whether Farrer would return to the office this way or from the back entrance but that would mean he needed to go around a block to get to the back door and in this rain, he would not be that stupid. Mike was really agitated and was mumbling to himself something that was incoherent to Ray. Ray was starting to get agitated as well and knowing he should not say anything but did anyway;

"Mike, do you think this is a good idea today of all days why do we not come back some other time?", as soon as he said it, he regretted it as Mike threw him a look of complete anger and there was rage in his eyes. Mike grab at Ray's neck with his left hand and squeezed hard, scaring Ray. Mike shouted or so it seemed;

"If you have not got the balls for this then get of the car now and walk away but remember this you had better make yourself scarce as the next one on my list will be you."
Ray slinked back against the door of the car as Mike let go of his neck and returned to looking out the window at the front door of the police station. Mike adjusted the rear-view mirror so he could see out the back window also to see when Farrer may be returning. It was getting on in time and Ray was not game to say another word or to even move just in case Mike retaliated in a forceful manner as he had just done. Ray had not seen Mike like this in all the years he had known him and was wondering what had snapped inside him to make him like this. Was there something he was not telling Ray and the way he ordered Shaw to make sure Forrester turned up at the causeway also flashed into his mind. Was Mike going to kill those two as well, his mind raced with doubts as well as questions, but dare not to think about it too long.

Mike again looked at his watched and said;

"What the fuck is taking him so long, it does not take this long to get a bloody coffee. Come on Farrer you bastard return to your place where revenge will be sweet." Ray looked at him and knew then that this was more than just revenge more like a vendetta and there was going to be bloodshed whichever way this went down.

Suddenly Mike sat up straight and placed the rifle barrel just below the window and opened it making a small gap the rain came in but that did not seem to worry Mike. Ray looked in the side mirror of the car and saw Farrer half walking half running across the road and then lost sight of him.

"Be ready to go when I say said Mike," and Ray put the vehicle into gear. Mike raised the rifle up and aimed it across the street lowering the window just slightly and turned himself sideways in the seat to be facing across the street, the barrel was not quite outside the window at this point then as Farrer approached the door, he stopped and looked straight at the car, Mike poked the barrel out the window and let off two shots, neither hit their target, they were above Farrer's head.

Ray hit the accelerator and the car jerked forward sending Mike hard into his seat and the gun hit the window as it retracted back inside the car.

"What the fuck are you doing" Mike shouted;

"I missed the fucker, go around the block I need to get him", Ray ignored him and sped around the corner the car's rear end sliding on the wet road, he took the next turn and sped down the street towards the set of lights they changed to green luckily just as he reached them. Passed the intersection he spun the car hard left and then right back onto the South Arm Road. The car was sliding and fishtailing all over the place on the wet road. Mike had regained his seat properly and belted himself in;

"Go back you fucker I need to finish the job,"

Ray ignored him and continued, then suddenly he felt a sharp pain in the side of his head, Mike had punched him and for a few seconds he was bewildered at what had happened.

"I am not going back, you missed, and he is now aware of someone wanting him dead. I do not care what you want or why you want him dead, I am going back to the house and getting ready for Shaw and Forrester, packing up the Ford and then getting ready to head to the border. You are on your own after that." Ray shouted at Mike.

Ray, almost livid with anger and his head hurt was in no mood for anymore of Mike's hair brain schemes. He wanted out and as soon as he got back to the house, he was grabbing the money leaving Mike with and the drugs and splitting out of there. Mike had gone off the deep end and as far as Ray was concerned, he was not safe to be around.

They reached the Southern Outlet bridge and headed to Pullman's Point, the rain was still heavy, and the wipers were working hard to clear the water. They raced past Pullmans and Lookout Cove the Old Mill, just then a police cruiser came into sight and passed on the opposite side of the road. Ray then remembered that Mike had loaded the bags into the trunk of the Camaro, so there was no need to return to the house, as money, guns, and drugs were in the car. Ray drove through Talon Point and passed the house driveway heading towards the Causeway.

Mike was noticeably quiet, but Ray knew he was angry and that no matter what he said or did was not going to calm him down, so they just drove on in silence. Five mile up the road Ray found a layby off the road and hidden from the road by trees, and he felt this was a safe place to hold up until the time came to meet up with Shaw and Forrester. They had stopped when finally, Mike said something;

"I have not finished with Farrer and I will not be going anywhere until he dead, his family are dead, and anyone connected with him are dead."

"What is going on with you Mike, you do not need to do this and doing anything else is just going to make things worse. Killing Farrer will achieve nothing."

15

The two deputies returned to the office which at this stage was in a stage of high alert as well as disarray with what had just gone down. They came straight to my office to report on their visit to the properties on the far side of the lake. They reported that all was clear except for Bernie Talbertson's which was strange as he was not around, and the place was all open. They reported that they had checked the place and there had been somebody there and that

Bernie's basement had been ransacked as was his upstairs. They checked the sheds but could not get into them as they were locked and the glasshouse also. There were fresh tyre marks around the back leading to the front and then heading for the driveway, but no sign of Bernie. They did not call it in as he may well have just been down at Talon Point or here in town, so they thought they would check with me first and maybe get some more men on the job to find him or what had happened.

I blew my stack at them and told them to get back out there and check everything break into the fucking sheds etc., if you must, but find him. I also asked if they knew anyone with a black Camaro and they said that Bernie owned one. I was livid by now and explained that someone in a black Camaro had just taken two shots at me out the front of the station. Then they told me they had passed the black Camaro when they were returning to the office but really paid no attention to it. They knew I was pissed at them, and they quickly headed out of the office and knew they had their arses in a sling. I then rang Hal, Ray, Bill, and Colin and told them to meet out back at the car park. Then called James and told him to try and see if there were any bullet fragments in the brickwork out front where the shots had hit the wall, he said,

"He was already on the job, but the rain was making it hard to get an unobstructed vision of where the shots hit. I told him;

"Forget the fucking rain just get me results."
He retorted;

"Do not get off your fucking high horse with me, just because some bastard wants you dead."

At that point I realised this case as with the earlier series of murders was getting to my psyche and I knew I had to get a grip or suffer the consequences, such as hitting the bottle and living in a fog all over again. If that happened, it would not be fair on Katrina or the kids. Why had these arseholes decided to return here and, on my watch, causing me all this upset, and brain drain.

This world was not big enough for me and the bastards who were going around killing innocent people for no real possible reason or benefit other than to satisfy a hunger they had to relieve themselves of internal belief they had a right to do what they were doing. Hal, Ray, Bill, and Colin were all in the carpark as asked, and I told Ray, Bill, and Colin to ride in one vehicle Hal and I in the other.

"Where are we going?" they asked;

"To a Bernie Talbertson's place. The Camaro with the person inside the passenger's seat, who shot at me earlier belongs to him, so I want needed answers."

We left the police carpark and headed out onto Endeavour Drive heading for the main road to the South Arm. My mind was racing with what would we find there when we arrived?

The radio squawked into life;

"Boss we are at Bernie's and have surveyed the place, his Camaro is not here but that fella's Jeep that went missing the other day was locked in a shed down the back of the property. The plates on it do not correspond with the

352

registration nor does the Ford that is here, someone has swapped the plates on both vehicles."

The radio went silent, not even a sign of static, my mind racing, suddenly I shouted;

"Fucking Grant and Beale have set up their escape and using this Bernie's vehicles for it."

Hal looked at me and I could by the look in his eyes that said it all, we may have a break that we needed. I now had to think if they were setting up to use those vehicles where was the Camaro and where was Beale and Grant, but more to the point where was Talbertson, or was he a party to all this? We were still a good fifteen minutes from Talbertson's place when the radio again squawked into life;

"You had better get the forensic boys here we have found stuff in the shed as well as in the glasshouse behind the main house. There are freshly made soil marks in the glasshouse, and the soil is mounded up in places. We will not touch anything until you all get here. The house has been tossed badly also."

The radio again went silent, I told Hal to call Andrew and to put on hold anything he was doing and get to the Talbertson place as soon as possible. We sped up and now had lights and sirens going as did the boys in the car following us. We passed Lookout Point and the Old Mill in record time and was soon at the entrance to Bernie's farm's driveway, I quickly turned the car into the entrance and sent it fishtailing slightly on the loose gravel as I put the foot down to accelerate along the long narrow drive.

We soon arrived at the house and alighted from our vehicle, Hal said;

"You can turn the siren and lights off now, we are here." Ray, Bill, and Colin got out of their car as they did Bill said;

"Fuck Farrer, you trying to win some type of rally or something the way you entered the driveway, spraying shit up everywhere," I ignored the comment.

I was more interested in finding out what the Deputies had found in the barn and glasshouse than worrying about what Bill thought of my driving. Andrew grabs his case from the trunk of the car and followed me into the main house, the boys were not wrong the place had been well and truly trashed, stuff everywhere and you could see by other areas of the lounge that Bernie did not keep an untidy house. I went ahead through into the small ante room off the lounge which looked like an office.

I put on a pair of surgical gloves and tried the filing cabinet in the corner it was locked. I then checked the draws of the large oak desk, to see if there was a key, I found a set of keys in the slide out area in the middle of the desk at the top. I continued through the draws which had been opened and rifled and found nothing but letterheads, envelopes, and coloured folders holding accounts etc. The filing cabinet key was not on the keys I had found so it was going to be a job for Andrew to try to open it, as I looked around at the bookshelves lining two sides of the room as well as a single bookshelf on each side of the large window that looked out towards the garden and glasshouse. The shelves had few books left on them the rest were strewn on the floor, magazines also littered the desk and the floor, flower, and plant journals. I left Bill to go through what ever there was in there and told Andrew to try the file cabinet. Hal had gone upstairs, I re-entered the lounge and looked around, photographs of family and of two weddings one looked like Bernie's the other may have been a daughter or sons. Paintings were hanging at a slight angle in some areas, but it was neat other than the cushions from the settee and chairs were spread across the floor, and we had to step over them carefully.

The mantle over the fireplace also had photos although lying flat and ornaments that had been on here, I suspect were now broken on the flagstone hearth of the fireplace, which was also made of flagstone. Each side of the fireplace stood a lion made from white marble and looked to me to be quite heavy in appearance and had not been moved. There was again papers, newspapers and other paraphernalia spread throughout the lounge, it seemed out of place. Heading through an archway into the dining kitchen area, the table was covered in ammunition boxes half full others empty.

They were for a variety of weapons; this made me shiver and a cold chill ran up my spine. The sink had dirty dishes in it as well as on the benches on either side, as well as on the table. There was a fry pan and a pot on the stove which looked like they had been used but had not been cleaned up. I looked back at the table and the sight of all those boxes and live ammunition made me think that Beale and Grant were now well armed and even more dangerous.

16

In the siding where Ray had parked the car he got out and was visibly shaken by what had just happened. He also heard sirens back along the way they had just travelled but they soon stopped, and he thought shit, they are at Bernie's place I would bet on it. Ray pulled out his revolver and checked it, Mike just sat in the passenger's seat door open and lit up a smoke, saying nothing, but with a fierce angry look on his face. Mike in the past days had turn into a narcissistic psychopath, and Ray was worried that he could turn at time on him. His whole demeanour was off, it was not the past or even what had happened over the past years, Ray had not seen him like this and wondered was it returning to Oemen Lake that turned him into this uncontrollable man with a thirst for vengeance against all. Was Ray on his radar to get rid of him too.

Grant finished his smoke took a swill of the whiskey he had placed in the car, and with menace in his voice said;

"We have to move this car nearer the causeway, I heard the sirens and I do not want to be caught with my fucking trousers down, so let's go."

Ray got back into the car and slowly moved out of the layby clear of the trees that had hidden them for the past couple of hours. He was afraid that leaving the place where they had been especially in the daylight risked everything, but he did not want to rock the boat especially with Mike's state at present.

As they drove along, Ray was constantly looking in the rear-view mirror for any sign of a police vehicle as well as looking for a place to stash the car before they met up with Shaw and Forrester. He was starting to wonder whether that was going to happen and whether Shaw and Forrester wanted anything to do with them after so long. What did Shaw and Forrester have to gain by meeting them, then again what did they have to lose if they did not. Ray's mind was racing with scenarios that he had never dreamed of happening and the way Mike was at present was not a good omen.

About a half mile from the causeway entrance Ray saw a car park used for parking up boat trailers after the owners had put their craft in at the boat ramp near to the bridge. He thought this was perfect hide the car and find another that suited the purpose they could use to head for the border, it also suited as there was an exit onto highway North forty-one. As the entered the area Ray remembered vividly that this was also a place where he and that other idiot Drummond placed one of the dead girls beside the boat ramp. Was it wise to again revisit this place? Ray thought that if he was a police officer and he had seen it on television that sometimes killers return to where their victims were, and from that they were able to relive the memory and get a kick out of the feelings all over again.

This Ray automatically dismissed as he was not going to get any kick out of returning to this place and if he had his way he should have been long gone from here altogether once they retrieved the bags from the Old Mill. Why did he not flee and leave Mike to his own little vendetta against Shaw, Forrester and Farrer, Ray did not have any harsh feelings towards them, and he was quite happy to leave well enough alone? Mike said;

"Park over their by that bunch of bushes and try to put the car behind them and that boat trailer."

Ray obliged and was able to manoeuvre the vehicle close by the trees and it was partly hidden by them as well the other vehicle. Mike got out of the car and walked over to the car parked near where they were, it had a dual axle boat trailer attached and was a SUV, so this would suit fine. The owner must have been a very trusting soul as he had left the vehicle open and keys in the ignition. Mike thought for a moment he has just launched his boat and will be back, so he ordered Ray to walk down to the boat ramp and see if there was anybody there and was the coast clear. Ray obeyed and slowly walked out of the carpark and across the road trying to remain hidden by the trees on the roadside and he kept glancing back down the road and back at Mike who had now lit another cigarette. Bloody fool thought Ray may as well send up smoke signals, if there was anyone around, they are going to see the smoke drifting slowly into the air. Ray clasps his pistol which was now neatly seated in his belt at his back, and his right palm became sweaty on the grip.

He reached the edge of the trees and had a clear view of both the boat ramp and the end of the causeway. There was no one in sight either on the causeway or at the boat ramp and he could hear no boat motor engine sounds, so he slowly walked into the open and viewed both left and right, spun on his heel and returned the way he had come back to the car park.

On returning to the vehicle, Mike had the trunk open and was sorting through the weapons he had placed in there the night before, along with the ammunition needed for each. He told Ray to pick out at least three weapons as he may need them if things go south with meeting. Ray was again disturbed at the way Mike said this and thought they were there to meet not for a fucking shoot out at the OK Corral.

He did as Mike ordered and pick up a forty-five and clipped the magazine out, checked it was full, then slid the loader back and ejected the shell that was already in the chamber. He juggled the bullet as it flew out and almost dropped the pistol in the pistol in the process but managed to regain the ejected bullet in his palm and slid it back into the magazine, pushed the magazine back into the handle of the pistol and cocked it to make sure there was one in the chamber then flicked the lever to put it into safety. He repeated this with another and placed one in his belt next to the pistol he already had there and the other in the front to his left in the same manner. Next looking at the multitude of weapons in the trunk he picked up a rifle, flicked out the magazine and made sure it was full, slid it back into the rifle's magazine cavity and put on the safety.

While he was doing this Mike was also loading up guns and placing them in his pockets and then also collected a rifle, Ray thought this not going to be good if they carry a rife down to the causeway for the meeting, Shaw and Forrester will just not get out of the vehicle and flee, they would have an open road to the South or even North, by the time Mike and he got back to their car the two would be long gone.

He asked Mike;

"Are we leaving the rifles in the car or taking them with us?"

"Taking them with us and planting them close to the meeting place so if needed they would be handy."

Ray nodded his affirmative and continued putting ammunition into his pockets.

He looked at his watch and it about two forty, twenty minutes before Shaw and Forrester were due to arrive, Ray had not asked Mike where the meet was exactly to take place so was a little in the blind as to what was going to go down and where. Mike closed the trunk of the Camaro and walked towards the road, pulling at Ray's arm to follow. The two men walked off in the general direction Ray had taken a little earlier, on approaching the boat ramp Mike crossed it and went under the causeway placing his rifle up against the cement wall, which was the start of the causeway bridge, he signalled Ray to do the same without saying a word.

Ray obliged and could see that disturbing look in Mike's eyes again, this was now starting to really disturb Ray and he finally said;

"What the fuck is the matter with you, you have been distant and moody, and I am not sure it is a good thing.

Why don't we just take what we have and get the fuck out of here. Fuck Shaw and Forrester as well as Farrer."

Mike lunged at Ray and caught him off balance knocking him to the ground with Mike beside him hand clasped hard around his throat so as make Ray gasp for breath.

"I am going nowhere until I get what I came for and what is owed to me. Shae and Forrester ripped us off, I knew it back then and I know it now. You can stay and be part of it and get your fair share or piss off and take nothing."

Ray pushed him away and asked,

"How do you know they ripped us off",

"I know how much Coke and how many women came into this place and what they were getting for the drugs in the big smoke as well as the crème off the top from the prostitution, you must have wondered why they always had bundles of cash on them and never seemed short".

His eyes narrowed and his breathing became rapid, but he went on;

"All right yes, they were rich anyway, but they thought they would take us all down and leave us with a pittance. Well today they get the drugs, and we get the cash for what it is worth, and God help them if the fuck around with me. You got that?"

Ray nodded and Mike released his gripped, and Ray took in deep breaths, he knew now what was driving Mike to this obsession and there was going to be no let up until he got what he wanted. Mike had become money hungry and no matter what he was going to get his pound of flesh from Shaw and Forrester come hell or high water. Mike his money obsession had made him into some form of a demon hell bent of revenge, which was not part of Ray's make up. Ray stuttered out;

"Why are you so determined to get Farrer, what has he got to do with all this?" Mike turned and finally he told Ray;

"Farrer, about fifteen or so years ago when he was a detective back in Philadelphia shot and killed my little brother who was unarmed, yes, he had just robbed a convenience store and belted the owner, but Farrer the drunken prick had no right to shoot him. He was blind drunk, and the hierarchy covered it up, they moved him to another city, and he eventually found his way here and became the Sherriff."

He stopped and took a deep breath and slowly exhaled;

"I set everything in motion, killing and maiming those girls to throw Farrer off the scent, make him think he had a serial killer loose. I even left clues for the dumb son of a bitch, but he never cottoned on his brain was too fucking pickled from the grog. The drugs, the money, they were just cream to me, he has always been my target. But the people I got to manage everything were fucking useless" he stopped and for a split second seemed to ponder what to say next, after a short while he continued; "McClean killed the wrong fucking cop, Drummond the dumb son of a bitch did not know what he was really into, and the others were just blind fodder for me, as are you. But I like you Ray you stuck it out went along with everything, but you make a wrong move or fuck me over and you will also pay the price."

Ray sat and listened to this in quiet bewilderment. He knew there was always something behind the murders and yes, the killing of the girls was for certain body parts which were sold, and for blood to help someone with an illness called Myelogenous Leukaemia or something to that effect but was never sure how far the whole thing was going to go. He now knew that there was more behind the whole scenario and that it was just a front for Mike's vengeance against Farrer. All those people died and sent to prison for one man's vendetta against a drunk who shot his brother. It was incomprehensible to think he was a part of this. Just then a vehicle entered the causeway from the other end, Mike stood up and peered over the edge of the roadway,

"It's time to pay the piper Ray" he sneered.

17

I stood in that room looking at all the mess and trying to contemplate exactly what Beale and Grant were looking for other than the guns and ammo. The amount of paperwork strewn all over the floor and the way the study was ransacked. I yelled out;

"Have you got that fucking filing cabinet open yet?"

"No," was the reply. Just as I was about to go into the other room off the hallway, one of the young deputies came in all flustered and looking like he had seen a ghost.

"What is the problem?" I asked; he could not speak, just stuttered, and pointed out the doorway toward the glasshouse. I took this as a sign he wanted me to follow him out there. As we crossed the porch and down the steps the other deputy came out of the glasshouse and spewed his breakfast up all over the side of the glasshouse,

"Well, that was a fucking bright thing to do," I exclaimed thinking that any evidence on that part of the glasshouse was now gone.

I entered the glasshouse and there before wrapped in linen sheets was what looked like bodies, one had blood stains the other dirty from being buried. The two deputies explained they noticed freshly dug ground and that the shelving had been moved slightly as well as that the soil was mounded under the shelves.

Curiosity got the better of them and like good boys they donned gloves and moved the shelves and as they did so the soil on the humps was soft and gave away slightly. They scraped the soil off and found the sheets when they pulled one back slightly there was the head of a partly decomposed corpse of what looked like a woman. They did the same with other and it was a man although he had not started to decompose, showing he had not been in the ground exceptionally long. I told them to find my CSI man and tell him to get out here, as well as Hal or Bill whomever they could find. I knelt beside the two bodies and yes, the odour was strong from the decomposition of one of the corpse and the other thankfully was still relatively fresh. The man had two bullet wounds from what I could see one in the upper left shoulder and the other in

364

the forehead. I knew this had to be the work of Beale and Grant. The others arrived at the glasshouse door and Bill entered along with Andrew;

"I think you had better call James, Hal," who was standing at the doorway,

"Tell him I have two stiffs for him."

Hal looked at me that contemptuous look he gives me when he is angry with me, a look I am sure he has used in many of his telephone book interrogations he was renowned for. He was a good detective but his manner and his methods, I had to make sure I kept in check.

He looked down again at the bodies as Andrew drew the sheet further back, then he sighed and said;

"Bernie, you poor bastard what the hell did you do to deserve this?"

I looked at him and he knew what I was going to ask;

"This is Bernie Talbertson, and I suspect that may be his wife, May, I think was here name," he said in a quiet tone.

"How do you know the Talbertsons?" I asked.

"Bernie played snooker every Thursday down at the Tavern and had a couple of drinks, nice fella never a bad word about anyone. I have known him since I first arrived here in Oeman Lake, and he was one of the first people I met. Never met his wife though, she had been extremely ill he told me."

Andrew looked up and told me;

"That Bernie had been dead based on his rigour and liver temperature about thirty-six hours, the wife judging the decomposition probably around two to three months but would know more once they were back at the lab."

365

He asked;

"If I had rung James as he will need to see these before we move them." I nodded and walked out of the glasshouse.

"Tear this place apart, I want anything that will give us clue to these two bodies and have you got that fucking filing cabinet open yet?"

The bodies were building up again and my head was starting to spin as I re-entered the house, walking through the kitchen and to the stairs. I needed to see what was upstairs and whether there was anything that would lead me to what I wanted to know. Upstairs was not much different to downstairs, things strewn everywhere, not a method or organisation in how the search took place. In the bedroom the drawers of both side cupboards had been tipped out on the floor, the wardrobe was empty the clothes spread across the floor. The bed was even turned up and revealed the slat base underneath. The ensuite was also a shambles drawers of the vanity pulled out and items spread on the floor. The second and third bedroom much the same, and the main bathroom for an unknown reason had not been touched. Maybe they got sick of finding nothing and decided this was a waste of time. Suddenly a voice from below yelled out;

"Filing cabinet open." I rushed downstairs and into the study, the four drawers of the cabinet just held files of accounts, bank statements, paid invoices, and investment bonds.

The third drawer had a small metal box which had a lock on it, I tried to open it but was unable to and then remembered the keys I had found in the desk, the first one I tried opened the box and there was another set of keys and a small black pocketbook as well as a diary. I told the boys to put it all in evidence bags and take them back to the office. Bill had returned inside and had bagged all the evidence from the kitchen and the other room, he noticed that a panel in the woodwork in the study was out of place, he pushed on it and there was a clicking sound, then the panel flew open. It was a compartment like a wardrobe but whatever was in there was gone. It was where the weapons that we found in the kitchen and whatever Grant and Beale had taken were kept in there.

I told the guys to make sure everything was dusted for fingerprints and any other forensics we could find. I also instructed them to bag everything from the filing cabinet and the desk draws, leave nothing behind. I pulled off my surgical gloves and put them in my coat pocket and went out the front door. The coroner's van was just coming up the drive, I pointed to around the back, and it disappeared. I took a walk over towards the shed with faded red door, took out a clean set of gloves put them on and slowly opened the door.

There were bales of hay and farm implements in there also what looked like small pools of blood, I radioed Hal to get the CSI boys over here to check this shed out. I surveyed the shed as thoroughly as I could and as I was leaving noticed a spent shotgun cartridge close behind the hinged side of the door, taking my pen from my lapel pocket I picked it up and turned back toward the rear of the shed, as I did, I opened the door right up and pushed it back onto the outside wall. Something laying in the hay just off to the left of the door caught my eye it was a shell casing, I pulled a small evidence bag from my inside pocket and slid the shotgun cartridge inside, retrieved another bag from my pocket and using my pen again slid into the casing in among the straw, lifted it up it was a nine millimetre, I put that into the second evidence bag.

I heard someone behind me it was one of the forensic boys whom I did not know but he introduced himself as Michael Burrows and stated that Andrew had called in a couple of favours from the forensic group in Helena to help out as he was a bit overwhelmed at the amount of work that had arisen in the past few days, I thanked him and gave him the two plastic envelopes I had collected the shell casings in, and pointed to what I thought was blood. He nodded and said he would process the shed and its surrounds. I asked;

"How are the others were doing inside and in the glasshouse?" he replied,

"They have things in hand, but Andrew is going to call for a couple more guys as there is so much to process and he still has not finished on the vehicle apparently."

I decided to leave them to it and return to the office. I still wanted to know if they had retrieved anything from the wall where the two shots had hit above my head earlier. I also needed to ready myself as I was going to have to apologise to the crew for my behaviour after the shooting. It was not their fault and somehow, I had to work out why me? I took the first car parked in the driveway and sat in it for a short while. I rang both Bill and Hal told them I was returning to the office and would see them there later. I also stressed to make sure they got everything from this place as we need to know what happened here and what clues could be found about the bodies and the vehicles in the barn as well as any photographs that they could lay their hands on. I wanted the whole place and all areas thoroughly photographed as well. I started the car and drove off towards the main road, my thoughts trying to figure out how and why the woman's body was in the glasshouse and if it is Bernie's wife what was the reason she was in the glasshouse.

How long has she been there and what or why was Bernie in the same place. Had Grant and Beale been in town longer than just the few days since they signed into the motel and doing that was a ploy to throw us off. Had Grant or Beale murdered Bernie's wife to get him to co-operate and when his usefulness had run out, they killed him? Did Bernie know either of the two bastards, and was he connected with everything from years prior. I do not remember his name coming up in any conversation or in any of the files, which is something I will need to investigate at the office. All these questions and more was making my mind race and give me a headache and I had not even reached the bloody main road yet.

18

Ray peered over Mike's shoulder as the black what looked like a Jaguar approached their end of the causeway at a slow pace. Mike laid his rifle down and made sure that the two pistols he had were well hidden from view under his jacket. Ray also double checked the three in his rear belt and moved the two at the front to each side also in his belt. He thought to himself, fuck I hope the safety is on otherwise I may shoot my arse or balls off, he smiled to himself as he thought about this but then there was no time to check. The sleek black car approached slowly and veered off the causeway into the car park where Ray and Mike had left their vehicle. They could not see who it was in the car as the windows were darkly tinted and from side on was impossible, they had been out of position to view through the front windscreen.

The driver of the black car entered the carpark and noticed the boat trailer and SUV as well as the rear end of a Camaro parked behind bushy trees. He looked in his rear-view mirror and noticed two men coming towards him from the end of the causeway from which he had just past, he turned the vehicle around, so it was facing out and the two men who had now stopped were blocking the entrance to the carpark. Both men had rifles hung over their arms and this made the stranger a little uneasy. Ray and Mike could see that it was Steven Shaw now and only he was in the car.

"Get out of the fucking car," Mike roared as he approached the vehicle.

The driver's door suddenly opened and out stepped Shaw, looking very pensive and not sure what to make of it all.

"Where is Forrester, I told you he was to come as well?" Mike asked Shaw.

"I was unable to get hold of him as apparently he is out of town for a couple of days according to his voice message." Shaw said with a slight stammer and hesitancy in his voice.

Mike was not mucking around he handed his rifle over to Ray and walked up to Shaw grabbed him by the shirt front and pushed him back against his car hard which made Shaw wince with pain. Ray looked on and was quite taken aback again by the force and anger shown by Mike. He really has become crazy, and Ray was not sure how to oversee this whole situation. He asked Mike to let Shaw go as this was not going to help the situation, just then Mike pulled a pistol from his belt and jammed it into Shaw's forehead.

"I told you to bring Forrester, he needs to be here as well, as you cannot do everything I need on your own. Not only that the cops are hot on our heels, and we need to split, we cannot wait around for Forrester to get back."

Mike was now what looked like a psychotic state he was rambling and to himself, shaking the pistol around at Shaw, he was on edge, and anything could go wrong at this present time.

Ray shouted;

"Mike put the fucking gun away there is no need for that we need to talk not blow the fuckers head off. Calm down we will get nowhere like this."

Mike stared at Ray and pointed the pistol at him,

"I gave this prick clear instructions he was to bring Forrester with him no matter what, now he is on his own what the fuck are we going to do. If you do not like the way I am managing the situation, then you can fuck off or I will blow you away as I am about to do to this fucker now."

Ray was shaking and had no idea why Mike was so enraged and would not listen to reason or even put the gun away. He then turned the pistol back on a now shaking white as ghost Shaw, who could not move. Shaw said with a very trembly and high-pitched voice;

"I have a place you two can hide out safely until I get Forrester and we sort out what it is you want. I can bring him to my cabin in the woods up along the Northern highway thirty-seven, it is fully stocked food, drink whatever you need for t days."

Mike lowered the pistol and glared at Shaw;

"Okay take us there and I will give you seventy-two hours for you and Forrester to meet us at this cabin. You and Shaw can have the drugs we have we just want two million in cash when you come back. Do you understand, there is three times that in the number of drugs in that bag as I know I packed it before all the shit went down and we had to hide it." Shaw looked at him;

"How the hell are we going to get two million to you in three days especially in cash?"

Mike looked at him and never said a word, Shaw glanced across at Ray who shrugged his shoulders and with a blank look on his face.

"You have three days and you had better bring Forrester as I need to ask him some things about the dealings he was having, as a lot of it does not add up. Also, bloody Farrer is on my arse now, I tried to get rid of him but that failed I missed him." Shaw looked at him eye to eye;

"That was you who tried to shoot Farrer in the main street outside the cop station. Fuck you are crazy man the place is crawling with deputies everywhere and old Bernie Talbertson has disappeared, and the cops are crawling all over his place at present just down the road."

Ray walked slowly towards the car with both rifles now over one shoulder, and he looked at Mike;

"We accept his offer to use this cabin of his and lay low for a few days, so the heat is off us a bit and Shaw brings us Forrester and the money. This way we can slow down a little and not be so panicky about what is happening, secondly you do not have to kill anyone else just yet anyway."

Shaw looked at Ray and Mike still had a good grip on his shirt, Shaw was going nowhere fast;

"You killed that young deputy at the Old Mill a couple of days back, have you killed Bernie as well?"

Ray nodded towards Mike with a look of agreement on his face.

Shaw said;

"No wonder the cops are all over Bernie's place and you killed a young deputy and then tried to kill Farrer, are you fucking mad. This is getting out of hand I thought all the killing ceased years ago when the others went to prison, and you dropped off the map."

With that Mike let go of Shaw's shirt and glanced at the ground, replaced his pistol in his belt and then looked at Shaw again;

"Take us to this cabin of yours and this had better be on the up and up as if it is not, you will be floating face down in that very cold lake over there. Do you understand me?" Shaw nodded and got back in his car, Mike stopped him closing the door and looked at Ray;

"You go with him I will follow in our car, if he so much as deviates from where he said we are going blow him away. Do you think you can do that, because you are starting to become a bit of a chicken shit."
Ray did not answer just went to the passenger's side and with the two rifles sat in the passenger's seat.

Mike went to the Camaro and reversed it out of the position it was parked, pulled in behind the Jaguar and both cars set off out of the carpark back over the causeway. At the other end they turned left and headed up Northern Outlet Highway thirty-seven. They travelled some five or six miles in Ray's calculation then turned left onto a gravel road narrow and winding among the tall pines on either side, some way up this road they turned off onto another less used track and travel for some two to three minutes then out into a small clearing where in front of them was a small but quite neat looking log cabin. It was on the outer edges of the town, and no one would know it was there if they had not been here before. Ray glanced at the side mirror Mike was right behind them as they came to a stop around the back of the cabin. Shaw got out of the car as Ray did also, picking up the rifles from beside the seat.

Mike alighted from the Camaro and walked toward them, Shaw mounted the three or four steps and stuck his hand in a hanging pot plant and retrieved a key from it. He unlocked the door and entered followed by Mike then Ray with the rifles. Shaw showed them around the place it was very neat and tidy inside, the kitchen was well appointed and the fridge as he showed them was well stocked. He showed them the two bedrooms and the rest of the house.

Told them there was firewood under the porch out back, and that no one would bother them here as he only comes up here when he needs to be alone and get some peace and quiet. There are only three people who know about this place, Forrester, his squeeze, and Shaw himself. He gave Mike the key and turned to walk out just then Mike grabbed his arm;

"You have three days to do what I said, so do not make me come looking for you otherwise it may be very bad for you." Shaw nodded and walked to the door, acknowledged Ray, and left closing the door behind him. Ray looked around and opened the curtains in the front room in time to see the black jaguar leaving down the way they had come in.

"Get the bags out of the trunk of our car and make sure that it is hidden right around the back from view from anybody," Mike continued in a much calmer voice.

"I do not trust that bastard, I am sure he is not really, going to do as I asked even though I threatened him. We had better be ready for anything."

Ray nodded and headed for door towards where the car was, he went ahead to park it around the back out of sight but sat in the car for a few moments thinking about the past couple of hours and what had gone down. Was Mike losing his grip on reality and his narcissistic side was really coming out or was he just a pure evil psychopath that Ray was going to have to deal with soon. Ray got out of the car collected the bags from the trunk and returned inside the cabin, knowing that if it come down to it, he may have to kill Mike to be free himself.

19

I returned to the office and headed straight for the conference room and our murder wall, I decided I needed to put all the murders from the old cases back up as they had connections with Beale and Grant and to solve this whole dilemma, I was going to need to close off any loose ends. I opened all the boxes holding all the evidence and took out the files, looking for the brief that we had on the earlier victims. On finding what I was looking for I assembled them on the wall in order from the newest to the oldest.

Firstly, the most recent Bernie Talbertson and his wife. Then the young Deputy Turner, shot by Ray Beale using the alias "Ian Sommers" and Mike Grant using the alias, Michael Adams." This was followed by the list from the earlier case.

Annabelle Tate, 24, Single, Blonde hair, Brown eyes, she had a cross on her back with one horizontal line. Had the same, as the others except, had only been dead approximately 48 hours before she was found. The word *"Limbus"* meaning *'Limbo'* was carved in her back. Was taken off the walking path along the lake in the early morning. No witnesses but her handbag and phone found in bushes along the path to the north of town.

Teresa Caldwell, 21, Single, Blonde hair, Blue Eyes, she had a cross, with a vertical line on the right of the cross. No distinctive marks except what looked like forceps had been used on her vagina, but this was inconclusive. Blood and toxicology test proved she had had a form of ether and other forms of anaesthetic administered and a form of poison on her wrist. Had been dead at least 2 weeks before found. *"Blasphemia"* was the word carved in her back, *'Blasphemous'*. Left her employment and went missing. Alert raised when did not turn up for work on the Monday morning.

Barbara Waite, 22, married but separated, blonde hair, brown eyes, had a cross with one vertical line, to the right and the word *"Dalus"* meaning *'Fraud'*. Been dead 72-96 hours, it was later found she had embezzled $35,679 from her employer. How did the murderer know? Her car was found near Talon Point, but no significant clues as to where she was taken from.

Natalie Benton, 21, Single, blue eyes, blonde hair, cross on her back had line, horizontal below the cross. Found in downtown Oemen Lakes had been dead no more than 12 hours. Word carved in her back *"Volentia"* meaning *'Violence'*, we knew she was Eugene's niece and had not been heard of for 4-5 weeks. No other information.

Catherine Rhind, 23, Single, Blonde hair, blue eyes, had cross on her back, and line to the right of the cross vertical *"Avoutrer"* meaning *'Adultress'*. Dead at least a week, injuries are the same. We know much of her background and who her friends and latest lover was, she was an adulterer.

Judy Hampton, 22, Single, Blonde hair, Brown eyes, had a circle on her back, had one line horizontal above the cross. Had *"Lascīvus"* meaning *'Lust'* carved on her back, dead at least 96 hours, we investigated and found that she was the town bike and would have sex with anyone, anywhere, anytime, again how did they know her background, unless they had first-hand knowledge.

Rose McHenry, 23, Single, Brown Eyes, Blonde hair, had a circle with two lines one vertical to the right and a horizontal one below the circle and again *'Angere'* meaning *'Anger'*. Had been dead approx.36 hours, this one was a tip off. Her injuries were the same the other victims. She had a police record for assault. Not known exactly how or where she was abducted.

Eugene Barrelli, 39, married, two kids, wife Katrina. Was having an affair with one of the victims. Former Navy Seal, with the Police Homicide for 7 years in the Special squad. Description of death was not needed the photo was enough and the memory of his heart sitting there with that note and the rest of him exposed was just too much. He had been dead about one to two hours.

Julie Ann Crow, 23, single, blonde hair, green eyes. No marks, just *Ha Ha Ha* inscribed on her back along with the word *"Heresy."* She had been shot with Farrer's gun at close range on the night of the incident with Farrer but had been dead at least three weeks. Full report and other information on her, from Majors were arriving by lunchtime.

Missing: *Sally Donald*, blonde, blue eyes. Although we now knew where Sally Donald was in the hospital under police protection. I surveyed the board in all its detail looking for something to jump out at me, but nothing did. They all in some way had organs missing or were defiled in some manner. I rang Katrina to see how things were and told her I would be a little late but not too late, I could sense she was smiling when I said that. I asked how the kids were and whether they would be home tonight or not. She did not reply. I wrote a mental note to myself to collect some flowers and a bottle of wine on the way home. I smiled to myself as I hung up the phone, just then Steve Barlow a lawyer and our legal advisor entered the room;

"What is all this?" he asked.

I went through the details on the board for him and explained that the rest of the crew were still at the Talbertson place and filled him in on what found there. Steve was about forty, tall, blue eyes and greying hair which was strange considering his age, and a Harvard boy, married with two children at school here in Oemen Lake. He had been here about two three years, travelled a lot between here and Helena doing work, was also attached to the District Attorney's office so a lot of his work was prosecutions. He listened intently to what I was saying while perusing the information on the board. I said;

"We have a huge amount of evidence to go through from the Talbertson's place as well as two bodies to be autopsied, including shell casings and blood splatter."

He stood there silent shaking his head, then said;

"Do you believe this all connected to the case from a few years back that drug ring, the mutilated bodies and the women that were being trafficked?" I nodded and told him that the two we never got to apprehend back then had slipped the net were back and we suspected they had murdered the young Deputy Turner and at least one of the Talbertsons, Bernie to be exact, the woman's body had been dead a lot longer. I explained how the two Mike Grant and Ray Beale had come in under assumed names and had tried to get rid of Sally Donald who escaped the clutches of Damien Bourke back then, she recognised them at a gas station thirty odd miles South of the town. They tried to run her off the road and she was now in the hospital under guard.

He looked at me with a quizzical look, so I continued, she had returned as she had received a letter from her friend here and was on her way here from New York to meet up, as this friend had told her things about Steven Shaw. I was not going into detail yet as we still must put together what we know, and the evidence shows that there were others involved in the carnage back then who we knew nothing about. He turned and looked at the board again and was silent for a long pregnant pause before saying;

"You have your hands full with this one alright. If you need me, you know where I am, but could you get one of your boys to put a small brief together so that I at least have a heads up on this if things come to pass that there is a case here as it looks like there is?"

I agreed I would and at that moment Colin walked in, our other CSI. Now here was a fellow that was hard to get a real read on, forty-six, single, not sure whether he had been married or not, and basically kept to himself. Another Harvard graduate and a University of Southern California graduate specialising in BSA, (Blood Spatter Analysis). He joined the team only this year and was already fitting in well, although as I said hard to really get a line on him, but I am sure we will get to know more. He was hired by the boys in Helena but seconded here as we were short a CSI on our quota not that we needed another as nothing ever really happened here before all this bullshit came about. He said that the boys were on their way back with a car full of evidence and he was to prepare for a long night, and was just checking if it was okay if he worked late on what they brought in.

He also looked at the board and there was a bit of a shock horror look on his face when he saw some of the photographs of the carvings in the women's back from the old case.

"Fuck, did the bastards really do all that to these poor females?"
I nodded in the affirmative;
"Told him that the files were on the table if he wanted to familiarise himself with all of it, as what was coming in would have some connection in one form or another to what we have now".

The look on his face was enough was enough to know that he was going to need Andrew's guidance in all this as he looked lost and bemused by it all. He was I believe having trouble grasping the concept of what had happened to the women on the board and how could another person commit such heinous crimes on a fellow human being. I was of course prejudging him but the stance and look on his face gave me that impression. We both stood there in silence for a few moments, he then seemed to gather himself and turned and started to look at the files on the table. I had a train of thought rushing through my mind when the bloody cleaner came in with a noisy hoover and all thoughts went out the window with that. I asked;

"Can you leave this room please, it is not to be entered by anyone other than those involved in this case. We will clean and empty rubbish bins in here when we need to."

He stopped what he was doing looked at me with a sour puss look, pick up his cleaning stuff and walked out of the room. I had never thought previously that this room was open to all and sundry so anybody could come in here looking at the board and files, which in hindsight was not a good thing. Colin turned and I had the feeling he wanted to say something but didn't and so I left and returned to my own office. There was a darkening outside that heralded the night in, as the streetlights would soon flicker into action, and then all would be quiet for another hopeful uneventful evening. I was really looking forward to a quiet night at home with Katrina and the kids, this will be a blessing in disguise, as the last few days have been extremely busy and there was so much going on.

20

Ray sat in the seat by the window that looked out over the driveway and appeared to be far away in his thoughts but was also aware of Mike was pacing the floor muttering to himself. He was becoming unhinged Ray believed and how was he going to keep Mike focused on what had to happen and when as well as how they could achieve their plans. There had been hiccups, Mike killing that young Deputy did not help and then taking pot shots at Farrer as well as killing Bernie, this was not in the plan and was not even a contingency. Ray did not want to say anything especially with the mood Mike was in and if he did say anything then he could tip Mike off and away he would go another tangent and hell knows who would suffer his wrath then. Meanwhile unbeknown to Ray and Mike, Shaw had left them at the cabin and went straight to Forrester's place. He had lied to the others as he was not sure in what matter of things would have happened if he had told Beale and Grant that Forrester was at home.

He thought to himself as he drove back through town and on his way towards South Arm where Forrester's home was hoping that Forrester understood what was going down and how Steven had put himself in danger not that would matter to Dean Forrester. The two million was also going to be a hurdle as Steven knew that the one thing Forrester did not want to be involved with or have any part of was the drugs. Dean Forrester was quite happy putting up the money and his contacts for the as others called it "Slave" trade in women, which Steven thought was a bit bizarre as dealing in women for prostitution and organ farming was in his opinion a lot worse than being involved in the drug trade.

Shaw pulled into the driveway of the Forrester estate between the two great redwood trees that made up the entrance to it. It was a place of about ten acres, and it was fenced in crisp white fences and green pastures. Forrester had horse interests and was quite successful in the racing game but also in the equestrian arena. Shaw was not sure whether it was he or his brother or another member of the family had represented at the Olympics or something big like that. He travelled up the well-groomed road and had to admire how Forrester like himself was self-made, not born with silver spoon in mouth or born into money. Shaw wondered if the money he had made was all legitimate considering he became involved in the ring some years ago but as a silent backer in the background and with nothing being able to connect him to anything. Shaw had made his money legitimately and was proud of it.

He reached the horseshoe turn around at the front of the massive house. Forrester came out onto the porch as Shaw pulled up. Shaw wondered how he knew but then he had forgotten that there were cameras at the entrance and at points down the driveway. For all the times he had been to this massive property he never seems to know just how Forrester owned and how well off he was.

He got out of the car and walked to the steps leading up to the porch where Forrester stood, shook his hand, and then said;

"We have a problem, bloody Grant and Beale are back in town and causing mayhem already."
Dean Forrester beckoned Shaw to come inside and put his finger to his lips not to say anything just yet. They entered the big house and went through the foyer to the rear of the house, on the way through Shaw noticed that there were no

longer any photographs of Forrester's wedding or family photographs, which had hung proudly in this large foyer. This struck him as strange, but he was going to keep that question for a later date as there was much more important things to discuss at this present time.

Shaw knew that Dean had had affairs and that his wife had found out about one of them, and whether this may be the reason for the missing photographs. Linda Forrester had died a years ago in suspicious circumstances, but that was a story for another day. Dean led Steven into a large oak lined study with a heavy door and bookshelves along two walls filled with books, there was a line of four filing cabinets built into one of the bookshelves and a large French window opening out to a patio that looked out over the sprawling meadows towards the mountain range. It truly was a breathtaking view. Forrester's desk was the same as the wall panelling large made of oak and was covered in files and papers.

Off to the side was a drinks cabinet which was open, and Forrester closed the door behind them and beckoned Shaw to be seated in the large leather chairs surrounding a small table in the centre of the room. Shaw as he sat down noticed the television screens on the opposite wall and that they were the cameras surveying the property, this is how Forrester knew he was coming up the driveway.

"Drink," Dean asked;

"Yes, whiskey neat thanks," was Shaw's reply.

Steven took the glass from Dean and started to go ahead to tell him about his meeting with Grant and Beale, and what

Grant had demanded. Forrester questioned why the two of them had returned as it was not z smart move on their part to return to the scene of their crimes and especially since Farrer was still the Sherriff. Shaw told him how Grant had shot the young Deputy at the Old Mill and shot Bernie Talbertson on his own property.

The one thing that Shaw was really perturbed about was Grant taking pot shots at Farrer in broad daylight in the middle of town in front of the police station of all places. Shaw took a huge gulp of his drink and then another and held out his glass for a refill. Forrester obliged, and then enquired as to what did Grant and Beale want with him.

"They want two million dollars in cash, and we can have the drugs they have, which total according to Grant about five million. They have given us three days to get it all together," Shaw said.

Forrester studied him for a moment then refilled his glass and sat in the chair opposite Shaw;

"Well, they can keep their fucking drugs as I want nothing to do with that side of things. I am out of all that now and Grant and Beale can take a long jump off a truly short pier. I do not care what they want I am not getting involved."

Shaw sat in silenced and was not sure how to reply to what Dean had just said. Suddenly Dean said;

"Where are Beale and Grant at the present moment?"

"In my cabin up in the woods below the ski field, I put them there out of the way as the area was getting too hot for them otherwise."

387

Forrester sat and looked out of the large windows again sipping his drink slowly. Then in a gruff belligerent voice,

"They can get fucked, I am not giving them one red cent and the threats they made to you about what they want from us or else, well they can whistle for it."
Shaw was taken aback as this now left him in an untenable position and what was he going to do as he three days to produce the two million as well as get Dean to front up to Beale and Grant. Then Shaw decided he had better tell Dean what Grant had demanded,

"Grant wants you to front up to him, he will not let it lie as he has a sort of beef with you. He has a real bee in his bonnet over you and I do not know why, and he scares the hell out of me as when I saw him earlier, he seemed unhinged and was like a firecracker about to explode."
Dean just sat sipping his drink and then stood and refilled the glass and offered Shaw another which he agreed to. Forrester was calm now and finally said;

"Well, I suppose I had better see him but not at the cabin, bring him here or both as I am not going to bow and scrape to him. He demands nothing of me, and I owe him nothing he needs to realise I financed his start and if anything, he owes me."
Steven looked at him, and was not sure, but nodded and said he would bring them to him, but he was also apprehensive as to what Grant would think of that. Steven was going to have to keep Grant calm and would need Beale to make sure he kept Mike in check until the meeting. Steven got up from his chair and decided he needed to leave as he had thinking to be done. Dean

showed him out of the study and through the foyer to the front door, shook his hand and again reiterated that Grant was to come to him and asked Steven to forewarn him when that was to happen.

Steven went to his car and drove around the rest of the horseshoe and headed out along the long driveway again, not even noticing the fences or the green meadows anymore. He looked in the rear-view mirror and Dean was still standing on the porch watching as he left. As Steven left the property he had so much going around in his head. The one thing that was worrying Steven the most was the two million dollars that Grant had demanded as it was part of the demands he had, and Shaw was of the feeling that if this did not happen then their would-be trouble. Shaw wishes he never had got involved in this whole saga from the beginning but unfortunately, he wanted the lure of the money he was going to be an extraordinarily rich man, and he and Isabella would be well off.

How the tide has turned and now he was in so deep he had no way out and with Dean not willing to heed the demands of Grant and Beale it left him in a catch twenty-two situation, as whichever way he goes he will lose out. He needed to really think about his position, and it had to be quick as Grant had given him three days to bring Forrester to him and the two million dollars. He was in a bind now and he needed help.

Could he go to Farrer and tell him everything and that would bring Forrester in as well as Farrer would be able to get Beale and Grant, but he would also implicate himself and that meant he would need to cop a prison term or negotiate his way out of it. There had been too many deaths and too much water had gone under the bridge since he became involved and was in so deep, he felt like he was drowning.

He had arrived back in town and headed for the tavern he did not really recollect how he had got there it was as if he was in a trance and not really remembering anything along the way to where he was now, it was as if he was in robot control. He decided he would sleep on it and see Grant and Beale tomorrow, pass on Dean's thoughts and then take the situation from there. He would not tell Isabella about the happenings of the past few hours, as it was too intricate, and he needed to thick about his next step. He was fearful for his life also as Grant appeared to be out of control. He decided that he would drown his sorrows in the bar and forget about everything until tomorrow.

21

I arrived home to warm and hearty welcome from Katrina and the kids, it was great to be able to relax, even if it was only for a few hours. I went had a shower got changed and came back downstairs just as Katrina had dinner on the dinner. I opened a bottle of wine for her and a tonic water for myself. I had been sober for so long now I had forgotten what it was like, but I did not want to go back there as I now had far too much to lose. Dinner was great the kids were great we had laughs and enjoyed the evening. I told Katrina to put the kids to bed I would clear up, she moved towards me and gave me a kiss on the cheek, saying;

"I will not be long," I smiled back at her and began to clear the dishes, rinsing and loading the dishwasher. The pots and pan I washed by hand and dried then put them away set the dishwasher going, grabbed the bottle of wine and Katrin's glass as well as mine and headed for the lounge room.

I found my own comfortable chair and dropped into it, grabbed the television remote and turned on the news. It was as usual full of shit except for one story about the shooting in town outside the police station. I thought how they got to know so many details about that as we had not made anything public, and we were trying to play it down for the time being. Luckily, the story had finished before Katrina came back down and into the lounge settling down on the couch. She grabbed her glass and took a long sip of her wine, then looked at me and said;

"When were you going to tell me about the shooting today?" I was shocked and enquired how she had found about it;

"It was on the radio news at about three o'clock this afternoon. They even named you."
This I was pissed about as we had not even had a press release or a press conference, there was a leak inside my department, and I would need to shut it down as soon as possible as this was something for which I was not

prepared. At that moment my phone rang, I looked at the number it was Hal;

"Hello," Hal replied.

"Have you seen the news boss, how did they get the bloody story so fast?"

I replied to him that I did not know but tomorrow was another day and I would follow up that point at the team meeting in the morning. I sent a text out to everyone to be in the office at nine as I wanted to go over things as well as see if anything had come of the Forensics so far. I knew this was a stretch as the guys had only just returned to the office as I was leaving so unless they decided to work late or through the night then I would have no results to speak of. I watched television for another hour or so but started to doze off and decided to go to bed, besides, I had so much gone around in my grey matter upstairs that I was not able to think straight, and a good night's sleep may be the answer.

I slept through to seven and arose showered grabbed a coffee, kissed Katrina goodbye, and left by eight. It was not an enjoyable day; winter was coming, and the sky was a dark grey with rolling clouds and a strong wind cutting the lake from North to South down the valley between the Oemen Mountains and the Big Bear Range. I arrived at the office about fifteen minutes later and headed up to my office to clear any messages and prepare for the briefing. I sat in my chair and swivelled around looking out over the lake through the window which now had hard rain hitting it, I thought to myself I got inside just in time.

Time seems to stand still as I stared into nothing and felt a kind of melancholy as my mind wandered. I suddenly was awakened from my daydreaming by thunder and the white curls on the lake were now like waves upon a beach, I thought about the five pillars on the Southeastern side of Moonsun Island as they stood out from the island itself by a few metres causing a rip between them and the island. I imagined as the waves surged across the lake what it would be like in the space. I must one day pluck up enough courage to go to the island with the reservation Chief as the island encompassed part of the reservation and see for myself what it was like. I had been here a long time and up until now have not really given the island a thought.

There was a flash of lightning and another clap of thunder that made the windowpane rattle, I thought I am glad I am in here today and not out in this. I hope the boys at the Talbertson's place had got all they needed as this weather was not going to help. Just as I turned back to my desk, Hal walked in and told me all was ready in the conference room. I drank a swig of my coffee, stood up and walked behind him down the corridor to the room where we had all the files and board. There was updated information and new photographs on the board which now encompassed part of the wall behind it. We had so much now I was feeling the cases from some years back and this one was so entwined like a spider's web that we had central characters and from them spread out the strands of the web forming a never-ending circle as each strand led to another then another and so on. Everybody was seated around the perimeter wall, I started at one end and called on Hal to report on his progress, he reported;

"That he had followed up with Ruby from the motel on the two gents who had checked but nothing sat right there, and we now know that it was Ray Beale and Mike Grant. Then there was the mystery man who registered under the Ashley Collins from San Diego, but at this time had not been seen and Ruby was keeping an out for him".

He continued;

"Sally Donald was still in the hospital under police protection and she had confirmed the identities of Beale and Grant who had registered at the motel under assumed names of Ian Sommers and Michael Adams. They had traced the vehicle that was registered with the motel, and it was stolen and as you all know was found in the lake, but no evidence could be gleaned from it because of water damage."

He finished there for the time being.

Next was Ray;

"We followed up on the vehicle as Hal has mentioned and found that it was stolen in Colorado weeks prior. We also followed up on the aliases that Beale and Grant had been using, they had warrants outstanding Texas and Louisiana under those names. The other vehicle we found in the barn at Talbertson's place belong to a Terry Kamer, he was fishing when his vehicle was stolen. He has now been cleared of anything to do with the case".

He took a deep breath then sighed before he continued;

"Fingerprints and fibres found in the Jeep are a match for our two suspects Beal and Grant, they are getting sloppy as the Talbertson house was clean of prints no fibres nothing, we are still analysing the evidence from the house but so far nothing."

He finished saying;

"He had nothing more to add at this point in time."

I looked at Colin he started his briefing;

"We have so far found nothing from the house, although as Ray said there is a mountain of evidence to get through and luckily, we have now been given support to help wade through it all. I can confirm the shell casing found in the shed is from a nine-millimetre pistol and as you know had the same striations on it as was used some years ago in another robbery/murder, it may also be the same weapon used to murder Deputy Turner".

There was a slight pause;

"We are still working on that. The bullets extracted from the front of the building where somebody took a shot at you are almost indistinguishable as the concrete has stuffed them up, but we are trying. The thumb prints we have belonged to Mike Grant". He looked around to see if anyone was really paying attention, then continued in his monotone voice;

"We have Grant and Beale's prints on file as both have gun licences. Andrew, James, and I are going to perform the autopsies on the bodies later today and should have a report for you tonight or in the morning. As for the other evidence from the barn and the shed that will be a little while as all the guys are working hard and long hours to process it all and catalogue it. That is, it so far boss."

I nodded and thanked him. I next went to Bill, although new to the team he had been do some digging on the earlier case and finding out how all this might fit with what is going on now, he looked pensive but began;

"The evidence that I gleaned from the old files when all the earlier murders took place and the patterns, we have happening here are different in that there are only two men connected to the present crime as back then there was multiple persons involved. We know that two of the culprits from back then have return and are on a rampage of carnage and vendetta and collaborating with Ray we believe there may be others we are yet to know about that were connected back then but never saw the light of day in the investigation".

I stopped as suddenly I felt all alone and vulnerable, I still do not know why. I must have had a blank look as Hal asked;

"You alright Boss?" I nodded and continued;

"The backers of the earlier crimes are money men only; they do not get their hands dirty or get involved in the running of whatever may be happening. They just cream off the top the profit whatever that may be. The first case we know had drugs, prostitution, human sex trafficking, money laundering, and organ selling on the illegal market and involved high-ranking personnel."

There was silence and he shuffled papers before he continued;

"We now believe we may know two who were behind the first case and why the two we know of have returned. With your permission boss Ray and I want to interview the mayor, Dean Forrester, and Steven Shaw. The mayor was never interviewed in the first cases, but he had a vendetta against you and how you went about that investigation, this makes him suspicious. The other two are self-made millionaires and have the money and resources to fund the whole thing. I realise we need to tread carefully but we are going to dig a little deeper before going ahead with the interviews."

He stopped and looked at me, I was a bit set aback by this finding as I must admit I never thought our illustrious mayor could be involved. The other two I had made notes somewhere in the file about my suspicions. I began;

"Thanks everybody I know this is hard when so much is going on, you have done well and there is so much we do not know now. As far as the mayor, Shaw and Forrester are concerned you will need a bit more rather than hunches or gut feelings. The autopsy reports will be good if we can have the as soon as possible, also we need to know the movements of Bernie Talbertson's black Camaro, whether it has been seen in the area lately and who may be driving it. It was used to shoot at me but as to who was driving, we have no real idea although I have my suspicions considering it was not Bernie as he was in a hole in the ground."

I stopped and took a deep breath;

"We need to follow up on this Ashley Collins as he may have nothing to do with all this, but we need to either connect him or clear him. Okay that is all, any questions, oh and another detective from Helena will be joining us Chris Mills in the next day or two."

They all shook their heads in the negative, so I closed the discussion and returned to my office, but as I did, I asked Ray if he would see me. I sat in my chair as Ray entered;

"What's up boss?"

"Do you believe the mayor involved. I know that we always thought Shaw and Forrester but had no proof?"
He stood silent for a moment as another clap of thunder rang out, then;

"I had my suspicions back then Ian, he was too involved with McLean and what happened to Barelli, he also road the shit out of us all to kill the case, as he believed we were dragging our feet and tourist season was coming as it is now. I just have this feeling."
I nodded to him;

"Did you see the news last night about the report on this case, we have a leak in this office, Hal rang me last night just after it was on television, it was not something I wanted to hear or see broadcast. There is someone who knows what is going on and leaking it to the press it appears, we must close it down and quick or else there is going to be hell to pay if anything else gets out and tips off Beale and Grant. Although they surely must know that we are onto them and we know who they are, but still to have the case broadcast like that does not look good. I should have said something in the briefing about it and warn them to not to speak to anyone about the case." he nodded, and he left.

I must admit thinking back the mayor did have a fair amount to say back then I will do a memo about speaking to the press out of school and any questions from the press there is to a "No Comment", about anything at all even the slightest detail that they may question there will be silence on what we are doing, otherwise this will turn into a bloody circus all over again just like it did back then, everybody putting the fucking two cents worth in and crank calls about who is doing or causing the problems. I remember back then we were like the fucking Dodo bird running chasing our own arses half the time almost disappearing up them because of the shit that was spread and what went down.

I do not want that this time I close this off finally there is going to be no murmurs from the grave on this one, once completed it is finished for good. If Ray is right and the mayor is involved that would tie up loose ends for me that have gnawed at my gut for years, and not being able to get rid of that feeling that we missed something that was right there in front of us. I turned and faced out the window at the storm, which was now raging, and it was like evil was settling upon the lake once again and our demons had returned, I felt helpless at that very moment to correct it. In a way I wish Joe were here as these two Sociopaths/Psychopaths I needed to really understand their motives and direction they were going.

22

Steven Shaw decided he was going to go to the cabin and try to convince Mike and Ray to go with him to meet Forrester. He knew from the mood Mike was in when he left that was going to be a tall order and that it was not going to be an easy road to get them there. He also feared for his own life as Mike seemed unhinged and if he did know better was strung out on his own drugs. But that could not be true as Ray would not allow that as he seemed the level-headed one and maybe if he can convince Ray then Mike would agree. The two million though was a problem and he would not tell them what Dean had said about not paying up the money as he was not interested in the bloody drugs. He also needed to contact the other party involved in all this and had he realised who was back in town. The mayor had kept his nose clean and right out of sight for all these years, you hardly saw him only at official functions then he was there but not there if you get the drift.

He had covered up so fucking much and streamlined the judiciary and had the past judges and some of the lawyers in his pockets, paying those arseholes with my money thought Shaw, but things were different now. He decided the mayor was his first port of call this morning, he knew he would be home, as he rarely went into the office before noon unless there was a council meeting or big shindig he could get pissed at. Since the fiasco of the murders etc he had kept a low profile and the one thing Shaw knew he did not have the new Police Commissioner in his back pocket he was a hard arse and been sent from the capitol to take over the role. Take over he did, he had got rid of the corruption within the two counties and had promoted Farrer to the head of the Homicide task force, which pissed the mayor off no end as he knew he could no longer control or have any influence over Farrer. Although the mayor still had a few in his pockets he was not as influential as he had been.

Looking back the mayor collected the profits from the crimes and remained out of the spotlight but could have brought down the whole operation with his stupidity about McLean and that cop Barelli at the time. Shaw knew the mayor would not be happy at the return of Beale and Grant and that could be a way of getting them to see Forrester, use him as leverage.

He drove on through the driving rain, the spray from the foamy heads of the waves on the lake was blowing over the road along the esplanade and he was in two minds whether to go to the cabin or visit the mayor. Grant had not made things any easier by shooting at Farrer, that threw a real spanner in the works, maybe if he could have shot straight and got rid of Farrer then things might have calmed down a bit as then the mayor could have put pressure on his contacts and the investigation would have stopped at Bernie's death, but not then there was the fucking deputy that Grant shot at the Old Mill. This was fast becoming a nightmare and he felt he was losing a grip on his sanity.

He called ahead to tell the mayor he was on his way and be prepared for a shock. He arrived at the house and quickly alighted from his car and ran through the driving rain to the front door, banging hard on the door knocker. Even though he had run, the rain was so heavy he still had become very wet, and water dripped incessantly from his hair down his face. The door was opened and standing there with a glass of what looked like scotch in his hand was the mayor. Come in and take your wet shoes off, I do not want wet foot marks on the carpet. Shaw ignored the request and went straight thru to the mayor's study which was off to the side from the foyer, he had been in this room on occasion. Bookshelves floor to ceiling filled with law books, encyclopaedias, and novels as well as ornaments strategically placed in different areas.

His desk was a large oak one with four huge wood turned oak legs, on the top was a pile of books and files and a half empty bottle of Glenfiddich. The mayor took a seat behind the desk, it made him look miniature in size compared to it. He beckoned Shaw to have seat and asked if he wanted a drink, Shaw replied;

"It is fucking ten thirty in the morning and you're drinking already."

The mayor just looked at him, that is when Shaw noticed that the mayor was only wearing a tracksuit and slippers. From that he gathered he was not going to the office today, also as he looked around, he realised that the place was untidy which he had always found everything to be neat and in its place.

"I see you have redecorated slightly," he said with the tongue in cheek remark.

"Don't be a fucking smartarse, my wife left me a year ago and I have been unable to find a housekeeper, do you want a job?" he asked Shaw. Shaw ignored the question and realised that the mayor was serious;

"What happened?" he asked.

"She came home and found fucking the young housekeeper we did have here in the office on this desk as a matter of fact. I had been doing her for a while without my wife knowing then she came home early from one of her women's meetings, a book club thing I think and there I was chocka block up the housekeeper."

Shaw started to laugh and knew the mayor was full of shit, as that would not have been the case as the housekeeper Shaw knew was not that stupid to get involved with this old drunk and anyway, he would have had to pay her pretty penny to let him do her.

Shaw did not carry on the conversation about the wife but took it for granted that she had gone and that he was in fact on his own as his ex-wife would not have let him drink at this hour and then Steven looked at the sideboard and there was empty beer and whiskey bottles there as well as dirty glasses on the far edge of the desk.

"Well, I have some bad news for you that you are not going to like, and this will sober you up in a hurry," to which the mayor tried to stand up but fell back in his chair,

"What the fuck are you on about Shaw?"

"Beale and Grant are back in town and causing chaos already and only been back two or three days and already killed a young Deputy, Bernie Talbertson and took a couple of shots at Farrer outside the police station right in the middle of town."

"Fuck" said the mayor who had suddenly gone very pale the redness in his cheeks had disappeared.

"What the hell are they back here for?"
Shaw slowly and very deliberately said;

"They want two million in cash, and we can have the drugs they have which are worth a lot more than the two million. They want Forrester and I to meet them and finalise the deal, but Forrester will not have a bar of it as you know he is not into the drugs."
The mayor sat in silence for what seemed ages before suddenly pouring himself another half glass of scotch and waved it at Shaw, who again declined.

"Why won't Forrester meet with them, he needs to get rid of them or else we are all going go down the fucking shitter with them." The mayor now seething, and Shaw knew this was not a good thing, as he had seen this before when the old man gets upset or angry, he can be a bloody handful and being half drunk as he will make it worse.

"I want Forrester to get his arse here now, and I will convince him that he must do as they ask, or he puts us all in jeopardy as we got through the last skirmish without a scratch although that bloody Farrer suspected something but could not prove bugger all. Forrester needs to get his fucking priorities right."

Shaw agreed to get Forrester to the mayor's house that afternoon, but he also told him that Grant had only given them three days to produce the money or else there was going to be trouble. He explained to the mayor that Grant was off his meds he was psychotic, ranting, and raving, he did not know how Beale was keeping him from doing something stupid even though he had already murdered two people. Shaw was at his wits end and noted to the mayor that if Forrester does not do as Grant asks, then both he and the mayor's life could be next on the chopping block.

The reason Grant had a real beef with Farrer and anybody who did not do his bidding or held up his plans for Farrer was playing Russian roulette with their life.

"What is his beef with Farrer?" the mayor asked.

"I do not know replied Shaw but it must be pretty serious as to take a couple of shots at him in the middle of town in broad daylight and outside the cop station it must be bad," Shaw said in an unconvincing voice.

The mayor stood up this time and stayed standing,

"Get Forrester here we are going to have to nut this out as we cannot afford to let Grant go around killing people and implicating us in this whole affair as we will go down the river for a long time probably longer the other bastards that Farrer put away".

Shaw stood up and left the room vowing to bring Forrester back that afternoon. He let himself out and the rain had not eased off any, running to his car and getting in he saw the mayor standing at the window looking out across the lawn in front of his house, Shaw pulled away from the mayor's house and headed for Dean Forrester's. He was not sure what to make of the mayor and his state of mind or whether he was even capable of making rational decisions. Shaw decided he would call into the chambers and just query was the mayor in and if he could see him, he was having this moment of unsureness as to whether the mayor was the mayor anymore, although he had heard nothing of him retiring or resigning. He drove to the centre of town and turned down French Avenue towards the main Council building, pulled into the carpark and stopped sat for a few moments was this the right thing to do? He finally plucked up the courage got out of his car the rain was still heavy and ran to the front revolving door went through into the reception area. He walked up to the counter and knew the young lady on the desk, she was the daughter of an old friend Julie Ashcroft.

He walked over and said hello to her and told her he wanted to see the mayor, she had a blank look on her face and then said;

"The mayor has resigned some six months ago, he had some personal problems, and his wife has left him, we have a Deputy mayor now, would you like to see her?"

"No" said Shaw;

"I wanted to see him on a personal thing, it does not matter I will catch up with him at home, thank you anyway." Shaw spun on his heels and headed for the door, went through the revolving part as fast as it was possible and headed for his car, got in and thumped the hell out of his steering wheel. The old bastard had not told him he had resigned, and we do not have a new mayor, only a deputy. Steven felt betrayed by the mayor for not being up front and honest, this made things difficult now he was going to have to tell Forrester, but should he go back and have it out with the old bastard beforehand or leave it till he and Forrester were together. He decided he needed time to think so he headed for his office and would lock himself away and try to make sense of this whole mess which had now become an absolute fucking shit show.

He arrived at his office and went upstairs telling his secretary that he was not to be disturbed by anyone. Just as he was about to enter his office his secretary said,

"There is a man waiting for you in your office he said that you both had an appointment, but I could not find it in your diary or on the system",

"It is okay", he told her and headed down the corridor to his office. Who the fuck would this be now as he never saw any cars out front that he did not recognise, he entered his office and there standing staring out the window toward the township was Dean Forrester.

"What the fuck do you want?"
Shaw said with a menacing tone.

"Did you know the mayor has resigned and we will not have a new mayor until the fall."

"I just made an absolute dick of myself and went to his chambers to see him and was told he had resigned, and his wife had left him, and he had personal problems. I went to see him at home this morning and the arsehole never told me he had resigned but I knew something was not right as his house was a mess."

Shaw looked dishevelled and wet as he glanced in the mirror over the top of the large wooden sideboard on the western wall of his office. Forrester remained looking out the window which was behind Shaw's desk. Shaw asked;

"How long have you known about our illustrious mayor?" Forrester did not turn around but replied;

"A couple of weeks, I have thrown my hat in the ring for the job."

"Well fuck me, and you knew this yesterday when I spoke to you, and you never thought to give me a heads up. Well thanks a bloody lot, I walked right into this shit show didn't I."

Just then, Dean turned and looked at Shaw;

"How the hell was I to know you would go to see him of all people about what was going down, and beside why the fuck would we want him involved anyway?"

"Because I was hoping he would talk some fucking sense into you about what we needed to do before Grant goes off half-cocked and kills us both, which he is likely to do in the state he is in."

Shaw was in full panic mode his voice raised and trembling, Forrester put his finger to his lips to quieten Shaw;

"You going to tell the entire world about it. The way you are going on that secretary of yours will know about everything the way, you are shouting, and you know what the typing pool gossip is like the whole town will know before happy hour tonight. This news will travel faster than a baby with diarrhoea, shut your mouth and listen. I will go with you to see Grant and Beale and we will deal with them both my way, then there will be no connection for Farrer to investigate as I suspect he already knows that

Beale and Grant are here as I said, and that they handled the murders. We will see Beale and Grant tomorrow, got it?"

23

Ray Beale was at his wits end and was trying not to engage with Mike as little as possible, Mike was really on edge he could not sit still, and would pace about incessantly, mumbling to himself and then he would sit down roll his fingers on the table or the chair on which he was sitting. He would then take out his gun and play with it like a toy all the time as if he were waiting for someone or something to arrive or happen. Ray was really on edge and wanted to leave the cabin and Mike to his own devices, but knew that if he did that, he had nowhere to go or could not trust anyone that was part of his former life. As far as most of his family or friends were concerned, he was either dead or never to return home. He had through the grapevine that his business had been brought out from under him and his family was the recipient of the proceeds of the sale, he had no idea of what they received.

He was brought back to reality quickly when he heard Mike growl at him;

"We just cannot sit around here playing with ourselves. We need to do something as I do not trust Forrester or

Shaw, I will make sure once they fulfil their obligations to us that is last, we will here of them."

Shaw sat for moment thinking hard about what Mike had just said and realised he may mean to cut them from the picture. He was not going to be part of that as it was dicey enough now and after Mike had shot that police officer and then Bernie both in cold blood, he did not feel safe himself around Mike. He also started to pace the floor as well and kept looking at Mike, making sure he did not suddenly take the gun to him. Mike was now making a fire as the temperature in the cabin had dropped and the rain outside was getting heavier and the thunder was much louder before. Ray said;

"We cannot start a fire what if someone sees the smoke, there are heaters in the rooms we can bring in here."

Mike looked at him and agreed and went off to find the heaters. Ray was thankful for the little bit of peace and distance for a brief time between himself and Mike. Ray went over to the back window in the kitchen area and peered out through the rain, which was now a torrential downpour, there was lightning again accompanied by large bursts of thunder. Ray wondered if this storm spelt the death knell for them both or just one of them. Ray decided to check his guns which he had removed from his belt on arrival at the cabin and sat them on the table in the living room, but they were gone. He took a deep breath and realised Mike now had his weapons to.

Hell was upon him he thought, just then Mike came back into the lounge with a heater under each arm, he set one up in the lounge and one by the breakfast bar near the kitchen.

Ray decided he was going to grow a pair and ask Mike what he done with his weapons;

"Where are my guns, Mike?" which Ray thought was a reasonable request. Mike looked at him and said he had put them in the cupboard over by the front window with the rifles, as leaving them on the table like he had was not good especially if Shaw and Forrester turned up unannounced. His explanation sounded reasonable, but it begged the question why he still had his so Ray asked;

"Why have you still got your gun, if you put mine away?" Mike with a curt reply said;

"Get your fucking gun and keep it with you if it makes you feel safe but remember we do not trust the other two to come through for us so if we must then you must use the fucking thing and not just have as a show piece, like you did in El Paso and Allen, just waved the fucking thing around like you dick".

Ray was taken aback a little by this statement as in both those places neither had to use their weapons at all, or even show them.

The El Paso job was an easy threat and rob without violence or even showing the guns, Allen was a bit different as the gas station owner tried to pull his shotgun out and Mike pistol whipped him. They found out when they got to Colorado that there were warrants out for them, so they stole a vehicle and drove North into Wyoming and laid low for a couple of weeks then onto Idaho before ending up here in Mantana at Oemen Lake. This was a place that neither wanted to return to, but they had become short on cash and knew there was over two million at the Old Mill in the hidden tunnel as well the drugs.

Ray would have been happy to have collected what they had and left, but Mike the fucking big hero thinking he was some kind of fucking gangster had to shoot that deputy. Then when Ray had arranged for them to stay at Bernie's all went to shit there because Bernie had changed and wanted nothing more to do with them and pulled the bloody shotgun on them, so Mike shot him twice. When we buried him the glasshouse we found May, Bernie's wife and I suspect Bernie may have killed by euthanasia as she had been sick for long time. Ray was just guessing now, but it seemed on the cards, as no one had seen May for a long time Ray suspected so Bernie could just go about his daily business as he lived out in the never never and no one would really worry him, as Talon Point was just down the road, and he would not have to travel into town that often. The one thing that Ray did not calculate into this was that May would need hospital visit how the fuck did he pull that off and what if a doctor came to the house, which was rare but saying he did what was the result there.

He will never know as Mike blew Bernie away in a fit of rage all because Bernie wanted them off the property and he pulled the gun on them. Ray collected his gun from the cupboard and went looking for a radio to listen to any news or at least something to not only break the boredom but the continual silence and uneasiness in the cabin. Mike finally sat down in the lounge room he made no attempt to look at Ray, but Ray was silent not looking at Mike either the more

Ray searched for a radio the more frustrated he became with the quiet atmosphere within the cabin.

The two sat there in complete silence you could have heard a pin drop; the silence was deafening this made Ray even more edgy. The rain could be heard on the roof of the cabin, and it just seemed to get louder and louder, and made even worse because of the silence. Finally, Ray could not take anymore and decided he would go outside on the veranda even though the rain was so heavy.
Before he could leave the room Mike said;

"Where the hell do you think you are going?"

"To get some fresh air it is stifling in here," said Ray. Neither said another word.
How were they going to last another two days couped up in this cabin if this is what it was like after just one day. Outside the air was crisp and the wind was cutting, just like a mother in laws breath as some would say goes through you instead of around you. Ray only spent a couple of minutes out there it was too cold and wet and was even more miserable than inside the cabin. He returned into the now warm lounge room and again started a search for a radio, he was sure that Shaw had said that there was one here somewhere.

There had to be a television also as there were cables laying on the floor on the far side of the room. He went into each of the bedrooms and finally in the cupboard in the hallway hidden behind extra blankets and pillows was a television and radio. Ray pulled them out and carried them to the lounge room. He sat the television on the small table in the corner near the cables and put the radio on the breakfast bar. He then returned to the television plugged it in and connected the cables, turned it on and the television came to life. He tried the radio and found a station, luckily it was about two o'clock so there should be news on hopefully.

The television was on some soap, it looks like 'Days of Our Lives' or something of that genre. The volume was turned down so there was no tangible way of knowing. Mike sat there staring into space and was far away with his thoughts. Ray returned to the radio, turned up the volume, and scanned the channels until he found one luckily it was about to present the hourly news. The headline was that the police are looking for two armed men in connection the murder of a Deputy Sherriff and a yet to be named local. Anyone seeing or knowing any information are asked to contact the local police station.

24

I was seated in my office; it had just gone four o'clock and James brought me the preliminary results of the autopsy on Bernie Talbertson. I had the radio going in the background and the news came on, I suddenly sat up when hearing the report about two shooters the police were seeking in connection with the shooting of a Sheriff's Deputy and the shooting of yet an unnamed victim. Police were calling for any information to be reported to their local police station. My blood boiled again the media had details which we had not released for good reason. I quickly put the file down and phoned Hal and Ray to get the team together there was briefing at five o'clock in the conference room there had to be an end to these leaks.

I decided to set up a sting and quickly typed a scenario which I was going to leave openly on the table in the conference room. I had to believe that none of the team was involved, it had to be someone who had access to the building and to this floor. As I made my way to the conference room it suddenly hit me, the cleaner who had an interest in the murder wall as we call it, and what was on the table the other day when we were in there discussing the cases just after I had put the earlier case photographs up on the wall. His interest was I felt a little unhealthy and would he have the brains or the intestinal fortitude to sell it or give it to the media. I arrived at the conference room and the whole team was assembled even the forensic boys who must be so swamped with work were there.

I began by telling the team about the news broadcasts and that we had a leak within our team which did make me an unhappy camper, and if I found out it was one of them you would be off the team and could face disciplinary action even sacking. They all looked at each and around the room, all had blank looks on their faces, this made me feel a bit of idiot as it gave me the impression that not one of them was involved. I then noticed that there were two cameras

415

in each corner of the room facing the wall and table. Why had I not noticed these before maybe because this room is not usually used as much as it has done in the last weeks. I dismissed the group and told them to keep their eyes open and if they were talking to the media cease and desist at once.

 I acknowledged that I trusted each one of them, but this put a little doubt in my mind, so I implored them not to breach that trust. I asked Hal and Ray to stay behind and pointed to the cameras and asked where they are connected to as I wanted to view the footage. Ray said they were held in the communications room and that a deputy staffed the special room where the cameras where fed into on eight-hour shifts. The room covered all areas within the building as well as outside on all four corners and the carpark. I at once went downstairs and found this special room which was set up with about eight screens and each intermittingly change from one camera to another. I asked the young Deputy sitting in front of the screens reading a book and not really paying attention to them did the footage from each camera get recorded and stored. He pointed to a bank of recorders in the other corner of the room. I went ahead to request he mention the recordings for the conference room on the first floor from 2 days ago.

He looked at me and asked;
 "What time exactly are you looking for?" I said;
 "I do not know but we need to go through all the tape recordings for those days."

He suddenly had a look of 'what the fuck' all over his face as it meant he would have to do some work. I told him that I want it by the morning, and he was the only one to do this for me. He complained that his shift was about to finish, and I looked at him and said;

"Not today sonny Jim you will do as I ask and when you find what I am looking for transfer it onto a disc and then find me with that disc, do you get the point?"

He nodded his agreement, so I turned and left, as I did, I could see his reflection in the glass partition that separated this room from the main communications room, and he had a look of absolute bewilderment. I left him with his thoughts knowing he would do the job asked of him.

I decided that I was going to the motel with Ray and interview this Ashley Collins from San Diego, he is not connected but he is, I wanted to find out one way or another. Ruby had said it seemed strange especially for this time of the year to have two out of state people check into the motel in the off season was weird. If anyone was going to recognise who should be in the motel and when it was Ruby. During the busy season there would be people from all over the state and the country heading here for the skinning at Big Bear. To get people from outside of the state was rare, mostly from within the state was normal because of the tourism side of things. I had to agree with her as we would notice when there was a natural influx of people during the off season and then when the ski season started it was a huge influx and we would have to employ more Deputies.

As we approached the carpark and headed to the car, I asked Ray if he thought at all that one of the team was a leak to the media. He looked at me with a look of disbelief that I would even ask such a question. I took that, he believed there was no-one he did not trust. We got into the car and headed out of the carpark heading to the motel, I even thought, once we have finished with this fellow Collins, we might grab a bite at the Tavern/Diner and have a little talk to the owner Greg Manns as he was a bit like Ruby, sees and knows all that goes through the doors.

As we drove through the town and past the other bar and tavern as well as the plush hotel owned by the owners of the ski field. It was a reasonable price in off season but in ski season you would need to take out a mortgage to afford a one night stay there, it was ridiculous how the price fluctuates. It is unreal how this happens, and I cannot really get the gist of this. Ray was talking to me as we drove on while my brain was having those thoughts. I had mentioned this to the Psychiatrist when I visited about how my mind wanders at times onto to completely unrelated topics. He said that it was just human nature and was an automatic response when we were under pressure or to spend time thinking pleasant thoughts about something you would prefer to be doing or something you would like to achieve in the future.
Ray was looking at me quizzically when I turned to look at him and he said;
"You are away with the bloody fairies' mate, I bet any money you never heard a bloody word I was saying to you."

418

I nodded in agreement that I was a bit distracted. We arrived at the motel, and I swung the car into the carpark beside the office. I went in and asked Ruby if our friend Mr Collins was in, she replied he was. I signalled Ray and we went up to his room in one- one-two and knocked on the door.

He opened it and was a gentleman about forty-five slightly built with greying hair and piercing blue eyes, well dressed and I must admit he would have looked better in the Big Bear Hotel than in this motel as the surrounds did not suit his demeanour. I introduced myself as did Ray and he introduced himself as Detective Ashley Collins of the San Diego Police Department, homicide division. I must admit I was a bit take back by this and asked for his identification which he went over to the decide table and retrieve his police badge and identification wallet, presented it to us. I also noticed a holstered gun on the table as well.

After the pleasantries were over, I asked;

"Why did you not identify yourself to us when you came into town, as that would have been the courteous thing to do?" He replied;

"I am not here officially and yes I am out of my jurisdiction, but I am looking for a fellow by the name of Mike Grant, I had a snitch in Colorado who told me he was headed this way with another bloke by the name of Ray Beale." My interest peaked I questioned why he was after those two fellows.

He explained;

"Mike Grant was mixed up in some drug dealing with a guy in San Diego some years ago, but we could not get enough on him to nail him. I know all about what went down here some years back and the confidential informant I had left San Diego and resettled in Colorado, and it just so happens Grant and Beale stole a vehicle there and was seen crossing the border into Montana. I put two and two together and realised he was returning here to Oemen Lake. If I could prove that it was him then I would have approached, you for a warrant to arrest him and send him back to San Diego for trial on drug and sex charges."
I looked at him, then said;

"You know he is booked into the room underneath you and so is Beale. But they are booked in under assumed names and I can confirm they are back here and already having murdered tow people, a Deputy of mine and a civilian."
He looked at me in horror and said he was sorry that has happened. He asked;

"Have you got him in custody?" I replied that we did not, and we had no idea as to his whereabouts or that of Beale, only that they were still in town somewhere and they had help from others who we believe were also connected to the murders and the macabre goings on from years ago. I suggested we pool resources and he come into the station tomorrow and we can brief him on things so far.
I asked;

"Have you eaten?" he nodded saying that he had not so I suggested we go to the Tavern and have a meal and we

420

can go over things in general there. He agreed and the three of us left his room and headed for the tavern.

Back at the communications room it was abuzz with movement as there had been a so-called sighting of Grant and Beale at the causeway carpark, Hal was on the job and was trying to ring me, but my phone was turned off for the time being. He did not realise Ray was with me, so Hal took Bill with him to talk to the witness and to see if there was anything in the information that had been telephoned through. The young Deputy looking through the tapes for me of the periods I had given him had also turned up interesting footage and was transferring it onto a disc for me. He took the disc and placed it in an envelope on my desk, as he was leaving my office, he noticed a cleaner in the conference room looking through the paperwork on the table. He walked in just as the cleaner shoved something into his pocket;

"What the fuck are you doing in here can't you read the sign that says, "NO UNAUTHORISED ENTRY," that means you."

The cleaner quickly grabbed his stuff and left by the other door entry into the room, but the deputy had his name from his identification badge. It was a Gary Marsden. I did not know it the time, but this name was going to ring a few bells for me down the track.

25

Shaw and Forrester drove through the morning gloom, with rain, wind, and sleet hitting the windscreen and the wipers were battling to cope with the onslaught. Shaw, who was driving, was apprehensive of the upcoming meeting with Beale and Grant, and now knowing the mayor had resigned long ago was a shock and it made things even harder to swallow, and with now no real power behind them Dean and himself were going to have to go it alone and get rid of the Beale and Grant problem. Steven was not killing people, and even being connected to the thought was not on his mind, where as Dean had no problems with it as he had already proven in the past when all those poor women were murdered. Steven knew he has always been a great negotiator and hopes that he can do the same in this situation.

The biggest problem was Mike Grant's short fuse and his narcissistic psychopathic attitude. Dean had never seen Mike in the frightful state that Steven saw him in that day in the carpark at the causeway. The weather was making both feel a little on the gloomy side as this grey, wet, and windy weather had been around now for two days and it was becoming a real effort to get oneself fired up of a morning even if it were to go to work at their own individual businesses. Suddenly there was a flash of lighting across the lake and the boom of thunder, Steven in his daydreaming thoughts, suddenly hit the brakes hard causing both he and Dean to be catapulted forward with their seat belts grabbing tight and jerking them back in their seats.

"What the fuck are you doing?" shouted Dean from the passenger's seat looking rather flustered.

"I was not really thinking clearly, and the thunder brought me back to reality rather quickly and I panicked," he rebutted with a tremble in his voice. "Do you want me to drive?" asked Dean.

"No" replied Steven.

"I am okay."

Steven put the car into gear, and they moved off again towards their destination in the woods. Both took deep breaths. They were both aware that this meeting at the cabin with Beale and Grant was not going to be easy, and they needed to buy some time so they could work things out, especially with the mayor as he knew everything and in the pickled state, he was in twenty-four hours a day it seemed, they needed to sober him up or all hell could come down on them at once. Dean reflected on what had happened years before and that with time he surmised it had all calmed down and basically gone away, but no, the demons had returned in the shape of Beale and Grant. Things could be better by the end of today or bloody worse thought Dean. They drove on in relative quiet except for the car radio sending out music in the background although barely audible.

Steven was concentrating hard on the road ahead now as he was wide awake and alert after their little shake up back in town. They left the town limits behind and headed North, past the reservation and the turn off to Big Bear Ski field, the causeway was about another ten miles further on and the cabin some eight after that. Steven was hoping that Beale had had a chance to calm Grant down and that Grant was not in a trigger-happy mood on this dark and wet day. He thought this could all turn to shit with the moody Grant in charge of things, and what is he going to say when they tell him about his good mate the mayor. He will most likely blow a gasket as they had known each other since high school, but they had gone in different directions after that, although stayed connected. Grant was High School football quarter back and could have been anything except for his temper and his love of the drink.

The mayor on the other hand was a goody two shoes, did nothing wrong, straight A student and drew the girls like ducks to water, although some of the lads thought he may have been gay as he never really went out with any of the girls. Even the graduation dinner he was very withdrawn and seemed out of place, yet he was voted most likely to succeed. Mike was never a scholar he was the football hero and how that got him through school Steven did not know. Steven, Grant, and the mayor all attended school together Dean was an outsider from another state but came to Oemen Lake with his business to start up a franchise here and never left.

As they neared the causeway and turnoff on North 37 towards the cabin, Dean final spoke;

"Do you think that Beale and Grant will listen to reason, I mean think about what really needs to be done and how we have to go about it, we do not want Mike attracting any more attention than he already has, and I do not need any more shit to hit?",

Steven paused for a moment then in a calming voice;

"We just have to convince them both that we need mor time and cannot do anything without the mayor anyway as he has the final say in a lot of this, after all he brought us into this whole scenario?". There was silence for a while just as they reached the turnoff to the cabin Steven said,

"You were all for not giving in to the demands and leaving Grant and Beale to their own devices what the fuck has changed your attitude?"

Dean sat silent saying nothing and this worried Steven as to what he had in mind.

They reached the cabin and Beale was standing in the doorway with a rifle pointed at them, Steven flashed the lights a couple of times and Beale retreated inside the cabin. Next thing both Beale and Grant appeared at the doorway, Grant did not look in good mood, he had a distinct look of disgust on his face and his body language that of a very agitated man. Dean was first to get out of the car and slam the door shut, Mike Grant yelled at him,

"Where is my two million you mother fucker, you better have it or else one of you aren't leaving here alive today." With this Dean remained close to the car and finally Steven got out of the car and shouted;

"We are here to talk, we have not got your money as we have had a hiccup,"

"Hiccup my arse, you fuckers get in that fucking car and get my money as I want out of this place. You have one day to get and be back here by eight in the morning day after tomorrow, I am sick of this fucking weather this fucking cabin and Beale so fuck off and do as I ask." Just then he pulled a pistol, and a shot rang out going between Steven and Dean over the top of the car into the bushes behind them.

Beale grabbed Grant's arm and as he did Grant turned and threw him back against a chair on the porch, with Beale falling to the floor. Grant raised his pistol and put a shot into the floor beside Beales right hand.

"Touch me again fucker and the next one will be in your fucking head; I am sick of all this shit and the fuckers who do not follow fucking orders." Beale lay there on the porch shaking with what had just happened. In the meantime, Steven Shaw, and Dean Forrester had taken cover behind the car. Forrester pulled a pistol from his belt and fired at Grant on the porch missing him and the bullet slammed into the door frame behind him.

"You fucker, have the balls to shoot at me, I will fuck you up you shithead," yelled Grant.

"For fucks sake calm down everyone, we need to talk this out or we get nowhere and then one of us or three could end up dead," shouted Beale from his prone position on the floor of the porch. Shaw yelled at Forrester and Grant;

"To stop being fucking idiots put the guns away and let's talk." Finally, Grant raised his gun in the air and put it back in his belt, as did Forrester.

Forrester and Shaw came out from behind the car and stood in front of it, they took a couple of steps toward the cabin and Beale had finally pulled himself onto the chair on the porch, just as he did Grant shouted;

"Where is my money and what the fuck are you doing here if you have not got my money".

"That is what we are here to work out with you Mike for Christ's sake calm down and let us go inside and talk about this we are getting fucking soaked standing here in the rain and the longer this goes on the longer it will be before you get your money." Yelled Shaw back at him.

Mike Grant was not in a happy mood, but he calmed down enough to allow Shaw and Forrester to come up the steps and enter the cabin as Beale got up from the chair and followed. Grant looked around to make sure there was no one else around.

26

After the events of last evening and having had dinner with Collins from San Diego, Ray and I were convinced that Mike Grant had been a remarkably busy boy not only from our case but across five states it seemed. I grabbed a coffee as I entered the office area and went straight to my office where on my desk was the morning paper and the headline read;

"Police at a loss who is the Murderer."

Now my sting had worked all I needed was to find out who the prick was who was leaking the information to the press. There was also an envelope on my desk under the paper I at once put it into the player and watch the segments the Deputy had recorded for me. What a surprise when I saw who had been in the conference room staring at the board and searching the files spread out on the tables. Just then the young Deputy who had been doing the surveillance of the tapes for me came in and asked if I had viewed them.

I acknowledged and he told me that he had caught the young cleaner in there last night looking through things and he was quite sure that he took something from the table but could not be sure but had a bit of film I might want to see. I followed him through to the recording room and he played the tape for me showing the cleaner pick up my piece of bait paper and stuff it in his pocket just as the deputy entered the room. I asked;

"If he had gotten a name and he told me Gary Madden," I thought fuck this could not possibly be related to the Marsden involved in the murders from the earlier case.

My mind racing, I hurried back to the conference room and started to search through the files until I found the one, I was looking for. Stewart Madden, he was mixed up alright in the first case and had connections to all parties. There was also a Victoria Merrin who worked for Steven Shaw and was somehow connected to all this as well. How they fitted in with Madden meant I would have to go through the files closely again, and if I am right about my gut feeling this Gary Madden is related to Stewart Madden, and he could be trouble, as if I did not have enough already with Grant and Beale on the loose and two dead bodies, and why would Madden be back here now.

Armed with this information I knew that I had to interview this Gary Madden and soon as he was going down for interfering with a police investigation so he could join his brother looking through bars for a time and say goodbye to his fancy cleaning job. This was becoming a bloody nightmare all over again and something that I really did not want. I called Ray and then Hal to see if they could get hold of this Gary Madden and find out where he lived, how long he had been back in town and what was his reason for being here. I was also going to advise him that his little snooping job and leaks to the press was going to cost him unless he some information that would help me.

Looking through the files the name Isabella Shaw and Victoria Merrin also popped up and I was not sure yet how or why they were connected to all this as the files were vague in their actual documentation as to how and why they fit into the scenario but that was another lead I would need the team to chase up on. This whole case was again becoming a nightmare, and at least there was one consolation in all this we only had two bodies now, was it a blessing or a calm before the storm. Just then Ashley Collins the detective from San Diego knocked on my door and came in;

"Thanks for the dinner last night, and I apologise for not letting you know earlier of my presence here. It was unprofessional and extremely discourteous." I waved it away saying;

"We are all working for the same outcome here and hopefully another set of eyes might help in this situation anyway."

I showed him to the conference room, and we collected a coffee each on the way, he looked at the board and I could tell by his face he was a bit shocked at what he saw.

He took a couple of minutes to gather his thoughts and then in a rather timid like voice, like that of a child who had be scolded for doing something wrong;

"Fuck, I did not realise just how much mayhem this case had back then and now these two arseholes have brought all this back here again it must be frightening to think what they may be capable of".

I looked at him and nodded my agreement, but also informed him we still only had two more deaths at this point and both point to Grant.

The autopsy results were here, and I read them aloud to Collins;

"The Deputy, Bernie Talbertson and his wife were laying there as well, and it had been confirmed by dental records and fingerprints that the woman in the grave in the glasshouse was in fact May Talbertson. The toxicology report from the bone marrow and cells showed she had been given a lethal dose of a cocktail combining Fentanyl and Morphine. She was an extremely ill lady with advance stages of cancer and must have been in excruciating pain."

He paused for a moment before continuing;

"It seems like Bernie had euthanised her some weeks prior although the timeline was a bit sketchy as the lime which was spread over the bodies as well as the temperature within the glasshouse had slowed down decomposition greatly. The coroner proved though that her death would have been quick and painless, she died sometime between eight and twelve weeks ago."

I took a sip of coffee a long breath and continued with the report;

"Bernie died from two gunshots, one to the right upper quadrant of the left side of the body penetrating the Pectoral Muscle and Left Lung upper lobe and lodging in the Pulmonary Artery, basically killing him from blood loss. The second bullet penetrated in or around the second and third rib and lodging in the Costal Cartlidge, if this had been the only shot, he may have had a chance of life, but the other bullet was the murder bullet."

I again sipped my coffee and saw Collins who was in deep thought and saying nothing so I continued;

"The Deputy unfortunately was shot in the forehead just above the right eye socket and penetrated the frontal lobe lodging in the front area of the Parietal Lobe of the brain, death would have been almost instantaneous."

I acknowledged to him what the rest of the report was about and did he want to peruse them further as the rest of the reports were mostly about stomach contents blood workups and other medical jargon which I was not interested in now. He showed he did not as he had the picture. All I knew was we had three victims two by murder and the other by what may or may not have been aided suicide. Bernie had already paid the price for his wife's death and that was a costly one with that of his own life.

We still did not have a connection between Bernie, Grant or Beale or was it just random. We do know that the two murders were committed by Grant and Beale as it was proven, they had the means and the opportunity, now was the problem proving which one pulled the trigger, my feeling was Grant as he was an unstable fucker back years ago and I doubt he would have changed. At that point Hal rang and informed me we had Gary Madden in a holding cell downstairs, and did I want him brought up to an interview room.

I stated yes and asked Collins did he want to sit in on the interview with Stewart Madden's brother or so we believed it to be his brother, we were yet to confirm that although it seemed strange same surname and he was here in town and so interested in the information on the table and the board. He acknowledged he would, if it were okay, I nodded and we headed for the interview rooms further around the other side of the building, calling via my office first to gather the press stuff we had compiled as well as my notebook and diary.

I also collected a recorder even though the interviews were videoed, and voice recorded I wanted my own. We reached interview room number two and entered, Hal already had this Gary Madden seated and looking very full of himself. He was very much like his brother very defined features, blue eyes, and dark hair, he seemed tall although he was seated, well-built but he had that schoolboy overall look. He had a distinct air of arrogance which pissed me off, as I was about to put a dent in that arrogance.

27

Isabella Shaw was not quite sure as to what her husband Steven had been up to but was sure that he and Dean Forrester were mixed up in something that was not good. But for the time being she was more worried about Ms Victoria Merrin who she had found out had been sleeping with her husband and that it been going on for years. Although the affair had seemed to have fizzled out, she could not be sure as Ms Merrin still worked for Steven. She had kept all the ingredients she needed to fix her up and be rid of her hidden in a lockup in Big Bear Village, Steven had no idea. She was a very driven woman and what was hers remained hers, she was not going to share anything, especially her husband. This rival for her husband's affections had to go.

Isabella wondered what Steven was up to he had left early this morning no breakfast and it was strange he did not even have coffee, so there was something wrong, she knew it was not the business as he would talk about that and ask her advice if it was anything that needed attention. This was not a usual Steven and it worried Isabella, that maybe the affair had recommenced, or he was in trouble with that bloody Dean Forrester again. She thought Steven had left all that shit behind him years ago, even though she did know the full extent of what was going on back then, but it had caused both to be edgy and very unresponsive to each other. The two of them had only just rekindled their relationship with a Mediterranean cruise which seemed to be the tonic they both needed.

Her plans for Victoria Merrin she decided that today was the day and if Steven were involved again with her then so be it, she would kill two birds with the one stone and have no regrets. She showered and dressed quickly in track pants loose hoodie and runners, rushed down to the garage opened the garage door and entered her very distinctive black Range Rover, reversed out of the garage onto the gravel driveway, the rain was persistent and although was not the best day to be travelling or even being outside she had a goal and not the weather or anything else was going to put her off. She pressed the button to close the garage door and as t was closing drove away down the driveway towards the main road.

Once on the main road she headed for Big Bear Village where a long time ago she had hired a lockup. As she drove along through town and heading North, she contemplated exactly how she was going to get Miss Merrin back and make sure that she never had a chance with Steven again. She passed the entrance to the reservation and continued her journey. The lockup was just this side of Big Bear Village, and reached it quicker than she thought she would, pulled into the driveway got out unlocked the gate and drove around the first two blocks of lockups and found the block her number thirty-nine was in. She got out and the rain seemed heavier, she covered her head with her hand and entered the code which opened the door to the corridor that led her to the doorway through which she found her lockup. Upon opening the door, turned on the light and shut the door behind her.

On the long bench she found the box of surgical gloves and put a pair on, then grabbed a bottle about the size of medium sized perfume bottle, continued to the other side of the room where there was a small upright steel cupboard, from there she gathered two bottles of clear liquid. Putting on a mask she opened one of the bottles carefully pouring a small amount into the empty bottle a small splash of a drop fell on her upper arm, she wiped it with a disinfectant swab.

Then emptied an amount of the second bottle of liquid into the same bottle. She now had both liquids mixed in the same bottle, removing the gloves, and putting on a fresh pair, from her handbag she withdrew another bottle pouring a small amount into the bottle holding the two other liquids, she hoped she had correctly remembered the exact amount to use, noticing that it had a slight yellow hue and an odour of acid. With a small spray bottle of which was perfume she got out of her handbag, spraying some into the bottle that now held the three liquids, she sealed the bottle tight and removed the gloves.

Putting on a fresh pair she carefully recapping the two bottles and returned them to the metal cupboard, upon which she checked the piece of paper she pinned on the wall that what she had done was correct and that the right amount had been mixed. She knew the perfume was not necessary but if this plan were to work, she wanted to make sure that Steven and no other man would look at this bitch ever again. Turning off the light she locked the door and turned and walked the corridor with the suspected bottle in her still gloved hand, placed the bottle into the small calico bag she had brought with her, removed the gloves dropped them into the rubbish bin beside the door and re-entered the code for the external door and exited the building, making sure the door closed behind her and out into the rain again, getting into her car had a smile of some satisfaction on her face.

 Starting the car turned it around and headed for the main gate which automatically opened this time as she was exiting and did not have to enter a code, turned South onto the main road, and left Big Bear Village in her rear-view mirror. As she travelled along, she wondered how Steven would react when he found out what had happened to his precious Victoria. Again, she passed the entrance to the reservation and continued to town, upon passing the boardwalk entrance she turned right into Grove Close, stopped the vehicle of about four houses from the end of the cul-de-sac.

Getting out of the vehicle grabbing the bag with her precious cargo in it, walked to the block of apartments at the very end of the cul-de-sac, entered the pathway which took her down the side of the building to back stairs where Isabella mounted the stairs to the first landing. On the landing went right and found number three, from her purse she took out another pair of surgical gloves, a gauze cloth and carefully opening the bag wearing the gloves, unscrewed the cap of her bottle of potion and dampened the cloth with the liquid. She rubbed it on the door handle and around the area, making sure to get a good coverage. Then along the windowsill and around the door jam, emptying the bottle of liquid in the process.

Placing the bottle back into the calico bag and removing the rubber gloves placing those also into the bag. Isabella turned and walked back along the landing to the stairs and descended back down to ground level. Made it to her vehicle and turned around and headed back out of Grove Close, turning right onto the main road again, heading through town towards home, but before making it there she stopped by a rubbish bin and placed the calico bag and contents into it. Returning to her car she returned home and all the way with a smile of contentment and satisfaction.

When she arrived home parking her vehicle in the garage and closing the door, went inside and poured herself a wine, saying to herself bugger the time of day I deserve a drink, I have rid myself of that bitch once and for all. She walked out onto the patio and with a sneer of sheer glee skulled the rest of the wine and headed for a refill. At that moment Lucy their housekeeper came out of the bedroom with the vacuum and was startled not only to see the madam home but also drinking.

"Are you alright Mrs Shaw?" she asked in a timid sounding voice. Isabella answered;

"Never been better Lucy, my dear, the day has started off fantastically and can only get better."

Lucy turned and began vacuuming again not answering or even glancing back at Isabella. The rest of the day went as normal answering emails and bringing the books up to date for the business, also sending out invoices to whom had ordered products and processed the banking online.

It was a day full of joy Isabella thought to herself she had achieved her goal or so it seemed, but the full enjoyment of her exercise would be when it was announced or Steven informed her that Victoria Merrin was dead, gone, never to be seen or heard from again. She continued with her tasks and made lunch for both her and Lucy and invited Lucy to join her on the balcony, again Lucy was taken aback by this as this was the second or third time that Mrs Shaw had invited her to dine with her, and it made Lucy uncomfortable as she was not used to this and it was out of character for the lady of the house to dine with her.

Anyway, Lucy obliged and joined Isabella on the patio, and they chatted about the world and what it holds for them both. Luckily, the patio can be enclosed as the weather was not good and the rain could be heard on the glass roof of the patio as it pounded away trying to break into the serene peace that was under it. Isabella even thought that maybe a few days up at the cabin might be an effective way to relax over the weekend coming up, they had not been there in so long.

The weather would need to improve although she did like it up there when there was snow around it made it feel very surreal. The other good thing about the cabin in the snow was it was not far from the Big Bear Ski Field which both her and Steven enjoyed. She had been able to ski since she was young her father teaching her and her sister. Isabella had to teach Steven as he had never been to the snow until they moved here and brought the cabin which was their first home, it was cheap, and both found it comfortable but when the business was flourishing, they decided to move to town and build the house they now have.

Both had wanted children but due to a curse of nature were unable and they had made the decision not to try or adopt. She often felt that children in this house would have made it a real home, but she was now too old, and they had not discussed the subject in ages, years even. Isabella never broached the subject, and she could not remember Steven saying anything about for such a long time she had forgotten the last time he said anything. It was good when Lucy brought her two young ones over, to swim in the pool they made up for not having their own as they could give them back when the time came with no guilt feelings. Isabella often thought whether that was feeling selfish, but the feeling was soon dismissed from her mind. Her thoughts suddenly transferred back to her little escapade of earlier in the day and when she would hear of her triumph, she dares not raise the matter with Steven, but then he was too engrossed in whatever it was he was doing at present, it was nothing to do with the company she repeated to herself otherwise she would have known and now her mind raced with untold imaginings.

28

At the cabin, things had become a little more placid and Mike Grant had calmed down compared to his original barrage when he arrived, and all weapons had been placed in safe places so no one could be tempted.

Dean asked;

"What is it you want after all this time Mike, I honestly thought you were free and had no reason to return here." Mike stared at him up and down, then with a menacing tone said;

"I came back for the money that Beale and I had stashed as well as the drugs also", Dean looked at him with astonishment;

"What drugs and money, as far as we knew that was all separated and dealt out when the others were caught and the case was closed, or so we thought and you two skipped," nodding at Dean and Steven.

"We took what we could easily and stashed the rest in the locker room in the end of the tunnel number eight."

"Fuck if I had known that or even thought that" said Steven

"There would have been nothing there now".

Mike scowled at him, and Dean gave Steven an evil stare that without saying was not the thing to say with how volatile Mike was. Dean taking charge was not in a mood to give Ray or Beale anything considering what they had retrieved from the Old Mill, also he was unforgiving considering that these two had already murdered two people from the media reports, and how many more were going to die before this whole mess was put to sleep. Steven sat there very pensive mulling over his own thoughts and what it meant that Mike and Beale had that extra money and drugs that they had told him about that first day he had met them at the causeway carpark.

He then spoke up;

"What exactly is it you want, you told me you wanted another two million and we could have the drugs which were worth a lot more than that." Dean said;

" I do not want any drugs, you can keep them and stick them up your arse for all I care and you are not getting two million not from me anyway and I do not think Steven is going to give up two million or even a million for that matter."

With that Mike Grant stood up and walked over to the breakfast bench picked up his gun and aimed at Steven,

"You will go and get the two million or I will drop you where you sit you fucking arsehole, and do not tempt me as I am not in the mood to be fucked with."

Steven stood up walked a couple of paces closer toward Mike and with a gesture;

"Come on you are fucking nutter, you are a fucking psychopath and need to be locked up", Steven yelled;

"No don't shoot I will get the money somehow there is no need for any more bloodshed, and we can surely work this out as grown adults. Let's keep thing a little civil and talk about this as we are all in a bind here."

Dean glanced at Steven and was almost telling him to shut up and that Mike Grant was not going to shoot him. Just then there was a loud bang and a flash from the end of the pistol's barrel. Steven suddenly had a look of extreme anguish on his face as he grabbed at his chest.

"You fuckwit," shouted Ray;

"What the fuck are you doing, we were getting somewhere."

As he spoke Dean Forrester fell to the floor, and blood started to pool around his right side as he gasps for breath. The cabin fell silent for what seemed ages but it was but a few seconds, Steven raced to Dean's side and put pressure on the wound but could see it was a lost cause as Dean faded, he felt for a pulse and there was none, Dean lay there with open eyes and a deadly stare. Steven wiped his hands over Dean's eyes to close them then stood and stared at the end of the gun, while saying,

"Mike what the fuck have you done, I suppose I am next am I, you are a fucking idiot you have just made this whole thing so much more difficult and more complicated than it ever had to be".

Mike Grant cocked the pistol and looking at Steven said,

"Do not tempt me arsehole, I will have no hesitation in putting a piece of lead in you too, both you and that arsehole treated me like shit all those years ago and he thought he could be my lord and master, so he got his wish, he is now with his lord and is master of no one".

Ray Beale sat with his head in his hands and shook uncontrollable at the scene that unfolded before him. Mike still pointing the gun at Steven said;

"You now get the two million and bring it here three days from now, and if not, I will come looking for you and your bitch and will have no hesitation in topping both of you." Steven looked at Mike and said;

"I cannot get that amount of money together in that time as it is Friday and the banks do not carry that sort of cash on hand here, I would have to go down to Helena, then they would need notice of me wanting to draw that amount, also there would be questions asked about taking that much out of the account at once. Also, you know the mayor who would owe you something is no longer in that position he is a fucked-up alcoholic and does not even know what day it is let alone give me the time of day, or you any type of plausible answer."

"I do not give a fuck about the mayor or your fucked up excuses you get me the two million you get the drugs or as I said you die as does anyone else who gets in my way now. I have nothing absolutely fucking nothing to lose"
Mike said with real malice in his voice. Finally, Ray stood up and at once Mike swung the gun on him,

"What the fuck are you going to do or say you chicken shit. You have let these arseholes run shotgun over you for so many years now and we have the upper hand, so you either go with it or end up on the floor with that arsehole."
Ray took a step back and looked at Dean's body lying on the floor in a pool of blood asking himself how the fuck did it get so bad, three dead now and they were no closer to the extra two million, had the law chasing them, and on top of that Mike had this fixation on Farrer and seems to have settled on getting Farrer above all else. That is the one

443

thing Ray has yet to really come to grips with as to what Farrer had done to Mike to cause him to have this vendetta. Finally, Ray spoke up,

"What are we going to do with that body now, we cannot exactly bury it in the glasshouse and out here in the middle of bloody nowhere." Steven said;

"You can't bury him on this property, there would be hell to pay if it was found as Isabella knows nothing of what I was into those years ago or still now."

"Well, isn't that fucking fantastic," said Mike;

"We will drop him off the causeway into the icy lake and let the wind or whatever carry his body wherever."

With a look of unknown anger Steven was not going to have anything to do with that and looking at Ray who was now beside Mike, and then Ray said;

"I will take the body tonight and dump it over the causeway to get rid of our problems hopefully. We need to get a few things straight before I do this though."
He continued;

"Mike you must drop the thing with Farrer and the two million as I can see Steven is not going to be able to get the money without raising red flags, secondly, the drugs will bring us more in Chicago or even New York I am sure we can find a buyer even it is only fifty or seventy percent of what it is worth, lastly, we need to get out of this place or we are going to get caught and I do not feel like going down for a period of time in jail that will probably see me end my life inside". Mike looked at him and with a voice of absolute sound of dissatisfaction in it declared;

444

"I am not dropping the thing with Farrer, he owes me more than I wish to talk about, secondly, the drugs are not really my worry but I agree, we may be able to sell them, but what we get for them is not going to make up for what we have lost or more over what I have lost".

Ray finally decided to get up the balls to ask Mike what it was with Farrer and why his vendetta was so strong. Mike went to say;

"That the robbery that went horribly wrong in which a person was shot by Farrer was Mike's little brother and he had never forgiven Farrer for that as he got away with the shooting as a clear and justified shooting, which Mike did not agree with as he was a part of the robbery and Farrer did not have to shoot as his little brother Ely was giving himself up and he was unarmed. Farrer planted a gun and was pissed out of his brain at the time, but they covered it up and he was allowed to resign and ended up here as the fucking sheriff of all things."

Mike went on to tell them why he was here;

"That is why he came to Oemen Lake for no other reason that making money through his contacts got the whole drug thing going, the bodies were unfortunately not really his thing but it helped to get more to hopefully in the end to frame Farrer for the whole thing but McLean and Bourke the fucking idiots went too far with the sex slave thing and the body organ bit. Then Madden got involved and the slave trade for sex got out of control the mayor and two other police got involved in the finish it was just too big and we started to lose control as the bastards from overseas became involved and we had Interpol and the FBI all

445

chasing their arses to catch us. Then McLean killed Barelli and that fucked everything."

Ray and Steven then knew there was no tangible way of Mike stopping his rampage as it was too personal and how the fuck were they going to stop him. The mayor got Steven and Dean involved as well as Beale as they had the means and money to finance the projects and skim off the top and help with laundering the money through their various businesses. Steven looked at Mike;

"Why the hell did you shoot Dean, he could have helped you get out of this mess he has more contacts and is better connected in many ways than I am." Mike looked at him for a moment then said;

"He challenged me and I do not like people who believe they are better than me especially when they front me like he did talk down to me thinking he was the big man and was challenging me to act on my convictions so I did what was necessary to put him in his place, that is it and nothing else".

Ray helped Steven wrap Dean's body in a sheet off one of the beds and took it out to the car and loaded into the boot of the car. The rain was still pelting down and did not look like it was going to let up at any time soon, which suited Ray to get rid of the body later. The darkness then coupled with the rain would help cover up what Ray had to do, even though he did not like it as he did like Dean, he seemed a fair enough guy even if he could be a bit of a martyr at times. Returning inside Mike had started to clean up the blood mumbling something discernible and trying not to act as though this was his doing or his problem.

Ray went into the room to gather a jacket while Steven announced he had a few thousand in his safe at home and would try and bring that as well try and get to Dean's as he knew he had plenty of cash at home and Steven knew how to get to it, although he was unsure of what amount was there. Also, Dean kept money at his safe in his office so there was another avenue that could be looked at. The one thing Steven did say to Mike;

"If he got this money then the thing with Farrer was to go and get out of town without any more death or trouble." Mike was non-committal.

29

In the interview room, we started the questioning of Gary Madden, Hal had read him his rights and he had refused his right to a lawyer as far as he was concerned he had done nothing wrong and did not realise we had the film of his activities in the conference room, or that we had contacted the press outlets trying to find who had told them about the investigation, we were going to bluff him on this matter as the press would tell us nothing as they would invoke their right to protect their sources. I started with the obvious question,

"What relation are you to a Stewart Madden?" he looked at me with a look of complete awareness that we already knew who he was and what that relationship was. His answer was one of contemptuous attitude, he was going to play this out to its fullest, he surmised they had nothing and that was his persona until Hal started the video. This whole time Collins was seeing with interest Madden's body language.

I opened the file on the desk and read from it as he, eyes glued to the screen watching the video showing him on several occasions entering the conference room and rifling through the papers and even taking photos of the board with his phone. My commentary was read in unison Gary Franklin Madden, born Alabama, son of Noel and Francis Madden, one brother Stewart Madden. I did not go right into the file his juvenile record for theft, driving under the influence and spending time in Juvenile as well as six months for drug possession. I looked at him as he still watched with intent the video and without any movement I stated to him;

"Well Mr Madden, what have you got to say for yourself?"
He turned looked at me, and gave me the finger, I turned to Hal;

"Lock him up and charge him with obstruction, theft, interfering in an investigation and suspicion of murder," the last one was to see if there was a reaction and it worked.

"What the fuck is this murder bullshit?" he said,

"Well, we have a body and you have been extremely interested in our investigation that we believe you are our number one suspect in the murder of a Deputy."

As I finished, he shifted in his chair and said;

"I murdered no one and was only trying to make some extra cash as this reporter offered me a hundred dollars for each piece of information, I gave him. That is all, I promise."

He looked at Collins as if asking him for a comment or to back him that he was telling the truth. I looked at him and said;

"You are still interfering in the process of an investigation and would have to face that charge as what the press printed was a fabrication especially the latest as that was a sting to see if could catch the leak and we hooked a big fishhook, line, and sinker, you!"

Hal took him by the arm and took him out of the room to be charged with the impeding an investigation charge, I stopped the video and collected the disc and file and looked at Detective Collins well what do you think of that as we returned to my office, grabbing a coffees on the way. Ray came in just as we returned and I beckoned him to sit. Collins sat in the rear of the office as Ray handed me the files he had been perusing and had produced a plausible scenario as to why Beale and Grant were back in town and there was something else that had been bugging him for some time. He started to tell us how he had always thought that there was one maybe two persons in town who had the influence and the backing money wise to fund the enterprises that went on back at the time. He did not believe that we rounded up all the culprits when the case was closed. I looked at him and showed that I have had that gut feeling for the same amount of time, I had my suspicions but nothing to really go on or to follow through with what I thought, but this was about to change I thought especially with Beal and Grant back on the scene. They came back to town for something and it was not to just murder a Deputy and Bernie. Collins looked at us both and asked;

"Who do you think was the money men if you want to share?"

I looked across at Ray and then Collins and was unsure if I should tell who my suspicions were about.

Ray looked at me and I felt he was in the same frame of mind but I decided bugger it I would tell him my thoughts if it stayed here in this office as if my gut feeling was correct, I did not want to scare them off this time as I wanted to take the whole lot down this time.

"Steven Shaw and Dean Forrester are involved as well as a high-ranking public official, and he I also believe to be the mayor. But as I stated this is only a gut feeling and will take a lot more than that to make the thing stick." Ray shifted in his chair and moved it so he was facing both Collins and I, nodded in agreement with what I had just said;

"You are right Ian we have nothing at present but all roads seem to lead to those three as not only do they have the funds to finance this operation but they have a hell of a sway of power in this town, considering both are major employers and make a huge contribution to the town and

450

no one would suspect them, except for a small-town Sheriff and his right-hand detective".

Ray stopped short of saying that we should bring them in for questioning but like me we did not want to stir the pot and scare them off. We had to solve where Grant and Beale were to start with then bring them in and hopefully one of them would break and give us the main characters in this drama. I knew deep down the one to crack would be Beale as Mike Grant had too much stubbornness to give in and he would not want to appear weak. His narcissistic attitude would not allow him to wilt.

I looked at Collins and asked what he thought but there was no comment from him even though he had been through the files at length, also he only wanted Grant as that was his main reason for being here and Grant was the centre of his attention at this present time. I knew though that we would have first crack at Grant as he had committed crimes here long before he had out East and what we would have on him here would be enough to put him away for a long time. I asked Ray if he could find out where Mrs Shaw was and that squeeze of Dean Forrester that we found out about during the last inquiry, her name has slipped my mind for the time being. He said;

"You mean Victoria Merrin?" I nodded that's her we may have to have a little talk to both and see if they have anything to say about the whole situation, as they may now know more than they did back when.
Collins looked at me and said;

"Sometimes the partners know a lot more than they let on as a way of protecting their loved ones but also to cover their own arse in the long run."

I had to agree with him as that had been my thinking back when we first interviewed them but they had alibis and really did know nothing of any importance. Maybe now years down the track they may have found out things and from memory was it not that Mrs Shaw knew Merrin was tonsil tickling the husband but could not prove it or had paid a slob call Mews to do the job on him or am I getting confused. Ray was of the opinion, that it was Linda Forrester who had paid Mews to knock off Merrin, but there was such a tangled mess of who was doing who and it had no real bearing on the whole case overall anyway as that was not the focus back then.

I finally got it straight that Linda Forrester was having the affair with Stewart Madden and Cerise Blackwell who I think if I remember correctly was Ray Beale's niece and worked at Beale's Transport business and was sheet shuffling with Dean Forrester. Cerise was killed by Linda Forrester who died. We also found out that Dean was Stewart Madden's adopted brother or vice versa not sure exactly. Then I thought hang on if that is right then Gary Madden must be related with Dean Forrester, and so the spider web gets even more tangled and entwined. Ms Merrin was Steven Shaw's squeeze and his sheet shuffler which meant I am sure Isabella Shaw may know about those two so she may drop the hammer on Shaw.

Holy man this was becoming a nightmare of who was with who and how we were going to sort it out. I decided I would get the two Deputies down stairs to go through the files and try to put together a sequence of who was involved with who and how it was connected and put it all on a new board in the conference room then we could interlock what we have now and how it all connected to the past, although I was not keen on bringing the past into it except for linking Beale, Grant and then Shaw and Forrester and whomever the higher official was if any.

The two young Deputies came to my office and explained what I wanted them to do, they would need to see the Sergeant downstairs and tell him I had cleared it for them to do this job as it was going to take a little time. They seemed keen enough as it meant they got to work on a murder case instead of just handing out parking tickets or pulling over speeding or drunk drivers. It was good to see keen young officers coming through the ranks, even though this may have seemed a minimal task to me as a lead detective, this was going to be all new for them especially when they caught sight of some of the photographs in the files and those already on the board. Ray left with Detective Collins once I had briefed the young Deputies. They were going to follow up on some leads as well as call on Mrs Shaw and Steven as well as Dean Forrester. Make a call to Ms Merrin and interview them all, and hopefully shake something loose, although I did not hold out a lot hope we were going to have to shake the tree firmly to get the acorns to drop into place.

I went to get another coffee when there was a commotion downstairs about a body being found I went down to investigate what the ruckus was all about. Hal and Ray as well as Detective Collins were there as well as the rest of my team all listening intently to the police radio call that a body had been found near the Western side of the causeway. The officer calling it in was unsure but reported he believed it was Dean Forrester, he had been shot.

I at once grabbed Hal and Ray by the arms and called the team to order to get to the causeway as soon as possible. I called back to the officer on the other end of the police radio call and told him to secure the area, do not let anyone near the position of the body and make sure no one crosses the causeway from either directions until we arrive and that we were on our way, I rushed out to the carpark, got into the vehicle with Ray and Hall and sped out of the carpark sirens and lights going, heading North to the causeway, we passed the reservation at speed and other vehicles were pulling over out of our way as we screamed through Big Bear Village, soon arriving at the scene. I at once jumped out of the car put on surgical gloves that I had in my pocket and went ahead down to the shore where the body was. I shouted out in an angry enraged voice;

"Fuck me" it was Dean Forrester, there goes my thoughts of questioning him and hoping to get something that would connect him to all this mess. It looked like he had been shot at close range and there was blood all over his clothing but none where he had been found which meant he was murdered somewhere else and dumped here. Colin our CSI had just turned up as well as James the coroner. They looked the body overturned him on one side and told them the bullet had penetrated through the front but no exit wound, was killed somewhere else and had been dead about ten hours roughly.

The cold had preserved the body so until they did a postmortem there was no way of really telling the actual time or anything else for that matter as it was so cold and wet. I did not even realise it was pissing down with rain and that the scene was basically being destroyed by the bloody weather. This place was really starting to get to me and this whole deal was a proper mind fuck and that it was frustrating the shit out of me. Hal and Ray stood there dripping wet like myself;

"Well," said Ray.

"This is a proper cluster fuck and where the hell do we go from here, now one of our main suspects has been taken out of the picture?"

I looked at him and I knew deep down this was the work of Mike Grant and I was more determined than ever to hang this prick out to dry now. I had no second thoughts that this was Grant and not Beale and my thoughts of Forrester and Shaw being connected to all this with Beale and Grant was now even more vivid in my mind and my doubts were washed away with the rain that was cleansing our crime scene here. I knew in my heart that things were far from being easy to understand and the amount of loose ends this whole case was now causing were never ending and I had lost control of the situation in a way I did not like.

People were being murdered and we knew who the culprit was but had no idea where he was or what he was planning next. His partner Beale I felt was really an unwilling partner in this whole escapade, and Shaw would have to be involved and would undoubtably be fearing for his life seeing his friend and former business partner was now lying dead on gurney heading for the morgue.

We now had four dead bodies, three murdered by Grant and the death of May Talbertson which was a mercy killing but it still had to be fully investigated, but how as the person we were looking at was murdered himself. It was a shit show and the demons had well and truly returned home. Home for me was not going to be for a while so I phoned Katrina to tell her I would be late maybe even an all-nighter as we have another body, she understood and would see me when she sees me.

30

The cabin was silent, they had disposed of Dean Forrester, but should have been further down the lake on the other side as Steven thought just dumping it at the intersection of the causeway and the Northern outlet was too close to home to be safe. Mike disagreed as he was of the opinion it did not matter where they put Forrester's body Farrer would eventually find it and then his arse would be hanging in a sling as he again had another murder on his hands and no clues, no evidence, and no clue as to where they were and how long they intended to stay in the one spot. Beale was shaking like a leaf amid an Autumn storm, he was uncontrollable at this time he was sick of the death, the carnage that they had caused and the senseless killings as he could so no sound reasoning for it all. Grant made fresh coffee and came and sat at the table telling Beale to sit down and drink his coffee, Grant added a shot of whiskey into his cup as well as Beale's and Shaw's.

"I wish you would grow some balls" he scowled at Beale;

"You also need to get a grip and remember you are both up to your neck in this and what happened years ago is going to come back and haunt us all if we do not finish this and then get the hell out of Dodge".

Shaw looked at him in realistic disbelief at how calm he was and that he did not seem to care what he had done and the shit show he was creating for them all. Steven did not say anything though as Grant had the gun sitting close at hand and if anything were said out of place, he had no fear that Grant would put a bullet in either he or Beale as Grant was truly out of his tree, not only with his thinking but also his whole rationale of what was happening. Steven believes truly that Grant would kill both he and Beale just to get rid of a pair of problems as he saw it that if they were breathing, they were a liability. Finally Grant skulled the last of his coffee and looked at Steven and said;

"You had better get going Mr Shaw, you have two million dollars to find and as well as that you need to shut

that mouth of a drunken mayor up in case, he decides to start shooting his mouth off in one of his alcoholic binges."
Steven looked at him in complete disbelief and stuttered as he tried to ask Beale what Grant meant. Beale just shook his head and said;

"You need to do this you know the mayor better than we do also you will be able to get closer than we can to him to do the right thing."
Steven reeled back against the wall and shook his head;

"I am killing no-one do you understand. I was in this for the money from the drugs and the other illegal pursuits. I stated from the start I wanted nothing to do with that maniac Bourke's little game of just killing woman and taunting Farrer. Then he started selling body organs and trying to find a cure for a disease I had never heard of this whole thing has become an absolute horror show that you would not see play out in a television series".
He took a deep breath, you could hear the breathe being sucked in through his clenched teeth,

"No, I will not kill anyone, I will bring him here and you two can decide what you do with him."
Grant jumped up grabbed the gun and quickly crossed the floor towards Steven who panicked and tremble at the knees. Pointing the gun at Steven's head he shouted at him even spitting in his face he was that angry;

"You will do as you are fucking told and you will not bring him here or anywhere else. You will pop him in his own castle of shit and make sure you do it properly."
At this point Beale intervened and stood and looked at the pair by the wall;

"Come on Mike if he cannot do it do not make him do it, he is like me I cannot kill anybody, I do not have that in me," he stammered as he blurted it out.

Grant swung around and one step and hit Beale across the face with the pistol, Beale fell to the floor bleeding from the cheek.

"You two weak kneed arseholes are going to do as you are told or I will fill with you both a bullet and dump your bodies beside the causeway and think nothing of it. Do you understand me? Secondly Beale you will never come at me again or I swear you will go down like a sack of shit so quick, I have had a gutful of you weasels. Ever since this whole thing started years ago none of you except Damien and McClean have had the guts to do the right thing and take responsibility for your share for it all. I swear my patience is wearing very thin."

Grant was red in the face and livid with rage as he voiced this at both Shaw and Beale.

Finally, Steven said;

"Okay I will try and get you your money, and attempt to get rid of the mayor, but remember it is with protest that I do this." Mike shouted;

"Protest what fucking protest, you will do this and be done with."

With that Steven left and headed for his car, the rain was now turning to sleet and was getting very thick and the temperature, had dropped dramatically. In his car Steven turned it around and headed back down the driveway or road whichever you would call as it was so long, it also has become very slushy with the rain and sleet. The wind was

459

also getting stronger and this was not good as it meant the lake would be treacherous and the waves would be crashing against the sea wall along the esplanade and if they became too bad, they would break over the boardwalk. Steven finally made the highway and headed South toward town. He drove along in silence turning the radio off and all the noise he could hear was the windscreen wipers slashing against the rain and the sleet. He wondered what would happen to him if he did not carry out the orders of Grant and just tell the mayor to lay low or take a long one-way trip. Killing was not in Steven's vocabulary and even any form of brutality was not in his make-up. He would need to consider the alternatives as well as this he had to try and find two million dollars, this would mean he was going to have to talk to Isabella and basically tell her everything as she would need to co-sign for a withdrawal that big. He also did not have Dean around anymore to bounce things off. It was a loose situation for him and he could not see his way clear to resolve any of this.

Before he knew it, he was at the edge of town and decided he would head home and speak with Isabella about the whole thing first before he did anything, next he was going to have to see the mayor and hope he was receptive but most of all bloody sober so he could talk sense into him and explain the situation and what was to come if he did not listen. He continued through town, Mike Grant's words ringing in his head repeatedly;

"You two weak kneed arseholes are going to do as you are told or I will fill with you both a bullet and dump your bodies beside the causeway and think nothing of it."

Steven knew he meant every word he said as he had seen how he shot Dean with no second thoughts when Dean had stood up to him, his mind flashed back to the view of Dean's body lying there on the lake shore with rain and sleet falling, the edge of the lake lapping at Dean's feet and the wind howling through the supports of the causeway. This all started to bring Steven to tears something he had not done in a long time and was hard to hold back the tears as his lower lip started to quiver. Why did Beale and Grant have to come back they could have the drugs and money from the Old Mill and left no one the wiser. He then thought no because Grant had this fixation against Farrer. Suddenly it hit him, maybe he could talk to Isabella, and then go to Farrer and spill the beans tell him everything and appeal to his sense of reality, maybe even try for a deal of immunity if he spilled his guts to Farrer on all that he knew.

Maybe this was a pipe dream, but it was something he may have to try, and even talk to the mayor and get him to do the same, as two sides of the whole macabre and tragic story would go down better than just his side of things, besides the mayor knew a lot more than he did as he had been a part of the whole situation from the beginning. First thing though was to talk to Isabella and ask her what she thought. He knew he would probably have to serve some time in jail but a reduced sentence would be better than life, anyway he had murdered no one and yes, he was there and maybe could be classed as an accomplice but he did not murder anyone intentionally. He would sleep on his conversation with Isabella and decide on what he will do in the morning. He had decided he was not going to give Grant or Beale any money and knew the consequences all too well of this decision.

31

Victoria Merrin arrived home very cold and wet as she had been caught in the storm just walking from her car to the apartment block where she lived. Wearing a thick coat hat and gloves she was still shivering by the time she reached the door of her apartment. The rain and sleet were being blown into her front door almost at right angles and the water dripping off the door onto the concrete balcony, as well as off the windowsill like a small waterfall. Victoria hated this weather as it sent chills all over her body and even made her teeth chatter due to the cold. It was not so bad when it was snowing as there was a feeling of contentment and something special about snow.

This weather though was not any of that but it had to be before the snow season arrived. She fumbled in her bag for the keys and with the gloves on made it difficult to grasp the keys but she was not going to remove them for fear of the cold even it was making things difficult. Finally, she managed to get the key for the door handle lock and then the dead lock and was quick to move inside, quickly shutting the door behind her. She noticed a kind of sticky substance on her gloves and removed them and took them to the laundry where she placed them in the tub with some powder and ran warm water on them. I will let them soak while I have a shower then put them on the heated towel rail to dry by morning.

Victoria undressed and went into the bathroom, decided she would have a soak in the bath and not a shower. She started to run a bath, grabbed a bath towel, and wrapped it around her tight, walked back into the living room and then the kitchen opened the fridge and grabbed out a bottle of wine, collected a glass from the shelf and went ahead to the living room, grabbing the remote on the way to the sumptuous couch turning on the television and was lucky enough that the news had just started. Suddenly Victoria was taken aback by a picture of Dean Forrester on the screen and she turned up the volume as a ticker passed across the bottom of the screen saying;

"Local business identity and millionaire, Mr Dean Forrester was found shot dead near the causeway in Oemen Lake earlier today".

Victoria grabbed at her chest as the news reader announced;

"That the police were looking for the following two men Raymond Beale formerly of Beale Transport in Oemen Lake, and Mike Grant also of Oemen Lake. If anyone has information in connection about these two men or any witnesses to the occurrence, could they please contact Sheriff Ian Farrer of the Oemen Lake police with the information. All information will be treated as confidential."

Victoria suddenly felt very cold and a shiver spread across her body, Dean of all people what had he been into that had caused him to be shot and was Steven involved as she had not seen or talked to Steven in weeks, even though she worked for him. He had been very conspicuous in his absence over the past weeks, and everyone wondered whether he was ill. Nobody answered the phone at his home or his mobile phone went straight to voicemail. Victoria wondered whether Steven had met the same fate as Dean and if so, where was his body? She returned to the bathroom turned off the bath and decided now a shower was quicker, draining the water from the bath, she quickly showered and dressed in a comfortable tracksuit and returned to the living room.

Slowly sipped her wine and pondered what had gone on to get Dean shot. She had an inkling that Beale and Grant may have been mixed up in all that shit from years ago when all those girls were murdered and there were drugs involved. There were rumours that Beale Transport may have been carting the drugs and that there was also human trafficking of women for sex was involve. It was horrible time for this small town, and now she wondered if maybe Dean and Steven were involved in some way. She remembers that when Steven was with her and they were cuddled up in bed that he was very distant at times but she put it down to the pressure of work as the business was doing well and had just received a huge contract from the Government, even when making love he still seemed to thinking about something else or there was more on his mind than her.

At this point in time, she went her bag and tried her phone to ring Steven but again it went to voicemail, she tried again and same result. At this time Victoria started to think the worst and was hoping above all else that it was not true that Steven was not mixed up in all that and he was okay that he had not befallen the same fate as Dean. Lucky, she thought that Linda was dead and did not have to suffer the heartache of Dean's death. Then her mind went to Isabella, what would Isabella do if the same fate had happened to Steven, how would she feel, after all her and Steven were still an item but not as intense as it had been, and he was not coming around as often.

She often wondered whether Isabella knew or even suspected about them and the affair. Then again, she could not really count it as an affair as they only tumbled in the sheets now and again as it was only an occasional thing nothing serious although she wanted it to be, but it never eventuated, not from Steve's point of view anyway.

She finished her wine and poured another in the kitchen, then went to the laundry to retrieve her gloves, and there was a distinct odour, and the gloves still had a sticky appearance as well. It worried her as to what was happening as she had touched nothing to cause that. Victoria decides not to touch them or do anything with them and was going to call the chemistry guy at work to come and have a look as it looked suspicious considering she had not touched anything that she could think of that would cause that kind of thing. Also considering what was on the news and what she knew about Steven and Dean's friendship. Was this all to do with the happenings and was she in the firing line as she worked for Steven, did someone know about her and Steven? Questions that Victoria had no answer for at all. At that moment there was a clap of thunder and a flash of lightning that shook Victoria back into reality and out of her daydreaming and the thoughts she was having.

It was all too much for Victoria, so she rang Rowdy at the factory hoping he was still working and would he come around as soon as possible. Luckily Rowdy had a thing about Victoria and she knew she could get him to come over as soon as possible. The phone rang then Rowdy answered;

"Hello,"

"It is Victoria, I need a favour can you come around and have a look at something for me as I am not sure what is going on and I am a bit panicky" she exclaimed. Rowdy asked;

"What is the problem?" Victoria quickly explained the events and the gloves and the odour that was now in the laundry. Rowdy explained he would be about an hour or so and would bring some items to test what it may be. He was of the opinion she may have just picked something up at the factory that has reacted with the fabric of the gloves but warned her not to touch them with bare hands until he arrived. She promised she would not do anything until he arrived.

Rowdy arrived as promised and rang the doorbell, as he did, he noticed what looked like a sticky substance on the handle and lock of the door as well as the window ledge and it had a slight yellow tinge as the rain was still coming down hard and the wind would cut through you. He did not touch it but as Victoria answered the door, he asked her if she had touched the handle or lock with her bare hands. She told him she had not so he placed his case on the ground and opened it taking out some surgical gloves, mask, and swabs. He swabbed the lock and handle then asked where the gloves were and told her not to touch the outside of the door. He went into the laundry and saw the oily look to the water as well as the distinctive odour and a slight yellow tinge.

He recognised it straight away as what he thought was glycerine as it is miscible in water with an acid smell. He was horrified and told Victoria to ring the police at once while he tested what he had on the swabs from the door handle. He did not elaborate but realised that someone had tried to cause harm to Victoria by putting a mixture where she would touch and she could be at once hurt by the mixture, as if it were a contact with the skin poison it was deadly. He heard Victoria talking to the police, and he returned to the living room, leaving the gloves in the tub.

Rowdy Bryant, six foot four all muscle and blond hair, with piercing brown eyes. He was a catch for any woman but Victoria had only interest him as a good friend and work colleague although Rowdy wished there were more. He waited for the police and had kept the front door open although the rain was beating in grabbed towels from the bathroom and placed them on the floor in the doorway. The Deputies arrived and Rowdy warned then not to touch the door or windowsill and walked them through what he had found, took them to the laundry and showed them the tub with gloves in. He then withdrew two plastic bags from his case and a pair of tweezers, lifting each glove and placing them each in a separate bag. He then stickered each and gave them to the younger deputy as he placed the swabs in another plastic pouch and named and dated that one also. The deputy remarked about the smell of acid and Rowdy explained he thought it was like sulphuric acid but could not be sure but it was mixed with glycerine and some other substance he had no idea of and would need to have it tested.

The two deputies then took statements from both Rowdy and Victoria, and said, they would send it off to the lab and not to touch anything that may have been contaminated. Rowdy told the police he would wash the door and windowsill as well as the tub with a neutralising agent later but Victoria will need to stay somewhere until he can get that done and the results of the lab tests come back. Rowdy knew whoever had done this had a real grudge against Victoria and as he thought he knew what the substance was they would have been careful not to touch anything that they put the chemical on or get it near their skin. The Deputies left and Rowdy told Victoria to pack a bag and stay at the motel or the inn for the night until the results came back. She agreed and asked if he would drive her to the motel, which he did and stayed until she was safely booked in and then returned to the factory. Rowdy had not given the police all the swabs he had kept two back as well as a water sample from the tub.

32

I returned to the office and I needed to speak with Gary Madden again. Ray came in and told me of the call about Victoria Merrin and that two deputies were on their way there now. What the hell has happened now I needed to talk to her after I had finished with Gary Madden, and hoped above all else she could tell me where Steven Shaw was as he was one, I really needed to interview and as she was his secretary and the rumour was his tumble between the sheets partner would have the information we need. I went to the interrogation room where Collins was waiting for me, a deputy brought Madden in and he sat opposite us at the table.

I switched on the recorder and again we introduced ourselves, the date and time;

"Mr Madden," I began with a rather stern voice;

"Who did you give the information about this case to and exactly how much have you supplied prior?" Collins then interrupted and asked;

"How long had he been employed to work here as a cleaner?" Madden remained staunch and refused to answer.

"Well, you are going to be charged with interfering in a police investigation and refusing to cooperate with police. So how are those apples and have you got anything to add?"

He again sat there with a blank face and I knew he was going to give nothing up, I wish we had a chance for Hal to use his old tactics on him the phone book questioning technique, maybe then he would tell us, but that was out of the question and I would not allow it anyway, even though this little prick was frustrating the hell out of me.

I returned to my office via the coffee machine in the lunchroom and Ray and Hal were there talking with two deputies, I asked;

"What is the news?" The younger of the deputies filled me in on their trip to Victoria Merrin's house and that they had collected samples of what looked like an acid substance and delivered it to the lab. They also went on to say that a chemist from Steven Shaw's factory was there and he had already bagged up some of it for us we only put it in evidence bags. I was now triggered into thinking was this Grant and Beale getting back at Shaw, but that is not Grant's style, poison he just shoots them. I pondered was it Shaw trying to get rid of her as she may have known too much. I thanked the two deputies and asked Ray and Hal to meet me in my office if they could find Collins and bring him also, please.

Shortly after sitting down, Ray, Hal, and Collins came in sat themselves down and I went over what the two deputies had just told me, at once Collins said as to what I already knew that this was not Mike Grant's style. Poison for him was too slow a bullet is much quicker and cleaner and I had to agree. Ray and Hal asked if I wanted them to interview Merrin and I replied yes if they could and was, she safe. Hale remarked that the two deputies had recommended she be placed at the motel or inn until the results of the substance found came back. Rowdy Bryant from Shaw's work was going to take her there. How does this Rowdy fellow fit in to all this? Apparently Merrin called him when she noticed the yellow tinge in the water in the tub in her laundry where she had put her woollen gloves to soak because they had some sort of sticky substance on them.

Okay, I thought this is a new twist, someone is trying to get to Merrin and I was near positive it would not be Beale or Grant, I was also of the opinion that it could not be Shaw as she was his squeeze, also it may have been Forrester then again, he was dead so why would he want to harm her, jealousy perhaps? Then the penny dropped, Isabella Shaw, she had everything to lose if Shaw went off with Merrin and everything to gain if Merrin was dead, but why go to all the trouble that it sounded like she had if she wanted Victoria dead, she could have gotten Grant to do it for her and there would be no qualms. Pay him enough he would do anything if the money were right, but I think shooting a woman may be below him as they do not fight back like a man would be his thinking. I looked at Ray, Hal and

471

Collins who had sat there rather quietly while I had summarised all this in my head. Hal broke the silence and said that we would need to wait for the toxicology report on the substance whatever it may be before we could jump to any conclusions anyway. I had to agree.

The autopsy for Dean Forrester was due and although I knew what it would be, I was still interested as to whether there was any fibres or evidence as to where he may have been killed was available. Why would Grant shoot Forrester he was like the golden goose, he and Shaw I was now convinced of that as there had been no sightings of Shaw at his factory for a few days and Shaw and Forrester where seen in the Tavern two days ago and there was a report that they had been seen heading North out of town yesterday morning. I looked at Ray and, asked;

"If we had checked if there were any properties that either Shaw or Forrester owned North of town and whether Forrester had been at work in the past few days."
He replied;
"He would get straight on it".
I told Hal;
"Book young Mr Madden on the interfering charge and leave the paperwork on my desk", at that point I had an idea of how I could flush out his press person but it was going to need a bit of planning.

We needed to know who it was as they may have more information than we have as well as that they could jeopardise the whole case if they printed anything that was sensitive and we needed to keep it under our hats for the time being. Hal jumped up and left to begin the paperwork, Ray followed to see what properties were around that either Shaw or Forrester owned North of town and was there a possibility that Beale and Grant were held up in one. This weather was starting to get me down also as I looked out through my office window across the lake which now you could not make out the other side or the mountain range. The waves on the lake were now continuous flowing heads of white foam and the rain, sleet and wind were consistent with no let-up in sight.

James and Andrew brought me back to reality as they entered and I turned to face them, they had the report on Dean Forrester. I opened and read slowly through the preliminary results that showed he was shot at close range there were powder burns around the wound, the estimated time of death was withing twelve hours of the body being found but could not be proven accurately as it had been in the rain and sleet as well as the lake water for a period. The bullet was a forty-five millimetre and was of comparable size and characteristics that was registered to Bernie Talbertson. This meant that Grant and Beale had raided the weapons cabinet of Talbertson, and he had quite a collection of weapons looking at the list the boys had compiled for me. If it came down to a raid on wherever they were hold up it could be like shooting apples in a barrel and with the number of weapons they had and amount of ammunition it could end up being a blood bath which I desperately wanted to avoid.

Hal returned from booking Madden and was holding him downstairs, I decided to let him sit for a while before putting the paperwork through to the District Attorney for a formal hearing on his plea, which of course he would plead not guilty and cause the county extra for a jury trial. I was of the opinion let him sweat it out down there for the next hour or so and see if his harden nature and staunch resistance to admitting what he had done would shake a few brain cells into realising he was in an inconvenient situation. I went back to the newspaper clipping we had from the news that Madden had released and found a name, Rosalie Mathews, I knew of her was a good reporter and my thinking was maybe shaking her tree a little and she may give me the evidence I need to hoodwink young Madden into talking.

It was a longshot as the media were very reluctant to give up sources easily as there was this confidentiality thing of protecting one's sources. The thing in our favour was we knew the truth and we had the source and now the end of the confidential trail maybe we can come to some middle ground to save this from being a complete fiasco. I need her to retract the last story as it was not correct as I had planned the sting and the information, she printed was a lie and it could work in one of two ways, it either made Beale and Grant flee or it would send them on a rampage of further death and destruction. I believe the latter as they had nothing to lose three dead and we were no closer to catching them and they could play us in a game of cat and mouse. Ray came back and told me that Forrester and Shaw owned fourteen different properties around the county, they of course owned their factories and the land they were on, they shared in the motel and tavern, they were shares in the Cone and Pine, which I did not frequent as much now I was more of a tavern lad. They owned separately with their wives the houses and land that they were on, Shaw owned a log cabin up in the woods about twenty-five to thirty miles North of town, Forrester owned a share of Big Bear Ski Field and a shareholder in the lodge up there.

Dean and the former Mrs Forrester owned an apartment in Seattle and another property in Helena. They also owned parcels of land around the County which were earmarked for development of condominiums. The one that interested me the most was the cabin North of town as it was perfect and provided a close easy access to both Northern Highways and the causeway as well as being able to cross the causeway and head South. I told Ray to apply for a search warrant for the cabin, but also both their homes at this point, if we find nothing then the factories were our best bet next.

He turned and left the office Hal was still there and he seated himself in the bigger chair opposite and stared out the window behind me I could see his mind racing and finally I asked;

"What is the problem?"

"Just this weather and how it has come in so suddenly considering this is not due for at least for another month, if it keeps up ski season will be early and the town will be

475

buzzing and we do not want that if this shit show is still happening."

I must agree with him and nodded my head. I picked up the phone and dialled the newspaper office, asking for Rosalie Mathews when the operator answered. Fortunately, she put me through and it went straight to voicemail so I left a message to ring me as soon as she received this message as the matter was one of urgency. Ray was still staring out the window when the young desk deputy came in with the lab report on the samples taken at Victoria Merrin's place. I quickly opened the envelope and I must have had a complete look of amazement on my face as Ray asked;

"What is it mate?" I glanced at him then back at the document and said;

"The substance found was Thallium and Acid with a glycerine base and perfume. Someone was trying to kill her."

I looked at Ray and grabbed my coat we were on our way the Merrin's place with a CSI and then on to interview her.

33

Isabella Shaw was not feeling well, she had this feeling of nausea and terrible pains in the stomach. She had felt unwell for a couple of days since mixing up the chemicals in the lock-up. She had now severe abdominal pain, nausea and was vomiting rather badly for the past few hours se also had some blood in the toilet when she just used her bowels. She needed Steven she rang again but still no answer and it went to voicemail again. There was pain especially on the soles of her feet when she walked and on the palms of her hands. She tried to lay down but that was uncomfortable as well, she rushed to the bathroom and vomited again. She had now developed weakness of the lower leg, she was confused, and started having bad convulsions. She called out for Lilly who came running into the room and was shocked to see her laying on the floor at the foot of the bed vomit coming out the side of her mouth and Isabella unable to talk. By now Isabella also was finding it hard to breath and her vision was impaired she was seeing double.

Lilly rang for an ambulance and explained the symptoms as best she could understand them from Isabella who was now almost unconscious. The ambulance was sent and they told Lilly it would be ten or so minutes until it arrives. Lilly rushed to the bathroom to grab a wet cloth and some towels, there was a terrible smell of vomit and it made Lilly dry reach. She quickly gathered three or four towels wet a face flannel and rushed back to where Isabella lay motionless and with heavy breathing.

The ambulance arrived and Lilly went out on the balcony and shouted the door was open and that they were upstairs in the main bedroom. The two officers came in with a stretcher and quickly took blood pressure and placed an oxygen mask on Isabella. They lifted her onto the stretcher as one of the officers asked if Lilly knew what the lady had eaten in the past few hours, Lilly explained that she had eaten nothing no breakfast or dinner last evening.

In the ambulance on the way to the hospital, Lilly was trying to get hold of Steven, but to no avail. Isabella was white and breathing extremely hard even with oxygen, she had a rash on her right forearm and her eyes watering. She kept saying over and over in a muffled voice caused by the oxygen mask;

"I shouldn't have done it," her heart rate on the monitor was fluctuating badly, the ambulance officer increased the number of probes on her from six to twelve. He looked at Lilly and asked;   "Has Mrs Shaw taken an overdose of something?"

Lilly looked at him with a very worried look and said in a strained voice;

"No, I do not think so, she has been very worried the past few days though, as Mr Shaw has been away a lot and not home much".

The ambulance finally arrived at the hospital, Isabella was rushed in the emergency room and into a bay where she was transferred to a bed and a doctor was at once by her side.

The ambulance officers explained how they had found her and had taken blood, put up a saline drip, taken her blood pressure and transferred her here, her heart rate had been irregular and was breathing with some difficulty. The doctor asked for more blood tests as well as cultures, and, if possible, a urine sample. Isabella kept on saying the same thing;

"I shouldn't have done it," the doctor leaning over and lifting the breathing mask slightly asked Isabella;

"Done what?' but Isabella did not answer and fell into a coma. The doctor quickly called for and intubating tray and laid Isabella flat and inserted the tube into her mouth and connected to a line giving her air straight into her lungs. Her blood pressure was steady although low and she was sweating. He examined the rash on the forearm and asked the nurse to take a scraping and send it for analysis. Over an hour had past and the bloods had come back and showed that Isabella had been poisoned but as to what they were still working on that, they had managed to place a catheter and get some urine which was a greenish tinge and this also was sent to lab. The doctor again asked Lilly;

"Where does Mrs Shaw work?"
Lilly shook her head saying;

"She does not work anymore full time but sometimes helps out Mr Steven at the factory".
He asked what was produced at the factory and she thought it was some form of electronics but was not sure, just then

Steven came around the corner of the curtain of the cubicle and asked the doctor;

"What is wrong with my wife?''

"We are yet to determine that Mr Shaw we are running a barrage of test and I have just taken a new set of bloods and sent them off".

Steven looked fatigued and worried, and looked at Lilly,

"How long has she been like this?" he asked her;

Lilly could not answer as the tears were running down her face and she left the cubicle. He continued to ask Steven;

"Whether there were any drugs such as cocaine or heroin in the house even strong barbiturates, as Isabella has ingested something that has made her extremely ill and we are at present at a loss as to what is wrong other than she has been poisoned by something."

Steven looked at him and just nodded in a manner that he did not know. Then a nurse came in and told the doctor the results of the swab and urine had come through, so the doctor looked at Steven and said he would be but a few minutes.

He returned with a look of disbelief on his face, turned to Steven and said;

"Your wife has been poisoned by an acid of some kind and we also suspect Thallium poisoning but that is yet to be established, but I am going to start her on a course of Prussian Blue just to be on the safe side." He ordered the nurse to start the course as he wrote up the order in Isabella's notes and told Steven he would return as soon as the full results were ready. Steven sat in a chair beside the bed and held Isabella's hand the other forearm had been cleaned and bandaged where the rash was and it was covered as a precaution. Steven looked at his wife and the state she was in and could not understand the thought of losing her. He knew in the back of his mind he had been unfaithful but had broken that off months ago.

Did Beale or Grant do this to her if so why, he was going to get the money or go to the police he had not decided as he was going to talk the whole thing over with Isabella last night but he slept at the office as he needed time to think and clear his mind. How would Beale and Grant get hold of Thallium anyway as at the factory it is kept in a special container under lock and key. They used for the semi-conductors, and that it is rare that someone outside of that area would have access to it. Anyway, that was now a matter to sort out later all that mattered now was Isabella and getting her well.

In the meantime, Beale and Grant had decided to leave the cabin and ventured to Big Bear ski field and the lodge they believed that the cabin may have been a little hot because of the finding of Forrester's body. Upon arriving at the Lodge, Beale parked the car well out of sight down behind the ski lift building which was well out of sight of the road and the lodge.

The only problem with being here was there was only one way out the road they came in on, but then again it was same at the cabin but there they had the woods to disappear in here it was just mountains and snow. The weather was also worse up here and Beale thought to himself they were lucky to have got up that road to here considering the rain, sleet, and ice. Grant had found the mains power box and was going to cut the alarm power but knew that it also had a backup system so that was out of the question.

He rang Shaw and at once Shaw answered asked,

"What have you done to my wife you bastard, she is dying in hospital and they do not truly know what is wrong with her."

"Grant replied in a vicious voice;

"I have done nothing to your wife, and if I was going to it would be a bullet and nothing else so do not accuse me of anything arsehole, remember you need to do your duty or I will kill her."

Steven told Grant;

"To go fuck himself and he was not doing anything until his wife was well as she was his priority not him or Beale." Grant explained, they had left the cabin and were now at the ski lodge and needed to know how to get in and not set off the alarm. Shaw told him he needed the keys and the alarm key, which were in the lift house in the control room in the locked cupboard and with that he hung up.

Steven had made his mind up now that as soon as he knew Isabella was out of the woods, he was going to see Farrer and tell all, he had no reason not to now with Isabella's life at stake and he realised he had caused this as well as many other lives being lost. It had been almost three hours since Steven had seen a doctor and went to find him, he did not have to go far as the doctor was at the emergency room desk reading a file. He looked up when he saw Steven standing at counter, Mr Shaw;

"We have confirmed that your wife was poisoned by Thallium and an acid suspended in glycerine, she must have spilt some on her arm and that is what the rash is, we will continue to watch her and keep up the treatment with Prussian Blue. You know we will have to report this as it is a restricted compound."

Steven looked at the doctor and just pleaded to him to look after her. He would be back soon as he needed to follow up on something as to how she was able to get the Thallium. The doctor rang the police and reported the incident as well as the poisoning authorities to alert them to the poisoning. Grant found the keys just as Shaw had explained where they were, he and Beale unlocked the lodge front door and then put the key into the alarm and turned it off. Beale went and turned on the heaters at the bank of switches by the entrance, then headed for the kitchen to see if there was any food in the place. Meanwhile, Grant went to the bar and found a bottle of whiskey and poured himself a large glass.

He leant on the bar and had grave thoughts about Shaw and where it leaves them, he, and Beale, they should maybe cut their losses and leave this place all together or stay and finish what they started. He wanted Farrer so he was not keen to get out just at this time. Beale returned from the kitchen and told Mike that there was no food in the kitchen and they should have probably grabbed some from the cabin, Mike smiled and told him there was a bag in the trunk of the car as he thinks of everything. Beale thought shit I have to go out again in that shitty weather and walk all the way down to the lift house, but if they want to eat, he will need to go, because if he fought Mike on the matter then Mike could and most probably would lose it again like he did with Forrester.

He went and retrieved the two bags from the trunk of the car and felt this weather would freeze the balls of a pool table and he was so sick of the rain and it was so bloody cold. He returned to the lounge and opened the bags and they both had enough food for at least three days, which he hoped that would be enough and they could get out of this place altogether. This was at this present time a fleeting thought as Mike was too fixated on Farrer and the two million dollars he was after. On this Ray was not fully committed anymore not after what he saw with Mike and the way he dealt with Dean Forrester for no valid reasons.

Ray was really scared of Mike for the first time since they fled from Oemen Lake years ago. He again went back to his thoughts of why they had not left once they had the bags of money and drugs and just go. He walked over to the window which looked out over the lake which was not really that visible through the mist and even the village below was covered in mist and only glimpses of the village lights could be seen. In the distance the lights of the town were also just visible as the wind blew the rain and sleet around the building in a violent way. He was feeling rather uncomfortable in this place and was not as confident as Mike. Ray had the feeling there was going to be a bad ending to this whole scenario with not a good outcome for anybody. He returned to the bar where Mike had poured him a large whiskey and refilled his own.

Ray finally asked;

"How long are we going to stay here, as we are more vulnerable here than at the cabin, at least at the cabin we could have scrambled through the woods and out on to the highway, here must go down the way we came up."

Mike nodded in agreeance as he swallowed the last of his drink and went over to the window looking out at the same sight Ray had just been looking at. Back at the hospital Isabella's symptoms had improved slightly and seemed to be responding to the Prussian Blue but was not out of the woods yet as it was unclear what damage had been caused to her organs or even her brain. The doctor returned to check on the condition and to take some more blood and get the nurse to empty the catheter bag and send it to the lab. The doctor was still worried that he may lose this patient especially with how far gone she was when she arrived at the hospital. They had found a bed for her in the Intensive Care Unit and would be transferred there as soon as possible and would be transferred to a specialist in poisonings. He was hoping that the husband would return soon as he needed him to complete some paperwork to do with the poison and how his wife came to have access to it.

34

Ray and I were on our way to Victoria Merrin's residence when we received a radio call saying that an ambulance had been called to the Shaw residence in an emergency. I at once called back and asked to be kept informed of what was happening at the residence and if they could get any information from the hospital. I had no sooner finished the conversation than we pulled up outside Victoria Merrin's residence, we got out of the car and ran through the rain to the stairs and up to the balcony along to where there was red danger tape and police tape covering the doorway. There was a sticker covering from the doorframe onto the door thus preventing opening of the door.

We noticed that the windowsill also had a protection sticker on it preventing it to be opened. I realised we would be better not entering the apartment and wait until the test results come back. I felt this may have been a wasted trip but realised that it was serious and was this all connected to what is happening now. I looked at Ray and said we will go and interview Merrin at the motel and see what exactly happened.

As we entered the car again and Ray turned around and we headed for the motel. The radio again squawked into life and it was the communication desk, telling us that the hospital had rung that Mrs Shaw had been poisoned by Thallium and some other acid and was in a serious but stable condition. My mind suddenly thought of the apartment we had just been at and the lab results had returned the same diagnosis, only in this case Victoria Merrin had not touch anything with bare skin which may have saved her.

We still needed to know who may have a grudge against her and did she know anything about Thallium and was she able to gain access to it. It was also interesting that she was able to realise that something was wrong and called out Rowdy Bryant to investigate whose advice was to call the police. We arrived at the motel and I entered the office and asked Ruby which room Merrin was in, she answered three, and we parked right outside the door. We saw Merrin peak out the curtain and then open the door, we rushed inside quickly and she closed the door behind us. She asked if we would like a coffee, I obliged but Ray declined the offer. While she made the coffee, I asked her about how she discovered the substance at her apartment and what made her ring Bryant?
Victoria said,
    "That when she went to rinse the gloves out after she had opened the door and lock, she realised there was a sticky substance on then and put them in the tub in the laundry to soak, then was going to wash and dry them. The reason I called Rowdy was that there was a yellow tinge in the water and on the gloves themselves and a putrid odour. I did not know what to do so I called him."
She finished preparing the coffee and handed me mine as I sat at the small table by the wall Ray sat opposite and she seated herself on the bed. She was a little shell shocked by it all and tears started to well up in her eyes, and her face

was ashen, this was all too much for her to take in. I then continued to ask about her job

"As to what her main job was at the Shaw factory and she replied she was Steven Shaw's personal assistant." I at once asked the obvious,

"Was she and Shaw intimately involved in anyway, she hesitated for a moment then nodded and stated they were some time ago but he broke it off weeks ago maybe months she was unsure as she was not thinking straight after this ordeal that someone had tried to hurt her." I followed up by asking;

"If she had any enemies at work or was there anyone, she thought may want to hurt her?" her reply was,

"No, not that she knew of."

"Was she familiar with Ray Beale and Mike Grant and did she know they were back in town?"

"Victoria admitted knowing both men Ray Beale through his transport company and Mike Grant as an associate of Steven's. She had not seen them or heard from them but had heard that they were back in town."

I paused for a moment and took a deep sip of my coffee and then asked her about the news of Dean Forrester and

"Did she know he had been murdered?"

Her answer was;

"She saw it on the news and the report that the police were looking Beale and Grant."

She asked;

"Do you think they have anything to do with my situation, although I do not know why as I have had nothing to do with them?"

I was satisfied that she did not know who had made this attempt on her life and that she would still be in the motel until her apartment was cleaned up and we could safely say she was in the clear. I finished my coffee and told her that a deputy would be posted outside for the duration of her stay at the motel and most likely when she returned home until we could safely guarantee her safety. Ray and I left the motel and headed for the hospital to interview the doctor that was treating Isabella Shaw, we also needed to talk to Steven Shaw as soon as possible.

On arriving at the main entrance to the hospital luck would have it we were under cover of the large veranda and the rains and sleet could be seen like walls of water dripping down over the two sides. I must admit I was sick of this weather the cold and wet was starting to get on my nerves. We entered the hospital and as I did my phone rang, I answered it was the reporter Rosalie Mathews who had been the contact for Gary Madden and she had printed the stories. I explained to her we had charged him with interference in a Police investigation and that the last piece she had printed was a lie as we had set him up to catch whomever it was leaking the information to the press and that she would need to print a retraction and that I was charging her with the same charges as we had against Gary Madden.

Her reaction was of course one of defiance and that I could not prove he had given her the information, to which I stated the stories were in the paper under her name so therefore she handled what had gone to print. I told her to have a good think about what I had said and I would be in touch, but she needed to retract the last item. We headed for the lifts, but first we needed to find out where Isabella Shaw was and who the treating physician was, the young nurse at the desk told us she was being transferred to the ICU at that time and that a Dr McMichael was her treating physician.

Ray and I looked at the list of floor names on the wall by the lifts and found that the ICU was on the fifth floor, the lift doors opened and we entered, I still have thoughts of travelling in lifts after what happened with the body hitting me upon my exit back those years ago. We reached the fifth floor and Ray went first I quickly followed, we reached the nurses station for the ICU and asked about Mrs Shaw, and could they page Dr McMichael for us please? Isabella Shaw was in a private room with machines all beeping and lights flashing, she had tubes coming out of her everywhere as well as a breathing tube which was connected to a respirator. Dr McMichael met us in the room and quickly told us that Isabell a was still touch and go but was improving slowly that the next thirty-six to forty-eight hours were critical. He was not going to be her doctor up here as he was the Emergency Department Consultant.

He was unable to advise who her doctor would be for the time she spent in ICU but she would be here for a while then transferred to a ward once she improved. I asked if Mr Shaw had been in and he recommended he had but had gone back home to get some personal things for his wife he thought. He left us with the noise of the machines and our own thoughts, as I saw the bandage on Isabella's forearm but was unable to ask him about as he had already left and I was too slow to get to him. Ray and I left the room, continued to the lift doors, and pressed the down button, the second lift arrived and a ding alerted us to its arrival.

The doors opened and out stepped Steven Shaw carrying a bag, I looked at him and said;

"We need to talk and sooner rather than later," he nodded and asked if it could come to the station in the morning as he wished to be with his wife at present.

"I asked him about his cabin and could we go check it out as we believed that Beal and Grant may be using it", he agreed, and told us were the spare key was situated. He looked a bit sheepish when telling us.

35

Hal had called to say he would meet us at the cabin with Colin and James and that we had the full toxicology report back from the samples taken from Victoria Merrin's apartment, it was confirmed that it was Thallium and Sulphuric Acid as well as Glycerine and "Rose of the Isles" perfume, it was a volatile mix and if it encountered any skin, it would cause exceptional bad side effects and even death in the strength it was. He also explained that Merrin's gloves were covered in it and most probably due to their makeup saved her life. We explained about Isabella Shaw and the state she was in so someone has tried to do both Merrin and Shaw, but who. We could not see Grant or Beale doing it as a bullet was more effective as far as Grant was concerned and I do not think it was Beale as I do not think he would know enough about the chemicals or how to mic them as Grant would probably not either.

We travelled on through town towards the causeway and the police tape was still up around the scene where we had found Forrester's body, suddenly my phone rang and it was the reporter saying she had typed a retraction to the story and after talking to her boss and the legal department it would be better to confirm that it was Gary Madden who had supplied her with the information. I agreed that was the best course of action and she would need to come to the station tomorrow to make a statement to the fact, she agreed she would be there just before lunch. Hal then called asking where the key was for the cabin as they were there and the place was deserted although it looked like there had been recent activity as the place looking through the window was a mess. I advised where to find it and told him we were not far away from them.

James examined the outside and although there had been a lot of rain etc there seemed to be three different sets of tyre tracks recently two were very fresh, the other older. The two fresh sets were no more than a day old and looked like they came into the cabin then back out again around a tree that was centre of the driveway. He could not be sure of course but believed they were fresh. He told Hal to tell us to park away from the tree as he will need to get some photographs of the tracks before, they are muddied more or the rain and sleet washed them away. He went to his case grabbed his camera and went back to where he thought the tracks began and where they left the property, we pulled up just as he was taking photos of the tracks at the entrance to the cabin. He waved us on saying he had all he needed and was looking a bit worse for wear with the rain and water dripping from his hair down his face.

We pulled up behind Hal's vehicle and went inside making sure we stepped on the grills that Colin had laid out so as not to contaminate the areas. Even though we were dripping water in areas he had already photographed most of the living room and was now in the kitchen. He asked if someone could bring over another crate of grills so he could go to the downstairs room and then the bathroom. In the meantime, James was back inside and wiping his face and trying to dry his hair a little before he started on the stairs. Both were taking photographs of everything and they asked us to done shoe covers and gloves which we did.

The cabin smelt of wet clothes and had musty smell as well, there was also the smell of alcohol and that quickly was shown when I reached the kitchen and found empty Glenfiddich and Teachers whisky bottles in the bin as well as food leftovers, there was also empty cans of beer on the bench and in the sink with unwashed dishes. Colin said that someone had been here within the past four hours as the heater was warm and the food on the plates in the sink was also fresh.

I looked in the pantry off the kitchen there was cans on the floor and it looked like someone had cleaned it out in a hurry. Colin and James had photographed everything and was now starting to look for fingerprints and any trace evidence that may have been left behind. They turned on the lights and aske Hal if he would collect the spotlights from the car. He brought three sets in plugged them in and switched them on it lit the place up like a circus tent, but James asked for one to be set up upstairs, which he did.

With all the lights and especially the spotlights we could see there was a blood stain on the floor near the table, which the boys had already sprayed with luminol and under the ultraviolet light of our torches it was a rather large area. Samples had been taken and I wondered if this is where Dean Forrester met his demise before being dumped near the causeway. There was not much Ray or I could do here so I suggested that Ray, Hal, and I head back to the office and leave the boys to it. Make sure you seal this place off when you leave as we do not want anybody coming in here uninvited also bring the keys with you, James acknowledged they would so the three of us left them to it. On the way back I thought that we were close to Beale and Grant and that they had been hold up there for some time and I was bloody sure that Shaw knew about it also. Hal, raised the question should we not pick Shaw up for questioning, but I told him about his wife and he had promised he would be in the morning and I believed him as it was in his best interests to come in.

Ray agreed from the back seat saying that his wife was ill and that Shaw was really cut about her being close to death. I was still unsure as to how she got the Thallium and how it became a problem at Victoria Merrin's place also. I had logically ruled out Beale or Grant but was Shaw out to get Merrin because maybe she knew too much, but then did he have the knowledge to mix the chemicals. I thought about Merrin staging the whole thing herself and was getting rid of Isabella and needed to make sure that it did not come back on her. Then there was Isabella Shaw, who had motive as her husband was banging his secretary, she had opportunity and access to the chemicals, but how did she get it on herself surely, she would have known the risks also where she had stored it. I then aloud repeated my thoughts to Hal and Ray, and asked if they would get a search warrant for the Shaw residence. I also asked that he organise one for the Forrester's residence as well as both Shaw and Forrester's Factories. Upon arriving back at the office, the rain had finally abated but the wind was still chilly and to stand in it too long you would have become a frozen popsicle. I made my way upstairs to the office and grabbed a nice hot coffee on the way, seeing Detective Collins in the conference room asked him to join me in my office. I sat down and opened the file on my desk which was the one I had requested on the death of Linda Forrester and whether within this I could find some form of motive as to why Dean Forrester was shot and left like he was considering the fact we were dealing with an absolute

Sociopath and Psychopath all rolled into one in Mike Grant.

There was nothing that gave any indications as to what Forrester was up to or whether he was even involved in the goings on from the past. I still could not grasp where he and Shaw fitted into the whole scenario other than my unsubstantiated idea that they were the money men behind the first crimes, and we never actually at the time gave them a thought. Now we had another three deaths all attributed to Mike Grant with Ray Beale as an associate in some form, and of course there was May Talbertson, who by all accounts had been murdered or aided in her death by her husband. This was still to be formally proven but the forensic report and toxicology confirmed how she had died. Linda Forrester was an aggrieved wife due to Dean's playing around with Cerise Blackwell, who was Ray Beale's Secretary. All these players in a game of murder and mayhem and I was left to clean up the mess from years gone by and now everything was rearing its ugly head all over again.

Ashley Collins came in with a coffee and sat opposite me. I asked him if Grant was the sort to fight it out if cornered, I knew in the back of my mind that it was a stupid question to ask as I knew the answer to be yes. Mike Grant would not go quietly and he had an axe to grind and I needed to know what it was about me that he had such an unfavourable feeling and vendetta against me, for where or what I was supposed to have done to him in the past, as it was surely not here in Oemen Lake, it had to be in New

York or Philadelphia. Collins looked at me with a solemn look of aggravation as he too knew I was asking a question I already knew the answer to. But he spoke up and said that if we cornered Grant, he would go down fighting and he would not care one little bit who he took with him. His own personal safety was of little concern to him.

Collins, sat quietly for a moment and sipping his coffee as did I, then we both went to talk at once, but before we could ask each a question the phone rang, I answered it,

"Hello, Farrer", the other end was the registrar at the court and informed me that my warrants for the Shaw, Forrester, residence were ready and for their factories were also available. I thanked him for his call and hung up. I looked at Collins and asked;

"You feel like a drive?"

he nodded and I told him that the warrants we had applied for were all ready and did he want to take the Shaw residence with a deputy, Hal would look after the Forrester Residence, Ray the Forrester factory and I would concentrate on the Shaw factory. We would all need at least two deputies with us and one of the CSI fellows as what we find we need to process and put into evidence. I knew I would have to corral a couple of Deputies of other duties to help but this was more important at this time.

An hour later we were all on our way to our designated places, warrants in hand and I prayed that we found something to link all the happenings together. I arrived at the Shaw Industries factory with Colin whom I had called in from the Shaw cabin to help with the search of the factory. He informed me that they had completed the cabin search and evidence collection anyway and they were all back in town, so I spread them among the others to carry the searches of the premises that their respective warrants named.

Colin told me that they had plenty of fingerprints and some shoe and boot impression from the cabin, some hair and blood samples, but the analysis of such would have to wait until we had completed what we were doing now as we were all stretched a little thin on the ground. We reached the Shaw Industries factory main gate and the guard allowed us in after I produced the warrant. I parked outside the main reception and entered the building with Colin in tow and his forensic kit. This was going to be interesting.

36

Ray Beale was shaking with cold, as the heaters had not really warmed up the ski lodge a lot now, but Mike Grant was still pacing the floor wearing a well walked trail across the entire length of the lodge, muttering to himself the whole time, and Ray could see he was getting angrier and angrier with every pass. The rain had stopped but the wind up here on the mountain was still strong and was swirling around blowing the light dusting of snow that had fallen into small whirlwinds which seemed to encircle the lodge and make a whistling sound as it did so. Mike finally stopped looked at Ray and stuttered slightly;

"I do not trust Shaw to do as he said he will, I am sure he would betray us at the first chance he got and the bloody mayor would not get his hands dirty for any amount of money."

Ray answered by saying;

"But the mayor is not the mayor anymore so does not have the clout or the authority he did have, Shaw told us he was now an alcoholic and was not even in his right mind."

Mike took in what Ray was saying and this made him even more angry and filled with rage, he started pacing the floor again until Ray finally said;

"Will you stop the pacing for fucks sake you are driving me bloody crazy, with your muttering and your to and fro movements."

Mike looked at him, pulled the gun from his belt and pointed at Ray;

"For your sake I hope Shaw comes through because if he is not here by tomorrow evening you are a dead man and I will go after Farrer and God help anyone who gets in my way. Do you understand?"

Ray was now in no doubt that Mike was off his tree and his obsession with Farrer and getting this extra two million dollars had clouded any resemblance of clear thinking that he may have had prior to coming back here the town that was home for so long. Ray now had the feeling it may be better to shut up and just go with the flow and not rock the boat in anyway as he did not want a bullet in the head.

Ray's phone rang and he quickly looked at the name who was calling, it was the gate guard at Shaw's factory who once worked for Ray. Ray answered;

"Hello," the guard filled Ray into what was happening in that the police were searching Shaw's factory and they had a warrant to search everywhere including his office. He also informed him that they had warrants for his home, Mr Forrester's factory and home. He asked Ray;

"Was there anything he wanted him to do?"

Ray answered they would find nothing at Shaw's or Forrester's and that he was okay and thanked him for letting him know. Mike looked at Beale and asked what that was all about, Ray informed of what was happening and Mike blew a gasket, which means Shaw will not do what I want as he will be too shit scared of the search and that they may find something that could incriminate Shaw. Mike was of the opinion now that he and Beale had to get out of the lodge and find somewhere in town to fix up Farrer and then get out as quick as possible. Ray did not agree with that plan, even though he knew it may mean his life, he just wanted to go and leave the whole thing behind take the drugs and the two million they had and get out of this place as fast as they could, dump the car before the border get another and be free of anything. Before Ray could say anything, he felt a burning sting in his right arm, he looked up and Mike had shot him in the lower left arm. Grant aimed the gun at Beal again and said menacingly,

"Shut the fuck up, that is flesh wound the next you will know nothing and be like Forrester a very dead man. I am sick of your whining and moaning about my grudge with Farrer, you had better go and fix your arm as you are bleeding all over the carpet."

Ray walked slowly towards the toilet area and knew he had to get out and if it was going to happen it had to be now before he was used as target practice, for a man that was completely out of control and had lost all sense of reality. Ray did not have his gun it was in the other room and to get to it he had to pass by Grant and he did not fancy the idea as Mike would sense what he was about. Ray made the toilets and rolled up sleeve, luckily the bullet had scraped the fleshy part of the forearm and Ray was able to stem the blood flow with a handkerchief and clean up the rest of the arm with some paper towel.

He looked in the mirror and felt he needed to piss, so he had one then came back washed his hands and again looked in the mirror, he did not like the person who was looking back at him. He there and then decided he was going out the back door cross the open ground between himself and the car, drive into town and throw himself on Farrer's mercy, tell him the whole story of what was going on. He would have the drugs and money in the trunk and would just hand them over as this might help him towards whatever was going to happen to him.

He left the bathroom and slowly and silently found his way through the kitchen and the back door. He noticed though the push bar to open the door was also an alarm so he was going to have move quickly if he was going to make the car before Mike found him and maybe finally shoot him. He counted to three and pushed the bar, opened the door quickly the alarm at once started to go a loud siren was going off, he stepped through the door and started to run across the ground between himself and the car. He made the car in record time, swore to himself as he fumbled with the keys and finally opened the car just as he glanced back and saw Mike coming out the same door as he had.

He quickly started the car put it in gear and flattened the accelerator the car jerked forward and swerved slightly as he took off, a shot rang out and hit the side window behind him showering him in glass pieces, another hit the rear window, shattering it too, two mor shots but they missed he slid slightly as he turned onto the ski field road and headed downhill as fast as the car would go, another shot rang out this time coming through the back window and hitting the windscreen, shattering it and covering Ray in glass, he felt some hitting his face and it stung as the cold bitter wind crashed into his face he glanced into the rear view mirror and Mike was running after him but making no ground him and still shooting but by this time was hitting nothing but thin air and then there was silence from the gun, Mike had ran out of bullets.

Ray steered his way down the winding road then suddenly out of nowhere Mike was there, he had run down over the side of the hill and had reloaded the gun, he started shooting again but thankfully hit nothing on the car but Ray saw small flurries of snow burst into the air as bullets crashed into the snow mounds. He again pressed the accelerator hard and was quickly moving away, he again looked back and saw Mike running but knew he was now in the clear. He reached the bottom of the mountain and turned right onto the main road, sliding on the icy surface, he came to the causeway entrance and where he and Mike had dumped Dean's body onto Big Bear Village, making sure to drive slowly and to the speed limit.

His phone went and it was Mike, he did not answer but pressed the hang-up button, a few seconds later the phone again vibrated into action this time telling him he had a message, he pressed the message button, Mike sounded livid and his voice full of anger;

    "You are a fucking coward, you will pay the same as Farrer and the rest of them only you will suffer a worse fate as I will do it slowly to you because of your betrayal you son of a bitch".

The phone went dead but Ray did not slow down and headed for town. The town came into sight and he knew he had to make it to the police station to be safe and that what was ahead of him was going to hard but he had resolved himself to the fact that he was going to jail no matter what the consequences.

As he approached the town he turned right into the avenue where the police station was, parked in a carpark opposite and got out of the car. He went to the trunk and retrieved the bags from it and crossed the road leaving the trunk up with the rest of the weapons on show. He entered the police station and approached the front reception desk, dropped the bags, and announced to the desk sergeant who he was and he had better get someone out to the car to collect the weapons in the trunk and he wanted to see Farrer straight away.

37

As we searched Shaw industries the office area first, we made our way to the factory floor, there was a tool room and several production cubicles as well as roller lines with plastic containers on them. Across from the lunchroom was a room with Danger in red and Keep Out on the door as well as it being heavily locked you needed a swipe card and a code to enter. The office person with us a Helen Noble, when asked was not able to gain entry and advised us there was only five people who had access to that room, they are being Mr and Mrs Shaw, the General Manager, Production Manager, and the shift boss. I asked who was available right at that present time and was informed the only one was the General Manager back in the office. I told her to get the GM as asap as I wanted into that room.

She quickly went back to the office while we investigated all other areas of the factory floor, finally she reappeared with a smartly dressed man in a three-piece suit, tall and greying hair which looked odd as he did not seem that old. I thought maybe the job had sent him grey, he had piercing blue eyes and very distinctive facial features, strong jaw line and rather thin lips which did not suit the rest of him at all.

He approached us and I told him I wanted into that room, he explained he could not as it said it was dangerous and that the warrant, we had would not cover that room. I told him to open the fucking door or I would charge him with obstruction, he pulled a blue swipe card out of his jacket pocket and swiped it the light on the card swiper turned green he then punched in a four-figure number and the door opened.

Inside were cabinets with glass fronts and at the rear was a stell cabinet with again a swipe card and numerical pad. He swiped the card, punched in another four-figure number and the two doors opened revealing small bottles varying in size from two hundred and fifty mils to one litre. They were marked with labels of contents as well as stock numbers and identification numbers. On the side of the door was a clip board with three columns, the first showing the name of the liquid, second the quantity of bottles in the cupboard and the third the identification numbers.

I perused the list as Colin who had done gloves at this stage went to the bottles marked Thallium, he counted fourteen bottles, I looked at the list there was supposed to be fifteen in there, we then compared the identification numbers and sure enough there was one two hundred and fifty mil bottle missing. The same for the Sulphuric Acid one missing same size. I asked who would have signed for the missing bottles, he replied on the back page.

There were no signatures for the past four weeks, he explained they had not needed any as they were now on a different contract and that they would not be needed for what they were working on. How do you know who had access to this room in the past month, he replied that the computer in the office show who owned the swipe card that enters and locks the doors.

We at once re-locked the room and headed to the office, my phone rang, it was the desk sergeant he informed me that he had a Ray Beale locked up in the cells he had turned up with bags of money, drugs, and weapons. I told him keep locked up we will be back shortly. Make sure they keep a watch on him I stressed. In the office the General Manager mentioned the list for who had used the room recently, it showed only the shift managers and the production Manager except three weeks ago Isabella Shaw entered the room and there was no record on the clip board of her entering or leaving, but her card had been used. I at once phoned Collins and told him to look for a swipe card and any type of keys at the Shaw residence.

He queried why and I told him, he said they had found a swipe card in Isabella Shaw's beauty case as well as a receipt for a lock-up in Big Bear Village. I told him to check out as I had to return to the station and explained why. He would go straight away and check out the lock-up and meet us back at the office. I told him make sure he takes his CSI partner there with him and bring back anything they find. I then rang Hal and they had left the Forrester's with nothing of interest except bank statements dating back ten years and substantial amounts of cash being withdrawn at various times around the time of the murders. My interest was at once heightened and I knew that things were starting to fall into place.

With Beale about to spill his guts and we knew Shaw wanted to come clean it was only going to be a matter of time before the final pieces of the jigsaw puzzle fitted together. I was feeling rather pleased with myself, even a slight smile must have shown on my face as Colin recognised it and asked;

"You must be happy about something, as you look like the cat that swallowed the canary."
I replied;
"More than the bloody canary mate, I have swallowed the whole cage full of the bastards."
We left the factory armed with copies of the clipboard notes and a copy of the computer entries to do with the missing Thallium. I now knew that Isabella Shaw was the one who had tried to poison Victoria Merrin and somehow had injured herself and was in hospital because of jealousy and stupidity. I really did not need her to tell me that but I would wait till she had recovered if she did and then asked her the obvious and charge her with attempted murder, theft of a dangerous product, and whatever else I could think of before the time came. I was feeling rather proud of myself as we drove back to the office and as we arrived Shaw was pulling up outside at the same time.

This was going to be a wonderful day as I entered the office. I told Collins to put Shaw in an interview room and

I phoned Ray and Hal, told them to return to the office and informed them of what we were about to uncover. I could tell by their voices they were as excited as I was. We all had a great anticipation of what was to come and that it would end long years of not knowing and desperation, especially on my part. The interview with Shaw was to be first as I needed the background to the whole thing before I tackled Beale as I was not sure whether he would fill in the blanks truthfully or just lead us down a garden path to give Grant time to get away. Entered my office grabbed two new tapes from my top drawer and the files I would need as well as a note pad, left and collected a coffee on the way to Interview room three.

Upon entering Shaw looked very sheepish and was staring down at the silver top of the table, I told the guard to remove the cuffs they were not needed and asked if he had been searched? The guard nodded yes and removed the cuffs, Shaw rubbed his wrists still not looking up. I placed the tapes in the recorder and waited for Hal or Ray to enter, Collins came in first carrying a coffee closely followed by Hal. Ray was staying behind with Beale, Ray informed me. I pressed the recorder button and the tape started going, I pushed the microphone closer to Shaw as I did not want to miss a thing in this interview.

I read him his rights just then the door opened and in walked Clayton Hill, lawyer for Shaw. He said,
   "Has my client been charged or spoken to yet?"
I looked at him and said;

"No, we have not even started we just repeated his rights to him."

Shaw looked at his lawyer and said;

"I rang you to be here but keep your mouth shut I am going to tell them all I know I need to get this off my mind as for years it has just caused me no end of worry, stress, and problems. It all comes back to haunt me every day."

His lawyer agreed. I started by asking Shaw;

"Tell me about eight years ago when this whole mess started?"

"He stammered as he started, he had tears in his eyes, and I could tell he did not want to be here and this was not supposed to be how the thing went down.

"Dean Forrester and I gave the then mayor who is now a sodden alcoholic, a considerable amount of money to buy into a drug ring and hopefully make a small fortune as the whole thing was explained to us." He stopped and asked for a soda, I signalled the guard to get him one and then looked at Hal,

"Can you get a warrant organised for the mayor and send Ray in."

I had forgotten to stop the tape but it did not matter we wanted everything on tape.

Ray entered and informed that Hal was heading for the courthouse to get a warrant signed by the presiding judge for the mayor's arrest. The guard came back with Shaw's soda, he opened it and took a long swig. I asked him to continue,

"Well, we did not know that there were others involved in this whole deal, the mayor had told us about Beale as he was the transport guy, which we understood but Madden, Bourke and McClean were never made known to us. When those young women started turning up dead and the macabre way, they were murdered Dean and I became suspicious that there was more to this whole thing than what was being told to us."

He paused and took another drink of his soda. I said,

"Go ahead," he began;

"Well, we fronted the mayor on what was going on and he told us about a meeting that we were all going to have to show us as the investors what was happening." He went silent for a moment and the tears welled up in his eyes. He started again,

"The meeting went ahead at Beale's transport, there was this Bourke and another we came to know as Mike Grant, the mayor, a Carl Manning and Dewey Sheldon." I stopped him there;

"Who is Carl Manning and Dewey Sheldon?"

He looked at me and laughed;

"You mean to tell me you have not known about them, well that is a turnup for the books. They were the ones who cased the woman and along with Bourke and McClean would organise the capture of them for Bourke to perform his sick shit on them."

This was news to me and I needed to know more about this Carl Manning and Dewey Sheldon. He continued,

"Dewey Sheldon was also the drug man he handled bringing the drugs to Oemen Lake, then they would be distributed throughout the state and Washington State and Canada all through Beale's transport. Carl Manning, he

510

brought in the girls that would be trafficked in the sex rings, again with Beale's help of his transport."

I was staggered this was going on in the background while we were chasing our tails on the murders. I said;

"Was this going on as well as the murders?"

He looked at me and stared straight at me;

"The murders were to confuse you and the police you dumb bastards were chasing the murderers and they were right under your own bloody roof the whole time."

I looked at him and wondered what he meant.

He continued;

"Bourke was looking for some cure for some illness which we were not interested in but the woman was being tested and then discarded with the markings to throw you all off. Mike Grant did the dumping of the bodies and Stewart Madden was laundering the money through his business. Grant became an integral part of the whole thing as he knew when and where to dump the bodies to throw you blokes of the scent".

He stopped and looked at me with a slight grin on his face then continued;

"When you found the tunnels and where Bourke had been doing his bloody cutting and slicing, it was Grant who tipped you off through that Barelli bloke as he was humping some chick who blew the whistle as she worked for Beale."

He stopped and took another sip of his soda, his lawyer was squirming in his seat as he knew Shaw was hanging himself but if what he told us then I might be able to talk

511

to the District Attorney about it but I was not making any promises and I was not saying that out aloud. He went on for another three hours and two more sets of tapes. He basically solved the case for us except we still did not know enough about this Dewey Sheldon and Carl Manning. Those two I was going to have to really follow up on as we had no idea where or who they were. It unsettled me that we had two loose ends that we would have to investigate further.

I knew then we would have to get the FBI involved as this would mean a country wide manhunt and wider if that was necessary. Shaw had filled in the gaps and he did not even ask for anything at this stage. I collected all the files tapes my notes and told the guard to put him back in a holding cell. His lawyer asked;

"If he may talk to him for a moment?" I nodded to the guard that would be okay;

"But you stay outside the door and he goes to the cell when finished okay?"

38

Next stop was Ray Beale, Ray had already started and he had been read his rights and was lawyered up. Ray was also on his second set of tapes with the interview. I asked Beale,

"Where is Grant?"

"He is hold up at the Big Bear Lodge, he has no way of escaping from there other than on foot as I have the car, which is parked outside, all shot up as he tried to kill me. I tell you he is nuttier than a squirrel's shit, he has lost the plot and he want you dead more than anything"

I looked at him;

"Why me what did I do to him, he has been on the run for some eight years and hurt so many people including killing one of my deputies and Bernie Talbertson, Dean Forrester, so why me?"

He looked at me and was shaking as he was clearly scared of Grant and was not sure of what was going to happen.

"You killed his brother, his little brother years ago in New York at a robbery that went wrong and his little brother got shot and you were the cop that shot him and he wants revenge. He wants it so bad man, he can taste it, as he reckons his little brother did not have a gun, as he was the one with the gun."

I pondered on this and my mind could not recall the event he was talking about, as when I was a cop in New York there was armed robbery after armed robbery sometimes three to four a day and I must admit I had shot four or five but in self-defence and I would need to go back through my files to check on this. If he was correct then that makes sense what Grant had come back to Oemen Lake, it was for revenge.

I told Beale;

"He was to tell us everything from the murders years ago, who was involved and what was it all for in the end and who was involved, I wanted everything. He was on thin ice as Shaw was here and had told us all we needed to know but he can confirm things as he was the transport man."

His lawyer looked at me and asked;

"If he tells all is there a chance of a deal in it for him?"

I looked at his lawyer and in a contemptuous voice said;

"Deal, a fucking deal, this man has been involved in God knows how many murders and his partner in crime Grant has now murdered three more people, and I do not know whether he was involved with pulling the trigger or not and not only that I two other people I knew nothing about are running around the country maybe causing mayhem. If he tells us what we want then maybe, just maybe I will talk to the District Attorney about a deal, but you and Shaw are going to do serious time."

His lawyer who I had not caught his name, but later found out it was Douglas Brandt from Helena, some big shot law firm represented Beale's company. It did not matter anyway as we had him now and he had answered what we wanted and we were going to throw the book at him and Shaw.

I left Ray to finish as we would all have to listen to the tapes and once, they were transcribed read them and anything we needed to clarify, we could question them again, we were also awaiting the arrival of the mayor who I was not really looking forward to interviewing him. I would have to get all this to Steve Barlow our legal man to peruse and help sort out anything we may have left out of the information or the interviews that we would need to present to the District Attorney. Just then a young Deputy came in and reported that I was needed at the mayor's place as well a forensic person it looks like the mayor had been shot.

"Fuck can nothing go right in this case," I blurted out, I signalled the deputy thanks and got on the phone to call Colin and explain I would pick him up as we needed to get to the mayor's place, I then phone Hal and told him to meet us in the carpark telling him what had happened.
As I approached the back door Colin caught up with me and said;

"We are so fucking snowed under we have all the evidence from the cabin, Shaw's house, Forrester's home, and Dean Forrester's autopsy to complete, as well as that we have not finished at the lockup in Big Bear Village, that Mrs Shaw had rented".
I had forgotten about that, I asked Colin;

"Did you have the keys etc for the lockup?"
They were in the lab, so he returned and collected them in the evidence bag and rejoined Hal and I in the carpark. I phoned Ray;

"When you have finished with Beale, take some deputies, and go up to the ski lodge and see if you can find Grant you may have to get some help up from Helena like

SWAT as will be heavily armed. I will join you there as soon as finish at the mayor's."

He agreed and I left it to him and we drove away heading for the mayor's residence.

We arrived and there was a policewoman out front consoling a lady who I presumed to be the housekeeper and as we approached the front door another policeman appeared;

"Not a nice sight in there man, he blew his brains out and it is all over the place."

I pushed past him and crossed the foyer, towards the study on the right, on entering the young policeman was right there a sight to behold, brains splattered from arsehole to breakfast time all over the large window behind the body of the mayor, blood splatter all over his desk and there was not much left of his face at all. I felt my coffee I had earlier come up to the back of my throat to say hello again. Colin heaved, he said;

"Shit I have not seen anything that bad ever."

I crossed the floor to the desk and the mayor's hands were by his side and I noticed that his left hand was holding a note.

I put on a pair of gloves I retrieved from my pocket and gently prised the note from his hand, there was a double barrel shotgun laying at his feet under the desk. The note was more of a letter than a note, I unfolded it and it was a letter or confession however you want to look at the situation. It was basically all that Beale and Shaw had told us. With this, it confirmed that we had all but finalised the case but then I remembered Dewey Shelton and Carl

Manning as well as that we still did not have Grant and he was the worry.

I left Colin to do his thing with the body just as the coroner's van turned up and two attendees got out passed Hal and I and acknowledged us as they passed. Suddenly my phone rang, it was Ray;

"We are at the Lodge awaiting SWAT, but there is no one here, we did a sweep of the place as the front door was wide open and not a soul to be seen anywhere. If Grant was here, he is well gone now and there are no tracks to follow as the rain is falling up here again,"

I heard him swear in a quiet breath. Shit where was Grant, and now he was on the loose, I had real problems as he could be heading for town or the border, I had no way of knowing. I rang Ray back;

"Told him to get SWAT to cover the place and make sure they check everywhere, I was going to Big Bear Village to check out Isabella Shaw's lockup."

Hal and I headed to Big Bear Village with the keys to the lock up and the whole way I was starting to think this whole case is again becoming a mess.

We reached the lockup premises and asked the manager to let us in and to take us to Isabella Shaw's, he walked along and turned down a corridor then left and stopped outside a steel door, I fitted the key in the lock and turned it, the door opened and we went inside there was a bench on one wall and a steel cabinet on the other side wall. I turned on the light the fluorescent flickered into life and showed the full contents of the lockup. I told the manager he was not

517

needed anymore and he turned and left. I used the keys on the steel cupboard opened it, there was a box of surgical gloves inside, a bottle labelled Thallium, one labelled Sulphuric Acid and another Glycerine.

They matched what was missing from the store at Shaw's factory as per the inventory and we now needed Colin to go over this place although it was clear that this is where Isabella Shaw created her concoction that she tried to murder Victoria Merrin with. My phone rang it was Steve Barlow;

"We just had a phone call from San Diego, asking whether we had a man by the name of Ashley Collins here, I told them we did and when he described the person to me, Ian the bloke we have let be privy to everything is not Ashley Collins's his body was found shot about two miles outside of San Diego four days ago,".

My body went numb what the fuck was going on, he had the credentials and passed himself off as a cop and he was not, who the fuck was he? I asked Steve;

"Is this Collins there?"
he replied;

"That Collins had left after we finished with Shaw's interview, and he took one of our cars, it had been tracked to the mayor's house and was then at the ski lodge but now was off the radar."

"Fuck, can you check the motel and see if his stuff is still in room one one two, get Ruby to let you in.
I have feeling this is either Carl Manning or Dewey Sheldon", why did I not check with San Diego and make sure of who we had. The phone number he gave me as his

boss was a phoney and was a complete set up, I had been played.

It was eight years all over again and there were so many loose ends that I thought we had cleared up but they were coming back to bite me on the arse in a big way. Why did I not see this? I passed it on to Colin who had packed up the bottles and tested for prints and any other forensics, but I knew we would find nothing there as what we had was enough to charge Isabella Shaw with attempted murder, theft of dangerous goods, and misuse of dangerous chemicals under the law. An hour had passed and I was itching to get back, I still had to go the hospital and charge Isabella hospital check in on Sally Donald who I had almost forgotten about. It was imperative I also get to Victoria Merrin to a safe house as this was now a dangerous situation as this 'Collins' was with Grant and that was a powder keg, and from what Beale told me about how Grant had revenge on his mind about me, there was Katrina and the kids I had to think of as I was sure he was not going to hesitate to hurt anyone connected to me.

I returned to the hospital with Hal and sent Colin on to the station to finish processing the evidence and that was going to take a while as well as the confessions from Beale and Shaw all were important to get it all finished as I wanted this out of the way to concentrate on Collins and Grant and Sheldon or Manning. I arrived at the bedside of Sally Donald and asked how she was doing she was quite well, the doctors were pleased with her progress, and she was to be discharged tomorrow. I told her what had gone on and I was having her placed in protective custody, until we sorted things out.

The guard would remain outside her room door until she was discharged, there would be a shift change but she can trust the men I send to look after her, and I or Hal or one of my trusted men would collect her tomorrow and take her to a safe house. Hal and I then went to Isabella Shaw's room, she was still in a coma and the nurse told me there had been no improvement, I told the guard on her room to handcuff one of her hands to the bed, he did so as I watched. I explained to him why and he was to keep her under close watch and I would organise someone to relieve him and they were to serve shifts. I returned to the police station with Hal and we made our way to my office, then thought I need to get a coffee so Hal joined me. This whole situation was a pure cluster fuck, pure and simple, there was no other way of putting it. How things had spiralled completely out of control, when I thought I was on top of the situation, only to be out played.

Part Two Epilogue

In this part two of the trilogy of the Farrer files, Ian Farrer confronted the demons within and when they returned to cause such mayhem, and further murders and a vengeance by two men who were part of the whole cartel of drugs, human trafficking, and prostitution, where out to retrieve what they had left behind and to make sure that those who went against them in part one were to pay the price for their disloyalty.

Mike Grant and Ray Beale returned to Oemen Lake with one thing in mind that was to retrieve their drugs and money and to make sure that Farrer paid his dues for the shooting of Grant's brother years ago in New York in a botched shooting.

The problem here was that Grant had not counted on Farrer being ready for him even though years had passed since their fateful encounter. Grant had also brought in help from outside to rid himself of Farrer and to make sure the money men behind the whole macabre set-up in the first place paid up a pretty penny for their betrayal in him as well as the others who were involved. They also wanted to rid themselves of Sally Donald who had recognised them at a truck stop outside of town and this tipped off Farrer as to their return. Despite this Beale and Grant carried on with their murderous trail, all the while Isabella Shaw was steadfast in carrying out her jealous vendetta against her husband's lover but failed.

This spurred Farrer to make sure that all those that had suffered at the hands of these perpetrators would fully pay the full price of the law. Ian Farrer knows that death and revenge are closer than he really wants.

"Satisfaction lies in the effort, not in the attainment."

- Mahatma Gandhi-

Part Three

A Deadly Revenge
"MURDER"

1

I needed to find my feet again, as I had been hoodwinked and played properly by Grant and this fellow Collins, also I needed more on those fellows Dewey Sheldon and Carl Manning. We had Sally Donald and Victoria Merrin in separate safe houses, as well as Isabella Shaw had been charged with attempted murder even though she was still in the hospital in a coma. I had invited Chris Mills who was up from Helena and had completed some work in the background for us on the Beale and Grant cases if he would join the team permanently. I had rung his superior and the transfer was finalised. This gave us three exceptionally good detectives I now had a huge team, which was good as it looked very much like this case was going to take a whole new outlook with what had eventuated.

The team now consisted of Hal Myers, and with Ray Barry, they have become invaluable. Steve Barlow stayed on as our legal advisor as well putting together any legal documents we may have, our CSI's were Colin Miles who was in charge James Simmons and Andrew Brian were there as pathologists and James was now the assistant coroner. Bill Durham had joined us as well from Helena as he was born here in Oemen Lake, Gary Mathews had stayed on as the pathologist and had just been appointed the official coroner, he had also had on a part-time basis help from Rowdy Bryant who once worked for Steven Shaw's Company as a chemist, which was now under new management and ownership due to the impending court cases against Steven Shaw and his wife. The Police building had been refurbished internally with a new reception area, our office had been extended onto the third floor which gave us all separate office areas, the conference room was now downstairs on the second floor with the operations room, and the files and archive section were now in the basement in a completely closed off area from the holding cells. Everything was now able to be fully functional and flow as it had been a complete mish-mash prior.

We needed to have coordination and complete autonomy from the everyday happenings of the other areas of the police department as we still had to follow up on Mike Grant as he was still on the loose and we were of the belief that he had teamed up with Ashley Collins, Dewey Sheldon and Carl Manning, whom all disappeared around the time we were starting to gain traction and charges had been laid against, Shaw, who had come to an arrangement with the District Attorney for a reduced sentence because of the information he had given us on Grant and Beale. Ray Beale was also lucky not to get a life sentence as he also corroborated Shaw's definitive explanation of events and thus helped with Mike Grant's arrest warrant being issued. We thought we had Mike Grant cornered up at the Big Bear Ski Lodge but he slipped through our fingers and we were of the belief he had had help from either Collins, Manning, or Sheldon.

We know they did not make the border or have left the state as information channelled into us was invaluable that they were sighted in Helena, Great Falls and Butte. The net for all three was thrown far and wide. I wanted Grant more than anything as he was just a cold-blooded murderer and he had no time for anyone as his narcissistic demeanour made him more dangerous each day, he was free. Little did we know or could foresee that another body was about to be dropped into our laps with all the markings of a Grant murder.

How can this man just continue a spree of killing people and not have a conscience? I was bewildered by his nonchalant attitude and could not for the life of me understand how Beale and Shaw became involved with him, even more so Dean Forrester whom Grant killed because he would not bow to his demands. What sort of man just kills for the sake of killing and never looks in the rear-view mirror let alone any mirror to look at his own reflection and sum up the person staring back at him? Grant had a real grudge against me as I was supposed to have shot his brother in cold blood and he was the instigator of the robbery back in Yonkers, New York that got his brother killed in the first place. He had no remorse for his brother or the two people he shot during the robbery. He left his brother to die, and to blame everybody else except himself.

To expand on that, I was a detective with the homicide robbery division and we had cause to follow up on several leads that a gang robbing convenience stores, leaving wounded and dead in their wake. They were just on a spree to cause havoc throughout the Lower East Side and anywhere else they could possibly cause a wave of destruction. The whole investigation was a city-wide one, with more than forty detectives working on the case at one time. I was a drunk living at the bottom of a bottle any chance I got, my marriage was dead and gone and I really was working on instinct ninety per cent of the time. My partner had been wounded by this gang in an earlier encounter at a Seven-Eleven holdup, I made a determined effort to catch the perpetrators before they could hurt anyone else close to me. I was cleared of all blame in the shooting, but it played on my mind as this was a kid, a child of just eighteen years old who had been brainwashed by his eldest brother into committing those crimes. An innocent life was gone in a moment, but if I had not taken the action I did I am sure Mike Grant would have shot me at that moment without hesitation, as it was, he ran like a coward and left his brother to bleed out on the street.

This whole scenario kept playing over and over in my head for nearly ten years before I left New York and I headed to this tranquil place to hopefully live a quiet life. I became Sheriff after much pushing from the locals and thought at the time this would suit me down to the ground, with no idea of any major trouble brewing, I was still drinking and finding it hard to really clean up my act, but, then the only real trouble in this town was a few drunk and disorderly, parking tickets and domestic squabbles. We had when I first started a small team and how this was going to change and change in a big way. Now Grant had caused mayhem

527

in Oemen Lake eight years prior as he had followed me with this full-on revenge against me.

Upon arrival he colluded with many others all connected with drugs, sex trafficking, and prostitution, but the worst of all the people who were killing young women for just murder's sake of which he was the ringleader of, as well as the twisted idea of trying to find some cure for an incurable disease that someone connected with these murderers suffered. Yes, I felt sorry for the person who was suffering from this cancer, but there was no need for the murder of so many innocent young women. This was the sad thing about this whole situation, so many suffered for no good reason and the worst of this whole scenario was that there would be more to die and families to be divided if we do not get Grant and his crony friends before mayhem recommenced. The team and I knew that things were about to get hectic and my gut feeling which I always believe in, was that things were going to happen, especially if this crew were still in the state.

If ever I was going to hit the drink again now would have been the opportunity as I let Grant slip through my fingers weeks ago, he was a Sociopathic person consistently showing no regard for right and wrong and completely ignored the rights and feelings of others, I would also class him as a Psychopath although a Sociopath and Psychopath sometimes overlapped, Grant showed the tendencies of both as an egocentric and antisocial person marked by his complete lack of remorse for his actions, and the absence of empathy for others, and this showed in his unrelenting criminal tendencies. His narcissistic manner also did not go down well with his fellow cohorts. I was taken in by his offsider Collins who we found out to be a dirty rogue cop, from San Diego, he only came to town to find out why his shipments had stopped and his money train had dried up.

He was convincing and had all the right mannerisms, but my mistake was I never took the time to check him out, as I was just too focused on what Shaw and Beale had divulged to us as well as that of their involvement with the whole sordid mess, not forgetting that Dean Forrester was also a major cog in this wheel of deceit, murder, and complete mayhem. Another question I had to ask myself was Isabella Shaw in on all the death and illicit going on and was she complicit in Linda Forrester's death as well as was Linda Forrester part of this and knew too much so she had to go? This past eight years although we had suspects and there were perpetrators in jail for the crimes. others within the department, myself included thought that there was more to this whole saga and there were other victims as well as persons of interest still to be found. We had primarily closed the case but with the return of Beale and Grant, along with Collins and Manning the whole can of worms opened again and this time I was going to put an end to it one way or another.

I knew though that I could not go back to drinking as I had to think of Katrina and the kids. We were happy and contented and for me to start the drink again was not going to be a good thing and, in the end, would most probably destroy another relationship. The job was hard enough on the family let alone becoming a drunk all over again. I had seventeen further deaths on my conscience because of my past and living with that was hard enough let alone going back to the bottle, although it would be easy to slide back into that way of life, a drunk, and bumbling my way through life and investigations. It was not going to happen.

2

The phone rang loudly as I was far away in another thought process. The light on the panel showed line three the front reception desk, I picked up the receiver and answered, the young-sounding voice on the other end explained that a call had just come in that another body had been found on the Northern Side of the causeway, it was found by a couple walking their dog. I asked if he had any other details but could only say that two deputies were on their way there at present. I rang Ray and asked him to grab Hal if he was available and meet me in the car park as we had another body in the lake. We all met in the car park and made our way in a swift purposeful manner to the farthest vehicle in the park. Hal jumped into the driver's seat and I went shotgun in the passenger seat while Ray and a young, uniformed Deputy by the name of Adamson joined him. We left the car park and Hal swung the vehicle hard left then right out onto the main road heading North. We past the Indian village and then through Big Bear village at this point Hal started to speed up and the scenery became a blur as the car travelled the winding road around the lake's edge toward The Causeway. A few minutes later, but it seemed like hours we finally reached the destination and there were flashing lights from the police vehicles that had already arrived and cordoned off the area. I quickly alighted from the vehicle and with a rather quicker pace than normal approached the scene.

The photographers and CSI were already there as I made my way down the small rocky embankment to where the body lay. There was a feeling of hope that this was Grant and he had crossed someone and had become a target of his own misdeeds, but that was too much to hope for. I finally reached the area where the body lay, bloodstains on his white shirt and trails of blood like small rivers flowing from a wound to the right side of his forehead. I did not have to look twice to know that it was not Grant but Ashley Collins the crooked cop from San Diego, it appears he may have caught Mike Grant on a difficult day. Two gunshot wounds to the chest one close to the centre of his chest, the other in the stomach. The third is to the head near the right temporal lobe. His eyes are wide open and staring into the abyss that is death.

I quickly glanced across at James Simmons, who was our pathologist and I asked if he had any sign of the time of death.

"Hard to say but maybe six to eight hours ago, rigour was setting in, but will know more once I get the body back to the lab", he said.

I nodded and asked if he could let me know as soon as possible as I was going to need that timeline to be able to tie down whether Grant and Manning were still on the run or were held up somewhere.

My thoughts at once started to think that maybe the ski lodge, which was not that far from where we were, could be the perfect place for them to hold up and stay unnoticed without any problems. The trouble with that thought was for them to have dumped the body here, which appeared to be the case, as there was no blood at the scene, so Collins was killed elsewhere and transported here, thus they took a huge risk of being seen by someone in Big Bear or on The Causeway around the time James estimated time of death.

We would need a concerted effort from all to canvas the village and surrounding areas for anything that may have looked out of place. I knew that if they were held up at the ski lodge, we would have a tough time trying to take them down up there, as there was only one way in and out and the terrain around the lodge was open, so a surprise attack or trying to enter the lodge would be near on impossible. Mike Grant had done his homework, and I was left lamenting as to what I would do next, as I did not have the troops or the ability to carry out an operation on the lodge, I was going to have to call on support in the form of SWAT from Helena.

We knew though that the body that was being transported to the morgue was not an Ashley Collins as his body had been found about two weeks ago in San Diego. I suddenly thought that the two with Grant were or had to be Dewey Sheldon and Carl Manning. I at once rang the morgue and told them to fingerprint the body, but that had already been done and the prints came back to Carl Manning who had a list of convictions and outstanding warrants for suspected armed robbery and attempted murder in five states. I had allowed this prick to pass himself off as a good San Diego police Officer when in fact, he was just a hitman for some cartel and was here to either sort Grant out or carry out the orders he was given. Unfortunately, I would never know the truth now unless I have Grant and Sheldon alive and the ability to get some form of the truth out of them.

3

Mike Grant was looking out across the driveway of the Talbertson property, he knew that Farrer would work out that he may have been held up at the ski lodge, but Grant was hoping that Farrer would take the bait and raid the ski lodge and of course, find nothing. Mike Grant was not stupid and was quite the planner and manipulator, he knew the police had finished at the Talbertson property and that he and Sheldon would be able to return there as the police would not believe he would return to an earlier crime scene.

Just then his thoughts were brought back to reality by a voice in the background, it was Sheldon;

"How long are we going to stay here, as the cops will surely check the lodge and then retrace their steps?" he stuttered slightly as he said this to Grant. Grant sensed the slight fear in his voice and glanced at Sheldon with a menacing look. Dewey then asked;

"Why the fuck did you have to kill Manning, he could have helped us as he had passed himself off as a cop and he could have got us across the border without any trouble?"

Mike Grant, thought for a moment before answering and then with a rather vile sound to his voice;

"Manning was a liability, he had cops after him in most areas as well and he murdered the real copper Collins in San Diego and we do not need the heat that would bring. Plus, he wanted a bigger stake in the money and the drugs we have, which I was not willing to agree to".

He stopped, thought about his next statement, you could see it in his eyes, "Besides Beale is probably in the custody of Farrer at present and spewing his guts out about us. I want Farrer dead and once that is carried out then we move on, not before".

Sheldon looked at him with bewilderment, thinking to himself that Grant was on a lone wolf vendetta that was going to get one or both killed in the process, but he bit his lip and said nothing, waiting for a later time to express his concerns, as at this moment Grant was far too volatile to even listen to reason and the way he murdered Manning was blood-curdling. Sheldon had watched in horror as Grant with no remorse put two into Manning's chest, and as he sat there bleeding out Grant then put the gun to Manning's forehead and pulled the trigger without so much as a blink of an eyelid.

He was 'old callous and unyielding and Dewey Sheldon knew there and then at that very moment, cross this unhinged sociopath he would be next for a bullet to the head. Sheldon turned and went towards the kitchen, just as Grant said;

"Cross me and you will feel my wrath as did the others who have crossed me. I have no remorse for the killing I have done as I know that my revenge on Farrer and probably my own death doing it will be the fulfilment I am looking for and the revenge for my baby brother who did not need to die in that way."

Sheldon did not stop or turn around but just kept walking toward the kitchen, the whole time thinking he was going to feel the pain of a bullet hitting him between the shoulder blades. Once in the kitchen, he let out a large sigh and realised he was shaking from the encounter that had just taken place.

Grant was nuttier than a fruit cake and he was not going to die because of this bastard's unhinged vendetta of revenge, which had nothing whatsoever to do with him. He would go along but as soon as he could see his way clear he was gone, he would split up the money and drugs and go, where he did not care he just needed to get away from Grant before the shit really did hit the fan.

As he put the kettle on to make himself a coffee, he could hear Grant in the other room talking to himself, about how things were going to be and that revenge was going to be bittersweet. As the kettle boiled Sheldon searched for the bags with the cocaine and the money in them, he knew he had brought them in with him and put them in the cupboard under the stairs, but they were now gone. Grant came into the hallway and looked at Sheldon as he remarked;

"Looking for the loot and coke, I thought you might try and do a runner so I moved it?"
Sheldon must have had a look of shock on his face and he stammered;

"I want my share now and if things go South then at least we can go our separate ways and that way there is less likelihood of either of us getting caught".
Grant laughed out loud, then with a stern and menacing voice;

"You are in this for the long-haul man and I am not splitting anything until Farrer is dead and you are going to help me achieve that. So, any thoughts you may have of taking your share and running off, you can get them out of that fat head of yours now, because if you cross me, I will blow your fucking brains all over this fucking house. You got that clear in your head?"

Sheldon just nodded closed the cupboard door and headed back to the kitchen leaving Grant watching his every move. The kettle whistled and Sheldon felt some relief, poured his coffee, and went out onto the back porch where he sat with his thoughts, his coffee, and the fear that Grant had put into him. The air was crisp and Dewey knew that the start of real winter weather was not far off, Snow would soon be falling and the roads and hills surrounding the lake would become white like the backdrop from some idyllic postcard. He hated the winter and the cold, which is why he was going to make Trinidad-Tobago his place to be when all this was over, he did not want to die here in the snow and be buried with the cold earth surrounding his body even though as he knew he would feel nothing being dead.

He started to chastise himself for thinking so irrationally and wondered if some of Grant's mania was rubbing off on him and he was going to end up like Mike Grant, a bitter, vengeful man with no real outlook for the future or plans that had any real meaning. He slowly finished off his coffee as he watched the sky darken with the oncoming of nightfall. At least if he got some sleep he may start to feel differently about the present and moreover the future.

Tomorrow was another day, but he had to get through tonight first. Back in the living room, Mike Grant sat in the large armchair he had shifted closer to the main window, where he could see right down the driveway at the yellow tape as it fluttered in the breeze that was coming from the East, across the lake and up through the trees that lined the driveway to the Talbertson home. He was now cautious and worried that maybe he had shot the wrong man and maybe Manning would not have given him so much trouble as Sheldon had. How long would it be before Sheldon cracks and makes a run for it with or without his share of the money and drugs? Sheldon was also curious why Grant had disappeared for three days just saying he had to run an errand and upon his return, he had a new vehicle and no explanation as to where he had been or what he had been up to.

The reason though was to become obvious within hours of Grant's return, Sheldon went to the vehicle and there in the rear seat was a black body bag. Sheldon unzipped the bag and to his horror there was the body of a woman inside, he felt a presence behind him he turned quickly and with a startled cry and look of sheer trepidation Grant was standing there holding a handgun.

"Who the fuck is that?" he stammered, Grant sneered and in a very nonchalant tone said;

"It was the former Mrs Farrer".

Sheldon reeled backwards against the car and he then knew where Grant had been for the past three days, he had travelled to Billings and found Farrer's ex-wife and murdered her. Without thinking Sheldon screamed at Grant;

"Are you out of your fucking mind, we have enough on our plate without having Farrer breathing down our necks with certain murderous tendencies on his mind after this little escapade?"

Grant just laughed and mumbled;

"He takes a member of my family I repay the favour and besides I have some help coming in from Seattle who owe Farrer a little visit".

Mike Grant did not elaborate on who those people were and Dewey Sheldon was not about to ask!
Sheldon realised that Grant was now out of control and had become seriously unhinged mentally, with his thirst for vengeance against Farrer now so deep and extreme Sheldon did not know where this would end.

"We are going to lay her in front of the Cop station and sit back and watch Farrer's reaction when he finds her. I suspect he has found that Indian squaw by now after we made her an example of just how far we would go to get revenge and see Farrer squirm and really lose it. The more bodies we build up the more Farrer will realise that we are not fucking around and that I most of all will not be satisfied until he pays for what he did and got away with it". Grant screamed with an evil grin as he was saying this.

Grant's brother was really talking to him from the grave about just how far he would go to exact his revenge on Farrer. Sheldon realised that Grant was now completely out of control and this psychopath only had more death on his mind and was not going to stop until he had completely driven Farrer mad or drove him to his own grave, either way Sheldon was unsure of where he now fitted into this scenario.

They both got into the vehicle with the body in it and headed down the driveway of the Talbertson farm and out onto the main road heading for town and the main street. The air seemed heavy and there was a darkness surrounding the lake as they drove steadily along the winding road towards the southern end of the lake.

Both men never spoke and the silence was deafening within the vehicle, Sheldon dared not speak for fear of a rebutted reprisal from Grant. They continued the rest of the journey towards town and entered the main street, Grant pulled the vehicle up close to the Boardwalk in front of the Police Station and alighted from the vehicle, opened the back door dragged the body bag out and unzipped it quickly then tumbled the body out onto the grass verge, making sure she was lying face up. He attached a note to her blood-soaked shirt, which Sheldon had not noticed before. They then re-entered the vehicle and drove off towards the far end of the Boardwalk and parked in between cars but made sure they had a clear view of the body.

4

Mike Grant was a cautious man and someone who could not be trusted. I sat waiting for the phone to ring hoping that someone anyone had a lead on where Dewey Sheldon and Mike Grant had gone, there was a rumour that Grant had been sighted outside of Billings but this had yet to be verified by the Billings Police. We had set up roadblocks and there was no way out of the area as we had it tied down as tight as a fish's arse, so I was sceptical that he was in Billings. I kept thinking why would Grant kill Manning,

540

unless he wanted to throw us off the scent or to show that he would murder anyone who got in his way of achieving his penultimate goal, making sure I was dead?

As the hours passed and there was nothing, I decided to call it quits for the day and as I passed the conference room or should I say our briefing station, I noticed Bill looking very serious and in deep thought viewing the incident board on which we had set out all the information we had as well as what had been drawn from the earlier files on this case.
I entered and asked;
   "What was he thinking?".
He turned slowly away from the board and looked at me with quizzical eyes;
   "Why would Grant want to kill you and go to all this trouble unless he had some other ulterior motive, we may have to look back further into your career and see who you have put away over that time and had connections to Grant? I just do not get his logic or thinking. He had the chance to leave with the money and the drugs as well as Ray Beale and they both could have been free and no one would have been the wiser"
I am staring him straight in the eye and in as calm of a voice as I could muster, I stated;
   "I must admit I have to agree with you in principle but we are dealing with an absolute psychopath who feels murdering innocent people and seeking revenge for something that happened years earlier that was proven to be no-one's fault does not make logical sense but then what

does go on in Grant's mind? That is something we may never know, not at present anyway".

I turned and stared out into the corridor and thought about what life may be like if that shooting had never happened and I had not left the big smoke to try and live a quiet life. Hindsight was a marvellous thing, but, on this occasion, it did not matter and we still had this madman on the loose and I had to take the blame for that. I nodded at Bill bid him goodnight left the room and went ahead to the elevator. I pushed the button to summon the elevator and waited with bated breath for it to arrive. As the ding sounded and the doors opened there stood Chris Mills, his face ashen and a look of complete bewilderment on his face.

"What is it?" I asked.

He stuttered then in a very staccato voice said;

"They have found another body, it is hanging from a tree near the Indian reservation, and it has a note on it for you."

This I did not need, I needed to get home I was tired and my mind was not clear or even thinking straight, just then my phone rang and I knew it was going to be unwelcome news, as if I needed any more. Hal Myers was on the other end of the phone as I answered and he went on to explain about the body that I had just been informed about. He was already at the scene and informed me it was a woman, young and had no real markings other than a bullet to the forehead, and a large note attached to the front of her dirty and partially ripped dress. He went on to read the message to me over the phone as entered the elevator and pressed the button for the car park, knowing I was not going home anytime soon. The message read;

"There will be one death a day until I have my revenge on you Farrer, so prepare for the bodies to build up or give up."

I rang home to alert Katrina that I would be late and not to wait up or save dinner as I was not sure how long I would be. As the elevator reached the car park the doors opened and I stepped out going ahead towards my car, Andrew Brian appeared from the left carrying his pathology bag and stepping out of the distance quickly to catch up with me. Upon arriving at my car at the same time as Andrew, I asked him if he knew about the body, he told me;

"Yes, Hal rang me and told me to find you and to travel out with you as quickly as we can as this was not good".

We got into the car and quickly sped out of the car park, turned left onto the avenue then left again onto the main road heading for the reservation. It was a short drive but seemed to take forever and my mind was racing again as to who this victim could be what poor soul deserved this kind of ending and what about her family? It appeared Grant had lost all self-control and his obsession was now engulfing him to the point of absolute mental and physical breakdown.

We arrived at the scene and Colin Miles one of the CSI's was already there with Hal as well as two uniformed coppers and a person from the reservation. Bloody hell I thought do not let this be a woman from the reservation or all hell will break loose. My worst thoughts were soon to be realised as Hall broke the news to me as I alighted from the car;

"She is Sandra Numell, better known as "Sun Daughter" and the worst is she is the one and only granddaughter of "White Bull" or William Hatcher chief of the local tribe".
I looked at Hal and he knew by the look on my face that the shit was going to hit the fan big time on this one. Colin came over and handed me the plastic envelope with the note inside that Grant had left pinned to the body. I yelled at the officers to cut her down and do it quickly. I asked Hal;

"Had the Chief been notified of the death", and he said,

"He had sent an officer to inform him and to bring him to the scene".
It was going to be up to the Chief to inform the relatives and the repercussions for myself and my team were going to be enormous, and Grant knew this, killing one of the reservation residents was going to be a death knell on my head. The Chief arrived with two of his tribal officers, and I at once passed on my condolences to him.
He asked;

"The note that was left, was it to do with this man you are chasing for all the other murders?"
I replied to him in the affirmative and then to my surprise he said that Sally Donald, whom we had seemed to lose touch with and had no idea where she had gone after she left the hospital was staying at the reservation as she knew two of the women there one being his granddaughter.

I asked;

"Where was your granddaughter going or coming from, to end up here and was she with anyone?"

He was slow to answer but in a quiet voice and with tears in his eyes he told me that she had been sneaking out to meet a man from the town but no one knew who he was or where he was from. I hoped above all else that it was not Grant or Sheldon, but convinced myself that it would be neither of them as we would have heard about that sooner than finding this body.

My phone rang, and it was Bill manning the emergency switchboard, saying that there was what looked like the body of a person lying on the foreshore verge near the Boardwalk in front of the station. I felt sick in the stomach and if ever I was going to give up the sober life and return to the drink it was now. I called Hal over to let him know what I had just been told, he asked if the caller gave a name, I told him it was Bill, I asked Hal;

"Why?", He replied;

"Well, the duty desk officer was over there helping place the body into the coroner's van, and as we were short-staffed, Bill was manning the switchboard."

I grabbed him to come with me and put the system on answering service.

I wondered whether it may have been. I called out to Colin and told Hal to ring Bill who was in the conference room when I left to see if he could see anybody on the walkway or if there was a body. Hal came back to me and said;

"Bill is manning the desk and the switchboard and he called it in from the second-floor offices when he went to get a coffee, he also thought there was someone else in the building but could not be sure".

Colin arrived at my side and I stated we were heading back to town quickly.

Just as we were leaving Hal ran to the driver's door of the car and breathing heavily, Bill called;

"It was a woman he quickly ran across and sighted the body", I told Hal to get the boys to finish up here and to meet me back in town as soon as he could but go nowhere near the Boardwalk, come in from the rear entrance and we will see from the offices, until we have made the area safe. We do not know whether Grant or his cronies were lying in waiting for us to arrive.

This was Grant at his best he was really taking revenge for his brother's death and that revenge was coming from the grave in a big way. It was no longer just revenge as far as I was concerned it had become a personal vendetta for himself and not his brother's death, he felt responsible for what happened, that was abundantly clear as he was there and could have stopped the whole event from happening but did nothing except run like the coward he is. His revenge from the grave was going to be my vindication for the shooting many years ago.

5

Grant and Sheldon were waiting anxiously in the car park for the return of the police from the site of the Indian body out by the reservation when suddenly Grant started to smile and began talking to himself in a weird kind of voice. Sheldon appeared to be worried as he was not prepared for what Grant had done in killing that woman and hanging her from the tree, especially outside the reservation and that she was from there. He even felt worse whilst waiting in the car and watching everyone leave the Police station heading out towards the reservation and the body, and Grant suggesting they pay a little visit to the second floor.

"Why, they are all out at the reservation and we have laid the body out for them to find, why tempt fate and go in there", he said in a rather worried and unconvincing tone.

Dewey Sheldon could see lights on in the far end room on the second floor of the station and there was someone walking around up there. He could not understand Grant's logic in wanting to go into the Police station considering there were surely going to be other officers in there and they were looking for them both, but Grant was instant and Sheldon was too bloody frightened to go against this madman.

Both men got out of the car making sure they closed the doors quietly, then half running half walking across the road towards the side entrance to the police station, knowing that there would be a code needed to enter. Around the back of the station was a small window leading to the men's changing room and it was open. Grant quickly pulled the window open as far as he could and with a leg up from Sheldon was inside in an instant.

"Go along a bit further there is a back door I will open that for you" Grant said with a rather gleeful sound in his voice.

Sheldon found the door just as Mike Grant opened it, and he entered, the station was quiet and there were only minimal lights on in the corridor. They rounded a corner and headed towards another door with an exit sign above it lit in green. They quietly looked through the small, long window in the side of the door above the handle and it appeared all was clear that there was no one to be seen. Mike pushed the handle down and gently shoved the door open with his left shoulder as he reached into the rear of his belt and withdrew his Glock pistol, Dewey whispered;

"What the fuck did you bring that for?"
Mike Grant scowled at him and said nothing. They passed through this second door and found a stairwell, mounting the stairs and passing through another door they found themselves in the briefing room, which was only lit by one light above an evidence wall, where both Grant and Sheldon's photographs took pride of place at the top of the board. Below were differing pieces of paper and photographs of all the murdered women, as well as those of Manning and Beale. There was a hospital report on Sally Donald and on Isabella Shaw who appeared from the paperwork was in a Thulium poisoning coma.

Grant perused the board with extreme interest as Greg Mann's name the Diner owner, Ruby the Motel Manager, Dr Geoffrey McMichael the Doctor treating Sally Donald and some broad called Victoria Merrin, with an annotation beside it saying;

"Shaw's squeeze". There were red wool strands joining each photograph with a police report and other relevant information. Mike Grant took notice of the strand that linked Ruby from the Motel to Sally Donald. Dewey pulling at Grant's sleeve said;

"All right you have seen everything let's get the fuck out of here before someone comes along".

Grant hesitated for a moment and then turned and left the room via a door that led to another hallway. At the end of this was an open door and the room was fully lit and there was someone in that room. Grant could not help himself he had to see who was still in the station and if it was Farrer, although he believed in the back of his mind that Farrer would be attending the hanging, gutted squaw out at the reservation. Sheldon was now getting nervous and continually glancing behind him hoping above all else no one was coming up the stairs to the right of them or that the elevator was still on the ground floor as shown by the lit "G" on the panel to the left of the elevator doors.

They reached the end room and quickly glanced in, at the far desk with his back to the door and facing out the rather large windows that would be facing the lake and the Boardwalk, was an officer with his back to them, speaking on the telephone. Sheldon could only hear slightly the conversation he was having but picked up that he was looking at a body lying opposite the station on the verge by the Boardwalk and it was lifeless.

"No", he said and then;

"I am the only one here at present the rest are out at the reservation".

With that Grant turned and started to retreat down the hallway from where they had come from, through the conference room past the board that had created so much interest for Grant.

Finally, they reached the window to which they had gained access to the police station. Quickly both men scrambled their way through it one after the other with Dewey slightly stumbling as he hit the ground. Grant pushed the window closed and headed for the vehicle. Quickly reaching the corner of the building and making sure the coast was clear they ran to the vehicle quickly got into it and as fast as possible headed out of town back towards the southern end of the lake and back to Talbertson's farm. Rounding the bottom end of the lake Dewey finally had to ask who the men were that Grant had said were coming from Seattle within the next few days.

"They are former colleagues of a friend of mine whom Farrer put away for ten years on a trumped-up charge and planted evidence, which no one could prove".

Sheldon sat in silence for the rest of the journey to the farm not trying to utter another word as he was aware how short Mike's fuse was and that he could end up very dead like all those others pinned on that board back in the room at the police station.

Arriving at the farm, Grant quickly parked the car in the barn and headed for the house, Sheldon tagging along behind slowly not sure what the next move was going to be.

"Grab a couple of beers and meet me on the porch" shouted Grant, and Dewey did so like a good manservant serving his master obediently. On the porch with just the sound of some faraway birds and the rustling of the gentle breeze through the trees close to the house, there were no other sounds. Sheldon opened his beer and took a huge gulp of the chilly drink, all the time watching Grant, with a keen eye and wondering what it would be like when these other men arrive for their revenge on Farrer.

Sheldon knew that when Farrer discovered the body, they had left was his ex-wife that the shit was going to hit the fan and Farrer's blood would boil with a vengeance, and there would be no stopping him from seeking out both he and Grant.

6

I was not a happy man as we quickly made our way back to the centre of town and what would we find, as reported there was a body on the verge of the Boardwalk but we had no details as to whether it was female or male. The officer who called it in was the only officer on duty at the station and could not leave even to go across and check on what was supposed to be a body. He had to stay, as the station was the central switchboard for all emergency numbers, yes, he may have only been a couple of minutes from the station but the rules were rules and he did the right thing, and that way the system did not have to go onto an answering service.

We quickly drove the car towards town and hoped that no-one would touch or nothing was going to happen to the body before we were able to get there. As we approached town, I could see the outline of something lying motionless on the verge between the road and the Boardwalk. I was hoping it was not a body, but that someone had left a load of rubbish lying there too lazy to take it to the dump and do the right thing. It reminded in a way as I smiled to myself of the Arlo Guthrie song "Alice's Restaurant", and how they had dumped rubbish from Alice's place by the roadside. Quickly I was brought back to reality as we came closer to the position of the item laying there still as the drizzle started to fall. I along with a young officer stopped some metres from what I could now see was a body and I felt sick to stomach when I thought how I had hoped it was just rubbish. Just then Bill arrived with Hal close behind and I approached the body telling the young officer to get something to cover it up as we needed the area covered for evidence.
He at once ran off towards the station as I got closer Bill grabbed me and held me back saying;

"You don't need to see this",

I pushed him aside and looked at the body and the pit of my stomach was pulled out through my back as I fell to my knees and realised the corpse in front of me was my ex-wife. She had been brutally murdered with one gunshot to the forehead and then her dress was covered in blood which I at once realised she had been either shot or gutted due to the amount of blood.

My rage built up inside of me with an anger I was unable to describe to myself let alone put it into words. This was Grant's doing without a doubt and he was now going to pay with his life no matter what the cost. Hal tried pulling me away from the body saying,

"You have to leave this to us now, you are too close to the deceased and that could compromise any or all the evidence we may find."

I shoved him hard and he staggered backwards as Bill grabbed me and dragged me some feet away. The young officer arrived with one of those portable pergola tent things and he and another officer had gone ahead to erect the canopy over the body just as James and Andrew arrived with Colin Miles hot on their heels.

I was sitting on my knees just staring at the happenings around me and from somewhere deep inside I could feel the anger building and although I was no longer married to this lady, she had been a big part of my life for so long and the agony I had put her through over those years she did not deserve this type of ending. This was Grant really driving the knives into me and twisting them to my wits end and somewhere he was watching on with a wry smile knowing that the inevitable was going to happen, he and I would have it out. Just between us and no-one else involved.

Why did he have to bring Izzy into this she had nothing to do with my problems or the demons I faced. She did have nothing to do with Grant or any of his cronies, she had never met or heard of them. How the hell did he find her in the first place as I was of the belief she was still in New York, but apparently, she had moved out west at some stage and Grant had found her, now she was another victim of my ghosts and there were too many already. I bit down on my lip hard holding back not only the tears but the anger at the same time. This was going to be a confrontation between Grant and me, and no-one else was going to get involved, as there would be no more deaths because of me.

7

Mike and Sheldon were slowly sipping on a beer, and reflecting on their handy work back in town, although Sheldon was not at all pleased with what went down as he knew that Farrer would be out for revenge and God help anyone who gets in his way. Sheldon had no idea why Grant had to kill Farrer's ex-wife as it did not serve any real purpose other than to piss Farrer off and make both he and Grant prime targets for a vengeful Sherriff.

As the gloom and darkness fell around the pair on the porch, and the silence became a harrowing experience with Sheldon too afraid to utter anything in case Grant's temper was to boil over and he would be the next victim of this psychopaths rage. Sheldon was not even convince that Grant was going to leave him alive, the reason he knew all the dirty secrets, the full story on what Mike Grant had done and was planning. He finished his beer and slowly eased himself out of the chair and headed indoors;

"You no need to worry."

Grant said as he passed him and entered the cabin. Sheldon made no reply or sign he had heard Grant's words.

Lying on the bed in the second bedroom of the Talbertson's house as Grant had taken the Master Bedroom, Sheldon reflected on Grant's words and was even more apprehensive as to what was behind the statement. Dewey Sheldon had seen and heard a lot from Mike Grant and although he was an accomplice in Grant's deeds, he did not trust him and that was the worry going around and around in his head. He closed his eyes hoping he would be able to get some sleep, but he was not sure sleep was the thing he needed right now.

He awakened to doors slamming, and a loud grumbling coming from the main room area and as he attentively alighted from the bed and found his clothes and quickly dressed, the noise continued. Upon entering the hallway and walking towards the main room at the front of the house, Dewey Sheldon knew Mike Grant was angry and that something had set him off. He entered the room just as a bottle was aimed at the door which he had just entered through narrowly missing him.

"What the fuck is up with you?" he snarled at Grant.

"I cannot sit around here anymore debating on what that arsehole Farrer is thinking or going to do, I need to cause havoc and draw the bastard out."

Mike sneered with an angry voice and the look of a vengeful man who had lost it all. Dewey Sheldon knew that the end was near and either, he, Farrer or Grant was going to be dead by day's end, or all three would be seeking refuge with the grim reaper if he did not calm Grant down.

"You cannot just go blazing away hoping that Farrer will accommodate you in the way you want him to. You must be smart about this and make sure that you come out on the right side of this, plan your execution of this nemesis or all you have done to implicate him or to seek revenge on this man will be in vain."

Sheldon finished his small rant and looked at Grant and realised no matter what he said nothing was going to satisfy Grant at this point as he was fuelled by alcohol and rage. Grant opened another can of beer and took a huge gulp, then turned looking at Sheldon with a blank stare and again turned away to stare into nothing as he finished the can and threw it at the window in the kitchen causing the window to crack. At this point there was no stopping Mike Grant he was on a path of self-destruction and nothing or no-one was going to change his mind. Just then Grant turned to Dewey and said;

"You can leave if you want, this is not your fight, you can take the drugs and half of the money and disappear, there is enough there to set you up with a new identity and far away from here and the past."

Sheldon considered for just a moment the words that Grant had just uttered and the sensible logical part of him wanted to take up that offer but the other side of him the illogical thinking part said to him that he must help Grant complete this no matter what the consequences. This decision he knew would eventually be his downfall, but then if he ran, he would be looking over his shoulder for the rest of his life that somewhere, sometime, there would be a bullet or that one person who knew what he had been part of would recognise him and he would end up in prison or in a cold stark hole dead. Sheldon quickly replied;

"No, I am with you, we get this done then disappear on our separate ways and that will be that. We succeed in this or we die trying to achieve and satisfy your wrath for this man."

Grant turned to face him and smiled with a smile of gratification and one of thanks, if anyone can really describe what that might look like. Dewey made himself and Grant a coffee whilst they decided how to go about drawing Farrer out into the open, although that would not be hard now as Grant having served up his ex-wife dead, Farrer was going to be a willing participant in whatever was planned.

Grant then with a sneer and a slight joy in his voice said;

"I have stitched Farrer up with all that has happened, some boys in Rikers and here in state prison have put in appeals naming him the main man in all the events that have happened here over the past years and even the recent ones including that bitches death. He will pay either way spending time in Federal prison and be dealt with in there or I get him while he sits and waits for his trial. The prosecutor from Helena wants him badly as he sent his uncle or some prick relation away for life over all this. So, you see Mr Sheldon I have planned my revenge down to the last detail and this has been over a long time and my patience is about to pay off".

8

I sat in the office staring at the blank wall trying to expect what would be Grant and Sheldon's next move. They had murdered my ex-wife for no reason other than to get at me in the vilest sense. Even though we were no longer married and I had not seen or heard from her for some years, she was a part of my life in some way. To murder her in the way that they did, and to just leave her body in the state it was, made this whole case now seem so surreal and my thoughts and actions were not rational anymore. I was seeking severe vengeance but knew somewhere in the back of my mind that was not the way to go. I needed to punish Grant in a way that he would suffer long and hard for what he had done, the murders, drugs, trafficking, the trail of destruction and countless number of lives he had affected was inconsolable.

There were others involved, yes, but he was the main contender and the one who gave the orders for all this mayhem, murder and mystery surrounding the real reason behind all the events that had happened over nearly seven years. Suddenly Hal pushed the door open hard as it slammed against the wall, and the glass rattled as it did so, I stood up quickly;

"There are State Troopers and two FBI agents downstairs who want to arrest you for the murder of your wife and they say they have evidence that you are connected to this whole saga."
He had a look of real concern on his face as he told me this. I looked at him and must have had a complete blank look on my face as I was unable to speak or even utter a word.

How the fuck do they think I was involved in all this saga when I was the one who had investigated the whole thing. Just as I started to get my wits about me two suits appeared at the door followed by troopers dressed in uniform;
"Sherriff Ian Farrer, you are under arrest for the murder of Steven Shaw, Dean Forrester, Ray Beale, and Elizabeth Farrer as well as other charges."

I fell back in my chair in disbelief of what was happening here, the whole scene seemed like a dream that nothing was real. At that moment, the leading FBI suit read me my rights while a trooper placed me in handcuffs, luckily in front so it was not that awkward.

"Is there a room we can use for interrogation purposes?" The agent asked Hal? Who was still standing in the doorway absolutely bemused by this whole situation.

"Yes", he stammered as he turned and led us down the hallway to our conference room. In the room I was sat down on the opposite side of the table, the two FBI agents sat opposite as the troopers and Hal left the room closing the door behind them. There was a brief silence as I stared at the two suits looking at me with obvious feelings of self-satisfaction. I knew the old saying he speaks first is lost so I just sat there silent, but with an anger building up inside that was going to explode unless these two pricks in suits said something soon. Then the darker haired one said;

"My name is Special Agent Neil Broom, and this is Special Agent Colin Mason, from the Helena field office. We have been given evidence that since you became Sherrif here there have been several deaths, drug related arrests, prostitution, human trafficking, and organ harvesting as well as money laundering and it all started upon your arrival here in Oemen Lake".
I was livid with anger;

"I arrested the heads of those crimes and they are serving sentences for their crimes and the evidence was overwhelming as you will see from the court documents and case files if you want to look, or can't either of you read?"
Just then Steve Barlow walked in;

"I am Sherriff Farrer's attorney, he will be saying nothing more until I have had time to speak with my client. What are the charges and what evidence do you have of the crimes he has supposedly committed?"

The two agents looked at each other and then Mason said;

"We have been given evidence and statements by the supposedly guilty parties that Sherriff Farrer put in prison as well as a Department of Internal Affairs report on a shooting that happened in New York some years ago and there were suspicious circumstances connected with that." Broom continued;

"It seems rather strange that there was no hint of any of these crimes here in this town until you became Sherriff and that murders started happening as well as the drugs etc. We have been given evidence that you are involved in all of this and that you are even responsible for the death of one of your own officers by the name of Barelli, and then married his widow."

With this I jumped up and lunged across the table smacking agent Broom in the nose with my head as we both fell to the floor. He had blood pouring from his nose and upper lip, my wrists hurt like hell as I had fallen in an awkward position, just then I felt the barrel of a gun against my neck,

"Make one more move and I will shoot you without remorse, do you understand?" shouted Mason.
Just then Steve was at my side and helping me to my feet. I looked at Broom on the floor holding his nose, thinking, just give me one second to kick this arsehole's head in.

I was helped back around the other side of the table with my wrists hurting my head thumping and Mason still with his pistol aimed at me.

"You realise you just gave us more ammunition against you don't you attacking a Federal Agent is a felony," said Mason.

"I don't give a flying fuck" I said;

"You accused me of all that has happened here in Oemen Lake and then accuse me of murdering my own officer and friend, you two must be novices at this if you believe I could do that. Besides the inquiry into that shooting, I was exonerated of all charges and it was proven to be a fair and justified shooting".

Broom reseated himself at the table holding his handkerchief to his nose, and with a muffled voice;

"Five minutes alone with you Farrer and I will fix your little red wagon for you."

"Take these cuffs off and I will accommodate you gladly", I replied.

Steve waved his hand and calmly said, that the evidence the agents had he will need to see as I have alibis for all the events, they are charging me with and who or where did all this so-called evidence come from? I sat back in my chair with an uneasy feeling that this was Grant's doing or he at least had a hand in this entire process. Broom suddenly spoke with the handkerchief still to his nose and looking rather blood soaked.

"We were given a statement of things that had happened and how you were connected to all the happenings. When

562

we investigated, we found that timelines and events all line up". He wiped his nose and continued;

"Within the statement given it was shown that you knew some of the victims by association and that your colleague got too close to the truth so you had to have him silenced".

My ire was starting to get revved up again and he realised that he was stepping on some very sore points and that just the look on my face would have given him enough to know that I had nothing to do with any of this. Steve looked at me and held up his hand to say be quiet let me handle this. I sat there in silence while they went through all the evidence they had collected before coming to town. Steve asked;

"Why did you arrest the Sherriff without first interviewing him and given the evidence you have that apparently places him in this situation, I feel you may be barking up the wrong tree. I am sure that we that being the staff here can verify all events and happenings and verify that what you have is in contradiction to the real evidence".

Broom looked at Mason and they nodded to each other, there was a pregnant pause before Mason said;

"I was to be relieved temporarily of duty and that Hal was to be placed as the Sherriff for the time being. I was to be placed under house arrest and I was not to contact anyone or use phones or be seen to investigate anything concerning this investigation. Also, I would be put under guard by the troopers on a rotating shift and anywhere I needed to go they would need clearance from them before I could go".

Steve looked at me and I agreed to their terms but was not happy. basically, basically tying my hands so I could not defend myself legally and do my job. Broom got up and called in one of the troopers and told them what was to happen, I was also to hand in my gun and badge to Hal before leaving.

I asked if I could speak to Steve alone before I was taken home and could I at least go to the morgue to see my ex-wife's body? They left Steve and I alone and at once I started;

"They have nothing but some prison gossip and I bet I know who is behind all this along with Grant and Sheldon, along with Brian McLean who was put away for two life terms. He vowed in the court room that he would see me suffer intensely or in hell before he served any real time for what he had been charged with."

His final words were;

"You may have one this day but your time is limited".

9

Broom and Mason retreated to the squad room and tried to look at all the files the team had compiled on my office desk. They also informed them that they will be interviewing each one of them about this whole mess, and they were to speak to no-one or correspond in anyway with each other during this investigation. There was a list placed on my office window of when and who was to be interviewed, and what they needed to bring with them like notebooks and any other information they may have. Steve had left me with the trooper and re-entered the squad room calling all the team together. He let them know what had happened and Ray Barry exclaimed;

"That this is all Bullshit, and where was there proof?" Steve went through the charges and told them to cooperate in every way and do not antagonise the agents in any way that could jeopardise my career or the investigation. Colin looked at Steve and asked;

"What are your thoughts on this whole matter?" Steve gave him a blank look and replied;

"That as far as he was concerned the whole thing is trumped up to cause a fracas and to give Mike Grant and Dewey Sheldon a chance to get to Farrer easily. The evidence they have is from a prison snitch and the statements are from all the crew that Farrer put away connected with the earlier cases and this bout of murders. None of it will stand up in court as it is gossip and nothing else".

I was escorted out through the back entrance and into a trooper vehicle, which then took home where I was going to have to go through the whole saga with Katrina and that was going to be hard enough let alone telling her that they think I killed Eugene. As we travelled through town towards the Southern end of the lake and turned up Alpine Drive heading home, I was contemplating how I was going to be able to carry on with my own private investigation, dumping the troopers and paying a visit to Grant and Sheldon as I was convinced they were hold up still in the area and my gut told me they had returned the Talbertson farm as we had finished our investigation and the full forensic sweep of the farm and it's surrounds.

It was logical and I was of the assumption that that is what I would do, as the coast was clear for a period. But assumptions can become a real menace when they get in the way of facts and I needed somehow to find out if there was any life at all at the farm before I could make my move. We arrived home and the trooper pulled up the driveway beside Katrina's car and told me to get out. As I alighted from the vehicle Katrina was at the top of the steps at the front door and had a quizzical look on her face. I started up the steps with the trooper in tow and as I reached the top step, I told that the bench seat under the porch overhang was his cubicle that he was not entering my home, he went to reply but realised it was going to be a lost cause.

I entered through the front door and Katrina shut it behind us;

"What is happening?" she queried, so I set about briefly explaining that I was under house arrest while the FBI investigated the claims that I was the murderer the kingpin of the whole operation and that because Eugene was getting too close, I killed him or had him killed. A look of shock come over her face and she gasped in astonishment that they would even consider such a thing. I explained that I believed McLean, Grant and Sheldon were behind as well as the District Attorney from Helena as he had a real beef with me over the convictions of the mayor and McLean.

Upon saying this it struck me that maybe he was caught up in this whole thing also, and we never knew or there was nothing leading to him being implicated. That was food for thought and something I will need to somehow investigate without raising suspicion. Katrina asked;

"So that trooper is going to be outside the whole time, what about the kids what do we tell them?"

I looked at her that we just tell them it is part of my job for the time being and I will be working from home, and besides there will be a different trooper each day.

Back at the office Broom and Mason, had started their interviews with the staff, and first off was Hal who I knew would tell them what they wanted but it would be hard going for them to get him to say I was in anyway connected to this whole affair. Hal knew this was a complete setup and that it was a witch hunt, as they had no tangible evidence or anything that was factual. Hal turned his interview into him interviewing the agents and gained relative facts about this whole saga. Hal was not going to bow down to them and was if there was any way possible that he would be in contact with me. The agents continued with their interviews, Ray, Colin, James, and Andrew. Finally, they got to Bill who was reluctant to say anything and from all reports called them, "The scum of the earth" for what they doing to a good cop and someone who cared about this town. The agents left it at that knowing that they would get nothing from him, and as the files and the other's notebooks there was no corroborating evidence that I had done anything untoward.

Then they interviewed Steve who was my legal counsel at this time and although he was part of the team, he was still a lawyer and as such was privileged to information although as he told them he had nothing to hide and all the files and notes they had were all true and correct records of the crimes. He repeated that they were barking up the wrong tree with me, and that my ex-wife was a victim in all this, someone that I had no contact with or seen as far as he knew in years. Steve even reiterated that both he and I believed she was still living in New York.

Interviews over, the agents now had to sift through hundreds if not thousands of pages of file notes, photographs, medical and autopsy reports as well correlating all this with the investigating officer's notes. I am glad it was them and not me.

10

Sheldon was getting itchy feet as was Grant as they both needed to know if Farrer had been arrested or was, he still free? Grant decided to ring the police station and ask for Farrer and if anyone queried him, he would say, that Farrer told him to ring and ask for him if any relevant information to the enquiry had become available, or something to that effect. Sheldon was unsure even though he wanted to know to get this whole charade over with and high tail it North and then as far away as possible. Grant dialled the number and there was a rather squeaky voice on the other end, Ray had answered the phone call and was not really in a good place to be talking to anyone at the present as his interview with the agents was still going around in his head and he had not quite come to terms with the situation.

He asked;

"How can I help?" Grant replied.

"I was told to ring if I had any information about the murder of the Indian lady or the body on the boardwalk to ring him". Immediately Ray recognised the voice and said,

"That Sherriff Farrer is out at present, but can I take a message for him." The phone went dead.

Grant was furious when he hung up and threw the phone across the room;

"Farrer is still doing his job, nothing has happened to him and that means that what I had set in place has failed. Fucking Farrer is blessed with so much luck".

Sheldon was in shock and knew now that the whole thing was about to be turned on its head. He did not even try to calm Grant down as it would be a futile exercise.

His mind racing at a hundred miles an hour Grant was pacing the floor of the hallway from one end to the other, slamming his fists into the walls as he went along, hitting doors hard so they either opened with force or shut with a huge bang. Sheldon just sat in the kitchen knowing full well that sooner or later Grant was going to come storming in with some outlandish plan to go after Farrer there and then and that would be suicide, so he had to think of a way to deflect Grant's thinking, even if only for a couple of hours to get him to calm down. Ray went straight to Hal and told him about the phone call and believe it to be Grant's as he recalled Grant's distinctive voice from the taped messages that Ian had received some time ago about the earlier case. He of course could not be one hundred percent sure but was, in his mind had no doubt who it was.

He said to Hal;

   "They needed to get those tapes out and replay them and that would be all he needed to convince him either way as to whether it was Grant or not".
The big problem as Hal pointed out was the tapes were the evidence the FBI agents had and they would want to know the in's and out of a dog's arse why we wanted them. Ray nodded in agreement but Hal knew that the cogs were turning trying to find a solution to retrieving those tapes.

Meanwhile the report had arrived from the postmortem on the former Mrs Farrer, she had been shot with a nine millimetre to the forehead slightly above the right eye and had been suffered injuries to her wrists and ankles where she had been restrained for some period prior to death. Estimated time of death was between ten and midnight the night before she was found. Ray read the report with interest, as it meant that she had been killed somewhere else and then placed on the boardwalk to be found.

In the meantime, Steve had returned from the room in which he was going over the evidence the agents had presented and what exactly they had or didn't have. The one thing that is clear is that there is no real hard evidence against Farrer it is all circumstantial and based on prison gossip. The other thing is that the tip about Farrer's involvement in this whole saga had come through the District Attorney's office in Helena, which did not make much sense considering that office prosecuted those now in jail and they had no hesitation in doing so. Ray and Hal looked at each other and neither had to speak as they both were thinking the same thing that something stinks in this whole affair like three-day old dog shit.

Steve in the conference room was looking at the board trying to connect the dots as he had seen Farrer do on many occasions. What was the connection to all this baloney that the FBI believes connects Farrer to these murders and especially his ex-wife, the whole thing made no sense. After some hours and many dirty tasting coffees it finally hit Ray who had joined Steve in the conference room with his own mental anguish trying to piece the jigsaw together. Hal walked in just as Steve thought he might have an answer.

"What are you two up to?" he asked, as he entered the room. Well Ray;

"It appears there is one constant in all this, that is McLean, he was guilty of Eugene's death we know that Grant was connected to McLean. Then if we look back there is all the evidence that links McLean to Beale as well as Beale to Grant and Shaw along with Forrester are all connected to this whole thing, otherwise why would Grant kill Shaw and Forrester as they appear to be the money men and somewhere along the way they either double crossed Grant or he just got sick of them".

Ray still studying the board nodded in agreement and looked at Hal and then across at Steve;

"We must get to Ian and find out what he knows about Grant. I know he told us about the shooting in New York, but this is bigger than that, I am sure of it."

All three walked out into the central office area the agents were no longer in Farrer's office, Hal enquired as to where they were, the young officer at the front desk told them they had gone to apparently interview Farrer and his wife. Ray did not need an invitation and quickly went into the office and searched frantically for the evidence bag holding the recordings of the conversations between McLean and the other men that they had.

Upon finding them he signalled Hal and Steve to the conference room, he quickly opened the evidence bag and retrieved the tape numbered two, placed it in the machine and pushed play. There was a distinctive tone to the voice, and Hal was sure it sounded like Grant's voice, but then the tapes were a few years old and they would have deteriorated within that period to a certain extent so an exact match could not really be confirmed. They still needed to get to Farrer but now that the agents were heading to see him it was going to be a bit of a gamble as to how they were going to be able to get Farrer and run by him what they had come up with in their assumptions, which do not always pan out the way you want.

11

The FBI agents pulled up the driveway and alighted from their vehicle heading to the steps leading up to the front door. I met them at the door and asked;
"What they wanted from me now?"
"We need to talk to you and your wife about several things, mainly was you and your wife having an affair behind Officer Barelli's back, and if so, how long had it been going on?"
I was livid with rage and felt like really causing some shit, but calmly said;
"No, it was well after the funeral that we got together something like a year. We were good friends yes but nothing more than that."
Broom asked if they could come inside and I stood aside as they passed me and entered the hallway.
I said;
"First door on the right is the lounge we can go in there and talk". Mason asked;
"Where is your wife as we need to talk to her as well?"
I felt an invasion of our privacy was about to happen and that Katrina and I were to become victims of a horrible set

up which had no basis or truth to it. The allegations that had been made at me were to say the least flawless and I was willing to prove such. I acknowledged Mason and went to the kitchen to fetch Katrina, I introduced her to Mason then Broom and she seated herself on the couch next to me. Mason continued;

"Can you tell us when you and Sherriff Farrer became romantically involved, and how long after your husband Mr Barelli's death was that?"

I felt this was a double-sided sword question, but with great aplomb Katrina answered;

"It was some months after, maybe even a year. Ian had been great to me and the kids through the whole ordeal, and he was a good friend to both Eugene and I and the kids. He had been around here many times for family dinners and we all got on well".

Katrina was sure, was not only brave but exact with her answers and I could see that no matter what these two jokers were going to ask she would answer with dignity and make sure they knew that she was not happy with the situation they had put me in. The questioning went on for over an hour, and I was starting to get really agitated as they kept asking the same questions repeatedly, admittedly in differing formats but basically the same content.

They finally got up to leave and as they did so I asked;

"How long is this charade going to last, I have a job to do and I can guarantee that you have found nothing at all linking me to all this shit". Mason nodded as they both went ahead to the front door, where Broom turned and looked at me straight in the eye and said;

"Personally, I believe we were sent up here on a fishing expedition to see if we could find anything at all on you as you had made so many waves down in the capitol someone who does not like you wanted you out of the way".

Mason nodded in agreement and then spoke with a soft tone;

"All the interviews we have completed and sifted through the evidence from the cases that this involves, we found nothing that could even so much as link you or any of your officers and staff to this. Believe me when I say we are sorry but we must fill in the blanks and follow orders, and if it is comfort to you, I do not take any credence on jail house gossip which all these allegations stem from", with that they both turned and headed to the steps to return to their car.

At the top step without looking Broom said;

"You can return to work tomorrow, our investigation is over here, but we will find out why the District Attorney's office has it in for you and why they went off a hunch and really no concrete evidence".

I thanked them and turned to return inside, closing the door behind me and watched them leave through the side window. I now knew that the time had come for me to share my thoughts with the team about where I believe Grant and Sheldon were hold up as it had been worrying me for the past few days since this whole shit show started. I rang the office and asked for Ray, Hal answered the phone and I told him what had happened. He was also the bearer of good news that someone whom they believed to be Grant had phoned requesting to talk to me about the

575

body on the boardwalk and the Indian woman found up at the point.

Hal continued and asked;

"Was I going to be formally charged or had that all been sorted for sure and certain?"

I informed him that they had shown they were satisfied after all the interviews and based on the files and notes that they perused that this was a complete load of horse shit and that I could return to work tomorrow after they put their report in. I then explained my thoughts on where Grant and Sheldon could be and that if he could get the team together and meet me up here later in the day and bring the files on McLean, Rourke, Shaw, and Forrester as I was convinced now that they along with Grant were the ring leaders of this whole fucking circus.

I finally hung up and Katrina was standing behind me, the look she had on her face told me she had a burning question and deep down I knew what that question was, I told her

"Ask" and she hesitantly asked;

"Did you honestly, Ian, have anything to do with Eugene's murder?"

I looked her straight in the eye and without hesitation said,

"No, I did not. McLean was the guilty party there as we have Eugene's notes and notebook and he had the dirt on McLean and was about to blow the whistle as he had already been to the District Attorney to find out the course of action to take. That was his mistake as someone in the DA's office is dirty and informed McLean of what was happening and what Eugene knew".

I bent down and kissed her as she had tears in her eyes as I said;

"I loved and admired Eugene and would never have done anything to him. I have only killed one person in my life and still regret that to this day, and you know about the incident in New York".

She held her hand against my cheek, and softly saying,

"I love you, and I want you to finish this, get them all that have made your life a misery and made our home a target for the lies they have told and their own gratification". This was said with conviction and real earnest in her voice, so I nodded and promised I would do just that.

12

Grant had finally calmed down after the phone call that informed him Farrer was not at that time arrested or that anything was happening as far as he was concerned. He looked at Sheldon and with an evil grin which reminded Sheldon of the Jack Nicholson character "The Joker" in the Batman movie and said;

"We are going on a little trip and dance with the Farrer's of this world. I am going to cause mayhem, more murder and even a little intrigue, a little mystery maybe".

This statement frightened Sheldon as he knew Grant's state of mind was about tip over the edge even though he was no psychologist he could see that there was real menace in Grant's eyes and God help anyone who got in his way. Dewey Sheldon knew this was the time he would have to try and get out from under Grant's influence and maybe give himself up to the police and tell them everything as he now believed Mike Grant had gone too far.

The money, the drugs all of it mattered no more, now it was a case of self-preservation and no-matter what the cost. How he was going to achieve this feat was something he would need to figure out as getting away from Grant was the first hurdle the next was approaching the police without any ideas on either matter his options were limited. Just then Grant gave him a way out of the situation, Mike turned to Sheldon and said;

"We need more beer and food, you go down to Talon Point and get what we need. You're not that well known as my mug is plastered all over the place and I would be recognised at once".

Sheldon agreed and Grant handed him a bundle of hundreds and told him;

"To take what he thinks he may need. Get enough food and beer to last at three days and fill the car up as well as the gas can in the trunk".

Sheldon grabbed a fist full of notes and the keys and headed out the back door to the shed where they had covered and parked the car, as he opened the back door without looking back, Grant said;

"Do not get any ideas of pissing off and leaving me high and dry here as I have enough evidence on you to take you down with me, so get the stuff fill up the gas and get your arse back here, understand?"

Sheldon acknowledge with a nodding yes and hurried out the door closing it with force as he left, headed down the stairs and across the back lawn through the small gate then across to the shed. He pulled the sheet off the car and coughed due to the dust that had built up on the vehicle over the time it had been sitting here. He got in started the car and was surprised it kicked into life straight away. Putting the car in gear he headed for the driveway which wound round the side of the house and onto the main drive that headed between the pines and towards the main road.

He reached the main road and his mind racing he knew there was a call box at the service station and he would get what was needed and while the car was being filled, he would call Farrer and tell him everything. He was shaking both with nerves and adrenalin as he drove the two or three miles to Talon Point and the store and service station. He arrived and parked in front of the store, went in collected a trolley from just inside the door and headed down the aisle towards the fridges, he collected some frozen pizzas and then cans of beans, loaf of bread, butter, and other essentials. He then went into the walk-in cool room where he collected two cases of Budweiser and two Millers beer, he left the cool room and as he past the spirits shelves he grabbed a bottle of Jack Daniels heading for the checkout.

At the register was a petite young woman maybe mid-twenties with a pleasant smile and asked how his day was going?

"Fine, busy", he replied;

He glanced around the store and there was only one other customer in there and they were at the rear of the shelving near the family products as the sign showed. Behind the young lass on the register was a poster and it had a photo of Grant on it with a reward for information leading to his arrest, there was also a warning that he was not to be approached as he armed and dangerous. The young lady asked;

"You up here on holiday doing some fishing or hunting?", Dewey was caught out by this but stammered an answer;

"A bit of both actually", the woman smiled as she said that will be;

"One hundred and thirty-two dollars twenty cents, thank you". Dewey handed over two one-hundred-dollar bills and the woman gave him his change, he stuffed it in his jacket pocket and went ahead to load the goods back into the trolley, smiled at the woman and left the store. He reached the car and placed the beer, food etc., in the back seat and replaced the trolley outside the front door of the store.

Sheldon then drove the hundred or so yards to the service station and parked, opened the cars fuel tank screw lid, and placed the gas gun into the filler receptacle, pulling the lever and locking the handle on. The pump chimed for each dollar it filled and he went and retrieved the gas can from the rear trunk, the gun stopped and he tried again but the handle again stopped meaning the tank was full, he filed the gas can and replaced the pump handle, put the gas can back in the trunk and went to pay for the gas. There was an elderly gent behind the counter;

"That will be ninety-one dollars seventy thanks" he said to Sheldon. Sheldon handed him a hundred and received his change bidding a good day to the gent and returned to the car.

He drove the twenty or so metres away from the gas pumps to the side of the service station next to the telephone booth, sat there for a few moments although it seemed like hours, then decided he needed to do this and got out of the car and went to the phone picked it up and put two quarters into the slot. He dialled the number he had memorised for the police station and suddenly a voice answered;

"Hello, Oemen Lake police station, how may I help you?" was the reply on the other end of the phone, from a pleasant-sounding female voice. Sheldon froze for a moment then said;

"I need to speak to Sherriff Farrer urgently". The voice at the other end said that Farrer was unavailable but one of his homicide team was available if that was any help. Dewey agreed and was put through, Hal answered the phone;

"Hello Detective Hal Myers, here, how can I help?".

"This is Dewey Sheldon, and I need to talk to Farrer, Grant has gone psycho and is out for revenge. I cannot speak for long as he is suspicious and if I take more than the time, he believes I need he will kill me".

Hal realised he had the one person who may be able to lead them to Grant on the other end of the phone;

"Okay, where are you and where is Grant? I am at the Talon Point service station telephone booth and Grant is held up at the Talbertson's farmhouse and he is armed to the teeth and will not go easily. I am scared shitless that he going to kill me before this over as he has a death wish and Farrer is his nemesis".

Hal told him to stay calm and he will have a car sent at once, but before there was an answer the phone went dead. Somewhere from behind him a hand had hung up the receiver and Sheldon was holding a dead telephone then, Sheldon heard the click of a gun being cocked and slowly he turned and faced the person holding the cocked gun.

13

Hal could not believe his ears and still holding the telephone receiver in his hands, at once yelled out to Steve and Ray. They came into the office quickly with looks of bewilderment written across their face.

"You will not believe who just called me and told me where Grant was holding up?"
Ray asked;

"Who would know that except Grant himself and that Dewey Sheldon shit head?"

Hal took a deep breath and then replaced the receiver back in its cradle,

"The phone call was from Dewey Sheldon, and he was at the Talon Point Service Station phone booth, but we got cut off quick, so I am hoping that he was not caught in the act by Grant, otherwise, our hope of surprise has gone".

"Have you let Farrer know even though he is still under investigation?" asked Steve;

"I have literally just got off the phone with Sheldon and you two are the first I have told", remarked Hal. Just then the two FBI agents walked in and as if in unison both asked what the commotion was all about?

Hal quickly filled them in on the phone call but left out the bit of where Grant was and made the excuse they were cut off before he could say and he wanted to speak to Farrer personally about it no-one else. They seemed a little pissed at this and seem to scold Hal for not keeping him on the line longer to get a trace.

"Fuck you" Hal shouted;

"I barely had time to get his name before we were cut off let alone ask for a trace or his whereabouts. If you two are so fucking clever then use your connections to trace the call, I am sure you can do that without us being involved. What is the go with Farrer, you are charging him or not?"

Broom and Mason looked at each other and then back at Steve, Ray, and Hal, then Broom in an authoritarian voice said;

"No, we have not charged him, and most likely will not be, as the evidence we have is thin and besides it is cell block gossip and the DA in Helena seems to have a bug up his arse about Farrer. So no, we will not be charging him but will be continuing enquiries and for the time being Farrer is allowed to return to duty". Steve smiled and remarked;

"I told you pair of gumshoe suits there was nothing in the evidence you had and another thing at the time of the murders, Farrer's whereabouts could all be accounted for by more than one person. You see while you have been off interviewing Farrer and his wife, and I suppose you even broached the subject that Farrer was being investigated for Eugene's murder also?"

They both nodded the affirmative and Steve was livid;

"You pair of arse wipes, opening old wounds like that, you have no sense of responsibility, we all told you in our interviews that Farrer was here in the conference room with at least ten witnesses when we were notified about Eugene. He was pretty cut up over the whole thing and besides, you should have never suspected him in the first place".

Just then one of the new deputies knocked on the door;

"We have had word that Grant, Sheldon, Collins, and Manning were held up in a motel of the highway I-90 just outside Butte, and that Grant was spotted in Helena some days ago at an address in in East Helena, he was with another man which the eyewitness has identified as Manning. They went separate ways after arriving in separate vehicles and when Grant left, he had a woman with him". Well, thought Hal to himself how long have the Helena police been holding onto this information since we know that Farrer's ex-wife was found three days ago and she had been dead at least two.

Steve spoke up;

"I doubt that the person they saw with Grant was Manning or Collins as they would be long gone, and we have had all point bulletins out for them for months now so I doubt they would hang around with Grant or Sheldon as they are well known and there are wanted posters everywhere for Grant especially".

Ray agreed and he also wondered whether the two FBI agents may be better going to Butte and interviewing the witnesses as well as those in Helena because there have been other names pop up on the odd occasion that no-one seems to able to associate with Grant yet they have been seen prior to all this skirmish with him.

Ray delved into one of the files and found the three names that keep coming up in different areas of the case, a David Lawrence, Chas Bollington, and Avery Cannington, all have form and their charge sheets look like the who's who of crime. All three were in some manner connected to drugs, prostitution, human trafficking, firearms offences, and Cannington even had a warrant out for his arrest for attempted Manslaughter. Armed with this information Hal asked the agents whether they could follow up those three and the news that had just arrived from Hellena and Butte? He looked at Steve and Ray and with a wry smile we are going to see the boss and at least let him know what the state of play is. Ray, Steve, and Hal set off for Farrer's home to discuss their next move they had managed to keep the FBI off their arse for the time being but that would not last long.

14

Grant slowly took the receiver from Sheldon's hand and placed it back on the cradle, all the while keeping the pistol aimed at Sheldon's head;

"I knew you were a weak link and someone who I thought I could trust but it seems I cannot just like Manning and Collins whom I had to dispose of as they were jelly kneed arseholes".

The look on Sheldon's face was one of horror and Grant knew he had hit a nerve with that news. Sheldon was under the impression that when they left Butte, Manning and Collins had gone their separate ways;

"You see when I sent you to get the car filled up in Butte. I left Manning and Collins in that drainage ditch that ran behind that dive we were held up in. They must be getting high by now and I doubt if anyone who was staying at that dive would not be able to smell the aroma coming from that ditch".

It was now that Sheldon noticed the silencer on the end of Grant's pistol and at once knew that this was the end of his

586

road as well. Grant led Sheldon back to the car and made Sheldon drive the whole time keeping an eye on the road and the gun pointed right at Sheldon;

"You see Dewey boy, for some unknown reason down in my water I felt that you would turn at the best possible chance you got and I was right that is why I sent you for groceries and beer. You forgot that the other car was in the barn and when you left, I followed a distance behind, sat on the side of the road opposite the store and watched load up the groceries then fill the gas tank and the can in the trunk", There was a loud silence and then in a rather raised tone, he continued;

"Your next big mistake was going to that phone and calling Farrer. I hope you told him where we were as knowing that lump of camel shit, he as sure as hell will come looking and that is what I want. So, you see Dewey you in a couple of hours you are going to surplus to my requirements as I have some backup coming and you know them well also".

Sheldon shrugged;

"I have no idea who is coming you have told me nothing of your plans you psychopath and if you knew I would call Farrer why let me go to Talon Point?"

There was silence for a few moments then Grant said as they turned into the driveway of the Talbertson farm.

They pulled up around the back of the house and Grant signalled Sheldon to get out and take the groceries inside he would bring the beer. Once inside he looked at Sheldon and said;

"Oh, Dewey what am I going to do with you, Lawrence, Bollington and Cannington will be here within the next few hours, I need to fix up Farrer, so you are really surplus to requirements".

With saying that he pointed the gun at Sheldon and shot him point blank through the forehead, Sheldon's lifeless body fell to the ground in a heap on the lounge rug. How convenient thought Grant now all I must do is roll you up and drag your sorry arse out back and there will be nothing more to say or do on the matter. He rolled the carpet up and with the body of Sheldon neatly wrapped inside dragged it out the back door onto the porch and down the steps the body making a thumping sound as it fell down each step. Grant pulled the body across the small lawn area and behind the fence on the East side of the house, leaving it where it lay;

"I will bury it later, I need a beer", he mumbled to himself with a grin on his face.

He re-entered the house unpacked the groceries put the beer in the fridge a pizza in the oven and looked at the bottle of Jack Daniels sitting on the sideboard if nothing else he thought Sheldon had good taste. He seated himself in the large armchair facing the window that looked out over the driveway and cracked open a Millers, as he did so he found his cell phone which Sheldon knew nothing about, anyway it was a burner and he dialled a number, asking the person on the other end;

"How far away were they?"

"Well hurry the fuck up, I have got rid of the problem just now so you three had better get here fast. Don't give me fucking excuses just put your foot down and get here".

He hung up the phone and took a huge gulp of the beer just as the chime on the oven rang letting him know his pizza was ready. He got his pizza out of the oven and sliced it up into four equal quarters, returned to the chair took another gulp of beer and went ahead to demolish the pizza.

Some sixty miles South of Oemen Lake a car travelling at speed with three occupants was approaching the turnoff to Oemen Lake, but they slowed down and passed the turnoff as there were State Trooper vehicles across the access road to the lake. The driver headed North for about another four miles where he found a layby and pulled in. The person in the back dialled a number and upon the answering at the other end he went ahead to say that there was police at the exit road to Oemen Lake stopping all vehicles and that they had no way of skirting around the roadblock as they were still a good fifty mile from him.

Grant was the recipient of that call and he was not pleased he had not planned on there being roadblocks on the entrance roads, which meant the Northern side would also be covered. He snarled into the phone;
    "Use your fucking head and find a way here, walk through the forest around the roadblock and I will drive and pick you up".
The caller said;
    "You can kiss my arse, we are not walking nowhere, you did not tell us that the cops were onto him or them and they

were taking no chances as there was still a live warrant out for him".

"You three fucking stooges get here I need your help and you will be well compensated for your trouble".

The phone went dead. Grant squeezed the phone tempted to chuck it at the window but then he had no way of contacting the three in the vehicle. He knew he needed Lawrence, Bollington, and Cannington as all were good shots and they owed him big time as he had got them out of a few tight situations in the past and they knew he was good for the money or equivalent in drugs. The three sat in the car contemplating what their next move would be and when and how.

15

Arriving at Farrer and Kristina's home, Steve, Ray, and Hal headed to the front door, which was opened by Katrina, she showed them in and told them Farrer was in the dining room. She closed the door and headed for the kitchen and the bar fridge where she retrieved three beers and went into the dining room giving one each to the three men, Farrer already had one. Katrina turned and left the men to themselves. Ray told Farrer what the FBI goons had told them that at this stage there was not going to be any charges laid, and that as far as they were concerned Mike

Grant and the crew that we had caught and were either in jail of dead were in there minds the culprits. Farrer stood up and turned to them saying;

"There is another problem, I found out through my sources in Helena, New York and in Butte that Grant and Sheldon had three accomplices who were all wanted by the FBI on various charges ranging from, drugs, prostitution, Human trafficking and murder or attempted murder. They were David Lawrence, Charles (Chas) Bollington and Avery Carrington". Ray interrupted Farrer to let him know they had already found out about those three as they were in the files from the old case and Manning had spilled the beans on them as a way of probably getting a lighter sentence.

Ray continued;

"We also know that Grant, Sheldon and those three were in Butte staying in a Motel off I-90 and have been spotted in Helena in the past weeks also".

There Farrer was not pleased that those three were so close as it meant there was going to be mayhem if they caught up with Grant and Sheldon and decided they were really going to make things difficult. Hal then said;

"We know that Grant was at your ex-wife's home and he was spotted leaving with her some days ago".

"How the hell did he manage to get through the cordon we had all the roads covered with troopers and our deputies?"

Steve intervened and told Farrer the FBI when they arrested you and kept you for that few days had lifted the cordon, but somehow Grant had got through prior to that and all we know is he stole a car in Helena to bring you ex back here. Farrer turned and looked at the fireplace as Ray and Hall knew he was now contemplating what to do, or even how to make sure the three did not connect with Grant or Sheldon.

Farrer turned back to face them and looked at the three blank faces sitting in his dining room.

"Do we know where possibly Grant and Sheldon may be hold up and where they might have been?" asked Farrer in a rather soft seemingly lost tone. For the first time Ian Farrer felt vulnerable and was afraid for his family.

Hal then spoke;

"We received a phone call it was from Sheldon and he was scared, he wanted to talk to you as he wanted to spill the beans on everything that had gone down. He sounded worried and his voice gave him away as he had trembling in it and was breathing hard".

"Did he say where he was calling from?" Farrer asked;

"Yep, the service station telephone booth at Talon Point, apparently Grant had sent him for groceries and beer but before he could say anything else the phone went dead suddenly". Farrer thumped the table;

"Grant does not do things by half we have already seen that and this was a classic, Sheldon is dead as Grant would have been setting him up to test his loyalty knowing he three fellow bastards close if needed. The Talon Point service station you say, well I think I know where Grant is hold up".

Ray and Hal looked at him quizzically, as Farrer outlined his thoughts;

"Where would you go if you were being chased by the cops and knew it had plenty of cover and hiding places that you could set up and ambush. You said the phone call with Sheldon stopped suddenly before he could tell anything more, correct? Grant had two cars the one he stole from the Talbertson's and the one he stole he Helena, he has used one for Sheldon to get groceries and he has followed in the second car to make sure Sheldon was with him or against him. He had feelings I am sure that Sheldon was worried about the situation he was in, remember",
There was a pause;

"Grant had killed his money lamb as well as the dirty cop from San Diego and the hitman he sent for me not counting the woman from the reservation and finally my ex-wife, all to bait me. He also made sure that from prison gossip the FBI would become involved and that from that I would be made the patsy in all this".

Farrer stopped took a long breath and looked hard at the dining table, took a drink of his beer, and then continued;

"Grant is hold up at the Talbertson's farm, we had cleared that both forensically and all other evidence was collected. So why not go back there the place was clean no cops would suspect that you would go back to a place where you murdered two innocent people, and now he would have Sheldon's body he could hide anywhere on that farm. That is why Sheldon called from the pay phone at Talon Point as it is just a couple mile up the road from the farm".
Steve nodded and asked;

"What are we going to do about the three associates of Grant's ?" Farrer took a moment to think, then looking again at the files and papers on the table, asked;

"I'd the cordon back in place?"

Ray nodded in the affirmative and said;

"We put that back as soon as the FBI told us that you were clear, that is why we are here now".

Farrer looked up at the three men staring back at him just as Katrina brought in four more beers, and asked;

"Do you want anything to eat?"

Farrer looked at her and smiled;

"No thanks sweetheart, we are fine. We have everything we need thanks, love you", she smiled and left the room.

Ray started;

"We need to bolster the cordon do we not?"

Farrer looked at him and with a grin and a long sigh said,

"Now we lift it in an hour. In the meantime, Ray you get young Cotterall and head to the old sawmill and park up on a stakeout, as if the three are coming as I am sure as my gut tells me they are, they will be coming that way. To make sure Hal you take Coventry and make a stakeout at the causeway on the Northern side just in case they come from that way. Steve you and I and two other officers are going to Talon point and sit in the diner along with the two FBI goons if they are still in town? Once we are all in place, I will give the word for the troopers to lift the cordons and head back to town but be on alert as we made need their services later".

With this all four prepared to leave and as Farrer went to find Katrina, Steve seated himself back down and finished

594

his beer, he wished now he had something to eat as this could end up being a very stake out. Ray and Hal left and headed back to town to let the others know what was about to happen and this time include the two agents. Farrer found Katrina in the lounge watching some rerun of NCIS and he told that all was okay the FBI had dropped the charges as they had found the evidence that had was very thin and did not stack up to the evidence we had and it was all prison cell gossip.

There was one thing still nagging at the back of my mind what involvement did the District Attorney from Helena have to do with all this, considering he was the one who tipped off the FBI presumably, and why he was so fanatical that I, Ian Farrer was the person who had committed all the crimes in the first place. That will have to keep for another day, I kissed Katrina and told her not to wait up as this could take a while, she cuddled me tight kissed me and said she understood but be careful. This I hope above all was going to be the end of this whole affair, as it was going to be either me or Grant that walks away from this, I had really wanted revenge but could not because of my position and family, but I would extract my pound of flesh out of Grant before this saga was over.

16

Grant sat in the still darkness of the farmhouse and sipped on his beer and ate his pizza. He was unsure whether the three would make it through or find their way to him and he may have to finish this whole thing on his own, but that would not worry him as revenge was going to taste sweet even if it did mean his life. He had made a lot of money here in Oemen Lake before Farrer had interrupted everything. We had a good thing going drugs coming in, women being traded, money from prostitution in Helena, Butte and here, body parts being sold to the highest bidder.

"Yes", he said aloud to himself, he continued to talk allowed to no-one except himself;

"A few sluts had to die, some arseholes got greedy and got caught, either ended up dead or in the can, the money men double crossed me so they paid the price, and their lives were fucked up as well, affairs and murder within their own families what a fucked-up world we live in. There was just two loose ends to deal with and I am going to leave this God forsaken place either in a pine box or on a flight to freedom where no-one can touch me. The two loose ends Ian fucking Farrer and that slut who caused me trouble Sally Donald, they both must pay the price for ruining a fucking good thing".

He stopped took a bite of pizza and a large guzzle of his beer which he finished off. He crossed the floor to the fridge grabbed another beer and returned to his seat jut as the phone rang;

"What", he shouted down to whomever was on the other end.

"Keep your fucking pants on, we are on our way the cops have left the roadblock and the road is now open".
Grant felt an uneasy feeling why suddenly would they remove the roadblock, he thought for a moment, maybe Farrer has worked out my three associates are coming but he has no idea from which direction. He said into the phone;

"Do not come from the South keep going North about another thirty miles and there is another way into this arsehole of a place, when you reach the causeway keep heading South through the shithole known as Talon Point and about two mile from there is a driveway on your left, come up the drive make sure you close the gate behind you and drive around the back of the house. I will be there".
The voice from the other end asked;

"Why are we having to come that way, there are no cops here now, that means we have to turn around and head back out to the main road, when we are already halfway in".

"Turn the fuck around and head the way I told you.
This copper here in the fucked-up town is no idiot and he would have worked out that you blokes would be coming from the South from Helena or Butte so do as I fucking say or so help me God, I will fuck up all three of you. You got that in your pin head brain, now do it".

Grant was angry and there was an agreeance from the other end of the phone just as Grant hung up. Grant started shouting to himself;

"Why is it no-one can take a simple fucking order and follow it?", with that he picked up the pistol on the side table and fired three times into the ceiling, took a large gulp of beer and returned to eating the rest of his pizza.

As Grant continued his dining his mind started to wander on the past exploits and how he had arrived at this situation. Was it pure luck, good planning, or just a pure figment of his imagination that this whole sage was a dream or maybe a nightmare and he would soon awaken from it? He gulped down the last of the beer and went ahead to the fridge for another, looked around and found the remote for the television, seated himself back in the chair and opened the beer whilst turning on the television and scanning through the channels, although out here in the fucking never, never, he thought there would not be much to watch.

He sipped his beer and then he found a channel showing a Clint Eastwood movie, well, he thought maybe I was wrong and he settled in to watch the movie have a few more beers and try and get some sleep. Then he was suddenly brought out of his thought pattern by the realisation he still had fucking Sheldon's body out the back and he would need to get rid of that as soon as possible as Bollington was Sheldon's brother-in-law and when he arrived, he did not want to have to explain why he was dead and who murdered him.

He turned off the television grabbed his beer and went ahead out the back of the house there lying in front of the car was the bundled-up carpet holding Sheldon's body. He finished the beer and went to the side of the house where he had left the shovel, laid it on the bundle and grabbed the carpet and pulled it towards the glasshouse. He thought well they found two bodies there before, maybe they will not look there for anymore, or if they did, he would be long gone from here anyway.

He dragged the rolled-up body through the door and along to where the body of old man Talbertson had been, he dug out the hole a little deeper and rolled the carpet body and all into the hole. Quickly covering up the hole as he was getting thirsty and he was beastly careless how well he tried to inconspicuously hide the body. He was done, grabbed the torch that was still sitting on the table behind the door and left the glasshouse.

He returned to the house just as the light was fading and the sun was slowly sinking behind the pines off in the distance. He felt a wave of satisfaction roll over him at that moment, grabbed another beer from the fridge and hoped the movie was still showing on the television.

17

Back at the office we all got our bullet proof vests, rifles and a shotgun. I made sure all were armed with sidearms and that the radios all were working properly. As we left and separated into our individual groups as had been worked out earlier at the house, the FBI agents asked me,

"What are you going to do when you get the chance to arrest Grant?" I paused for a moment and then said;

"If he comes quietly then good if not then it is his funeral and I am at this point in a could not care less mood to worry about him. He has taken so many lives and caused so many heartaches and left a trail of destruction in his wake he will either get the needle which would not be my choice as you and I would be paying for his keep for years while he appeals and drags the whole thing out or my preference is a bullet to the head, quick and easy".

Broom and Mason stared at me and both started to say something before I put my hand to my mouth for them to be quiet as I said;

"I know what you are thinking that I will deliberately kill Grant for what he has done to me as an act of vengeance. I am an officer of the law and will carry out my duty as I see is necessary to get the job done. Do you understand? If he comes quietly then good but otherwise, he shoots I shoot back".

With that they nodded and went ahead to the rear door and out into the carpark, there already loaded up in the cars was the rest of the team. We left the carpark and taking the different directions to where we would wait the arrival of the three and in that time be keeping a close eye on the main road just in case Grant decided he was going to move on. It was getting dark which was going to make matters worse as we have no real idea what vehicle the three were in and this whole situation was a lot of guesswork on my part. As I drove along in silence North towards the causeway, which was the quickest way to Talon Point from town, we passed the entrance to the reservation where we had found the Native American woman strung out in a horrible and degrading manner. Grant was a psycho and no mental hospital or jail would be a place this arsehole deserves to go. We passed the road leading to Big Bear Lodge and onwards further until we reached the causeway crossing it the FBI boys following as was Hal and Coventry who pulled off to the side. Hal radioed;

"We have a place so will hide out here and let you know if there is any action, good luck boss".

I quickly radioed back affirming that was the first part complete, just then the radio burst into life again as Ray and Cotterill recommended they were at the old mill and were able to see all from both directions.

Steve and I and the Agents arrived at the Talon Point diner which was attached to the Southern end of the store and after parking the cars at the rear we entered and took up two booths both facing the road. The waitress asked if we wanted coffee or to order anything from the menu, I declined anything to eat but coffee would be fine. The others ordered same.

Every five minutes I radioed the others to check in and so far, all was good. Four hours had passed and nothing was happening, the agents wondered whether it would be wise to just leave the two cars at the causeway and the mill and we call it a night. I scowled at them;

"You want to catch these bastards, or are you afraid of missing your beauty sleep? There is a motel one hundred yards up the road which we passed if you don't want to stick around here then go get a room and play with yourselves as I am and my men will be here for the long haul".

"Fuck you Farrer", Broom said, with malice in his voice. I ignored him and kept watch sipping on my third coffee.

Just as we were ticking over into the fifth hour, the radio came alive it was Hal;

"SUV just passed the causeway heading your way, dark coloured, three men inside, the vehicle has Idaho plates on it".

I radioed back that we will watch for it, I radioed Ray to let him know that maybe they were here and he could slowly make his way towards the farm, keeping an eye out for any vehicles that go past heading South with description Hal just gave us. Ray acknowledged and was on the move. Twenty minutes later the dark SUV passed us and headed South, Ray came on the radio that vehicle just turned into the Talbertson's place, we are coming to you.

Within fifteen minutes Ray and Hal, Coventry, Cotterill, Broom and Mason were all sitting around in the diner with Steve and I.

"How are we going to do this boss?" Ray asked.
I looked around trying to make decisions on the best form of tactics, then said;

"Broom you and Mason, park two or three hundred yards past the driveway on the main road, park the car at an angle across the road and then on foot circle round to the rear of the property and watch yourself as there are fences everywhere, try not to use torches unless you must. There is a full moon so that will help with light. Hal you and Coventry, park the same distance on this side of the driveway and do the same park the car at an angle across the road leaving enough room for a vehicle to arrive as I have the troopers waiting back at the office who were on the cordons, then circle around to the Northern side of the house".
I took a deep breath and looked at Steve;

"I want you to stay here and coordinate things keep in radio contact at all times, use your earpieces not the radio's speaker, okay?"
Steve nodded in agreeance. I continued;

"Ray you and Cotterill and I will come from the front through the trees along the driveway on each side. Hal we will get a lift with you to the driveway, okay? We need to make sure all are in place before we do anything. All agree?".

There was nodding of heads and mumbled yes from the group. We left the diner and went to the individual vehicles and slowly one by one left the diner carpark heading to the positions we had arranged. Upon arrival at the designated spot Ray, Cotterill and I headed for the cover of the trees, it was a long walk from the main road to the house but the way through the trees was clear and the mottles light from the moon through the treetops gave us some cover as well as enough light to see where we were going. Suddenly in my earpiece Broom's voice came;

"We are on our way to the rear of the house will let you know when we are set".

Hal had also radioed that they were making satisfactory progress to the Northern side of the house and would notify once they were in position. The three of us were now only about fifty yards from the edge of the tree line and it was about another fifty to seventy-five yards to the steps leading up to the porch. Just then someone was on the porch as they struck a match to light a cigarette, it lit up a face I did not recognise and suddenly through the trees with the moonlight beaming down on the accessible area I could see at least two sitting on the porch smoking and drinking although not saying anything but there was shouting coming from inside the house which I could not make out. I quickly radioed the rest and let them know that there were two on the porch out front, so be careful and keep your heads down.

My earpiece again came to life as all answered and agreed. I told Steve to be ready to ring the office and have the State Troopers on standby but warn them when we want them no lights or sirens as I want them to enter the end of the driveway and block it.

18

Grant heard the vehicle come up the driveway hearing the tyres crunching on the gravel and watched the headlights turn and go around the back, he quickly moved to the rear door pistol in hand. The vehicle stopped, engine off and headlights go off, the driver door opened and Lawrence stepped out as did Bollington and Cannington from the other side front and rear doors.

"What do you want that for?" Cannington asked in a rather sullen voice.

"There are too many undesirables around here and I have to be on my toes", Grant replied. The three men moved to the top of the steps on the porch where Grant stood and they embraced and shook hands;

"Good to see you old man", Lawrence responded. Grant at once asked, "Did you remember to shut the gate behind you?".

"Yes", was the reply in unison.
The four men went inside and Grant went to the refrigerator and retrieved them all a beer, while they all retreated to the lounge room and seated themselves so they were facing each other. Grant started the conversation by

telling them exactly what had gone on and where the situation was at present, each looked at each other and there was silence for a few moments but it felt like an hour, as the silence was deafening. Finally, Cannington spoke up;

"Why the fuck did you have to kill so many and Sheldon of all people he was not one of those arseholes?" Grant remained silent and threw a stare of utter contempt at Cannington;

"You doubt my methods", and quickly picked up the pistol and aimed it at Cannington. A shiver came over the others and they realised that Grant had in some way lost the plot and there may be no way out of this now.

"Chas Bollington the oldest of the group stood up;

"Calm down you dickhead, we are here to help, but I have to agree all the killing was a little over the top and has made the job at hand a little more difficult than what you had indicated when you called".

Grant was silent then with an evil sneer on his face he too stood and faced all three men;

"Farrer fucked up my family, then came here and fucked with our operation. We were making good money from our operations and our Italian contacts were enjoying the spoils of our labour. Okay the body parts thing was not my idea and it was probably not the way to go but it made money. The trafficking and drugs was lucrative and we had two cash cows who were pouring thousands into the operation and funding whatever we were doing as well as laundering the money through their business. It was a serene setup until Farrer arrived".

They sat looking at Grant who was now pacing the floor glancing every now and then at each of them. Finally, he stuttered slightly, but explained what he wanted them from them and how he was going to rid his life of Farrer and the only other person who could hurt him being that bitch Sally Donald who escaped because young Bourke was a fucking idiot.

He sat back down and laid out how he had found Farrer's ex-wife and left her dead on the boardwalk in front of the cop station and that was the catalyst to get Farrer where he wanted him. He wanted Farrer to come to him and he knew given enough time Farrer would realise where he was and then the end would be near for him. He wanted the three men to hide away in the woods and as Farrer and his cronies came up to the house, they would trap them in and that would be the ultimate, Farrer would be no-more.

"How are you going to get this Sally Donald?" Lawrence asked;

"She is not with the police but she is a nobody why would she be with Farrer?".

"I know where she is", said Grant.

"I killed this squaw by mistake as she looked like Sally Donald on the road to the reservation on the other side of the lake. A mistake I know but these things happen. Anyway, I found out through overhearing some gossip that she was staying with the Indians on the reservation and we are going in to get her as I do not want to be looking over my shoulder everyday knowing she is still alive".

The three other men stared at Grant and by their expressions he knew they would not be part of that, they were willing to help with Farrer but going onto an Indian reservation that was not on the agenda.

Lawrence asked;

"How long have you given Farrer to work out where you are?" Grant just shrugged his shoulders and said,

"As long as it takes". Bollington who had been rather quiet through all this finally uttered;

"Fuck this why not just go and get him now, sitting around here we are sitting ducks on a pond for him. We need to take the high road and be aggressive". Grant shot him a glance of contempt and made no sign that was what was going to happen.

"We wait", he said loudly. Cannington signalled Bollington to come with him out the front on porch, Bollington picked up his beer and followed, lighting a cigarette on the way.

19

The two on the porch could be seen smoking and drinking from their vantage point when Hal said;

"Grant is inside and he and Lawrence were arguing about Bollington and his reluctance to get with the project". This gave Farrer an idea and he radioed for the troopers to now block the driveway, but there was to be no lights, no sirens, and to also block the main road both North and South.

Farrer and his team moved closer to the house under the cover of the trees and small scrubby like bushes that were lined along the front of the like a hedge. Ray was in position and just waiting for my say so to hit the house, Hal was also ready and again was waiting on me.

I told them to wait as we needed the driveway and the roads blocked first, so we waited in the air of anticipation of what was about to go down. Ten minutes later the troopers reported they had the gate and main road covered. I thought to myself you arseholes were supposed to stay at the station and wait until I sent for them, they followed.

In a small way I was thankful but in another not so, all was ready then for what was going to be a takedown of real gratification to rid this town of all the mayhem, mystery and moreover the murder that had besieged this place. My first instinct was to get rid of the two on the porch as that would create a sort of advantage for us as then Grant and Lawrence would need to come out and see what they were up to and our actions would be simpler from there.

I now asked the group if anyone had any experience in stealthily taking out the two on the front porch without too much fuss. Broom at once replied;

"That he had been a Marine and could take one but two he would need help".

Young Cotterill suddenly came in my earpiece and said,

"I will help take one of the two at the front out but will need to be told what to do as to make sure it was quick and with little fuss. He had had training at the academy and it was fresh in his mind of what was needed".

I agreed and told him to go around the back as quick and as quietly as he could and meet agent Broom at the rear of the house behind the vehicles. I saw a shadowy figure move rather quickly in the dim light shining from the side window as the body moved stealthily along at a pace towards the rear.

Next thing was going to be a surprise for Grant as I was going in the front door as the others hit from the back entrance, I had to change the plans slightly because the two had come to the front as Hall had reported there was a bit of an argument going on which would I believed be a distraction to cover our entrance.

Within minutes I could see two figures creeping along the right side of the building from the rear towards the front porch. Then they disappeared underneath the structure and when I next sighted them, they were right underneath the porch steps directly beneath Bollington and Cannington. Cannington lit another cigarette and Bollington finished his beer and went inside the house, shit I thought to myself our advantage is lost, but the arguing whatever it was about could be heard clearly with the front door open.

Grant was not happy with what Lawrence was proposing and this was really going to be helpful to us if the argument continued as the din from their raised voices would cover what Broom and Cotterill needed to do. Within a short period, Bollington soon returned with another beer for each and he to lit up a cigarette.

"What the fuck are they on about in there?" Cannington asked Bollington as he took a long draw on his cigarette.

"Lawrence wants to go and front Farrer now and get it over and done with and to leave this Sally slut to her own devices that maybe one day she will meet an accident somewhere somehow", but Grant will not have a bar of it.

We also had a problem as when Bollington returned to the porch, and he had left the front door open so the quick surprise for taking the two out on the porch had to wait and with Broom and Cotterill under the steps they were in a precarious position as the light from inside the house was now streaming out across the front yard and we had to take cover under the low bushes as the light spread like rays of the sun across the expanse of the lawn and driveway, even though it was now getting dark as the sun sunk behind the hills, and with that cast an eerie uneasy feeling on what was to happen next. Suddenly the front door slammed shut and all was in darkness again, and the noise made me jump slightly as it did Steve.

Broom came over in my earpiece in a whisper;
    "When you're ready Farrer, now is the time to strike while there is so much noise inside".
I thought for a moment;
    "Hal move into the side of the house on the North side on the porch and stay under the window there, Mason make sure you cover the rear well now you are on your own, Coventry I want you to slowly go to the Southern side of the building and place yourself under on the porch under the window towards the front of the house facing the treeline, this way we have the four entrances covered",

611

I softly asked;

"Everyone understand, just say yes?", in a simultaneous chorus there was a plethora of yesses in my ear.

I waited for a few moments and suddenly the shouting got louder, and Cannington, threw his cigarette out onto the driveway took a swill of his beer placed the can on the handrail and went inside slamming the door behind him and shouting as he went in;

"What the fuck is the matter with you two, you keep shouting like this they will hear in the tin pot town down the road. Shut the fuck up and get over whatever is pissing either of you off".

At that moment Broom and Cotterill moved like black panthers, so quick and with little to no noise and any noise they did make was muffled by the shouting from inside the house. Bollington was taken completely by surprise and with Broom hand over Bollington's mouth and an arm twisted up his back they quickly picked him up, took him down the stairs and across the small piece of law into the bushes on the South side of the house. Next there was the sound of a thud like flesh hitting flesh. Broom came over in my earpiece, "subject subdued".

With that I quickly moved forward and signalled all the others to crash in from each side, there was the sudden crash of splintered wood and smashing glass, but no gunfire. I raced across the lawn to the steps and the front door as I ran up the steps the door flew open and before I could realise what was happening, I was hit like a steam train from front on. There was a gunshot but I did not know from where, I regained my senses and saw Grant jumping down the stairs, Steve jumped out from his position and yelled;

"Stop, where you are, put your hands in the air and drop your weapon", but before he could even get his final words out a shot rang out in the chilly night air, I saw Steve grab for his shoulder as he fell to his knees.

"Grant, you fuck, stop or I will shoot you in the back you are a fucking coward", I yelled. Grant stopped and slowly turned, his pistol still raised and I had mine centred on him. There was a commotion behind me and I recognised Hal's voice

"Take him down Ian, we have all under control in here". Just then Broom and Cotterill came into view with Bollington in handcuffs behind his back and Broom with a gun trained on him while Cotterill had a rifle trained on Grant. Coventry came out with both Bollington and Lawrence handcuffed and pushed them face down onto the porch floor on their knees, just as Broom did the same with Bollington to his knees on the edge of the lawn.

"The games up Grant", I shouted at him;

"You have no way out and you're finished in this town, the murders, the people you have hurt needlessly and the heartache to families you have caused. You are finished, so drop the gun and hands up".

He was standing maybe eight to ten feet in front of me by now and still advancing slowly saying as he did so;

"Farrer you must think I am a fucking idiot, I know that if I give up, I am going to get the needle but it may take years for that to happen and I have not got the patience or the need to wait".

"Your last chance Grant, drop the fucking gun and put your hands in the air". I yelled, he slowly raised his left hand and then within the blink of an eye he raised the pistol in his right hand and I saw two white flashes from the nozzle, instinctively I pulled the trigger on my gun just as a sharp pain hit my right shoulder, I dropped my gun, there was another shot from behind me and one to my right and as I fell to my knees, I was suddenly hit in the face with what I was later to find out was blood and some other matter, as yet I could not describe. Later I realised it was part of Grants skull and some of his hair attached to it. I saw Grant fall to his knees just then another shot rang out hitting him in the head again and his skull seemed to just explode with the force of the bullet. I looked across to my right I think unsure of my position, Cotterill had the rifle to his shoulder, he had fired the final shot as Grant's body fell forward hitting the gravel just in front of me.

I glanced at my shoulder with blood soaking my shirt and I could feel it trickling down my arm, I suddenly realised the pain I was in, Grant had almost blew my shoulder apart as the bullet had hit right on the point of my shoulder and I was on my knees leaning forward, blood trickling down my face into my eyes, when Steve came up to me and told me that an ambulance was on its way. I looked around and all I could see were blurry faces through the tears and blood that filled my eyes.

"Is it over?" I asked in a rather timid voice, then I saw young Coventry laying on the ground behind me as I tried to move, but before I could hear the reply or ask what was happening all went dark.

20

I awoke in a white sterile room with a shoulder that hurt like hell, and my head throbbing like someone was using my skull as a drum. I glanced to my left and there was a machine beeping and lines waving across the screen, then I sensed there was someone in the room. I glanced around the room and did this with great difficulty as my neck was restricted by the bandages around my shoulder. As I slightly raised myself up on my good side and found the pain rather crippling, so laid back down, and as I did, this beautiful face suddenly appeared over me and kissed me on the cheek, I then realised it was my wife and I managed to form a smile, I think, as the fentanyl was making me feel rather sleepy and I was not sure that I was not dreaming.

Katrina then held my hand and I knew that was real and reassuring, that all felt good. She spoke softly and calm to me, explaining what had happened, and that Grant was dead. Just Then Ray and Hal came through the door, and apologised for interrupting and turned to leave, but Katrina said;

"No, you two stay I will go and get a coffee. Do either of you want one?".

They nodded they did not, she gently kissed me again and turned and left the room. Just as she did a nurse came in saying;

"Ah, finally you are awake", and went ahead to check the machines I was hooked up to. Then she pressed a button and it raised the head of my bed a little and I could now see more clearly my surroundings, as well as focus on Ray and Hal. They quickly pulled up two chairs beside the bed and asked;

"How I was doing?", I tried to explain but I may have been a bit too groggy to really express what I felt.

Ray continued;

"Grant was dead, and his cohorts were all being held in Helena pending arraignment there".

Hal looked at me and had that look that there was more to say, so I said;

"Spill the beans".

"Young Coventry copped a bullet from Grant as he got off two shots one hit you the other hit Coventry".

I studied Hal's face through my slightly blurred vision, hoping he was going to tell me that the young officer was okay, but I could tell by the grim look on his face that all was not okay.

"He is fighting for his life boss, the bullet hit him square the chest and the stupid little shit was not wearing his vest, and he has just come out of his second surgery".

Hal explained in a rather sullen tone;

"We asked the doctor whether we should tell you and he indicated that if I was awake there would be no problem and that it would be better to know now than later".

I looked at the ceiling, and my thoughts went back to that situation, was I to blame for getting that young man shot and if so, was this another problem that I had caused? I was unable to clearly put things together as I had brain faze and there was parts of that evening I could remember clearly and others were just a blur.
I asked them;

"How long have I been in the hospital, what day is it?".
Hal responded saying;

"It was Friday and I had been out to it for three days as my surgery took hours to remove the bullet and repair my shoulder".
Just at that moment Katrina returned and came around to my right side and sat on the window ledge, she asked;

"Did I know about the young officer had Hal and Ray told me?" I just nodded in the affirmative as I was lost in my own pain but also that of the young officer who was my responsibility and his family. Ray and Hal stood up and placed one of the chairs back in the corner and Ray said;

"We will be back tomorrow to see you and how you are doing, I will leave this chair here for you Katrina. Bye boss, keep your chin up", they turned and left just as Katrina came back around and sat down in the chair Ray had left and took me by the hand.

For the next period nothing was uttered between us but I am sure she knew I was thinking of the young officer and

617

his fight that was going on for his life down the hall. The sun was sinking slowly, and the shadows were growing longer in the room as the darkness crept through the room like death again was on the prowl. Katrina leaned over to the panel above my head and turned a small pilot light in ceiling off to my left, I smiled at her and realised she had been here in my room before, probably since the day I arrived here. I asked her;

"How the kids were and how long had she been sitting here with me and how she knew her way around". She smiled and softly said;

"The kids are fine they are staying with friends, and I have been here every day since you were brought in after the incident".

I looked at her and smiled, with this overwhelming feeling just how much, I loved and appreciated this woman, with that thought I slowly drifted off, and was left to my own personal dreams and feelings.

Epilogue

Farrer recovered from his injuries and continued as Sheriff in Oemen Lake, but the town was never going to be the same after the mayhem, mystery, and murderous rampage that Grant and his cronies had been on for an extended period. Grant had caused so much heartache and loss for everyone in the town and Ian Farrer blamed himself for that, even though it was months since the final take down of the perpetrators.

The young Officer Coventry recovered but retired from the force on a pension as his injuries prevented him from carrying out his normal duties. This cut Farrer to the core because it was his doing that this young police officer's career had met an untimely end. Sally Donald had to undergo serious counselling for her ordeal and because of what Grant and the others had done to her and her friends, this was going to be never ending. Cannington, Lawrence, and Bollington are all serving life sentences in a federal facility.

Grant is buried in an unmarked grave in Butte, no-one claimed his body so it was returned to his birthplace and interred. Farrer continued his vigil of trying to understand why so many had to die, and for what reason, were the layers of Dante's reasoning of the seven sins true in this case or did it just come down to money, greed and a madman seeking revenge on another and was willing to do anything to achieve his goal? No matter how long Farrer tries to find the answers to his unending list of questions which he may never do now that Grant is dead, there will always be that nagging feeling,

"Did he get them all and what was next for Ian Farrer?"

NEXT IN THE

Ian Farrer Mysteries

The Cold Case

of

Jennifer Anne Murrow

By

D. R. McGregor

The Pocket Handbook to Life Solutions'

'We Pray To Die – A Convict's True Story'

Martin Bryant – Guilty or Not Guilty?
'A Review of The Crime – 28 Years On'

The Story Behind A Massacre
(Limited Availability)

We Pray To Die – A Convict's Story

The Life Handbook of Challenges

www.ingramcontent.com/pod-product-compliance
Lightning Source LLC
Chambersburg PA
CBHW071330020726
47502CB00001B/37